ROCK CREEK

RW Bennett

ISBN-13:978-1539039174
ISBN-10:153903917X

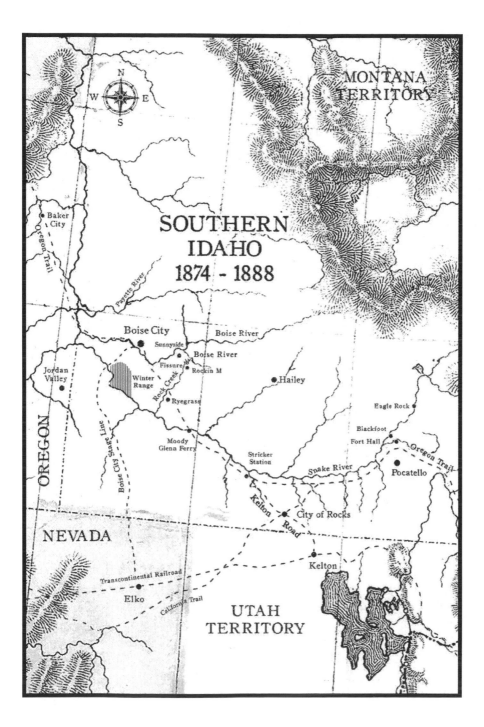

PART ONE

H2O

In unparalleled magic, you trickle
over barren lands creating lush forests,
fields of golden grain, green pastures.
Mystically allied with the moon, it caresses
your motion, divining tides.
You are the surf's curl,
the placid lake, melting snow,
an avalanche crashing down a precipice,
a terrifying flood, a river rushing to the sea,
a hurricane on the wings of wind.
You are the voice that sings
in a high country streambed,
the mist on the mountain,
a mirror reflecting the heavens,
a jewel on a rose petal at sunrise,
savior of parched throats
pain's release in cast-off tears,
mender of weary bodies.
You dance on tin roofs and flowers grow.
But for you, there could be no song,
no dance on this planet.
Men who search a lifetime for
the Elixir of Life never grasp -
the miracle is you.

Adelaide McLeod

PREFACE

On September 5, 1874, in the canyon forged by the South Fork of the Boise River, an earthquake created a fracture in the steep basalt wall that forms the river's south bank. The wide vertical fracture ran from the top of the canyon to the river bed far below.

The fracture found a weakness deep in the basalt and coursed its way six miles south until it stopped in a cave above Rock Creek. River water rushed toward the cave through the new passage formed by the fracture. The flowing water stopped when its level equaled the level of the river six miles away.

In a region where water can be as valuable as gold ore, the cave and the water within would be concealed from view for many years behind a thick cluster of sagebrush.

CHAPTER ONE

~1:14 p.m. September 5, 1874.
Northern Nevada/Idaho Territorial border~

Myra Gaines had become accustomed to the ground quivering and shaking. She'd spent her entire life in California. Nothing remarkable ever resulted. Regardless, earthquakes always made her edgy.

When the dirt floor shook inside the small juniper log stage-stop near the Northern Nevada border, she hoped her mother would utter a reassuring word or two but it hadn't happened yet. The driver had announced two hours earlier that they would stop for lunch at the stage-stop cabin and hitch fresh horses. After they'd arrived Myra thought calling the stage-stop a cabin was an insult to cabins – a shack would be a more apt description. Her mother remained silent so Myra shut her eyes, forced back tears and tried to ignore the dust from the shack's dried mud chinking that settled onto her hair and into her tin plate of putrid brown beans. Dust or no dust, she couldn't force herself to eat the foul-looking mass.

Hope still lingered for a comforting word so she opened one eye and glanced in her mother's direction but her mother sat mindlessly shoveling beans into her mouth and paid no mind whatever to Myra's fears. Disappointed, Myra brushed away a fly that was as unconcerned about the earthquake as her mother, closed her eyes and waited.

Six days had passed since their departure from Sacramento and nine-year-old Myra was still too deeply hurt to engage. She drew in a shallow breath and forced herself to remain stoic. During their three day train trip from Sacramento to Elko, Nevada, where they'd caught the Boise City stage, her mother and father seemed to purposely ignore her flat responses to their indifferent queries and dismissed them as pouting. Maybe she was, Myra thought. Now, three days after leaving Elko on the stagecoach, Myra felt invisible to them. Perhaps it was her own fault for being such a brat.

Moments before, when the shaker began, her father, in an attempt to quell the fears of his fellow passengers, calmly followed four panicked Iowa businessmen who'd bolted from the shack's blanket-covered doorway as if they'd be swallowed by the hard-packed dirt floor if they stayed another second. They'd never experienced the ground move beneath their feet. After they returned to daylight from the darkness of the shack and noticed the coach's tall lanky driver reassuringly stroke the neck of a flighty young roan gelding and heard the driver speak to the gelding in calm indistinguishable tones, the Iowans calmed a little as well. Still suspicious, they each surveyed their surroundings cautiously as if looking for evidence that the Nevada desert might have cracked away from the entire planet. The shaker stopped, the six-horse hitch settled quickly and the driver ambled casually toward the shack to fill his plate from the Dutch oven on the greasy Monarch wood burning stove. Without saying a word, Caleb Gaines turned and followed to join his wife and daughter and finish his lunch. The Iowa contingent stayed outside.

"Just a shaker," announced the driver matter of factly to Myra and her mother as if he'd lived through a hundred of them. "A little one."

~At the same instant 150 miles east near the Utah/Idaho Territorial border~

It was risky going downhill with a full load on this stretch of the Kelton Road so the driver of the mule-drawn freight wagon told his passenger to step out and walk behind, away from harm. The woman stayed further back than the driver suggested to protect the baby in her arms from choking in the thick cloud of hot desert dust kicked up by the wagon.

At the summit, to prepare for the descent down the long steep grade, the freighter locked each of the big iron-rimmed rear wheels in place with rough lock chains and attached drag shoes where each wheel met the road. The chains kept the rear wheels from turning. The skidding drag shoes protected the wheels from wearing flat spots as the shoes skidded along in the wagon's slow cautious slide to the bottom of the hill. Once the wagon was in motion, the skidding shoes added a new layer of intensity to the late summer dust on the Kelton Road, the main freight road in and out of Idaho from the Transcontinental Railroad stop in Kelton, Utah Territory.

Annie Chris Sproat and her husband, Ramsay, had stepped off the train in Kelton less than a week before and made arrangements to travel with the freighter, at least as far as City of Rocks, the crossroads of the southwesterly California Trail and the Kelton Road. The freighter had been their only choice as the stages had temporarily stopped running due to a recent surge in armed robberies.

4

Ramsay was sent ahead by the freighter to remove obstructions in the road. Once the eight-ton wagon started its descent, it would require all the freighter's years of accumulated mule driving skill to stop the wagon, if necessary, before it reached the bottom.

The panic began about halfway down the hill.

Startled, Annie Chris thrust her right arm out for balance and held her child tightly with her left. She stopped – spread her feet for better footing, and struggled to stay upright. For a moment she thought she'd been over-come by an illness or a fainting spell. Reality set-in quickly – the ground was moving.

Being alone with her husband and child in this strange rainless land, its endless expanse covered with nothing but rocks, sagebrush and random shoots of bunchgrass, was frightening enough. Now the ground itself was moving. She'd never experienced such a thing in Scotland, their homeland. She had no idea what was happening beneath her feet and didn't know if the rumbling and shaking would ever stop.

It was providential perhaps that only one in the small party was in-jured.

~   ~   ~

For three days Caleb Gaines paid scant attention to almost anything his fellow passengers said. He seemed distracted or agitated, more so earlier than of late. Caleb insisted on being seated in the stagecoach's forward seat next to a window so he could look back. More than once he had asked the driver if the pace could be quickened. What the traveling party didn't know was that Caleb Gaines, his wife and his daughter were on the last leg of a furious exodus from Sacramento and Caleb had every right to be nervous.

Six days earlier had been Myra's ninth birthday. A party was planned but was ignored in her parents' haste to leave. At the door of her class-room, her mother had embarrassingly summoned Myra out of school the morning before, less than thirty minutes after her father had rushed home from work. Myra was forbidden even to say goodbye to her friends. Her mother and father were desperate to pack, catch a train and leave their home, that night – forever. *Father's business* was the only explanation she was able to glean from her mother. So Myra sat alone, frustrated and angry, sketching a picture of a friend's puppy while her parents frantically packed.

Earlier that morning, her panicked father had discreetly left his office and raced to the depot to purchase train tickets to Elko, Nevada, the rail stop with the closest stagecoach service to Boise City, Idaho Territory, their final destination.

In Elko, after long stops and fifteen hours of rail travel, Caleb planned to buy stage tickets for the arduous five day, two hundred and fifty mile journey across the bleak Northern Nevada high desert plateau into Idaho Territory and beyond. From the Territory line, they'd travel through the rugged eastern breaks of the Owyhee Mountains, down Sinker Creek. Then, after ferrying the Snake River, they'd be only forty miles from Boise City. The entire trip would take nearly a week depending on a variety of indeterminate obstacles including weather, robberies and breakdowns. The quicker they arrived in Boise City the better.

Myra had been feeling less a child – the prepubescent stirrings of her approaching teen years had been slowly emerging. Her friends and school had become more important than ever. How could her parents have done this to her, tear her away from her life, so suddenly, never to return – the day before her birthday?

Her childhood had not been easy. It was true; she had not been an easy child – precocious and intelligent but quiet and pensive. But beyond those not-so-uncommon parenting challenges, to her parents, Myra had become an ever-present annoyance. They had bickered and argued incessantly, but not about Myra; they had other more serious problems and she'd been a distraction. Their exasperation, unfortunately, had often been directed at Myra and, as the most vulnerable years of her young life drew nearer, she'd begun to feel unloved and insignificant.

At the heart of it, Caleb Gaines and his wife had been frustrated with his floundering career and their inability to penetrate the shield surrounding the inner layers of Sacramento society.

Couched in disingenuous subtleties, the more the Gaines pandered for invitations to weddings and other important events the fewer they received. Their rented home had been modest, all they could afford, and far from appropriate for entertaining. Somehow, Caleb thought, through his job as a reporter for the *Sacramento Daily Union*, he would have to turn heads. Something would have to happen, something that garnered attention – something big, something important.

Caleb had always been a decent writer; he did his research and understood the issues and problems facing the community and the state. But here was his problem: Caleb Gaines could never recognize the fine line between eager and annoying. He reeked of ambition like a mule skinner reeks of tobacco and sour sweat. Politicians and influential businessmen turned on their heels and hurried in the other direction when they saw him coming.

Younger, less-experienced reporters had vaulted ahead of him, and built important spheres of influence. Caleb had become embittered to the point of desperation. He needed an important story and he needed one badly – so he made one up.

For years there had been rumors about a legislator's salacious and violent after-hours escapades in the shadowy back alleys and bordellos of Sacramento and San Francisco. The legislator, a State Senator from San Joaquin County, had managed to quell the rumors, thanks to the fortune left him by his deceased wife's family in Philadelphia. Caleb perceived the legislator as fair game, an easy target, a ticket to prominence and public esteem, perhaps even to editor.

Caleb had convinced his editor he finally had an exclusive. He'd interviewed gaming girls in San Francisco, he said, who'd swear they'd been roughed-up mightily by the good senator. Ecstatic, his editor told Caleb to publish it. The editor should have known better. It was the lead story in the August 28, 1874 edition of the *Union*. Street copies had sold out in an hour. Caleb Gaines could not have been more pleased.

Early the next morning, the day before his daughter's birthday, Caleb opened his dispatches and removed a note from a sealed envelope. It read:

> *Your despicable article is a lie and you know it. Here is the retraction that you will copy in your own hand and personally deliver to your editor. I expect it to appear in tomorrow's Union: "I, Caleb Gaines, as ordered by my editor, willfully and with malice, fabricated the August 28 story about a senator that appeared in this paper. I am aware that there has been a contemptible, ongoing vendet-*

ta against him by the editor of this newspaper. The Editor, Publisher and I are totally and completely responsible for the entire content of this vicious attack on the reputation of one of the most respected, honorable, effective and morally righteous senators the Great State of California has ever placed in the hallowed chambers of our legislature."

Please be aware, Mr. Gaines, of the sadness that could befall you and your family if this, WORD FOR WORD, retraction does not appear on the front page of tomorrow's, August 30, 1874, edition of the Sacramento Daily Union.

Good day.

It was unsigned.

One week later Caleb *Grant* (his name now, the name he'd given the Sacramento ticket agent after anxiously glancing at the photo on the wall of the bearded Civil War hero and current U.S. President) resumed his career as a reporter in Boise City. It was the capital of the Territory, a relatively new town platted just eleven years before, a town that was certain to grow because of the discovery of gold in the rugged mountains and scenic basins surrounding it. Here, in a town with so much promise, Caleb could begin again.

CHAPTER TWO

Caleb Grant was not disappointed. He found in Boise City the growing community he'd expected, far enough from Sacramento that he could safely start over – a town where he could achieve social prominence and make his mark. He was determined not to repeat his Sacramento mistakes.

Caleb accepted employment at one of the town's two newspapers and was quickly promoted to staff writer. He wrote many of the feature articles commenting on issues that affected community life. He had big plans: ownership of the paper perhaps and then, possibly, politics. The Grants rented a modest white frame house within walking distance of his work but didn't plan to stay there long. A year later he purchased a lot east of town along a street he felt would soon boast the town's most prestigious addresses. He would build a stylish Romanesque as soon as he was able to add the physical substance he felt was necessary to earn a place in Boise City society.

~   ~   ~

At times Myra Grant was ashamed of the feelings she harbored for her parents. She knew it was wrong to disrespect them but their pandering to the highly placed in the community was almost more than she could bear.

Status and gossip was all her parents could talk about – who had said this to whom and who had made a fool of themselves in front of this respected person or that, thereby ruining any chance the fool would ever have of being invited to this party or that event. It was so awkward and embarrassing that she would turn inward and disengage entirely. Her parents seemed to have no substance or core set of principles that defined them. They shifted like the wind to whatever cold front or warm front came through that day. They went to church to be seen at church but in the privacy of their home, it seemed they had not heard a word the minister had said about charity, forgiveness and kindness. They demeaned and insulted people with a gleeful unrelenting hostility but displayed a cloyingly disingenuous charm in public.

Myra came home from school one day despondent. At supper, in an uncharacteristic display of insight, her mother asked what was wrong.

She ignored her deep-seated reluctance to complain and said, "It's a girl at school. She's mean."

"Mean to who?" her father asked half interested.

"To me and other kids."

"What did she do to you?" asked her mother.

"When I picked up a stray kitten I wanted to bring home to feed," Myra fought back tears and continued, "she grabbed it from me and threw it against a tree. It fell to the ground and staggered away and she laughed. She does awful things like that all the time. I never want to be around her again."

"And her father is whom?" asked Caleb.

"Mr. Smith."

"*Jacob* Smith?"

Mildly interested until now, he turned in his chair, placed his elbows and forearms on the table and leaned in to her. "Now you listen to me young lady. Jacob Smith will be mayor some day. He and Mrs. Smith are hosting a gathering at their home on New Year's Day and we've been invited – the three of us. That means you are going with a smile on your face and you *will* be nice to his daughter. I don't care what she's done. Do you hear me?"

Myra attended the party but sat in a corner with a pasted smile on her face.

~   ~   ~

Myra grew into a striking teen which was, by Caleb's reckoning, a massive stroke of good luck and incalculably important to his career. At just the right time, and that time was drawing near, she would attract the eye of the son of someone respected in the community, someone whose coattails Caleb could attach himself to. Her only liability was, in his mind, her lack of charm, or more aptly, her shyness. If he was assertive enough, he was sure this minor problem could be easily overcome. Her marriage into a well-placed family could be his spring-board to influence and power and, if all went well, there would be no limit to his success.

To some Myra seemed distant and aloof but her kindness and modesty left most with a stately, almost noble, impression of her. As a young girl, she showed signs of being a talented artist. She drew sketches of horses, dogs, birds, any animal she thought beautiful and graceful. Recognizing

10

her talent, for Christmas one year her parents bought her a watercolor painting set. Her art graduated from pencil and charcoals to vivid lifelike color.

She began to embrace causes that struck at the evils of society and crimes against nature and humanity. Through the medium of watercolor, her causes became passions. The buffalo was first, then, a year or so later, she turned her attention to what would become her most passionate cause of all: the plight of the American Indian as seen through the eyes of an old Shoshoni woman who would become one of her best friends.

Patsy was an Anglo corruption of her real name, Pop-pank or Jumping Fish. She was one of the last of the Goslute Tribe of the Shoshoni Indians who lived near Boise City. Most Goslutes had been forcibly moved to the reservation at Fort Hall but Patsy was old and stubborn and would not move – too old, she knew, to live with the nomadic renegades who, in spite of all that had happened to their people, held out hope that their way of life could be saved.

She lived west of town in a bark and willow wickiup along the river near a community of Chinese gardeners. She traded fish with the Chinese for beans, corn and fruit. In the summer and fall she could be seen dragging her travois along the streets selling dried and smoked salmon and trout. The community saw Patsy's simplicity as a visual reminder of their superior way of life.

Myra was intrigued with Patsy and longed to paint her portrait but Myra knew her parents would never allow her to associate with such *an uncomely aberration*. So Myra, for weeks, went to the river after school for a stolen hour or two each day. She told her mother she was studying with a friend, a small but benign untruth. Patsy sat in exchange for a dime. Experimenting, Myra asked Patsy to sit in the shade one day and the sun the next as she struggled, trying to capture on canvas Patsy's alert but sad dark eyes set amongst the shadows and deep lines of her rich copper-colored face.

Replicating her snow-white hair was a much less difficult task. Its white richness was pulled back and clasped at her shoulders with a freshwater clam shell, held in place by a peg set across the back protruding through holes on each side. Myra loved the way Patsy's hair gathered at the shell then escaped to flare down her back like the tail of an enormous dove.

While she painted, Myra asked Patsy about her past – her customs, her family and her people's history. Patsy spoke a little English and knew a few French words passed down from the old days which, when mixed with Shoshoni, made communicating possible though awkward. Gradually, Myra learned enough Shoshoni for the two of them to converse in a kind of mixed language of their own design.

To Myra, an aura of profound sadness surrounded Patsy like a mist that never lifted. It was a private sadness and left a sense of shame in Myra's heart where a faith in the goodness of her white race used to be. The demise of Patsy's people, their proud customs and traditions and how cruelly they were moved from their ancestral home to the reservation left Myra more than just sad; she felt Patsy's deep loneliness as well. As she grew to know Patsy she waited for evidence of bitterness – it never came. It may have been there once, but over the passage of time was replaced with resignation. Myra tried desperately, in her portrait, to capture the essence of the proud old Shoshoni woman but found Patsy almost too complex to replicate on paper. As an artist Myra felt frustrated. In time, she came to an acceptance. She accepted the fact that she would probably never understand.

Patsy told Myra about her husband and sons who were killed in the Bannock War and how proud she was of Chief Joseph for his attempt to lead his Nez Perce people from their beloved Wallowa Valley in Northeast Oregon to Canada to avoid the confinement of a reservation. She tried to explain to Myra how her people's pride and dignity had been driven from their souls by these defeats. Although Patsy loved her people, she couldn't live in the midst of all that loss, watching boredom, the white man's illnesses and his alcohol reduce her people to total dependency. She preferred to be free and let the spirits of her ancestors do whatever they chose with hers.

CHAPTER THREE

~Eleven years earlier at Braeburn Castle,
Highlands of Scotland, spring 1872~

For months Ramsay and Annie Chris had caught glimpses of one another at the castle's back delivery gate but had never met. Ramsay occasionally brought the carcass of an old ewe to the castle, meat for the poor he was told but no crofter he ever knew received as much as a bone. That was exactly what he was doing one fine April day. He set the burlap sack in the shade and prepared to sit while he waited for Turpin, the estate's overseer. A slight movement from behind a stone pillar caught his eye. He looked closer and saw Annie Chris motion to him from the shadows.

He moved as discreetly as he could for he knew that if a crofter was suspected of fraternizing with a servant on the castle staff, both could be fired. He was at her side within seconds.

"Do ye own this place?" he whispered with a uneasy grin, immediately embarrassed at his awkward attempt at humor.

"What?" she whispered back, her right hand flying to her mouth to force back laughter.

"A poor joke. I am sorry," he whispered. "I've been watching ye for more than a year. I must know yer name."

"Annie Christine. I'm called Annie Chris. I have noticed you too. You are one of his lordship's crofters. What is *your* name?"

"Ye noticed me? I am sorry but I thought for sure ye did nae know I existed in this world." He lifted his head high and whispered proudly, "I am Ramsay Sproat."

"What a strong Scot name."

"I am proud that I am a crofter believe it or nae, though I wish I was more tae the world. Being a country lad, I am grateful I am nae starving."

"What work do you do on the estate, Ramsay Sproat?"

"I tend one of his lordship's flocks for ma rent and sell what I can from ma garden for ma needs. Ye are nae from here? Ye speak so fine with such flair with yere words."

"I'm from Edinburgh. I was sent here four years ago after my mother died. Her sister works here. My mother and the woman she worked for coached me to speak as I do but I'm afraid my manner of speaking is seen as haughty so regardless of how hard I work I am still a chambermaid."

"That auld butler is probably jealous and fears for his own job," whispered Ramsay. "I hope ye don't think me daft because of ma country ways."

"I do not, Mr. Sproat. Just because a person speaks with a trained tongue does not mean that person is more worthy. If I have learned only one thing in my life, it would be that. May I ask where you live?"

"Will ye call me Ramsay?"

"If that is your wish," she said shyly, her eyes cast downward.

"Aye, that is ma wish. I live aloone aboot three miles from here."

"Why are you alone? Where is your family?"

"Ma maw died giving birth tae a wee bairn who died as well. Ma pap died only months later. I have an aulder brother who left five years ago tae fish along the Outer Hebrides. I've nae heard from him since so it's just me and ma tykes."

"I am sorry about your family, Ramsay," she said softly. She glanced at the afternoon sun, "I must go before I am missed."

"I must see ye again."

"I have less than an hour late this evening between cleaning the kitchen after dinner and my rounds. There's no moon tonight – it would be a good time to go unnoticed. Can you meet me at ten-thirty next to the back gate?"

"Aye," he said smiling a toothy grin, knowing in his heart the answer would have been yes if she asked to meet him on the moon.

"I will be in my livery. There will be no time to change."

"A more bonnie sight I've n'er seen, just the way I see ye before me."

She smiled. "I must go."

They lingered for just a moment, looking timidly into each other's eyes. Annie Chris dropped hers, turned, walked quickly away then looked back across her shoulder at Ramsay. She smiled and waved.

Ramsay's heart raced. His feet barely managed to return him to the meat sack. He thought he might fall as he forced them to meet the ground on rubbery legs.

Turpin walked out the back door of the kitchen before Ramsay reached the meat sack. Ramsay stole a glance in Annie Chris's direction sighing thankfully that she had disappeared. He took a deep composing breath and prepared for Turpin's usual assault.

"What the bloody hell are you doing wandering around?" demanded Turpin, his chin in the air as he looked down and spoke over the top of Ramsay's head.

"Nae wandering sir, just walking around waiting for ye. Naw harm in that is there?"

"Next time you come here you stay right here and wait. You understand me?" Turpin demanded, poking an index finger into Ramsay's chest. "How would you like me to kick your sorry arse off this estate? Do you think I can't do that?"

"Aye, I know ye can do that sir," replied Ramsay, wishing Turpin was in jail where he belonged.

"You bloody well better know that I can and that I will."

Ramsay did not cower but stood straight and tall, looking directly at the crop of thick hair in Turpin's upturned nostrils.

Turpin slipped on a pair of gloves, opened the meat sack, reached in and squeezed the loins and legs and said, "Too damn fleshy." He opened the carcass's mouth, fingered its gums and continued, "There are still teeth! She could have made it another year you lout!"

"Mebbe so sir, but she did nae have milk enough tae raise her lamb and she had trouble birthing. I had tae graft her lamb tae a healthier ewe. This ewe is six years auld. She would nae make it through the winter."

"You give away good meat like this again and you'll be the next dobber in the sack. You hear me? Pick it up and follow me."

Turpin stopped inside the open doorway that led to the kitchen, turned to a closed door at his right, slipped a key into the lock, opened the door just enough for Ramsay to slide the sack through the opening and said, "Put it here." He wedged himself through the opening and over the carcass then slammed the door closed with a thud. Ramsay could hear a bolt locking from inside.

In spite of his age, just seventeen, lines from squinting into distances were beginning to appear at the corners of Ramsay's blue eyes. A wide-brimmed felt hat covered a thick thatch of blonde hair. The hat was peaked at the top to shed rain and add a measure of protection for his fair-skinned freckled face.

From daylight to well past dark, he wore his father's brown Harris Tweed coat, ragged and faded with age and exposure, its worn elbows and cuffs patched with canvas. An assortment of rips and tears had been darned into the garment over the years with whatever color thread was available at the time of the repair. The coat was made from the wool of the gentle animals who knew him by look, smell and the sound of his voice. Ramsay was a shepherd. He was their protector and the sheep knew it.

A tartan woolen scarf circled his neck, its knot always at his right shoulder, the bulk of the garment draped over his left.

Ramsay was stoutly built with broad shoulders, a thick chest and powerful legs. He walked with a sway, a habit formed by walking with his arms clasped around a walking stick pressed horizontally across the small of his back, as he slowly followed his grazing sheep, his big hands swinging freely.

He turned away from the mansion into the sunlight and left the mixed smells of the wonderful food being prepared for the tables of his lordship and his guests, food he had never once tasted let alone seen. The smell of the kitchen reminded him of the brief wispy scents sent by a breeze in his direction from the Earl's deer hunting camps he'd seen at a distance as he herded his flock.

He glanced back at the stone pillar where he and Annie Chris had just met. The memory of her scent, her dark hair and creamy olive skin, so different from that of most pale skinned Scots, seemed to linger like an apparition in the space she'd occupied only minutes before.

He walked through the courtyard out the rear gate to his waiting dogs, left the world of privilege and opulence and returned to the grim world of a Scottish crofter.

At the age of twelve, Annie Chris, also an orphan, was sent from Edinburgh to the Earl's castle. Before she died, Annie Chris's ailing mother taught her to read by guiding her through years of correspondence she'd had with a distant relative in America. Annie Chris continued the correspondence after her mother's death. Her correspondent wrote of the freedom in America to choose one's own future, a future not dictated by class, family or station in life. The woman and her husband had settled on land in the western Territory of Idaho, land given them by the government. There they raised cattle on what the woman called a *ranch*.

Over time, Ramsay had suspected that Turpin was skimming profits from the Earl's wool and grain crops, hiking charges from castle vendors and splitting the difference with them. But, because Turpin had paid for loyalty throughout the Highlands, Ramsay's punishment for revealing the crimes would be severe.

Ramsay wasn't the only one aware of Turpin's improprieties.

As a chambermaid, Annie Chris was required, by 5:30 a.m., to gather the chamber pots from Lord McIntyre's guests' and his family's bedrooms and haul them down the three flights of stairs to the scullery, empty, scour and return them to the rooms by 6:30. As she approached Lady McIntyre's bedroom one recent morning she noticed Turpin softly close the countess's door and tread silently down the hallway toward the grand staircase. Annie Chris waited a few minutes to avoid raising her ladyship's suspicion then quietly entered the bedroom to retrieve the pot. As she walked soundlessly past a bureau, her livery brushed against a sheet of paper and sent it cascading to the floor. She knelt, grasping blindly for it in the dark.

The sound of rustling paper startled the countess. She opened her drowsy eyes, lifted her head and in the dim light of the fireplace's dying coal embers said sleepily, "Be gone girl. Leave me – now."

"As you wish, my lady," Annie Chris whispered with the appropriate reverence, just as she'd been taught. Fearful the countess would see her replacing the dropped paper, she quietly folded it with one hand and placed it in the pocket of her livery, grasped the pot, stood and stepped silently backward toward the door so as to never turn her back on the countess.

"Go now," the countess murmured as she turned over in her bed. Annie Chris quietly shut the door.

What could she do? She couldn't take the paper back to the countess's room. She was filled with panic. She had to complete her rounds but if she was caught with the paper – the consequences would be severe. She rushed up the two flights of stairs to the servants' quarters, past her sleeping roommates, slipped the paper under her mattress and rushed back down to complete her rounds.

Later that night, alone in her room, she lit a candle, lifted the mattress, pulled out the paper and read. Her heart pounded faster with each vulgar word. It was a letter signed, *Your Darling Turpin.*

She had no idea what she would do. There were very few choices. She couldn't return it and risk being caught. If she destroyed it she could almost hear Turpin's exchange with his lover: "I left an intimate note to you right here on your bureau. Who has been in your room?"

Her worse fears collided with each other in her head. Imprisonment? That would be mild; people had disappeared from Braeburn for less.

There was no other choice. She had to leave. Leaving Scotland had been squarely on her mind that afternoon when, from behind the pillar, she motioned for Ramsay.

~   ~   ~

It was dark. She walked cautiously along the sides of the outbuildings. Ramsay was there when she arrived.

He removed his hat. They stood facing each other in the dark, hesitating, neither knowing what to say. Ramsay didn't know whether to hug her, shake her hand or just say hello. His mouth was dry; words did not come. He heard a barn owl hoot in the distance. It broke his concentration, making matters worse. He was the man; he knew he should speak first. He rocked sideways from foot to foot, his sweaty hands clasped behind his back.

Annie Chris broke the awkwardness. "I'm glad you came."

"Me too – naw, I mean I'm glad ye came here too. Naw, that's nae what I mean. I'm glad we both are here." He brought the heel of his hand up, smacked his forehead softly and said, "Ye know what I mean."

"You are funny when you're nervous. Do you know that I'm nervous too?"

"Ye are? Then ye don't think me a lug?"

"No, I do not. I think you are a fine man."

"Do ye think Turpin may have followed ye?" he whispered.

"Of course not. I mean nothing to him."

"Aye, that was daft. He thinks less of me. Yeah, Turpin – what a scunner he is."

"So you love him as much as the rest of us, eh?"

"Aye, mebbe it's his fancy clothes or his better than me bloody air aboot him that I loove so much." He puffed up his chest, stuck his nose and chin in the air and strutted in circles with his arms folded in front of him, like a rooster strutting in a barnyard lording over his hens. Annie Chris laughed at the mockery that did not seem at all like an exaggeration.

"I have tae tell ye, I am so glad ye came. I was nae sure ye would. It is so risky for ye. And, och, what a bonnie sight ye are. I hope ye don't mind me saying so."

"Thank you," she said blushing. "I don't mind. Kind words are few around here."

"What is yer last name?"

"Abernathy."

"Abernathy?" he asked, stifling a laugh.

"What is so funny about Abernathy?" she asked cocking her head pretending to be hurt.

"Sounds funny – I don't know . . . nae a name I would have guessed for ye. Surely naw dobber has ever called ye Aber-nasty."

"Only you, you dobber," she said with a grin. "What about Sproat?"

"Yere nae the first to tease me aboot ma name. It is a funny one. Ma pap and brother would fight anyone who teased them aboot anything. I like teasing as long as it's nae mean."

"Well then, I'm glad you won't be picking a fight with me because I'm not teasing," she said looking above his eyes. "*Sometime* I need to cut that crop of wiry hair that flops out of your hat when you take it off."

"If ye did that, how in the name of heaven would I keep ma hat on ma heid?"

Annie Chris laughed out loud.

"So what else aboot me do ye find so funny?"

"Well for one thing, I do not want to meet the brute that broke your nose and left you with that little scar. It's the funniest thing – it turns pink when you are nervous."

"Now, if I was a perfectly handsome laddie with nae a mark on me I'd be living in the castle now wouldn't I?"

"A good man does not exist that doesn't have a scar or two, but Ramsay, you could've lost your eye!"

19

"Aye, lucky for me. But the brute was a rock I fell on in the cairn when I was ten, nae a man's fist. Sorry tae say it but I suffered more than the rock."

Annie Chris laughed then became quiet. She sat. Ramsay sat across from her.

Earlier that warm afternoon while sitting by a stream with his dozing dogs lazily snapping at random flies, he'd practiced small talk. Although this particular moment hardly called for what he'd practiced, with little else to say, he decided he needed to go forward: "What do ye like tae do when yere nae working?"

"I read mostly – about America."

"America?"

She looked worried. Her dark eyes focused on nothing while she slowly rubbed her palms over her knees, "I have to leave Braeburn, Ramsay. I may be in trouble."

"What trouble?"

She reached in her pocket, pulled out the letter, handed it to him and said, "Here is a letter I found in her ladyship's room early one morning after Turpin sneaked out."

She told him the whole story then said, "Read it yourself. I cannot begin to describe what it says."

He turned his head away for a moment, closed his eyes then turned back. His eyes opened and met hers. He handed the letter back.

"I cannot blame you if you wish not to read it. It is so vile," she said.

"Annie Chris, I can nae read."

She put her rough calloused hands on his flushed weathered cheeks, gently lifted his face upward toward hers and said, "You have nothing to be ashamed of. My mother taught me to read. I will teach you. We'll find a time. But what will I do now? I can't stay and I don't have enough money to leave."

"Where do ye want tae go?"

"America, Ramsay…America."

"Can I go with ye? There's nae a thing here for me tae stay for." There was no hesitation in his voice. He asked her so quickly and so naturally, like he'd known her all his life. Her answer came back at him with equal conviction.

"Oh my Lord Ramsay, of course, but where will we get the money?"

Ramsay's freckled face brightened and with a dry half grin he said, "We got him now, Annie Chris. Turpin'll pay for it."

~   ~   ~

In Glasgow they bought steerage on an old sail ship. Two weeks into their voyage they asked the ship's captain to marry them. With the letters she'd saved from her cousin in America, Annie Chris spent the voyage teaching Ramsay to read. He learned quickly.

They arrived in New York harbor six weeks later and were dispatched through Castle Garden emigrant receiving depot, a converted fort at the southern tip of Manhattan Island. The fort was completed in 1811 to guard against the menacing British, hell bent to take back the "colonies" and return the people to the same life Ramsay and Annie Chris were escaping.

They worked for a potato farmer on Long Island for a year and saved for their eventual trip west to homestead where Ramsay dreamed of raising sheep. During that year they earned enough to leave. They ferried from Brooklyn to Jersey City then traveled by train to Pittsburgh and by flat boat to Cairo, Illinois, where they caught a paddlewheeler up the Mississippi to St. Louis and another up the Missouri to Kansas City. America was immense; rivers and trees seemed to stretch forever. What they didn't know was that there was about to be an abrupt change in the landscape. The verdant greenery and wide still rivers would soon be a thing of the past.

CHAPTER FOUR

They arrived in Kansas City in 1873. The town was a beehive of activity. Its primary existence for almost twenty years had been to accommodate the thousands of emigrants eager to make their way to a new life on a new frontier. Wheelwrights, brokers selling sturdy Peter Schuttler and Studebaker prairie wagons, stockyards, slaughter houses, harness makers, liveries, horse traders, cattle brokers and stores of every kind spread in all directions. A smattering of saloons, an opera house, whorehouses and dens with gaming chickens provided entertainment. There, the Sproats worked odd jobs for a year and saved for their trip west.

On May 22, 1874 Annie Chris gave birth to a little girl, Katherine Cora. Katherine was Annie Chris's mother's name and Cora was the name of the relative she'd been corresponding with for so many years. In August, they packed their little family and took a train to Omaha where they bought "emigrant class" train tickets on the Transcontinental Railroad to Kelton, Utah Territory.

Arrangements had been made through correspondence between Cora and Annie Chris to meet Cora and her husband, Hugh Calland, at the stage stop at City of Rocks about fifty miles north of Kelton. At City of Rocks they would decide to either continue west along the Kelton Road in search of a place to homestead or follow the Callands northeast and spend the winter on their ranch near Fort Hall along the Oregon Trail to learn as much as they could about homesteading.

At the local restaurant in Kelton, Ramsay and Annie Chris learned they faced a major obstacle. The stages had been shut down, they were told, due to a rash of armed robberies. Bandits had stolen over $20,000 in less than two weeks. Here was the Sproats' problem: without the stage coach, they had no transportation to City of Rocks to meet the Callands. They had to be there by the eighth of September. If they weren't, the Callands would assume the Sproats had changed their plans, would leave and return to their ranch.

"What'll we do?" Annie Chris asked after explaining their dilemma to Lou, the friendly proprietress of the restaurant. Lou was a waify, eager to please, brown-haired gal about twenty, close to her own age Annie Chris thought.

"You could just stay here and let me raise that cute little girl for you," Lou said laughing.

The Sproats' failure to see the humor in her remark was obvious. "I know you're in a bind. About your only choice is to hitch a ride with a freighter. I'm sorry but there's only one in town right now – name's Bill Judy."

~   ~   ~

By six-thirty Bill Judy was hungry. Drinking whiskey all day had dulled his appetite, then, quite suddenly, food was all he could think about. He rotated on the bar stool toward the front door of Homer's Saloon. Then with considerable effort, he lifted himself off the stool. At first his legs seemed unwilling to accept the weight that was expected of them and buckled to one side. He grasped the edge of the counter and managed to right himself then staggered out the door in the direction of Lou's restaurant without as much as a goodbye or a kiss my ass to ol' Homer.

Lou had designed her restaurant so that she, being a one-woman operation, could see the front door from about anywhere in the kitchen. In this case she heard Bill attempting to enter before she saw him. Her head snapped in his direction when he fell against the door. The door swung against the wall with a crash.

She walked toward the collision quickly but calmly trying not to alarm the diners who were enjoying the baked ham and yams she was serving that evening. The foul odors penetrating the air as she got closer to Bill caused her to swallow hard.

"Get the hell outa here, you're a damn mess," she whispered through clenched teeth, her jaw and neck muscles bulging like cables, straining the braids that followed the curvature of her head from temple to neck on each side.

"I suppose I am a mess, Lulu," he slurred, "I ain't arguing 'bout that but I ain't too messed up to oblige them smells coming off your stove. Me and Bob damn sure need a plate full of whatever the hell you got cooking. Been a long hard day with ol' Homer. You'd get drunk too if you had to spend all day with that son-of-a-bitch. Hee hee."

23

"Go back to the hotel and sleep it off. I'll bring you a plate after I close."

"Why the hell would I ruin a good drunk with a goddamn nap? Cost me a bundle to tie this one on."

"Get outa here – now! I'll bring you a plate at nine. Now leave."

"I know when I ain't welcome," he slurred as he reluctantly turned toward the cool evening breeze. Two awkward paces later he caught the heel of his boot on the top step and fell face-first into the dust. Bill's ever present black and white dog took a couple of paces in Bill's direction and looked up at Lou protectively.

Lou put her hands on her hips. *Help him or leave him lay.* She finally walked down the two front steps, leaned over, reached out her hand and said, "Give me your hand."

"I can take care of my own self – don't need no help where I ain't welcome."

"Fine with me."

Bill rolled over, managed to steady himself on his hands and knees and waited, braced on all fours for a couple of seconds, then staggered to his feet. He looked around to find the hotel. Once he had his bearings, he slowly and carefully headed that way without saying another word. His dog followed slowly behind.

Lou shook her head slowly. She walked back inside, grabbed a ham bone left over from a customer's dinner plate, turned toward the door and said, "Bob!" The dog looked up at her. Lou tossed the bone in front of him. He watched it sail through the evening air and fall within a foot of his head. He ignored it as if it were a rock, turned back in Bill's direction and continued in Bill's footsteps.

Lou shook her head again, walked back inside to tend to her remaining customers and prepared to clean up and close for the night. Just before locking up she placed three large slices of ham, two yams and two slices of bread on a dinner plate and wrapped it in newspaper. She closed and locked the door and walked in the direction of the hotel.

Bill sat in a battered oak chair on the hotel porch; its back leaned against the wall. The front two chair legs were about three inches off the floor of the porch. He was fast asleep, his chin resting on his chest. Bob was lying next to him fully awake, his chin on his paws, still as a statue, eyes focused on Lou.

"Wake up."

Bill opened one eye. The dog didn't move.

Lou placed the plate on Bill's lap. "Maybe this'll help sober you up."

"Marry me, Lulu," said Bill as matter-of-factly as if he were predicting the weather.

"I wouldn't marry you, Bill Judy, if you were the last breathing man on earth."

She waited for a reaction. None came so she changed the subject but not her tone. "Did you meet a nice Scotchman and his pretty wife at Homer's today?"

"I met a Scotchman this morning 'fore I took on this whiskey toot – he seemed all right to me."

"Did he ask you to take them to City of Rocks?"

"He did."

"If you as much as harm a hair on either of their heads and if you don't take them and their baby there as carefully as if that wagon of yours was loaded with dynamite, I will never speak to you or serve you in my restaurant again. You hear me Bill Judy?"

What little color was left in Bill's drunken complexion left immediately. "I'll take good care of 'em."

"You goddamn sure better." She didn't look back as she turned and marched in the direction of her restaurant. She stopped, picked up the bone that was earlier ignored, wiped the dust off with her apron and again tossed it in Bob's direction. It landed a foot from his nose. This time, he willingly accepted it.

~   ~   ~

At six-thirty the morning of September 1, 1874, Ramsay Sproat had everything they owned packed and ready for the freight yard except their tent and bedding which he would roll up early the next morning. He slung one of the loaded trunks onto his back and walked the three blocks to the freight yard. He spotted Bill Judy loading his wagon with a variety of crated items, implements and wooden boxes of things he had no way of identifying. Ramsay decided it best not to interrupt but wait until Bill turned to walk down the ramp off the back of the wagon for another load.

The black and white dog was sitting on its haunches near the rear of the wagon.

"Guid morning tae ye, Bill. Where do ye want our gear?"

"Over there." He squinted at Ramsay trying to remember. "Oh yeah, I remember you, you have a wife and a little – can't figure why folks don't wait to have them babies until they get where they're a going."

Ramsay made three more trips to the freight yard, hauling everything they owned on his back. One of those trips was for provisions Annie Chris had bought from the general store.

When his last load was neatly stacked in a pile Ramsay said, "Might I help ye finish loading? I've a strong back and would nae mind."

"I'll do it myself," said Bill softly. "My mules'll be harnessed, hitched and ready to go at seven sharp. You gotta a horse?"

"Naw horse. Just me, ma wife and the wee one."

"There's two for sale at the livery. Can't say much good about either one but I spect' either one'll make it to City of Rocks. My advice is you better get one of 'em. You could get damn tired of me or vice versa. I got no qualms about partin' company if we get sideways. Besides, my mules got enough of a pull – long damn way to the end of that road."

"I am nae a wealthy man, Mr. Judy."

"Walkin' with a wife and kid and everything ya own on your back'll make you wanna be."

Ramsay turned away so that Bill couldn't see his exasperation. After all, Ramsay was a Scot and parting with his money was not something that set easily with him. He looked back and said, "I'll take a look at 'em."

He crossed the tracks toward the livery to look at the two horses. The proprietor pointed them out. Ramsay looked them both over, checked their teeth and lifted each of their hooves. One's feet were better than the other's but neither was shod. Both animals' tails were knotted up tight with cockleburs. Their manes weren't much better. The one with the better feet had teeth in surprisingly good shape. She was a bay with one white foreleg.

"I like this one," said Ramsay. "What are ye asking for her?"

"Thirty bucks."

"I'll take her if ye'll throw in a saddle and shoe'er."

"Thirty bucks, five more for a saddle and two more if you want me to shoe her. Take it or leave it. You can shoe her yourself for four bits," said the liveryman.

Ramsay had shod a lot of horses working for a blacksmith in Kansas City. He realized he had no bargaining power. He gritted his teeth and said, "I'll shoe'er."

The burley liveryman nodded and pointed to an anvil and a wooden box full of shoeing tools and horseshoes and said, "Help yourself but pay me now for the mare – if you lame her she's yours."

"How much for a sack of oats?"

"A buck."

Ramsay pulled out his purse and counted out thirty-eight dollars. It hurt – almost a month's wages in Kansas City.

The poor mare's hooves were grown out, split and broken off here and there – it had been months since she'd been shod. It was obvious the liveryman had been hiring her out without shoes. Ramsay did his best to trim the hooves straight, true and level and was grateful that he was doing it, not this brute.

Ramsay saddled her, tied the sack of oats to the back of the saddle, put his left foot in the stirrup and swung his right leg over. The horse groaned when Ramsay's full weight came down on the saddle.

By mid-afternoon the wind had shifted and was coming from the east. The air cooled. A few hazy clouds appeared out of nowhere. He picketed the horse loosely to a steel rod he'd driven into the ground with the flat of his axe so she could graze on the dry grass near the camp he'd set up. He found an old porcelain pan, poured in a ration of oats and set it in front of her. She gained a new burst of energy when she got a whiff of the oats. She lifted her head, her ears perked up and her eyes seemed brighter as she stomped most of the dry grass Ramsay hoped she would have grazed on within the thirty-foot radius of rope he'd picketed her with. She devoured the panful within minutes in huge slobbering mouthfuls. When she finished she circled the stake and stomped the pan with a clatter at each revolution. He would have to move the rod, he thought.

Night was closing in on day. It was still and cool and seemed to be getting cooler. Annie Chris bundled Katherine in their tent with an extra blanket then husband and wife settled in for the night. Tomorrow would be a big day.

They were up and dressed at 4:30. Neither could sleep.

It was downright cold for an early September morning but they didn't mind. They hoped the cool weather would hold for awhile.

By five-thirty Ramsay had their bedding tightly rolled up in their tent and tied securely to the saddle on the horse's back. He stumbled around in the dark until he found the porcelain pan he'd used to feed oats to the horse and filled it half full. She ate with the same slobbering enthusiasm she'd shown yesterday.

"I think this horse is feeling better," said Annie Chris, her head cocked, her hands on her hips. "She looks like she has a little more life in her. Don't you think? At least she didn't fall over when you put the tent on her."

"Mebbe so," Ramsay said, "but we should give her a name. We can't just go on calling her *horse* or *nag*. What do *ye* want tae name her?"

Annie Chris paused a minute, thinking. Ramsay interrupted her mental search and said, "She's lucky tae be with us. Let's call her Lucky."

"That's not a mare's name. How about Lucy?" said Annie Chris as she picked up the cradle with little Katherine still asleep inside.

"Lucy – fits her just richt. Come on, Lucy," Ramsay said as he stroked her neck, untied her from her picket and took the first few steps leading her in the direction of the freight yard. "We have a long way tae go."

Ramsay, Annie Chris, Katherine and Lucy were there, ready to go at six-thirty, just as they'd promised. Bill had just finished hitching the fourth and last team of the most beautifully matched set of eight mules Ramsay had ever seen, each with a dark brown shiny coat, light brown muzzle and bred for power. Their collars, bridles and breeching straps were a well oiled shade of burgundy. Their hames and their tug and trace chains gleamed in the morning sun.

Bill's freight wagon was a barn-red sixteen foot California Rack Bed wagon, the wheel spokes and seat painted black. It looked clean and sturdy and freshly painted. The hard wooden seat in the front was supported on each side by two diamond-shaped steel springs. The springs were the wagon's only cushioning, intended to help absorb the shock of some of the roughest roads in the West. The wagon was capable of hauling eight tons of freight, a reasonable pull for four span of mules. It was loaded, covered with canvas and appeared ready to go. There were two full water kegs cantilevered on each side of the wagon. The wagon had not moved since Ramsay was there last.

"We're here Bill. Ready if ye are."

Bill cocked his head in the direction of Ramsay's voice, looked over at Annie Chris and Katherine and went back to harnessing without saying a word. The black and white dog was crouched to the side of the front pair. The two mules and the dog were in a silent stare-down: neither dog nor mules moved a muscle. The four span of mules stood motionless, hitched and ready with eight pairs of mule eyes focused on nothing but the dog.

Finally Bill said, "I'm leaving in fifteen minutes."

Ramsay untied Lucy's load, lifted it off the saddle and carried it to the back of the loaded wagon where he tossed it onto the top of his other gear.

Bill walked to Annie Chris and said, "Ma'am, my name is Bill Judy. I'll be the captain on this trip. We're gonna get along just fine as long as you and your man do as I say. Either of you is welcome to ride with me up front. I sec you got yourself one of them mares at the livery and just so you know, I don't give a damn which of you rides her or which of you rides with me but if the baby gets to wailing I don't want it up here. Ain't got nothing against babies, mind you, I just don't want the aggravation cause I'll have enough of my own. You got that?

"And, sorry to say so ma'am, but I have been known to curse in my life so you need to know that if my cursing is an affront to either of you, you got two choices. Choice number one is leave right now and find some freighter that don't curse, choice number two is tolerate it. Ain't no other choices. And just so it's clear, I'm my own boss – I do as I please."

Bill stared a hard stare at Ramsay, spit a stream of tobacco juice about six inches from Ramsay's boot, then asked, "Did you get that Sproat? I do as I please. Got any questions?"

"Nae a question but I do have somethin' tae say tae ye. I understand yer profession is a hard one but ye must know sir, that while we're on the road, if ye speak tae ma wife in a tone that is insulting tae her we will take our horse, part company and walk however far it may be. I don't mean that tae be a threat tae yer honor or yer profession but I have honor of ma own and ma wife is as wonderful a lass as there is on this earth and she does nae deserve tae be disrespected."

Bill stared at him for the longest time, cogitating on what he'd just heard from this plucky freckled-faced Scotchman. "Fair enough," he finally said.

"One more thing," he said as if none of Ramsay's admonition had registered. "Whoever rides with me's gonna have to share the seat with that there dog of mine. Name's Bob. He don't bite unless you bite him first. Now let's get the hell outa here."

Bill walked to the front of the wagon, stepped up the two wheel spokes that led to the board seat and whistled at Bob who until that moment was as still as death in his stare-down with the mules. Bob bolted back from the lead mule and with one acrobatic leap was in the seat next to Bill.

"Who's next?"

They looked at each other for a moment, then Ramsay took Katherine, grasped his wife's cold hand and led her to the wagon. Bill reached out for Annie Chris's other hand and pulled her up as she stepped up the two spokes and sat down. Ramsay handed Katherine back to his wife.

Ramsay hurried back toward Lucy, barely getting her untied from the back of the wagon when Bill slapped the lines twice over the top of the eight eager mules and spoke to them as calmly and gently as if he were talking to a basket full of puppies. "Hup mules, hup hup. That's it boys, pull pull." Then, as if the eight beasts were one, in a perfectly synchronized mighty strain against their collars, the mules responded to his cool but firm command and inched the eight-ton fully loaded wagon forward, increasing the wagon's momentum with each labored step.

At precisely seven the unlikely group passed through the freight yard gate on their way to City of Rocks and possibly many miles beyond.

CHAPTER FIVE

Even with the burden of Ramsay on her back, Lucy had no trouble keeping up with the slow-moving freight wagon. The sluggish pace left Ramsay with a peculiar feeling of impatience after having just arrived only three days before on a train that traveled over nine hundred miles in six days at speeds sometimes in excess of thirty miles per hour. *Annie Chris and Lucy will get along fine,* he thought.

He coaxed Lucy toward the front of the wagon to be closer to Annie Chris and Katherine. They'd been traveling for over an hour and not a word had been exchanged with Bill. The only sound was an occasional stream of tobacco juice exiting Bill's lips.

Ramsay knew that Katherine would want to nurse soon and would signal her demand with a high-pitched red-faced scream. He also knew that it might be folly to test Bill's patience so early in their trip so he asked, "Bill, can I ask ye a question?"

"Ask it," Bill answered flatly.

"Our daughter will soon be nursing. Would ye mind if ma wife moves tae the back of yer wagon?"

"No quarrel from me," said Bill. "Ain't nothing she can break back there 'cept maybe a leg. I'll stop the mules – make it safer for her, that way she can get off and climb in from the back. Hate to stop too long though; we gotta make fifteen miles today to a little spot with a spring and a meadow. We all might want to take a little nature call and this is as good a time as any.

"Whoa mules," Bill said calmly as he drew the lines. The wagon came to an abrupt stop. Bob was the first one off and bolted to a short sagebrush then lifted his leg. He ran to his position in front of the mules and the familiar stare down commenced.

Three of the eight mules immediately squatted, lifted their tails and watered the roadway, passing enormous amounts of gas as they did. Bill sat motionless in the seat staring forward over the tops of the mules' ears safely holding the lines.

Ramsay whispered to Annie Chris, "Would ye rather *stay* in the back ma loove?" She nodded gratefully.

31

He walked up to Bill and asked if he'd mind if his wife stayed in the back for awhile. Bill nodded with just the slightest hint that he might have been hurt a little and said, "There's a short grade we have to go up in a piece. Take us about an hour to get to the top. We'll stop there and rest the mules and have a bite to eat. You might want to draw a little water out of a keg while we're stopped so your missus can tend to the baby. Gotta do all that now cause we can't stop 'til we get to the top."

"Thank ye."

Bill acknowledged the thanks with a nod. "Once we're at the top we'll have a gentle go of it for a spell – mules won't have much of a pull, then you're welcome to ride up here with me and Bob. Bob ain't much for visiting. I'd welcome the company."

"That I will do."

It was a long two-hour pull to the top of the rise; the mules sweat profusely as they reached the top. The air was still comfortably cool with a light breeze from the west.

Bill found a level spot to stop and drew the lines. "Whoa mules." The wagon rolled to a stop. He climbed into the back and drew water from the kegs to water the mules.

Annie Chris spoke the first words she'd said to Bill since she met him earlier that morning. "Please Bill, let me fill the bucket and hand it to you."

"I got an easier way ma'am. Over there next to the kegs is a stiff canvas hose. You could stick it down, to the bottom of the keg, put your hand over the end and hand it to me. It'll siphon right on down then I can fill each tub from here and that'll make it a helluva lot easier on you, and would help me considerably."

Ramsay looked on wondering, *Is this the same lout I hired in the saloon?* With Annie Chris's help Bill made four more trips, and watered each team until they'd had their fill.

While Bill was busy packing water to the mules Ramsay stepped up onto the wagon, reached in one of the bags of provisions and pulled out the cheese and a rhubarb pie Lou had given them for their trip. He tilted it in Bill's direction as Bill returned from watering the last mule. "Would ye like some rhubarb pie? It's guid. Lou made it. We have cheese too if ye like."

32

"Don't mind if I do. I got some ham here. It's in a bag over there up toward the front. You can probably reach it from where you are."

Ramsay placed a clean tartan kerchief on a flat rock while Bill drew his long knife from its sheath on his belt, wiped its blade on his trouser leg and sliced off some ham for each of them. They sat in the noonday sun with a cool breeze coming from the west and ate quietly.

When Bill finished he looked across the countryside with a far-away look as if he was brooding over something. "You know," he finally said, "some of them flatlanders that get off that train pain me to no end. They think cause I'm an ol' mule skinner that I ain't got no worth at all and treat me like I'm some kind of a gutterpup. Folks that toughed it out to come hundreds of miles out here in an ol' Schuttler wagon know better. They've lived the rough life. But these carpetbagger types now-a-days coming off that train – nothin' but rakes and fops. Glad you folks ain't like them…most got their heads square up their sewer chutes, pardon me ma'am."

"No pardon necessary," said Annie Chris.

"I thank you, ma'am. Now that I got that off my chest we best be on our way."

Bill sliced off a piece of ham, walked to where Bob was standing guard, laid it in front of him and petted him on the head. Bob only moved his eyebrows and his nostrils, his gaze still squarely on the mules.

Bill walked to the back of the wagon where Ramsay was inside helping Annie Chris and Katherine get comfortable in their spots. "Like I said back a piece, Sproat, you're welcome to join me an ol' Bob if you want. I'd enjoy the company. You can tie your mare to the back – she seems to lead pretty good. If she don't she'll learn in a hurry, hee hee."

"The pleasure'd be mine," said Ramsay.

Bob only then, after the ham had been in front of him for several long minutes, in one lightning-fast move dropped his head, snatched the ham into his mouth and ran to the front of the wagon chewing and swallowing on the way. He leaped up into the seat next to Bill. Bill put his arm around his dog, patted him on the flanks. "Bob and me's ready if you are."

Ramsay stepped up two spokes, sat next to Bob and said, "Ready."

CHAPTER SIX

Bill slapped the lines over the backs of the mules. "Hup mules, hup, hup. That's it boys, pull, pull." With another mighty strain, the wagon slowly moved forward.

"So, Sproat, what are you after? Everyone out here's after somethin'." Ramsay gave him a brief summary of the last two years of their lives. He told Bill about wanting to raise sheep, Mr. and Mrs. Calland and that they were meeting them at City of Rocks.

"Ye've been across that land many times, what do ye think?"

"Can't say as I know much about sheep," answered Bill. "What's good for 'em and what ain't, but I can say that lately I noticed more of 'em in that country than before. Seen bunches of 'em here and there. Expect that means someone's doing all right. I do know that most years' winters ain't too bad down on the flat. That's gotta be a good sign for a sheepman."

"That's guid tae know. It rains more days than nae in Scotland – it's green the year round. It has nae rained here once since we left Omaha. Surprises me some that sheep could get by in this dry country."

"They get fat on green grass in the mountains in the summer, then in the fall of the year they get by on this dried-up grass like you see around us. Seen sheep down near the Snake in the winter – they seem to do all right on brush down there. Between the rivers in these parts there ain't much water, just springs and cricks mostly. Bad winters don't come too often but when they do most ranchers wish they had more hay. Takes irrigation water to raise hay around here and like I say, there ain't much 'cept near the rivers."

"Annie Chris's kin wrote us aboot the Snake. There are others?"

"The Snake's the biggest. The Malad, the Wood, the Boise and the Payette all run into it from the north and the east mostly. A few come in from the south. That's about it other than a few little ones that don't amount to much. Some folks do all right ranching on them little cricks but them ranches'll never amount to much without irrigatin'."

Bill paused a moment, thinking, then said, "Never thought I'd be the settler type – you know, a sodbuster or rancher, chasing a bunch of cows or sheep – never appealed to my sensibilities, being tied down. I always wanted more space – room to move around. But lately I've had my eye on a little piece a ground this side of Boise City. Nice little crick running through it out of the foothills. Ought to irrigate maybe a hundred acres or so, give or take. Kinda surprised no one's laid claim to it yet – might do it myself. Willow Crick it's called. That don't tell you much. I bet there's a hundred Willow Cricks in the Territory. You oughta take a look at it – worth considering."

"How would I find it – are there signs?"

"Wooo, weeh! – signs? Hey pard, you ain't in no big city. You may never see one again. Hee, hee!"

Annie Chris stifled a laugh.

"Awricht then, how would I find it?"

"It's about eighteen miles past the Rock Crick stage crossing I s'pose, about halfway between there and Boise City. After you cross Rock Crick you'll cross three little cricks, each of 'em about four or five miles apart – none of 'em run much water this time a year, enough to water a few mules is all. You keep on a going and you'll see it. It runs more than the other three put together but about half what Rock Crick runs. If you happen to go on by and miss it you'll know because the next one runs a little water but all the ground around it is nothing but gravel and rocks. Any ol' fool'd know it ain't worth farming.

"You look Willow Crick over when you get there – might not work for a sheepman, hell I don't know. I just might take it if you don't – might run a few cows. Not crazy about the idea but the notion of settling down is building inside me a little more every day. I got personal reasons."

Ramsay felt a pang of anxiety. The reality of how vulnerable and un-prepared he was began to settle in. All he could say was, "We'll find it." He considered the information for a moment then thought changing the subject might ease his mind. "How'd ye get into the freight business, Bill?"

"'Fore I got into hauling freight I worked the mines with a bunch of secesh war pals of mine – little place we named Atlanta up in the moun-tains on the Boise River. Bunch of us come out here after the war. All of us from Georgia – fought for General John B. Gordon through most of it. Sharpsburg was my first fight. Fought at Gettysburg too – took a ball in my leg the first day and missed the rest of the contest. Got back with General Gordon at Spotsylvania and stayed with him all the way to Appomattox. Lord did we fight for that man Gordon. I'd fight for him again if he called me, don't make no difference what the cause. I was there at the end, hadn't had a bite to eat in three days, spent to the bone, never been so wore-out – yes sir, I was there when General Gordon gave up the fight to Yankee General Joshua Chamberlain. He was a helluva good man that Chamberlain. Would have been proud to fight for him if I'd been a Yankee. He respected us Rebs as fighting men and all that we fought and died for whether he believed in it or not and he did not, no sir."

He gazed quietly over the mules' ears, spat, then continued. "I will never forget what he done 'til the day I die. As us Rebs was marching down the road to surrender with our heads down and our hearts as heavy as lead ol' Chamberlain ordered his men to *carry arms!* as a show of respect. All you could hear was steel being drawn out of scabbards and rifles bein' slapped against palms. Ain't ashamed to tell you that it made me weep from deep down in my soul. General Gordon returned the respect by unsheathing his sword and then slowly he dropped the point to his stirrup as he bowed his head. The whole valley was as quiet as death. Now them's real men, Ramsay Sproat.

"That was the saddest day of my life. No one but a secesh soldier like me knows how sad and weary we were. We damn near starved that winter of sixty-five in them trenches at Petersburg but we stuck it out and fought 'til April. Bobby Lee knew if the Cause had any chance at all we'd have to abscond from that trap we were in. We had to run all night and fight all day 'til Yankees by the thousands stopped us."

Bill became silent, his elbows resting on his knees, his hands barely moving, holding the lines limply, as if his reminiscing had been cathartic. Thoughts that may have been buried or troubling, it seemed, were now being released, some good, some bad. Ramsay barely moved, respecting the silence.

Bill spat and wiped his mouth on his sleeve. "You probably don't know much about our War Between the States, coming to the States after it was over. Maybe don't care. But you damned sure should care cause there ain't a soul alive in these United States that weren't tore apart by it somehow. You and your kids are gonna hear about it the rest of your lives. It was one fierce struggle – death everywhere. All us secesh fought for was the same as what George Washington fought for – independence. We call it the Lost Cause now, cause that's what it was.

"But it's over now. We lost. So a bunch of us come out here 'cause the South was torn inside out and it'll be that way long after I'm in the ground. Hurt too much to see beautiful ol' Georgia burnt and torn to shreds. Had to leave.

"How'd I get into hauling freight? Well sir, I just got plumb tired of digging in the dirt. That's about it. I haul ore and freight all over that Boise River country and it is damn sure a beautiful stretch. If I were looking for a place for sheep you couldn't do much better than some of that high country I pass through time and again."

Bill went on to describe the Boise River country and how to get there. He described the drainages, the roads and the passes and told Ramsay he'd do his best to draw him a map. He talked about the great salmon and trout in the rivers and the elk herds and the big mule deer and the beautiful stands of timber and the lush meadows and grassy hillsides.

"Tell me aboot the Indians, Bill. We expected tae see some on our way across the plains or even in the mountains we crossed. Have nae seen an Indian yet – even a buffalo and was told we might see millions of 'em. Will we come across Indians or buffalo before Boise City?"

"We might see a few Injuns but no buffalo. Buffalo need that thick grass country on the plains – too dry here. Never been any here far as I know. But as for Injuns, they's just like any other human anywhere you look. They fight for their land just like white men and yellow men and black men. The Injuns in the Snake River country are only here cause way back in time they got their asses kicked out of the buffalo country by tougher Injuns. That'd be my reckoning. Why else would they scrounge around here in the brush and rocks for rabbits and rock chucks and the like when there's fat ol' buffalo for the takin' on the plains? Just because you're an Injun don't mean you love all other Injuns. Times have changed for most all of 'em. The railroad opened up a market for hides and that brought out buffalo thieves by the thousands so there ain't hardly no buffalo left south of the Dakota and Montana Territories – all been killed or chased north with the Sioux that's been following 'em and a living off of 'em just like they done for centuries. But them Sioux kinda got sick of running north and the buffalo running out and started harassing the white sodbusters they thought had started it all. That brought the Army out and the Injun Wars started. Now guess who's getting' their asses kicked? Nothing lasts forever – s'pose someday someone'll kick the white man out. It's just the way it is. My daddy used to say, 'Time flies faster when there's less of it.' S'pect the Injun's a believer."

A cool cross breeze came up suddenly, prompting Bill to pause and inhale deeply, a fresh respite from the stale smelly air coming off the mules.

The breeze left as suddenly as it came. Bill spat without comment. "The Bannock and Piute had a few scrapes of their own with the Army. About seven maybe eight years ago was the Snake War. Injuns lost 'cause they live in bunches of not more than about a hundred and it was too damned hard to organize themselves into a fighting bunch, them being such an independent lot. That and the Army had General George Crook, a tough ol' son-of-a-bitch – ran up against Crook and his brigade at Burnside Bridge in the Battle of Sharpsburg.

"Now most Bannock and some Piute are on the Fort Hall Reservation fighting over their treaty with the Army, saying they got a right on Camas Prairie to dig camas roots to keep from starving in the winter. They're saying that them sodbusting whites and their hogs are eating and plowing up all the camas – could be a big war coming. You might be tempted some day to run your sheep on that prairie but I'm here to tell you right now it ain't yours. It belongs to the Injuns, at least for now or until they get kicked out, which seems to be their lot in life.

"Injuns left in these parts are pretty much a peace-loving lot – whatever deviltry was in 'em is long gone now but they'll fight if they have to just like anyone else if they get pushed around too much. Life ain't easy for an Injun in the Snake country. Guess that's what happens to the whipped in this here world – just like the South and Georgia."

Bill paused and again stared out over his mules' ears. "Too hot and dry in Snake country for buffalo. All there is is deer and antelope and they're both harder to hunt than chasing a buffalo on flat ground. There's elk in the mountains but that's the problem – they're in the mountains. These here Injuns in the Snake country, the Bannock and some Paiute, live off fish, a few deer, rabbits, burrowing critters like rock chucks, a few ducks and the like and camas. But if you leave 'em alone and they don't feel like you're stealin' from 'em then you'll get along. You might lose fifteen or twenty sheep a year but it damn sure is cheap rent for using their land. Don't forget that."

Ramsay and Bill were both silent for half an hour; Ramsay mulled all this over in his mind and struggled with conflicting emotions. Was he about to be a party to subjugating an entire people, a similar subjugation he himself had just fled only two years ago? *On the other hand,* he thought, *I'm nae going tae bother them and there's so mooch of this land. Why should they have it all? They don't even know how tae use it and, in the midst of all this plenty they are at risk of starvin'? That's madness.* He thought about it some more and realized he might be thinking like an American and he was all right with that, he decided. He knew he would always regard Scotland as his homeland but was beginning to think of America as his country.

Not far ahead Ramsay could see the road was going to gradually ascend, meaning the mules had a struggle coming up. He pulled his pocket watch out, clicked open its cover – it was three o'clock. About then Bill said, "Time to stop and rest these mules. Whoa mules."

As they came to an abrupt stop, Bob vaulted off the wagon, ran to the front and assumed his position.

Bill set the brake, tied the lines and said, "We'll stop for about a half hour, water 'em then head up that there hill – should get to the top by around six. There's a nice meadow there and a little crick where we'll make camp and spend the night."

They were all getting into a routine, just like Bob. First they would each find a discreet place to relieve themselves, Annie Chris always first. Ramsay would get his bucket and Bill would get his, Annie Chris would get back in the wagon, pull out the canvas hose and siphon as the two men hauled tubs full of water to the mules, to Bob and then Lucy. They made sure every critter got its fill.

When they'd finished Bill said, "This next stretch is a long one. Tires the mules out considerably so Ramsay, you're gonna have to walk and carry the baby and Mrs. Sproat you ride the mare. And I been looking at that there cradle and I got an idea. Let's tie it on your back, Ramsay. Got some rope here, let's give it a try."

Bill looped some rope over and around Ramsay's shoulders and tied some knots and within minutes the cradle was firmly in place on Ramsay's back. Annie Chris lifted Katherine in. She looked bewildered at first but once Ramsay walked around a little she seemed to like it.

"I got a couple of wheel chocks back there that I'm gonna drag behind them rear wheels," Bill said as he pointed to the big, heavy-looking wooden wedges attached to the back of the wagon. "I'm gonna drag 'em behind the back wheels so they'll stop the wagon from rolling downhill when we stop to give the mules a rest. I want you to walk to the side of the wagon, not in the back, just in case they don't hold."

Bill dropped the wheel chocks and climbed up into the seat. Bob, with no prompting, stayed behind with Ramsay and Annie Chris. He'd walked from this very spot many times over the past several years.

"Hup mules, hup, hup. That's it boys, pull, pull," Bill commanded.

It was a slow but steady climb. About every twenty minutes Bill would draw the lines, stop the mules and hit the brake. The wagon would slowly roll a foot or so backward until each of the rear wheels rolled onto a wheel chock and stopped. He allowed the mules to catch their breath for a couple of minutes then, "Hup mules, hup, hup. That's it boys, pull, pull," all over again until they reached the top.

The mules were lathered in sweat and breathing hard in long even pulls of air, their nostrils flaring with each breath. Within minutes they were eager to get going because, as Ramsay and Annie Chris were soon to find out, the meadow and creek were less than twenty minutes away and the mules knew it.

The road made a sharp turn to the east around a high rock embankment and then, in full view, was a green meadow oasis in the middle of nothing but rocks and sagebrush. A little creek ran the length of it. The creek crossed the road and was so small that, if allowed, the mules would easily stomp it into a muddy mess.

Bill guided the mules and the wagon to a wide spot off the road, just short of the meadow and the creek. "Whoa mules. Here we are – first stop.

"First thing we take care of is the animals. They been doin' all the work. We're gonna unharness and tie 'em to the wagon then we're gonna water 'em from the kegs cause there ain't enough water in this here little crick if we'd let 'em hit it all at once."

After the mules and Lucy were watered, Bill pulled out a sack of oats and gave each animal a pan full and said to Ramsay, "Grab that ax and go up on the sidehill and cut some sagebrush for a fire."

Ramsay unstrapped the ax from the side of the wagon and started walking. He looked back and saw Bill currying and brushing each mule. One at a time, Bill lifted all four of each mule's feet, cleaned out rocks as needed and occasionally hammered a shoe a little tighter. As he did, he stroked their necks and talked to each in soft tones Ramsay was too far away to hear. Lucy was last and received the same gentle treatment as the mules.

Bill climbed into the wagon and pulled out a sack of hobbles, climbed back out, untied each mule one at a time, led it into the meadow, buckled a set of leather hobbles to the mule's front feet, took off its halter and scratched gently behind its ears as each head dropped to the green grass beneath its feet. Lucy was last and was hobbled as well and for her, he had a leather strap with a bell that he buckled around her neck.

"They won't run off in the night?" asked Annie Chris after Lucy was released.

"Bob stays with 'em – keeps 'em close," said Bill. "They don't even know they're being herded. He raised hell one night about two years ago – a cougar had his eye on the mules. That cougar's hide's stretched out on a wall in a saloon in Boise City."

Bill walked back to the wagon, unbuckled the shovel off the side, carried it to a spot in the creek near the road and began shoveling big spades full of thick black mud from the creek bottom. Within minutes he had a good-sized hole the creek quickly filled. The water would clear up by morning so they could fill their water kegs before they left.

He went back to the wagon and pulled out a double-barreled shotgun and some shells from a box beneath the seat. Bob sat on his haunches looking up at Bill with a dog smile, his tail wagging in big sweeps across the dirt.

Bill laid the gun carefully on the seat of the wagon and reached behind for a wooden rectangular box filled with kitchen supplies. He set it near where he'd told Ramsay to build a fire.

Annie Chris approached with sleeping Katherine in her arms. She said quietly, "I hope I'm not being meddlesome Bill, but I overheard you telling my husband about the war – my word that must have been a horrible experience for you."

"It was a peculiar kind of war, more horrible than most wars I reckon. Many a time a man had to shoot across the battlefield knowing his brother or cousin or maybe even his daddy was on the other side. But you know, as bad as it was, I wouldn't trade a minute of it for a minute of not being there. That probably don't make no sense at all to you but that's how I feel and I know most vets, Yanks or Rebs, feels the same. Gives you a powerful appreciation for life when you're in the heat of battle knowing you might lose it any second. Maybe it's fear, I can't tell you for sure but it sure enough makes you feel alive. A vet never forgets that feeling ma'am – can't explain it any better than that."

"I've read some about the Civil War. We've been in America for over two years. The newspapers are full of stories about it. The aristocracy ruled where Ramsay and I came from. They kept the lower classes like us poor with no hope, so I'm partial to the Union cause and can't understand why those who weren't slave-holders would fight to preserve slavery. Why did *you* fight, Bill?"

"You think them blue bellies was fighting because they cared about slaves? If you do, you are darn sure wrong ma'am. They fought to preserve the Union. They thought breaking it up was like throwing away the whole damn idea of democracy and them kings and fancy fellas in Europe was right all along – common men can't govern themselves, they need kings or the whole damn thing'd blow up. Billie Yank didn't give one rat's ass about them darkies.

"Why'd I fight? Lincoln and his blue bellies invaded our homeland, that's why. They don't just march in on us without a fight, trying to make us like them with their smoking factories and all. No ma'am. They just wanted to shove their ways on us. They found out Johnny Reb could shove back pretty damn hard. Wooo weeh!"

"I don't understand. You approved of bondage?"

"Did you hear a damn word I said? I didn't give one piss in hell about slavery one way or the other – neither did Billie Yank."

"Well let me tell you something Bill Judy," said Annie Chris, her temper having exceeded its normal limit. "If you were ever enslaved you'd give a piss in hell about slavery. I wasn't enslaved but it was as close as you can get. Ramsay and I had to engage in trickery just to escape. If we'd been caught our fate would've been worse than a fleeing slave being returned to his owner."

"Wooo wee! You are a feisty one and might be right on that. But you know something, I had no more an idea what a slave was than Billie Yank and probably had less of an opinion on the subject. I will admit to this though: toward the end in them trenches at Petersburg, me and a lot of my sick and starvin' pals got to thinking about what in the hell we was fightin' for. We damn sure didn't want them Yankees running things but we got to wondering if we were suffering and dying just to keep them rich planters in charge. Seemed more and more like a rich man's war and a poor man's fight. Could be a lot like Scotland I expect. Them planters are probably a lot like them fancy pants e-ristocats in Scotland.

"Lots of Rebs up and down the line skedaddled. Looked to them like we was beat. Worried about their kin mostly but skedaddling weren't for me – no ma'am. I gave my word to Marse Robert and General Gordon. Way I figured, don't make no difference how the war shaked out, if you're cheating on your own word you just as well be dead."

They both became quiet. Annie Chris broke the silence: "You're a very good man, Bill. You've never found a woman you cared about?"

"I did ma'am, just once but she didn't see no future in the likes of me I reckon."

"Whoever she was, Bill, she made a big mistake."

Bill looked out toward the meadow. "Enough war talk, we gotta get our supper going. You can help me if you've a mind."

"Bill, we are fully prepared to fend for our meals ourselves. You explained that to my husband. We understand completely."

"And I meant ever damn word of it too. But what I didn't know at the time was what right nice folks you are. It is my pleasure to share what I got if you don't mind sharing what you got."

"We would be proud to share meals with you, Bill. Now what can I do?"

Used to doing everything himself, Bill glanced around the area temporarily at a loss for an answer. "Well ma'am, inside this here box you'll find a couple of Dutch ovens and most anything else you might need. Got a pan in there with some sourdough starter – you might want to whip up some batter for some biscuits. Bob and me's gonna take my shotgun and go get us some sagehens for supper. When Ramsay comes back with firewood you could get a fire going, grab that empty lard can there and set some water to boilin' for coffee then send him back for more wood. Can't have too much wood – takes lots of hot coals for a Dutch oven."

"Come on Bob," Bill said as he reached up on the seat for his shotgun. He walked off to the opposite side of the meadow from where Ramsay was gathering wood, Bob in the lead. His tail wagged happily.

Within fifteen minutes Annie Chris heard a boom and then another boom. In the distance she saw Bob sprint ahead of Bill. Five minutes later she heard another pair of booms. By that time Ramsay had made three trips for wood, had a fire started and had put up their tent. The high desert evening summer air felt crisp, clean and cool mixed with the distinctive smell of the sagebrush fire. Lucy and the mules had hardly moved from where Bill had freed them from their halters, their heads lowered, grazing on the lush green meadow grass. Other than the crackling of the fire, the only sound Annie Chris could hear was the occasional clank of Lucy's bell each time she hopped forward a step in her hobbles. Annie Chris had batter prepared for biscuits, water heating on the fire and was peeling potatoes as she looked over and cooed at Katherine, convinced the baby was smiling back. Annie Chris felt very happy.

Bob and his three human companions finished a supper as fine as they'd ever eaten just as the sun lowered out of sight. Ramsay put more brush on the smoldering fire.

Bob lay next to Bill dozing lightly and listened carefully for how distant the sound of Lucy's bell was becoming. Bill gently stroked the top of his head reassuring him not to worry, stay where he was and rest awhile.

Bill pulled a piece of wood from his back pocket, reached into his front pocket for a pocketknife and began whittling.

Annie Chris emerged from the tent having fed, changed and put to bed a very tired little girl.

None of the three felt compelled to talk as they sat consumed by their own thoughts silently staring at the fire. The companionship of a campfire does not always require conversation.

Annie Chris broke the silence as she looked across the fire at Bob and asked Bill, "Will Bob come to me if I call him?"

"Bob's his own self. Seems to ignore most everyone but me – you can ask him."

Annie Chris folded the top half of her body over her thighs and knees, looked at Bob, patted her right calf with the palm of her hand and said softly, "Bob, will you come and see me?"

Bob rose up on his haunches, looked up at Bill who nodded his approval and slowly walked around the fire to Annie Chris. He stood next to her while she petted him and talked to him. Within a few minutes he lowered himself to the ground and seemed to relax. Annie Chris stopped the rhythmic petting for only a few seconds. Bob nuzzled her hand with his nose and encouraged her to continue.

"In Scotland we have dogs like Bob who are very good with sheep. I think he may have some of the same instincts. Tell us about him," she asked.

"Ain't much to tell. About two years ago I was freightin' outa Boise Basin and camped for the night along a crick. Woke up the next morning and Bob was sitting next to me. Got no idea where he come from – just sorta hired on. He was pretty skinny, maybe a year old would be my guess. Limping pretty bad too – had a cut on his paw and bleeding a little from his right flank. I fixed us some breakfast, cleaned him up then he watched me hitch my mules. He just seemed to know what I was doing and did what he could to pitch in. Reckon he felt he owed me that for serving him his breakfast. He showed them mules his teeth when they tried to move too much and they been respecting him ever since."

In the dim fire's light Annie Chris saw a softness in Bill's eyes and slight quiver in his chin. He blinked twice and cleared his throat. "A man ain't never had a better friend than the friend I got in ol' Bob."

Annie Chris gave Bill a moment. "Why did you name him Bob?"

"Named him after the best man I ever knew, General Robert E. Lee."

They sat quietly, their talk spent for the evening, watching the last of the sagebrush flames turn to embers then, with the high desert night chill encroaching, Ramsay turned to his wife. "We better turn in, I'm sure the morrow will be a tester. How far will we be goin' Bill?"

"Gotta make about eighteen miles tomorrow – figurin' on leaving about seven."

"I'll have breakfast ready by six," said Annie Chris.

They each stood; as they did, Bob rose and trotted toward the meadow in the direction of the last clang of Lucy's bell.

CHAPTER SEVEN

The next morning as the mules were striding along on a fairly level stretch pulling without much strain, Bill asked Ramsay if he'd ever driven a hitch. Ramsay said, "I have nae and I best be learnin' soon. In Scotland only the very rich have horses. Poor crofters like us walked. Could I have a go of it?"

"Here you go," said Bill, handing over the driving lines. For the next two hours Bill guided Ramsay as the Scot learned to coax the mules to respond to his commands. Bill made a strong point of telling Ramsay that the biggest mistake he could ever make was to lose his temper.

"Animals, they got a sense for a man's fear and frustration. They ain't trying to be ornery – most times they're just confused by how dumb the man is. Getting mad at an animal never helps, only makes the animal lose respect for you and when you lost that you just as well go to selling rot gut for a living like the barkeep back in Kelton."

"Do the mules have names?" Annie Chris asked from the back.

"Yes indeed, ma'am," answered Bill. "Named 'em after some of Robert E. Lee's generals. You remember me telling you about General Lee – named Bob after him. You probably don't have no notion at all who he was. He was one helluva man. Us Rebs called him Marse Robert – like a father to us, at least that's what we thought. Ain't a man in his whole army wouldn't lay his life down for him.

"Abe Lincoln couldn't find a general in his whole damn Yankee army that Marse Robert didn't make a damn fool out of. Finally took Yankee General Grant and nearly four times the soldiers to take us starving secesh down. Nothing Marse Robert could have done about that. Numbers is numbers. They had 'em, we didn't."

Bill spat a long stream, wiped his mouth with his sleeve, lifted his chin proudly and said, "If Marse Robert would've had mules like these here, the South could've won that war – skinny starvin' critters, all of 'em.

Lead team is Tom on the left and Jack on the right. Tom is short for General Thomas 'Stonewall' Jackson and Jack is short for General John B. Gordon. Team behind them is Jeb on the left and Pete on the right, named after General JEB Stewart and General James 'Ole Pete' Longstreet. Them

47

four mules is the ones I trust the most. Team behind them is Baldy on the left and Jubal on the right, named after General Dick 'Baldy' Ewell and General Jubal Early and like Marse Robert, I get a little skittish 'bout them two sometimes. Team in the rear is Wheezy on the left and George on the right. Named Wheezy after General A.P. Hill – coughing and a farting all the time just like Hill. Put him in the back so's he won't gas the others – I can hold in my breath, they can't. Hee, hee!

"Notice anything different about ol' George here?" asked Bill with a chuckle, pointing to the mule directly in front of Ramsay.

Annie Chris looked up and down each mule then said excitedly, "Aye, I do, you've left his mane long but trimmed all the others."

"You got a good eye, ma'am." Bill spat then continued. "I left George's mane long cause Pickett's hair was as long and as pretty as any woman's hair you ever saw. George is the prettiest mule of 'em all. He knows it too. Put him last cause George was last in his class at West Point. That's my mules – Tom and Jack, Jeb and Pete, Baldy and Jubal then Wheezy and George. Finest mules in the whole damn Idaho Territory – not perfect, mind you, but put together they make as fine a pulling army as there ever was."

"Those are damned good names, Bill," said Annie Chris. "Sorry about the language but sometimes there's no substitute for a colorful word."

Bill threw his head back and laughed. "You're damned right ma'am. If colorful words is a good thing then goodness oughta be a dripping outa every pore in this ol' secesh hide of mine! Hee, hee!"

On the second day they met a teamster with a wagon loaded with ore headed for Kelton. They stopped and exchanged information about the meadows, the water, the condition of the road and all the other things men of their profession need to know. The teamster warned Bill to watch for rocks in the cut, gave Ramsay and Annie Chris a skeptical look and said, "See you got you a fare, Bill, hope it's going all right."

"Going fine – got me some right nice folks here."

Bill asked the teamster about John Hailey, saying he'd heard John had been injured somehow.

"Hailey's doing pretty good. Story I heard was that ol' John got a bit careless. As sharp as that cuss is, he made a bad mistake when some ol' guy asked him to help him with a mean stud. John knew that son of a bitch was a little surly but went in that damn corral leaving his better judgment behind. The stud took in after John like a bear goin' after fresh meat, bared his teeth and damned near ripped John's arm clean off. He crawled under the corral poles just in time or the goddamn thing would have killed him. Went and got his rifle, John did, and shot it dead. After he'd killed the son of a bitch he turned and gave that ol' guy a look like, *you're next you ass-hole.* Owner, he begged for his life – told John he'd pay for the doctorin' and all. John, he just lowered his rifle and walked away."

The teamster shook his head and winced as if in pain himself. "John didn't say a word – knew it was mostly his own damn fault. Anyway it's been over a month and he's back to freighting. Doctored himself. You know, ol' John's a goddamn good doctor – even brought a few babies into this world I been told. Sure you'll see him 'fore you get to Boise City – maybe even City of Rocks."

~September 5, 1874~

The next morning at breakfast Annie Chris asked, "Bill, can you tell us about City of Rocks? What's there anyway?"

"It's a stop on the California Trail – real pretty. Over the years folks have been writing their names all over them rocks. Lots of big tall rocks scattered everywhere. There's a stage stop there now about where the Kelton Road meets the California Trail. Nice meadow and a nice little crick called Circle Crick."

"My kin are meeting us at a spot called Camp Rock. You know where that is?"

"Yup, good spot."

Bill stood and stretched, prompting Annie Chris to start gathering up after breakfast. "Around mid-day we're gonna come up on a cut in the road – kind of a bad stretch, real narrow with lots of curves. Gotta watch for rocks coming down off the cut – had a big gully washer of a rain there about a week ago. Rocks'll fall off that cut for two weeks after one of them rains so you never know what you're in for 'til ya get there."

Bill put his hand on the big left rear wheel. "If a wheel catches one of them rocks it could cause all kinda trouble. The cut'll be on our left. Ramsay, when we get there I'll have you ride Lucy on up ahead of the mules and toss any rocks ya see outa the way.

"To drive mules you gotta think like a mule. That cut makes 'em nervous and a little spooky every time I go through it. It's narrow and they can't see what's ahead on account of all the curves and all, so ma'am, you and Kate stay behind and walk. Won't be for more than an hour – safer that way."

Annie Chris's head turned sharply in Bill's direction the moment she heard him say *Kate* but she said nothing.

"Once we're through the cut it'll be a pretty easy time of it all the way to City of Rocks."

"We're eager to get there and meet our family and introduce them to you, Bill. We've never met them ourselves so it's a big day for us."

"All right then – let's get this wagon on down the road."

After the camp was loaded and the mules were grained, watered, harnessed and hitched, Bill stepped up into the seat and said, "Ma'am, you and Kate come on up here with me and Bob. It'll be a couple of hours 'fore we get to the cut then you better get out and walk. Ramsay, you ride Lucy. I'll tell you when to go on ahead."

"Ye just tell me what tae do and when tae do it."

As they lumbered along in the crisp morning air Bill pulled the crown of his hat down to shade his eyes from the glare of the morning sun. Annie Chris did the same with her bonnet then covered Katherine's face with her blanket. The conversation was light until Annie Chris asked, "What was it like in Georgia when you were a child?"

"We lived up in the northern part near the Tennessee border, not far from Chattanooga. Most everyone was just poor dirt farmers like my daddy and his daddy.

"My momma and daddy had six kids – four made it past the first year, two didn't. I worked for my daddy trying to grow tobacco and corn and grain. We was so poor my daddy had to hire me out to the neighbors for wages most years. Went off to the war when I was sixteen. Came home after the surrender. My daddy was dead and buried and my momma found herself a new husband. Everyone else gone off to parts unknown, so I did too. Now here I am. Sorry for such a short story, ma'am, but that's all there is to it. I ain't got no regrets, no ma'am."

Bill called Ramsay to ride on over next to him and lined out orders for the coming hour. "We'll be going down a steep hill for about an hour so

I'm gonna stop and set these drag shoes in front of the back wheels and lock the wheels with these chains to keep 'em from turning. Then I'm gonna drop this here timber to drag in the back. Ma'am, time for you to step on down. Ramsay, you go on ahead now. Tie the shovel on your saddle so's you got something to help you move big rocks. If you find one you can't move come on back and get me."

Bill reached into his left trouser pocket and pulled out a whittler's work of art, a perfectly formed rattle with a handle small enough for a baby's hand on one end, a knob on the other and a thin shaft in the middle surrounded by four loose concentric rings that he shook and rattled with sheer delight. "Been whittling away on this last couple of nights – bet little Kate's gonna like it!"

"Och mercy Bill, thank you," said Annie Chris, as pleased as if it were made of pure silver. "Kate will be grinning and making a racket before you know it."

From that moment, Katherine Cora Sproat was known as Kate.

"Pleasure's mine ma'am." He walked to the rear of the wagon, locked the wheels with the rough lock chains, secured the drag shoes in place and loosened the big heavy timber from the back. It dropped to the ground with a thud and a cloud of dust. He checked all the chains to make sure they were secure, walked to the front, climbed back in his seat and coaxed the mules forward. "Hup mules, hup, hup. That's it boys, pull, pull." As the wagon began to move, thick clouds of dust rolled up from the drag shoes digging into the road, added to by the timber being dragged behind.

Ramsay trotted Lucy on up ahead. After he'd gone a ways he stopped and turned his head to look back. As the wagon slowly came toward him he could see the mules' heads held high, sixteen big ears stiff as boards, the mules' eyes bright with anxiety. He could hear them breathing in low rumbling snorts.

Annie Chris walked on the right side of the increasingly narrow road to avoid the dust until the road became so narrow that the only way she could keep herself and the baby from choking was to walk further behind. She walked along slowly at a distance following the cloud of dust, unable to see the wagon at all.

Ramsay found a few rocks, none too big to cause much trouble. Each one he came to he'd get off Lucy and roll it off the roadway down the embankment.

He'd moved a dozen or so rocks within forty-five minutes when he rounded a sharp turn and spotted a big jagged rock resting right in the middle of the left-hand track in the roadway. He looked ahead and could see the country opening up in the near distance. He was about at the end of the cut. He dismounted Lucy and untied the shovel. First he tried to move it without the shovel but couldn't budge it. It was resting on its flat side so he knew he couldn't roll it and would have to scoot it using the shovel as a pry, but as he increased the amount of force, he feared he'd break the shovel handle and stopped.

He stood sweating as the sun got hotter, scratching his head, wondering what he should do. Bill was far enough behind that he felt he had time to find a way to move the rock himself without going back for Bill's help. He knew he had no time to waste. Because of the blind turn, when Bill and his mules rounded the corner, the rock would be squarely in their path with no chance for them to stop in time or veer away from it.

Ramsay looked around for something to pry the rock with, not sure what it might be. He walked to the edge of the embankment and looked down into the steep wash below. About twenty feet down he spotted a small stout-looking downed tree not more than four inches in diameter. *I have time,* he thought.

He untied Lucy's halter rope from the saddle and tied it around his waist. He tied her reins around the rock, walked back to the edge of the embankment and side-stepped his way down to keep from falling. Within seconds he'd made it to the bottom and was next to the log.

He lifted the tree to test its weight. It was light enough that he thought he could drag it uphill. He tied the rope around the smaller end of the tree and tried to pull it straight up the embankment but was unable to get traction in the loose dry dirt. He realized he'd have to course his way along the side-hill gradually going uphill until he met the road. Time was passing too quickly.

Annie Chris felt it first. She thought the earth had moved beneath her feet but then thought the dust must be making her dizzy. The ground kept moving. Was she fainting? She squeezed Kate tightly and spread her feet to keep from falling. *My God, what is happening?* She felt helpless, nowhere to go to escape. Should she run? Should she stay?

Ramsay was struggling to make it up the embankment, slipping and sliding in the loose dry dirt. He managed to dodge two bucket-sized rocks rolling in his direction.

The wagon's slow steep descent along the cut was going fine for Bill until he was about fifty yards from the rock in the road that Ramsay had found, just short of the blind curve. He'd entered a portion of the road where the cut into the hillside was almost vertical from the top down to the roadbed, the upper part fifteen feet high, so close that he had to be careful steering the mules so the inside wheels of the wagon wouldn't scrape against the rocky embankment.

It was right there in absolutely the worst part of the road that the road itself moved beneath the mules' feet. Rocks rumbled and rolled into the cut from the hillside above. Baldy bucked when a fist-sized rock struck his rump. Jubal snorted a deep guttural mule snort as another hit him behind his left ear. They were both bucking now and straining to go somewhere to avoid the rocks that were falling on Jeb and Pete in front of them. The earth moving beneath them was the least of their worries as they panicked to avoid being caught in an all-out rock slide. Now all the mules were panicked, jumping and bucking, trying desperately to get out of the cut that their instincts had already told them to fear. They started to run.

Bill had no idea what was happening on the road below. All he knew was that rocks were falling and the mules were as hell bent to get out of the way as a sodbuster facing a tornado. He stood, pulled on the lines hard as he could and hollered, "Whoa mules!" His command was ignored; they were headed down the road as fast as thirty-two powerful mule legs could take them, the timber bouncing behind – eight panicked mules running to get out of that damn cut.

Ramsay had just made it to the top of the lower embankment and back on the road dragging the small log behind him when he saw, first Tom and Jack and, within an instant, the other mules and the wagon, come bolting around the corner. One quick glance and Ramsay could see panic in Tom and Jack's bulging eyes. Lucy was no longer tied to the rock. She had broken her reins when she jerked backwards to avoid being hit by a rock rolling off the hillside. He looked down the road to his right and saw her loping away from him as fast as she could.

Ramsay made a futile attempt to calm the mules thinking he could stop them by jumping up and down and waving his arms before they came to the rock he'd tried to move, the biggest one in a road now littered with more rocks that had rolled off the hillside. The panicked mules ignored him as if he wasn't there. He knew instantly that if he were to save his own life he'd have to dive off the embankment.

Tom, Jeb, Wheezy and Jubal (whose path the rock was squarely in front of) had no trouble jumping over the low flat rock. The left front wagon wheel, however, hit the inside edge of the rock. The wagon veered sharply to the right. Bill was standing now and holding nothing but the lines allowing him no stability. When the wagon veered right, Bill fell left and was vaulted over the side along the rocky cut. He reached out with his right hand on his way over and grabbed for anything that might break his fall. His hand latched onto a hook. When it did, the force of his own weight swung him beneath the wagon and caused him to lose his grip as his body slammed up into the wagon's underside. The force threw the trunk of his body clear of the left rear drag shoe but not his left leg which took the full weight of the wagon as the shoe crushed the leg just below his knee.

The timber bounced in the air just as Bill approached its path and came down with a dull thud on his right arm then bounced on down the road behind the wagon.

As Bill was being vaulted off the left of the wagon Bob leaped off to the right and rolled down the embankment. He landed at the bottom unharmed.

Bob picked himself up and sprinted back up to the road. He reached the road about the same time as Ramsay who had a much more difficult time of it.

Ramsay turned his head to follow the wagon's course and watched it slow to an eventual stop two hundred yards down the road. He knew Annie Chris would be behind somewhere and probably safe and thought Bill was aboard the wagon. It surprised him to see Bob running back toward the rock instead of in the direction of the wagon.

In the settling dust, his eyes focused on the two objects that Bob was running toward.

One was Annie Chris. Her bonnet had flown off and bounced on her back with each wild step as she ran with Kate in her arms toward the object lying crumpled in the dust on the road.

As Ramsay began running to meet her, he noticed his knee was bleeding and exposed through a tear in his britches.

He knew now that it was Bill in the road.

Bob got there first and stood over Bill licking his face. Annie Chris arrived next. She laid her baby down near the side of the road and rushed to Bill. Bob looked up at her and bared his teeth. Annie Chris ignored him just as she ignored Kate's screaming. Bill was not moving. Ramsay arrived, his chest heaving. Bob began to whimper and continued to lick Bill's face.

The Sproats dropped to their knees next to Bill. His eyes were open. He was breathing in short gasps. Both of their eyes were drawn to his lower right leg which was a mass of blood and dirt. With his knife, Ramsay cut across Bill's trousers at the knee just above the bloody mess, careful not to move the leg. He cut the leg of Bill's longjohns and pulled the garments down to Bill's boot top.

Annie Chris jerked the bonnet from her head and slid it under Bill's calf. His tibia was protruding through the skin. Blood oozed from the wound. A pool of red was building in the dirt. Other than his short panting breaths, Bill made no sound. He just looked up at the sky and tried not to move.

Annie Chris screamed, "Take off your kerchief and wrap it around his leg! Just below his knee. Tie it loosely. Go get a stick that we can use to twist it tight. Hurry!"

Ramsay jumped up and scanned the roadway looking for anything that might work. Nothing was within view. He spotted Bill's knife in its sheath and handed it to Annie Chris. She slipped the knife under the kerchief and began to twist.

"I think we've stopped the bleeding but I don't know why he's so still." She leaned over to Bill. "Bill, Ramsay and I are here. Can you hear me?"

In a barely audible voice he answered, "I can hear you. My right arm. Hurts like hell. Where's Bob? He all right? The mules?"

"Bob's right here Bill. He's fine. The mules are fine. We'd like to move you out of the road into the shade. Would that be all right?"

"Kate all right?"

"Everyone's fine."

"I need your knife," she said to Ramsay.

Annie Chris cut and tore about a one foot square piece of cloth from her skirt then tore off the hem. She folded the piece of cloth in fourths and placed it over Bill's wound. He cried out in pain as she carefully lifted his leg and wrapped the cloth around it and tied it with the hem.

"We need to move him to the shade."

"I can move my own self – which way's the shade?" Bill leaned up on his left elbow and tried to scoot.

"No you won't," Annie Chris scolded. "Ramsay'll help you."

Ramsay placed his hands under Bill's armpits and lifted.

"Careful there, goddamn it. I ain't no sack of beans. I think my right arm's broke. Leave me for a spell."

"Let's have another go at it," he said to Ramsay, after a few minutes.

"What happened tae ye?" asked Ramsay as he dragged Bill carefully.

"Hell if I know. Rocks falling everywhere – couldn't stop the mules." He tried to suppress a painful cough then said again, "Couldn't stop 'em."

When Bill was situated fully in the shade Ramsay kneeled at his side. "We need a doctor tae set yer leg. Is there anyone at City of Rocks?"

"Hailey or Alma Hawes – both of 'em set bones before," Bill answered, his voice oily, trailing off, harder to understand now.

"I'll ride Lucy in there and bring one of 'em back."

"It'd be dumb ass luck if Hailey's there. Ol' Alma's our best bet even though she ain't nothin' but a damn sawbones," said Bill, now speaking in a whisper.

"Go – Now!" hollered Annie Chris. "I'll get some water and make him comfortable. Hurry!"

"No, that don't make sense. Put me in the wagon. It'll be slow going but faster than you making two trips."

"He's richt," said Ramsay.

"Damn right I'm right. Now go get me a blanket outa my bedroll and bring it back with my axe and shovel. Bring the cradle too. You'll need it."

Ramsay hesitated and looked puzzled.

"Just do it!" Annie Chris yelled.

Ramsay turned and ran toward the wagon, two hundred yards down the road. He was back in twenty minutes.

"Now lay out the blanket next to me," said Bill, "and get that skinny little log you got there."

By the time Annie Chris had the blanket laid out Ramsay was back with the log.

"Now chop it in half. Put that shovel blade under my left ass cheek and line up the handle under my leg. Get that halter rope and wrap it tight around the handle and my leg, top to bottom. Then you're gonna fold the blanket in thirds and lift me on top. Then slip them two logs through the folds. Then you two are gonna pick me up and carry me to that goddamn wagon. You with me?"

Ramsay and Annie Chris had him laid out on the makeshift stretcher within minutes. Ramsay lifted Kate in her cradle onto his shoulders and was squatted down in front of the hastily made stretcher, his hands behind him grasping the ends of the logs while Annie Chris grasped the other ends.

"One, two, three," said Ramsay, then he and Annie Chris slowly lifted Bill for the two hundred yard walk in the direction of the wagon and the waiting mules. Bob trotted anxiously behind.

They gently laid Bill and the stretcher in the shade of the wagon, crawled inside and shifted some of the freight in the front to create a space large enough for Bill and his stretcher then rolled his bedroll out in the space along with their own. Together, they managed to place Bill in the space, remove the logs and set them aside for his eventual exit.

A tough ride lay ahead for Bill, sprawled out in a wagon without springs traveling an exceptionally rough road, suffering the pain of a compound fracture.

Annie Chris washed around Bill's wound, washed his face, arms and hands. She removed the makeshift bandage and did the best she could to wash dirt and debris from the wound then tore up more of her skirt for a fresh dressing. She eased the tension on the tourniquet which eased Bill's pain a little. "What happened back there? It felt like the ground was shaking – scared me to death."

"Hell if I know, earthquake maybe," said Bill, his face showing relief from the tourniquet. "Don't make no difference now."

Ramsay removed the rough lock chains and drag shoes, retrieved the lines, stepped up into the driver's seat with Bob right behind and situated himself so he could turn his body enough to keep one eye on the mules and one eye on Bill. He slapped the lines twice and hollered, "Hup mules, hup, hup! That's it boys, pull, pull!"

Bill tried to shift his weight each time a wheel hit a bump or a rock, his face wincing with the pain. After a half mile he couldn't keep his mouth shut any longer and said, "Goddamn it, do you have to hit every goddamn bump in the road? I got a broken leg here."

"He's doing the best he can Bill," whispered Annie Chris.

"Like hell he is. He could of drug me behind this goddamn wagon and I'd been a damn sight better off. You hear that Sproat? Do you think you can find a few more bumps? There's another one – wooo weeh, Lord God almighty."

"If ye don't shut yer mouth," Ramsay barked, "I'm gonna come back there and set that leg maself. Then ye'll know what pain is."

Annie Chris snickered as Bill rolled his eyes. She picked up Kate and got situated in the wagon. When they were settled Annie Chris asked, "Tell me about the woman that you were close to. Do you mind?"

"Yes I mind. Don't wanna talk about it. No use – plumb over."

"That's fine. I didn't mean to pry."

"Ain't prying, just don't want to talk about it. That's all."

Just then the wagon lurched to one side as a rear wheel slid off a rock with a bang and raised the predictable outburst. "Damn you Sproat, when I heal up I'm gonna bounce you off the tallest rock I can find so you'll know the pain you're causing me."

"If ye do," Ramsay laughed, "find me some green grass tae land on."

"Tough luck for you, Sproat – ain't much for 200 miles in every direction. You'll bounce like a rubber ball. Hee, hee!" The laugh made him wince.

"Yer making me a wee bit nervous aboot how dry it is here – for sheep I mean."

"Don't fret about it. If you get a place like Willow Crick you'll be fine." Bill hesitated. "'Cept in a drought."

"What's that?"

"A drought? You don't know what a drought is?" His pain coupled with Ramsay's naiveté was beginning to wear on him.

"Naw, I don't. Tell me."

"That's when it don't rain and it don't snow and the cricks dry up. That's what a drought is."

"How long can a drought last? Months?" asked Ramsay.

"Months? Hell, that's plumb normal around here. I'm talking about a couple of years."

"Ye mean naw grass – for a couple of years?"

"Sometimes."

"What do ye do?"

"You scramble best you can. Some folks sell out – pack up and leave. That piece of ground I told you about called Willow Crick, well that little crick just keeps on running – never does plumb dry up, least I ain't never seen it dry. Can't figure why some flatlander ain't latched onto it by now."

Ramsay was quiet. Finally Bill said, "Life's good out here but it ain't easy – you'll find out."

CHAPTER EIGHT

Bill closed his eyes – tired of talk. He thought, *Lord, I could sure use a whiskey.*

He was jolted awake from a half hour of dreamless sleep when he heard Ramsay ask, "Bill, I see rocks way oot there across the flat. That City of Rocks?"

"Shush," said Annie Chris, but it was too late.

"Now how in the hell would I know what you're looking at?" He pulled in a couple of labored breaths then asked, "How long we been traveling?"

"Aboot three hours," said Ramsay.

"I s'pose you oughta be able to see them rocks by now." He rubbed his right hand over his forehead then said, "Damn I got a bitch of a headache." He found his tobacco and bit off a corner.

"Where will you spit, Bill?" asked Annie Chris feigning sympathy. "You're flat on your back."

"That ain't worryin' me none. I got more problems than that."

Annie Chris lifted the canvas she'd covered his leg with, held it up to screen the wound from his sight and was alarmed by the swelling. She loosened the tourniquet a twist, removed the dressing and cleaned the wound again. She tore off more of her skirt and placed another square of cloth over the wound and tied it again with the hem. She washed his leg hoping the cool water would help.

An hour passed while Annie Chris intermittently wiped his leg with cool water. Bill had completely lost his mood for complaining, which worried her. He just lay there looking at the clouds drifting by in the late afternoon September sky, a slight grimace visible across his brow and dark eyes. His face was turning pale, rapidly losing its deep bronze tan.

"Bill yere richt, this place is nae much more than a lot of big rocks poking out of the hills," said Ramsay as the Kelton Road led them slowly closer. "Don't look like naw city I ever saw but these rocks, they *are* huge – great muckle and so heich!"

Bill tried to lift himself up on his left elbow to see out the wagon only to fall back on his back with a grimace. "What the hell kinda Greek is that?" he asked out of frustration.

"He means the rocks are big and tall."

"Why the hell didn't he just say so? Don't he got no control of his goddamn tongue? Rolling around in his mouth like it weren't tied down. Do ya hear me Sproat? A goddamn Chinaman'd be easier to understand."

Annie Chris giggled.

"What the hell you laughing about? You ain't much better. Where are we anyway?"

"Aboot a mile tae the rocks," Ramsay answered grinning.

"In about a half mile the road'll fork. Take the left and go another half mile and you'll see the stage station. Alma oughta be there."

~   ~   ~

It had been a quiet summer at Alma and Albert Hawes's two-story rock house. The stage line to Kelton had been shut down off and on all summer due to the robberies and what little law there was rarely stopped by in their haste to chase down leads. Why those idiots didn't just pack a stage with armed deputies and pull a surprise on the damn thieves was a mystery to Alma.

The "detectives" quit stopping at her place, preferring to chase stupid leads. They reminded her of ants running around in different directions with no apparent purpose.

The flow of emigrants in their wagon trains that went right by their place bound for California had slowed considerably, mostly because of the new Transcontinental Railroad. To help make ends meet, John Hailey had offered Albert a job driving a freight wagon from late April to late November from Kelton to the Boise Basin mining area. Albert came through about once a month and spent a few days doing what he had to do around the place to help Alma out. Other than that, she was on her own, operating the stage stop, taking care of the boarded stock, irrigating the pasture and tending the garden.

The house, with its two-foot-thick rock walls shaded by tall poplar trees, was cool in the summer and warm in the winter, a perfect haven for road weary travelers whether they be emigrants, freighters or stage travelers headed to and from the railroad at Kelton.

She kept two spare rooms on the second floor for guests and had a long table in the first-floor sitting room that served as many as eight guests at a time. A doorway led from the sitting room to the kitchen where a big Majestic wood burning range was visible from the front door. Behind the house, in addition to a rock barn and several outbuildings, was a large sturdy pole corral with three stalls on its north side to separate horses or mules that refused to be cordial if they were unfamiliar with one another. Next to the corral stood a stout hay shed full of loose hay to feed the stage line's replacement horses and the mules that would occasionally be boarded there. Behind all of this was a large fenced green pasture that was irrigated from the creek that ran near the house. The stage hadn't been by for ten days and only one freighter had come by, the same one Bill and his party met on the Kelton Road.

Alma was in her garden picking the season's last ears of sweet corn when she heard her old dog Buster barking in the direction of Kelton. She looked up and in the distance recognized Bill's wagon and mules. She smiled, glad for Bill's company; she knew he'd stay for a day or two. He was always good for a joke and never pestered her to hurry with this or get him that. He was just plain fun and easy to be around and spar with – never in a damn hurry like everyone else these days.

She'd met an older couple from Fort Hall two days earlier who were camped in a meadow down Circle Creek a couple of miles. They had two teams of horses pulling a buckboard with another hitched behind it. They seemed pleasant enough as they asked her to be alert for a young couple and their baby who'd be coming through from Kelton, possibly in the company of a freighter. When or if the young couple did come through, Alma was asked to point them in the direction of their camp. Alma said she would gladly comply.

Although Alma thought a lot of Bill, she hoped the young couple wasn't with him. If they were, she was sure they would've had their fill of his surliness. Though he rarely showed it, she knew Bill was as gentle at heart as a padre on Sunday morning. She just didn't want to be an ear to their complaining about Bill and have to again make excuses for his bad behavior.

She walked out of the garden toward the road to wait and tried to think of the rebuttal she'd have to come up with to counter the almost certain smart-aleck remark that always followed a stream of tobacco juice.

As the mules came closer she became alarmed. The man in the seat next to Bob wasn't Bill. *What the hell?*

"Who the hell are you?" she demanded over the noise of wheels rumbling and trace chains jangling. Ramsay drew the lines and the wagon came to an abrupt stop. "What'd you do with Bill?"

"Shut your damn mouth Alma and help get me outa here," said Bill from the back, still flat on his back.

"Mrs. Hawes, ma name is Ramsay Sproat. We had an accident. Bill here is hurt and needs yer help."

"Thank God I didn't have my rifle, young man, or you'd be dead right now. I've had a belly full of thievin' around here." She breathed hard, wiped her brow with her sleeve and hollered, "What'd you do to yourself this time Bill?"

"You'll find out soon enough when you get me outa this goddamn wagon."

With Alma's help Ramsay and Annie Chris reversed the procedure they'd used to get Bill in the wagon three hours before. "Let's get him on in the house and we'll take a look," said Alma as she took the back end of the stretcher from Annie Chris.

"You drop me Alma Hawes and I'll sick ol' Bob on you. He'll tear you to pieces."

"He's just like you, all bluff and no bite. Ask them mules."

"Just fix me up damn it and save all the yappin' for someone else."

"Hush now – stop your bitchin'. You'll have plenty to bitch about after I'm through with you."

"Let's just lay him out here on my bed. By the way, I'm Alma Hawes. Me and my husband Albert run this stage stop. As usual Bill ain't too sharp on his manners or he would have introduced us."

"This is ma wife Annie Chris."

"Pleased to meet you Mrs. Hawes. I'm going back to the wagon to get my baby. I'll be right back."

"Lay the little child out on the settee when you get back," Alma said. "What happened, Mr. Sproat?"

"I ain't dead yet Alma," said Bill. "I can talk."

"When I want to talk to you I'll tell you," she snapped. "Otherwise save what breath ya got, you may not have much more."

Alma went into the kitchen and brought back a bottle of whiskey, a knife, a bowl of hot water from the stove and some towels. She wet a towel, cleaned his wound then slipped the knife under the top of his boot at the back. "Don't move or I'll cut your damn foot off."

"One more time, Mr. Sproat, what happened?" she asked as she carefully cut open the back of Bill's boot then slipped it off.

"Aboot one, I went ahead of Bill through a cut in the road tae clean off rocks. Next thing I knew rocks were rolling doon the hillside then I saw the mules coming around a sharp turn fast in ma direction – had tae jump off the side tae keep from getting run over. Bill was nae in the seat. Then I saw him in the road, crumpled up like a dead man. Ma wife was running toward him."

She looked at Bill. "You got throw'd off, Bill? Wished I'd seen that."

"Sproat, tell her to shut her goddamn mouth."

Ramsay ignored him. "His leg is bad. We twisted a kerchief tight above the break tae stop the bleedin', cleaned him up and here we are."

"It was an earthquake. Felt it here too," she said offhandedly as she looked over the wound. She placed her palm at several spots on his leg above and below the break, placed her other hand over his forehead for a few seconds then glanced over at the alarm clock on a table across from her bed and lifted his wrist.

"Careful damn it," said Bill. "That arm hurts like hell."

She ignored him, placed a finger under his wrist and stared at her clock.

Annie Chris joined them in Alma's bedroom. She whispered, "I tended the baby. She's asleep."

Alma nodded and motioned for them to walk out of the bedroom, "We'll be right back."

"You level with me Alma Hawes."

"I will," she said as she and the Sproats walked into the sitting room.

She lowered her voice to a whisper. "It needs to come off. His leg is stone cold. You can see the swelling yourselves. His heart is racing too fast – should've calmed down by now but it hasn't.

"To set it, I'd have to open up the wound to see more of the bone so I can line it up right. There ain't much chance for it healing straight and true if he managed to survive. I expect he'd be just as much a cripple with it as without it but he'd have more of a chance of living if it were gone."

"It doesn't surprise me," said Annie Chris.

"Can ye cut off his leg?" asked Ramsay.

"That ain't no problem – done quite a few."

"Ye gonna tell him?"

"You oughta know by now that you don't *tell* Bill nothing. I expect he'll want it set. War vets don't take too kindly to having their parts removed. Seen too much of it. But you never know about ol' Bill. Let's go back in. By the way, you folks are Scotch. That right?"

"Naw ma'am," said Ramsay. "We're Scottish, Scotch is a whiskey."

Alma laughed. "Don't know if it's Scotch but I got plenty of whiskey."

They reentered the bedroom.

"I expect she told you it's gotta come off – didn't she?" Bill huffed.

Ramsay and Annie Chris were silent waiting for Alma to respond.

"You knew that already didn't you Bill?" said Alma.

Bill paused, looked at the ceiling, his eyes dim and unfocused, then said in a distant reedy voice, "I want to talk to Alma alone."

Annie Chris nodded, took Ramsay by the elbow; they turned and left the room.

"Shut the door behind you," he said, his voice gaining strength.

When they'd left and the door was shut he began slowly. "Alma, ain't no way you're gonna take my leg. Seen too many cripples wasting away, being waited on by kin hand and foot – I'd rather be dead."

He turned his head toward the window. His eyes moistened a little. He said, "I'm lonesome Alma. Lou don't want me and I don't blame her none.

"I want to have a life like you and Albert and these nice young folks outside your door. I'm getting on and had enough of the rough life. I seen it too many times – no woman wants a man she's gotta wait on hand and foot. The poor bastards can't earn a living and nobody wants 'em. Able-bodied folks looks at 'em with pity in their eyes and shakes their damn heads. Why, hardly no one wants me in one piece let alone all broke up.

"No Alma, you ain't takin' my leg. Set it as best you can – I'm ready. Gimme that bottle and let's get on with it."

"Your chances of getting gangrene are high, Bill. You know what that means."

"I know, now hand me that goddamn bottle."

She handed him the bottle, and walked out closing the door behind her. She whispered to the Sproats, "I'm gonna need both of you to help. We're gonna set his leg. Mrs. Sproat I need you to stoke the fire in the stove and fill the tank with water and fill the kettle on the stove. There's more towels upstairs – gonna need 'em all. I gotta sewing basket next to the towels. Bring me that too. If the baby needs anything you better take care of it now 'cause we're gonna be pretty damn busy for the next hour or two.

"Mr. Sproat, I got a sharp knife in the drawer over there. I'm gonna need it sharper. The whetstone's in the same drawer."

"Please, we're Ramsay and Annie Chris, Mrs. Hawes."

Alma nodded.

"I should unhitch and tend tae his mules."

"Be back in twenty minutes and, by the way, I'm Alma – don't answer to nothin' else."

~   ~   ~

For the last two days Hugh Calland had been spending most of his time sitting on a granite rock high above his and his wife Cora's camp, watching the road to Kelton hoping he would see a wagon or stage on its way in their direction. He passed the time whittling on a wooden form slowly beginning to resemble a doll baby. Earlier in the afternoon he'd been shaken by a phenomenon that had become all too familiar to him in Eastern Idaho – an earthquake. He had jumped off the rock he was sitting on and ran clear of what might be the path of any others, then sat back down to continue his wait and his whittling. This time he sat in the dirt.

By the time he saw Bill's wagon and mules it was late in the afternoon. The wagon was less than a mile from the crossroad where the Kelton Road met the California Trail.

It was only the fifth day of the month. He didn't really expect them this soon but this wagon was the only one he'd seen since they'd arrived at City of Rocks so he decided he'd follow-up.

It took him a half-hour to walk down to their camp, "Cora, a wagon passed by. We just as well hitch ours and see where it's headed – might be our folks."

Hugh could see no reason to be in too big a hurry. If the freighter didn't stop at the stage stop he was pretty certain Ramsay and Annie Chris weren't with him. Both Hugh and Cora were nervous, eager to meet their only relatives. Cora changed her skirt and spent some time fixing her hair. Hugh got one of the wagons ready and whittled while he waited for her.

"How do I look?"

"Never prettier," said Hugh, a mouthful for the quiet, hard-working cattle rancher.

The freighter or the man Hugh thought was the freighter, had parked his wagon in the open area to the side of the station house and was un-hitching his mules with his black and white dog beside him.

Ramsay looked up as he heard Buster bark and saw an older couple sitting side by side in a buckboard wagon pulled by a team of horses, one a bay the other a dun.

Ramsay tipped his hat as they approached. Bob was quiet, doing his job with the mules.

Hugh said, "Don't mean to be too forward, sir, but did you happen to bring a young couple and a baby with you from Kelton?"

Ramsay stared, "Did ye come here from Fort Hall?"

"Why yes, we did. How'd you know that?"

"Och, Ramsay Sproat's ma name. Ye must be Mr. and Mrs. Calland."

Hugh stepped off the wagon and offered his hand. "I am Hugh Calland and this is my wife Cora."

"Hugh, where are your manners?" asked Cora. "Help me down."

"Pleased to meet you Mr. Sproat," said Cora. "You've come a long ways. Your wife and her baby must be inside – is that right?"

"Aye, they are. I wish I had more time tae visit but the freighter we came with had an accident. He's being attended tae by Mrs. Hawes and ma wife. I'm needed in there as soon as I can get these animals stabled. Mr. Judy, the freighter, has a broken leg."

"You go on in," said Hugh, "I'll see to the animals."

"Can I help?" asked Cora.

"Ye could keep an eye on our wee one – that would help."

"Oh, would I love to do that. Just show me where she is."

Kate was asleep on the settee. Annie Chris had propped two chairs against it to keep Kate from rolling off onto the floor.

"This is our daughter Kate," said Ramsay smiling down at her.

"She is beautiful."

"I'm going in tae lend a hawn now."

"You go right ahead and please do what you have to do and don't worry about the baby."

Ramsay slowly and quietly opened the bedroom door. In one hand he held the freshly sharpened knife Alma had asked for.

"Come on over here so you can hear me," Alma said when she heard Ramsay close the door. "Annie Chris, I want you to keep some clean wet towels close and do the best you can to keep his wound clean and the blood away from what I'm about to do. Ramsay, when I say, I want you to pull hard on his foot.

"Here's a spoonful of laudanum. Swallow it all Bill. Now take another pull on that bottle then bite down on this here scrap of wood cause what I'm gonna do is going to pain you like you've never been pained before."

"Just tell me what you're gonna do. Your pain's gotta be easier to take than your lip."

"It don't line up good where the bone is broke. One end is over the top of the other. I'm gonna open up the flesh on your leg so I can line up the two pieces straight and true. Ramsay's gonna pull on your foot so I can line the bones up. Annie Chris is going to keep the wound clean.

"You're as tough as a boiled owl Bill Judy – *your* job is to hold still and not fight us. You can do it. When I get the bone back in place and lined up good I'm gonna sew you back up. You ready?"

"One more pull."

CHAPTER NINE

Alma carefully and deliberately worked on Bill's wound for nearly an hour. Beads of sweat dotted her forehead as she skillfully maneuvered her knife, separating flesh from bone. Bill's eyes were closed and his jaws were clenched on the scrap of wood. His face turned a dark shade of violet and the tendons in his neck bulged but he made not a sound. It took her less than five minutes to sew him up and five minutes more to bandage the wound. They wrapped his leg in a section of clean bed sheet, positioned six pieces of lath around his leg for a splint, wrapped that in burlap and bound it all snugly with twine. Around the wound, she cut open the burlap and the bed sheet beneath it, exposing the dressing.

"We're done Bill," said Alma. "You can start your bitchin' now. By the way, your arm ain't broke just bruised up some. If you die it won't be your arm that kills you."

"Where's Bob?" he asked, his voice barely audible.

"Dogs don't come in my house – even yours."

Bill tried to put some weight on his good arm but fell back. "Then I'm going where he is."

Alma looked at him and shook her head. "Annie Chris, get the damn dog."

Annie Chris turned to leave. Ramsay touched her shoulder and whispered, "I'll get Bob, there's something I have tae tell ye."

Annie Chris opened the bedroom door slowly.

Standing in the parlor with Kate in her arms was the woman she'd corresponded with for so many years, the same woman her mother had corresponded with, on whose letters both Annie Chris and Ramsay had learned to read. She looked exactly as Annie Chris had pictured in her mind's eye: short, white haired, a little plump with rosy cherub cheeks and a wide smile.

All Annie Chris could say was, "Her middle name is Cora."

"I know that dear."

Without another word they slowly walked toward one another and embraced with bewildered little Kate held delicately between them.

~   ~   ~

69

Ramsay knew he would find Bob lying quietly outside Alma's bed-room window.

"He's gonna be awricht Bob," said Ramsay. "He wants tae see ye."

Ramsay had to drag him by the collar around the house and through Alma's front door. He'd never been in a house before, but once over the threshold, he caught Bill's scent and was willingly led into the bedroom.

"Yer ol' frein is here Bill."

Bill patted the side of the bed weakly. Bob walked to him and licked his hand. "You doing all right Bob?" asked Bill trying hard to keep his voice strong.

"Leave us be a spell," Bill said.

Bill scratched Bob behind his ears and petted him lightly. "It's you and me Bob. You're all I got. No one else'll have me. Mules don't care much but I suspect you know that don't you. I don't reckon you understand what I'm telling you but that's all right. I just always felt better talkin' to you so I'm gonna talk to you again – just like old times.

"I might not make it but that's all right by me. I had a good life – some disappointments for sure but a good life just the same. You been the best pardner I ever had. If I don't make it, you decide for your own self who you want to own up with. Might not be too bad here with ol' Alma but them two Scotties in there might be your best bet. They been damn good to me and you, too. I just want ya to know I want the best for the days you got left."

Bob whimpered and nuzzled Bill's hand with his nose for more petting.

Alma told Ramsay to turn the mules into the pasture. It would be a couple of months before Bill would be well enough to even think about continuing on to Boise City. She said she hoped Albert or maybe John Hailey himself might be able to continue the trip and take the load on in, maybe sometime soon.

Ramsay told her that he was perfectly capable and very willing to take the load himself if their journey was to take them in that direction. He and Annie Chris hadn't decided whether they were going to travel on in search of a homestead site – Willow Creek maybe – or go with Hugh and Cora to their ranch near Fort Hall.

"Mrs. Hawes," said Cora, "I've got a pot of stew back at the camp. There's enough for all of us for supper. I imagine everyone is hungry."

"Why that'd be much appreciated. I wasn't expecting anyone and don't have much fixed." She did a quick survey of the guests. "Ramsay, you and Annie Chris can take a bedroom upstairs. Hope you're comfortable in your camp Mrs. Calland 'cause I don't have no more beds."

"We're very comfortable there. Please call me Cora."

"And I answer to Alma."

Alma turned solemn. "Annie Chris, you and me's gonna do a night watch on Bill. You stay with him from eleven to two – I'll take over 'til breakfast time. We gotta keep givin' him water and keep his leg up about a foot off the bed. We're gonna wipe him down to keep him cool. I got some quinine in case he spikes a fever. Most important, we gotta keep him from moving his leg. He might want to get more comfortable in his sleep and shift around. We can't let him do it. We'll have to help him when nature calls. Do what you gotta do, just keep that leg still."

"Is he going to make it?"

"All we can do is try dear – that and pray. He might, then again he might not. Only the Lord knows for sure and He knows we're gonna do all we can. I'd be lyin' if I told you I know it all cause I don't. There's an old doctor, Doc Webber's his name, that's taken up homesteading with his son near Pine Basin. If it suits Bill having me gone for a day or so, in three or four days I'm gonna go get him and bring him back just to be sure.

"You remember Pine Basin don't you?" she said looking at Hugh. "It's about thirty miles back toward Fort Hall. You came through it on your way here."

"I remember. Just a little store and a few cabins is all I recall."

Thanks to the whiskey and the laudanum and hour by hour care, Bill made it through the night.

CHAPTER TEN

"We have tae decide," Ramsay said to Annie Chris. "There's naw use in puttin' it off."

"Let's go over in the shade of Alma's barn and sit with Hugh," said Cora. "The four of us'll talk it out."

When they were settled in the shade, Annie Chris turned her back to the group so Kate could nurse.

"There's another wagon back at our camp," said Hugh. "We weren't sure what you two would decide to do so we hitched the second wagon and brought it along. There's another team hobbled near the camp."

"What for?" said Ramsay.

"The second wagon's loaded with farm implements – a plow and a harrow and a disc and a planter and a ditcher, some hand tools and other farm gear. It's extra on the place and I figured it ought to be put to good use so I decided to make you the loan of it all – doin' me no good rusting in the barn."

Ramsay raised a hand in protest but Hugh cut him off. "We're just loaning it to you – the team too. When you get settled and on your feet we'll want it all back."

"That is so kind of you," said Annie Chris.

"We're more than happy to do it," said Cora.

"You better decide if you're going on or coming back to the ranch with us – your call," said Hugh. "Easy enough to haul it all back if you decide to spend some time with us at the place – so, what'll it be?"

Hugh continued without waiting for an answer. "Don't mean to be pressing but we have to leave in a couple of days. I've got the last cutting of hay I got to get started on. Don't know that there's much more any of us can do here for Bill."

Ramsay looked at Annie Chris. "What do *ye* want tae do ma loove?"

"I think we should go with them," she answered without hesitating. "We have so much to learn and this will give us a chance."

"I don't want to confound this too much," said Hugh, "but wagon trains are coming through Fort Hall almost once a week and more and more folks are talking about Oregon filling up so they're asking about Idaho.

"Cora and I won't think ill of you one way or the other. I would hate to think that because of us you might miss some opportunity. But the time for cogitating is about to run out."

"If we chose tae go on, how much can ye teach us in a couple of days while we're all here?" asked Ramsay.

"Cora and I can talk to you about what you need to do, but experience is always the best teacher."

Ramsay looked at Annie Chris, who nodded slightly, then back at Hugh and said, "Awricht, we'll go with ye."

Later, Annie Chris and Ramsay stood next to Bill's bed. She spoke first. "Alma says that you're coming along fine."

"I'm doing *damn* good, I'd say."

"Six weeks or more of rest and ye might be up and around some," said Ramsay.

"Six weeks my ass – hell, I'll be on the road cussin' them mules in no time."

Annie Chris frowned. "I don't think that's a good idea."

"Alma's gonna get that doc from Pine Basin and bring him back here to take a look. Said if I'm doing good she'll go after him in three or four days when she goes for provisions – he'll turn me loose."

"I doubt it," said Annie Chris.

Bill rolled his eyes, "This bed ain't no place for me. Doc, he knows that."

Annie Chris swallowed hard not knowing precisely how she was going to share the news and drew in a breath. "We wanted you to know that we've made up our minds. We're going to leave with the Callands and spend some time with them learning what we need to know – six months, maybe more."

Bill raised a hand slowly to his forehead, closed his eyes, opened them again and pleaded, "Wait a week for me to heal up and we'll all head out together. I'll show you Willow Crick. I can teach you all you need to know while we're on the road. Might even stay with you to help you learn – how about that? We might even partner up on the place."

"Ye won't be going naw where for a few months," said Ramsay. "Alma will take guid care of ye richt here. Her husband or Mr. Hailey will take yer load on in tae Boise City. There's naw a reason tae hurry it."

"The hell there ain't! I could care less about that load right now. Willow Crick ain't gonna wait forever. May already be spoken for by the time we get there."

"If it's gone we'll find something else," said Annie Chris. "We're leaving day after tomorrow. Ramsay and Hugh want to spend tomorrow helping Alma get caught up around here. Then we're going to leave the next day, as long as you haven't had a setback."

"You're being fools. That's all I gotta say."

Annie Chris put her hand over Bill's. "We would never have made it this far without you, Bill. We'll find a good place for our ranch and you'll always be welcome there. I'm just afraid that if you don't take care of yourself we may never see you again. Promise me you'll do everything Alma and that doctor tell you to do. Will you promise me that?"

Bill slid his hand away. "I'm gonna tell you two things. First, I ain't making no promises and second, I don't want your goddamn pity so hang on to it and give it to someone that needs it."

She patted his hand tenderly. He pulled it away again, turned his face to the wall and was silent.

"Please don't be that way – we can't leave you like this."

"Like what? I'll be fine. It's *you* that worries me. You don't seem to believe me – seems to me you lost your nerve."

"Damn you Bill Judy," Annie Chris shot back. "That's the meanest thing you ever said. It is not true and you know it."

It was threatening rain the morning the four of them set off for the Calland Fort Hall ranch. Cora, with blankets ready, sat comfortably in the seat of the lead wagon waiting for Ramsay to hand Kate to her. He lifted her into Cora's outstretched arms then walked to the back of the second buckboard to make sure he'd tied Lucy securely. Annie Chris was waiting anxiously on its seat trying to hold her emotions in check. She was feeling guilty and unsettled about leaving Bill. In less than a week a bond had developed between the three of them. He was their friend and they owed him.

She thought of Lou and her cheerful hardworking disposition and of Alma standing only feet away. Alma, whose toughness and determined attitude inspired Annie Chris and strengthened her faith in herself.

Bill, Lou and Alma – all, in the span of one week, by example, had taught her that they could do darn near anything and survive.

Alma was quietly standing next to the wagon waiting to say her good-byes. Annie Chris's emotions swirled in her head as she waited alone on the seat. They had just left Bill. He had done his best to offer a cheerful sendoff but his disappointment was clear.

Other than the few things the Sproats had added to the load, the Calland wagon looked the same as it did the day it arrived at City of Rocks. Ramsay walked quietly past Alma and stepped up and onto the seat next to his wife. Alma could sense their hesitation, "Bill's gonna be fine if he does what I say. I may still need to take the leg but I'd prefer Doc Webber be the judge of that. You go on now and keep in touch. I'll send a letter to keep you up-to-date. So please, there ain't nothing you can do here. Go on now."

At mid-day, their second day out, they came through the little settlement of Pine Basin. The countryside was appealing with meadows and cattle scattered along the grassy hillsides. A large mountainous bluff rose to their left. Pockets of aspen and intermittent oddly shaped green juniper and mahogany trees added to the pleasant setting. They stopped at a log supply cabin to re-provision for the balance of the trip. There were three other log buildings nearby, one a school with children outside laughing and eating their noonday meal.

The store's proprietor welcomed them eagerly as if he hadn't seen a traveler for months. He seemed starved for news, wanting to know what Alma had heard about the robberies, was the stage running yet, was Hailey back on the road and more. Hugh told him about Bill Judy. The proprietor said, "Bill's the last one I would have thought to suffer a run-away. He's the best there is at avoiding such calamities."

"It was an earthquake we were told," said Ramsay.

Annie Chris advised the proprietor that Alma would be by in a couple of days to resupply her provisions and lead Doc Webber back to City of Rocks for his appraisal of Bill's condition. She asked if someone would alert the doctor that Alma would be on her way soon.

"He has six grandchildren in the school you just passed. When we're done here I'll walk on over and have them tell him. Doc's kinda give up on doctoring, being in his declining years and all, unless it's life or death of course. But I expect he'd be glad to check in on Bill. Should I have him just take off for Alma's soon as he can?"

"It would be best to wait for Alma," said Annie Chris. "Bill's doing pretty good and I'm sure she'd enjoy the company for the trip back home."

By mid-afternoon of their second day out of Pine Basin they arrived at the Oregon Trail.

Hugh stopped his team, stepped off the wagon and walked back to talk to Ramsay. "Let's stop here a spell. I want to give you some bearings. Our night camp'll be about three hours more up the trail. Not much forage here for the horses. All the stock from the emigrant trains has pretty much cleaned it up."

Ramsay stepped off the wagon into the powdery six-inch-deep dust churned by the wheels of thousands of wagons and the feet of their pulling beasts on their way west on the Oregon Trail. He would have been in one of them, he thought, if it weren't for the railroad. Wheel ruts were everywhere; wagons had veered this way or that attempting to escape the dust of those ahead.

"Whenever you and Annie Chris decide to head west you'll follow the trail," said Hugh. "Not even a blind man could get lost. You'll meet up with the Kelton Road again at a stage stop named Stricker Station two days from here. About three or four days later you'll come to where the trail crosses the Snake. There's a good ferry there run by a guy named Glenn and his partner Moody. Once you cross the river you'll be three or four days from Boise City.

"A long day after crossing the river you'll come to Rock Crick Crossing. Then there's another long day after that and you'll be getting close to the place that Bill keeps talking about. I'm not exactly sure where that is but I got an idea. I've only been through there once. Anyway, we got all winter to talk about it – time to head for the night camp."

~   ~   ~

Two days after the Sproats and Callands left, Alma sat at the foot of Bill's bed just as she'd done every morning since he arrived. Her routine was to open the bandage, check the progress of the healing, clean the wound and change the dressing. In spite of her initial doubts, his leg seemed to be healing. At least the wound looked good and there was no discharge. His leg and foot were still swollen but had not worsened and warmth had returned to his ankle and foot. The most encouraging sign of all was the absence of fever.

She started feeling pretty proud of herself, then thought of how close she'd come to amputating his leg. Too early for congratulations she told herself, removing the leg may still be necessary – after all, it had only been four days. Bill's progress made her feel more at ease about leaving him overnight to get Doc Webber. The best thing was for Doc to take a look, she was sure of it.

"I think you'll be all right at least through tomorrow," Alma told Bill. "I'll be leaving in about an hour for Pine Basin for provisions and I'll bring back Doc Webber – should be back by late tomorrow afternoon. I'll feel much better after he takes a look. I'll leave you plenty of water. You got them crutches to get to the commode – no further though, you hear me? And don't mess with the splint. I'll put some ham and bread on the table here next to the bed. Think you'll be all right?"

"I'll be fine if you leave that bottle. You go do what you gotta do. You tell Webber that we don't need him here unless he just wants to come for a game of cards. Remind him he owes me five bucks from our last game."

"You tell him yourself 'cause he's coming back with me whether *you* like it or not. Now don't you go doing nothin' stupid," she added turning away. "Don't you dare put any weight on that leg at all. Nothing, you hear? Use them crutches. Any kind of jolt and we'll have to do it all over again."

"Whatever you say – yes ma'am," said Bill saluting Alma as if she were General John B. Gordon himself.

"Anything else you need?"

"Yeah, bring me a paper and a pencil."

"You gonna write a letter?"

"You gonna do what I ask or ain't ya?"

~ ~ ~

Cora noticed it first. Hugh and Ramsay were standing next to one another in the dust pointing, talking about what lay to the west and how it was different from where they'd just come and where they were going.

77

Cora saw something and squinted into the distance. "Look! A rider, coming this way – fast."

All eyes followed Cora's stare and looked in the direction of Pine Basin and City of Rocks. "Hand me my rifle Cora," said Hugh.

As the rider came closer, his horse in a dead lope, they realized it was a youngster – barely a teenager. His horse was lathered, foam dripping from its bit. The boy drew rein. The horse's rear heals dug into the dirt as it came to an abrupt stop.

He was hatless; his wild blonde hair parted itself naturally down the middle as the horse jolted to a halt. He was as breathless as the horse.

"Looking for someone named Sproat." The boy's pre-teen voice cracked.

"I'm Ramsay Sproat."

"Well sir Mister Sproat, I been told to tell you that Mister Bill Judy up and left the Hawes's place. He weren't there, Grandpa told me, when he showed up to doctor him."

"There must be a mistake. He has a broken leg and could barely get out of his bed. He's *got* tae be there. Did they take a guid look around?"

"They did, sir, but he was plumb gone. Grandpa and Missus Hawes knew that 'cause he left a note saying he took the Wells Fargo buckboard in her barn. That and two of his mules and his dog was gone too. They told me that you oughta know in case you want to chase him down. Missus Hawes can't leave 'cause the stage is running again and Grandpa's too old for chasing – said his chasing days are past him. She and Grandpa are mighty worried that Mister Judy's gonna hurt hisself worse."

"Which way did he go?"

"Headed northwest on the Kelton Road, toward Stricker's Store they told me to tell you."

"Do they have an idea when he left?"

"Figured he musta took off right after Missus Hawes left to fetch Grandpa – that'd be three days ago I reckon. Got here as fast as I could – most everyone thinks highly of Mister Judy."

Frustrated, Hugh rubbed his brow and shook his head. "He ain't as smart as I thought he was – what, by God, would make him do a damn fool thing like that?"

"Willow Creek," said Annie Chris.

CHAPTER ELEVEN

"We owe him," said Ramsay, "even though all we're doin' is tryin' tae protect him from himself."

"My Lord that man can be aggravating," said Annie Chris shaking her head as if Bill were a three-year-old. She was at her wit's end.

"You better go," said Cora recognizing their leaving looks. "You'll never forgive yourselves if you don't."

"There's some reading for you on farming in the wagon," said Hugh. "Remember what I told you – most cricks are running low this time of year but if the place you like doesn't have water enough in the crick to fill a keg in a minute, just keep on going even if it is Willow Crick. And the other thing, tall thick sagebrush is a good thing – means the dirt is good and the brush is getting lots of water to its roots.

"I won't be able to tell you again so pay attention. The first thing you gotta do after you find the right place is clear the brush and rocks then plow the ground, disc it and harrow it to get it ready to plant. Don't try to do too much this fall. One man with a good team like you got here can clear and plow maybe sixty, seventy acres in about a month and a half I'd guess, weather permitting. In the spring, as soon as the mud dries up, harrow it again to knock down any weeds then plant about two thirds of your ground to oats and the other third to alfalfa. Oats'll be your cash crop that'll bring you enough to live on. The alfalfa will be for your animals in the winter. Each fall plow up a little more of the oat ground and plant it to alfalfa the following spring as you bring on more animals.

"Everything you need for your first year, including the oat and alfalfa seed, is in the wagon. And if you have time before the ground freezes, use that level I gave you to survey some ditches then cut 'em around your field with the ditcher. No use in putting dams or levies in 'til late spring after the runoff is done.

"As soon as I get my hay laid up and get the cattle home for winter, my hired man can take care of the rest then Cora and me'll catch up with you and help out for a while.

"Your tent will have to do for a spell. Most winter winds come from the west so in your spare time," Hugh said with a doubtful grin, "you can make a pretty good winter shack with cottonwood and willow laid up against the east side of a hill after you cut into it a ways with your shovel and pick. Then cover it with your tent."

He cast a hard parental stare at Ramsay. "Don't even think about sheep for a couple of years. Your plate'll be plum full just getting the place up and running. Your biggest worry is the same worry we all have in this country – water. This ain't Scotland. You can't count on rain. Whatever you grow will have to be irrigated. The crick you settle on is your life blood. Sure, sheep'll do good on grass in the mountains but it will be the hay you put up for the winter from your irrigated fields that'll make you or break you in a bad winter. Trouble is, you never know when it's coming. But you don't have no choice on the matter – you gotta be ready every winter. When you have a good stand of alfalfa then you can start thinking about sheep."

"Ye've been telling me that," said Ramsay. "Bill says the closer ye are tae Boise City the more likely yer stock can get by in the winter without hay."

"I know. That is true but it'll happen, maybe sooner, maybe later. Some brute of a winter'll come along and you'll be kicking your own ass for not having a big hay stack."

"Quit making them worry Hugh," said Cora. "They'll know what to do when the time comes."

She turned to Annie Chris. "I put in some recipes and directions on how to do a few things around the farm to get you through the winter. Get your garden in soon as you can with turnips and carrots and the other things I told you about that'll grow in the fall. The seeds are all in there. When we come we'll get started drying fruit. We'll make a trip to Boise City and pick up what we can. Oh, don't forget to get a couple of milk goats. You can get a cow later."

Cora turned to the back of her wagon. "Let's go through this food. Take as much as you need. I've got six hams in here," she said lifting the canvas, "some elk jerky, flour and sugar and dry beans. You'll see when you go through it."

"I wish we could send some money along," said Hugh, "but we ain't got much of that so what you got there'll have to do."

Humbled by their generosity, Ramsay said, "We were nae expecting a thing."

"Don't push yourselves too hard," said Hugh, ignoring Ramsay's discomfort. "If Bill's got a mind for traveling he'll make thirty, forty miles a day. I suppose he knows you'll be after him and won't want the aggravation of an argument. You'll find him all right but I suspect you'll probably find him holed up somewhere trying to heal up enough to keep going. I'd be surprised if he makes it as far as the ferry on the Snake. That's three hard days ahead and you know he's got a three day head start on you so if he's pushin' hard there ain't no way you're gonna catch him unless he's dead or laid up."

"Hugh's right," added Cora. "Don't push it. Think of the baby. Whether you find him or not, remember, you're welcome to turn around and come right on back."

"Thank you for everything," said Annie Chris. "We'll take good care of all the things you've loaned us."

"Getting those things back ain't my concern right now," said Hugh. "My concern is you getting to wherever you're going safe and sound, Bill or no Bill."

~   ~   ~

Halfway between Stricker's Store and the Moody-Glenn ferry, Bill noticed two riders stalking him about a mile to his rear. He knew they were stalking because every now and then they'd disappear about the time they came upon a big rock outcropping or they'd stay behind a rise in the road longer than what their traveling pace would account for.

He wished there'd been a wagon in Alma's barn other than the Wells wagon but borrowers can't be too choosey. The problem with anything as identifiable as a Wells Fargo wagon was that any idiot hooligan in the West knew he wasn't hauling potatoes. So, sure enough, these two thought they'd hit pay-dirt – a Wells wagon and only one man aboard. Bill knew his mules couldn't outrun them so he began planning his defense.

He knew the Kelton Road and every wash and gully in its path almost as well as Hailey, the man who built it. And he knew that about a mile ahead the road sloped abruptly down the high bank of a dry stream bed, a perfect place to pull over and ambush the bastards just as they came over the top of the rise in the road.

He put the mules in a fast trot to get there as soon as he could. He had to give himself enough time to crawl over the side of the wagon without doing further damage to his leg, get his Winchester and pistol out and crawl over the bank of the creek.

He got into position for battle where he could see not only the road but up and down the dry creek bed. You can't always assume thieves are stupid. He waited, knowing that the best laid battle plans rarely unfold as expected.

Sure enough, the larcenists weren't stupid. They knew the road and knew that the driver of the wagon had probably been on it before and knew the creek bottom ahead would be his best chance. They dismounted. One snuck up the dry creek bed out of sight from the creek bottom below, the other snuck down it. They planned to trap Bill along the bank, his only hope of escape being west across the creek bottom into the open.

"Bob, listen to me."

Bob whined, looked around, sniffed the air and tried to find the danger.

"Get in the wagon Bob." He commanded, pointing to the wagon. "Now go!"

Bob hesitated. "Go!" Bill said firmly.

Bob raced to the wagon, jumped on, nosed his way under the canvas and crouched.

When the bandits didn't appear over the rise in the road about the time Bill expected them, he knew he had to adjust his battle plan. He grabbed the Winchester and a crutch and dragged himself up the embankment to get the high ground. They saw him just as he approached the top. A shot rang out from upstream to his left and ripped through his left shoulder. He drew his pistol and whirled downstream to his right knowing the other one would be shooting next. Sure enough the guy was taking a bead – unfortunately for him, he took too long. Bill fired two shots; one hit him in the gut, the second in the middle of his throat.

As he shot, he threw himself to the ground and rolled back down the embankment landing in the creek bottom below with a thud. He cried out in pain as his tibia separated at the break, the bone re-piercing his skin where Alma had sutured it. He'd lost his Winchester but still had his pistol. He glanced at the wagon; Bob was looking at him from beneath the canvas. Bill motioned for him to get down. Bob lowered his head. Bill's leg was again covered in blood.

A shot rang out spitting dirt near his wounded shoulder, then another that must have gone over the top of him he figured. He couldn't see the shooter as he lay on the ground. He knew he'd have to stand and fight or lay there and be murdered. He got up to his right knee and as he did, a slug slammed into his stomach with the same dull thump he'd heard so often when a comrade fell during battle. He fell to his right and lay still.

Minutes went by as he tried to breathe and clear his head. His pistol had fallen out of his grasp. He drew his knife and waited. He heard footsteps but lay as still as death.

"Well I'll be damned," said the bandit, kicking the pistol further away from Bill's reach, "if it ain't ol' Bill Judy. Damn sorry about killing you Bill. If I'd known it was you I'd have just rode up to your Wells wagon here friendly as could be and asked you about the weather."

"Pencil Dick Johnson, you bastard," said Bill, in a small pinched voice fading at the end with pain.

"Now that ain't a nice thing to say to your old secesh buddy. Last person that insulted me with that name was you – now I'm glad I killed you."

"You skedaddled, you chicken shit. Shoulda heard what Gordon called you – you'd a wanted to kill him too." Bill stopped, tried to stifle a weak painful series of coughs but couldn't. Once the coughing ended, he continued, his voice weaker. "Damn good thing you taking your skinny yellow ass and leaving us didn't amount to no bad result. You being gone probably helped us more than hurt us. Gordon woulda hunted you down like a rabid dog – he and about fifty volunteers, me included."

"Enough of your sweet talk, Bill – what you got in the wagon?"

"Nothin' that'd interest a thievin' varmint like you."

"Well, why don't you let me be the judge of that?"

Pencil Dick walked to the wagon, stopped, looked at it with his hands on his hips, turned and said, like he'd forgotten something, "Where's my manners? I oughta be thanking you for sparing me the chore of killing poor ol' Floyd over there. Sure has been my lucky day. Saved myself a couple of bullets and don't have to share this here Wells load with no one. No sir, it's my lucky day. Think I'll go back to Kelton and cuddle up with that skinny little restaurant gal. Gettin' tired of the highwayman life. Flash her a few of the goodies from this here wagon and she'll follow me like a bottle-fed goat."

"You touch her," wheezed Bill through clenched teeth, "I swear, if there's a God in heaven, my soul will haunt your miserable ass for the rest of eternity."

"Pretty tough talk for a man lying flat on his back, blood spilling out his guts in the dirt."

Pencil Dick laughed a mean laugh, turned, stepped up on a wheel spoke and lifted the canvas to look inside. "Well, let's take a look here at what we got."

It happened so fast Pencil Dick barely knew what kind of critter it was that lunged at him from beneath the canvas and clamped its jaws around his throat. He fell from the wheel, staggered backwards and somehow managed to stay on his feet while his hands desperately grasped for dog hair, dog ears, whatever he could get a hold of. Bob's locked jaws closed on Dick's windpipe, and sealed it from ever drawing air again. Dick tripped after a few awkward steps backwards, turned and fell gut first onto Bill's waiting ten-inch knife. The blade entered his abdomen just below the rib cage then angled upwards with a little help from Bill and penetrated Dick's dark heart.

Three minutes later Bill wheezed to Bob, "You can let go now."

Bob locked his teeth around Pencil Dick's right wrist and pulled until the motionless corpse was dragged off Bill.

It was late afternoon and the sun was making its descent in a bleached hazy sky, the air noticeably cooler. Between stage stops, wagon traffic wouldn't begin to appear until the middle of the next day.

The bleeding from Bill's shoulder wound had stopped and the bleeding from his leg had slowed but it was the slug he took in his abdomen that prompted him to reminisce. He'd seen lots of gut shots in the war – the bleeding in most of them was internal and fatal.

He thought of his mother and how heavy-hearted and unsettled he felt when he returned from Appomattox to find her taxed with another man's hollow-eyed kids to feed. The last thing she needed was a half-starved vet to share the meager fare she placed before this war ravaged bunch each day. A mother too burdened to be joyful over his battlefield return would have little time now to be sorrowful over his demise almost ten years later. He didn't blame her; life is harsh enough for the living.

He tried to picture her in his mind but couldn't. He tried to shake the dullness overtaking his brain but still couldn't see her. How sad, he thought, for a soldier not to picture his mother when his time has run out.

Out of nowhere, Lou's lean smiling face, pulled tight by her ring of braids, floated in front of him, so vividly and so abruptly that for a second he thought she was standing over him. He blinked his eyes and she was gone.

He thought of his regiment and of Gordon and Lee – what would they think of him lying here dying at the hands of a deserting coward?

It was so unfair: this loathsome skulker had ruined his plan, his plan to reunite with Lou and finally have the love of a good woman, his plan to partner with two hard-working decent people who were only looking for a chance at an honest life on their own terms.

Enough of this, think about what you got not what you don't got. His thoughts turned to friendships and Lou and little Kate, camaraderie in the war, Bob, his mules and the beauty of the mountains and plains he'd shared with them over the years.

He could see Lou again now. They were sitting together in her restaurant laughing over a cup of coffee. *What were they laughing about?* Didn't matter.

He had no idea how long he'd been laying there; it wasn't important. He felt no pain now. All he could feel were the soft pleasant licks alternating between his cheek and his hand.

He heard Bob growl, then a familiar voice telling Bob to take it easy. His eyes had difficulty focusing on the bearded face looking down at him. He heard his name being called.

"Bill," said John, "Goddamn Bill!"

"Hailey? Is it you?"

"It's me all right. You've done the world a big favor, Bill. You've rid it of the worst murdering thieves the Wells line's ever seen."

Hailey lifted Bill's head and put his canteen to Bill's parched lips. He drank slowly.

"Listen to me John," Bill said weakly after his head was gently lowered to the ground. "I got some wants."

"I'll take care of 'em – you know that."

"Sell the load and pay Alma for my doctorin' and keep." Bill coughed and gagged barely able to continue. He paused, drawing in shallow labored breaths. "Sell the wagon and mules. Half to Lou in Kelton and half to two Scots that'll be showing up here directly – guy named Ramsay and his wife and baby."

"I will."

"But John, listen to me." He paused, waiting for a cough that didn't come. He felt a trace of new strength, a renewed sense of purpose and continued, his voice stronger. "Help them two find Willow Crick, you know where I mean, about a day's ride from Rock Crick. But don't give 'em nothin' 'til they get a good start on the place." Bill coughed and gagged. When the spell was over he forced his lungs to accept air before he continued. "They'll want sheep – don't give 'em nothin' 'til the place is ready. They're too young to have money dropped on 'em. Money ruin't more youngins than it ever saved."

Bill coughed another choking gagging cough. He recovered then said with tears in his eyes, "The woman, Annie Chris – I want her to have Bob. Bob'll be happy with her. She'll take proper care of him.

"Two more things – look in on 'em every now and then and bury me there – at Willow Crick."

Bill blinked twice:

> *That's it. I see it. The stars and bars; I can hear it snappin' in the wind. The cool wind feels good, like a dip in a crick on a blistery day.*
>
> *Beneath the flag, it's them. Do I look as tired as them two? Expect I do.*
>
> *Sayler Crick is behind me now, thank God: the heat, the horror, the screams, the terrible noise.*
>
> *Yes siree, it's them. They're waving me forward. I can read their lips. 'You can make it,' they're saying.*
>
> *But I'm so tired, so weary, so sad.*
>
> *'You can make it,' they say again.*
>
> *I can, I know I can.*
>
> *'Forgive me, I can't stand,' says I.*

'It is all right corporal. Rest easy – it is finally over,' says Marse Robert.
'There's no more fightin,' says General Gordon.
'You can go home soldier,' they say together as one tender voice, 'and rest in peace.'

CHAPTER TWELVE

After four days of hard traveling, following Hailey on the Wells buck-board, Ramsay and Annie Chris arrived at Willow Creek. Mid-way on the last day, the odor coming from the back of the Wells wagon had become so overpowering that Ramsay had to take the lead.

Hailey had pushed hard in spite of having to stop briefly at stage stops along the way to talk with people who used to work for him when he owned the stage line before he sold it to Wells. These were people he knew would be worried or offended if he'd driven right on by without stopping to share the bad news about their dead friend in the back of the wagon and allow them to pay their respects.

They came within sight of the Snake River on several occasions. Most often it was shrouded in rocky deep canyon walls. It was not as wide as the rivers they'd crossed east of Kansas City but much swifter with exposed intimidating rocks and white water. Annie Chris began to worry about crossing it on the Moody-Glenn ferry. Her concerns proved unfounded. The crossing was uneventful.

Hailey seemed to know everyone along the way and they all were pleased to see him doing so well after his near disastrous altercation with the mean stud horse. His discourse was pleasant and business-like and re-flected his years of experience all over the Pacific Northwest.

Annie Chris spent a good deal of each of the long four days reminisc-ing about Bill. Somehow she had known the minute they learned Bill had left Alma's that Bill's foolish departure would end in tragedy. She prayed Bill was not mistaken about Willow Creek. Hailey had passed by it many times over the years and said he thought favorably of it too. He told Annie Chris that it had never occurred to him to homestead there. His business interests at the time had taken him in directions other than homesteading.

She was not going to bring it up now, but she was prepared to tell Ramsay they should turn around and go back to Callands if, after they ar-rived at Willow Creek, she had a foreboding feeling about it, just as she had about Bill. Annie Chris's instincts rarely let her down.

"This is it," said Hailey drawing the lines on Bill's mules. "Couldn't be more sure of it. First thing we gotta do is get Bill in the ground."

"We'd like tae look around a tad," said Ramsay.

"Look all you want," he answered. "Take your mare and mine. Ride up the crick a ways. Take your time, but this is where Bill wants to be buried whether you like it here or not. I'll take him up the crick and find a peaceful shady spot and start digging."

Ramsay helped Annie Chris onto Lucy, strapped Kate on his back, untethered Hailey's mare from behind the Wells wagon and lifted himself into the saddle. He looked around in every direction. The valley floor ran east and west framed by gently sloping hills to the northwest and southeast. The creek ran through the valley, dividing it almost equally as near as he could tell from where he stood. Willows and cottonwoods lined the creek as far as he could see. Hailey shook the lines and headed up the creek.

Ramsay and Annie Chris rode across the valley floor in the direction of the sloping hills to get a better perspective. Bob could not be coaxed to follow. He stayed with Hailey and the wagon.

The grass was so thick and lush they had to kick the horses forward with almost every step to keep them from stopping to graze. When they were about a hundred yards up the hillside, they turned upstream. The valley floor was less than a quarter mile across, narrowing further upstream. Tall sagebrush plants with strong trunks were scattered randomly across the valley floor. The floor gave way to slowly rising hills covered with fescue.

It was a sunny fall afternoon. Shadows cast from the cottonwoods along the creek stretched eastward as the sun slowly made its descent. The sun bathed the entire valley in a softly filtered golden light. A series of mid-September showers had moistened the hillsides and valley floor just enough to restart the perennial grasses. They cast a faint green hue at the base of the sun-bleached spring growth.

They followed the creek a half mile upstream to where the valley floor turned gently northward and narrowed by about half.

Several irregularly shaped granite rocks appeared on the hillsides on both sides of the creek; the largest rose over thirty feet in the air and reminded Ramsay of City of Rocks. Between two of these rocks, a hundred feet up the hillside stood a patch of willows with green grass in the space from rock to rock. The grass extended down a depression in the hillside to the creek below. *A spring*, he thought.

John had stopped the Wells wagon just below. He stepped off and kicked loose dirt. He walked to the wagon, took the shovel from its carrier on the side and walked back to the spot he'd kicked.

"Look!" Annie Chris cried, pointing. "There, on the hillside my love! Do you see them? Deer! There must be a hundred of them!"

"Mule deer," said Ramsay.

"Look how big they are and those big ears! They're beautiful."

Hailey had Bill's grave half dug by the time Ramsay and Annie Chris worked their way down the hillside. Ramsay reached for a shovel and walked to the grave to help him finish.

"Have you presided over a funeral, Mr. Hailey?" asked Annie Chris.

"I have."

"Would you say a few words for Bill?"

"It would be my honor."

"Ramsay would like to add some music."

Twenty feet from Bill's open grave Ramsay stood a little uneasy about his soiled trousers and a faded blue muslin shirt. He wished he had his father's tartan kilt, sporran and bonnet but he was ready. Ramsay hadn't played his bagpipes since he'd left Scotland but felt he could get through the one piece he knew best, the one he'd played more often than any other.

Three feet from the grave he and Hailey had lain Bill's remains on a board Hailey had pried from the Wells wagon. Bill was wrapped tightly in a grey woolen blanket from his bedroll stamped "CSA."

Hailey began: "Lord, Bill was a soldier, a miner and a freighter and no matter which of these pursuits he happened to be engaged in, he was always the best. We know just as you do that when it came to temptations your servant Bill was not a perfect soul but he did his best. He loved good people and good animals and respected them both. He also loved and appreciated the beautiful country you allowed him to call home. He, by his own accord, picked this spot for his final resting place and picked these people here before you to join me in a final sendoff, back to you, his Maker. Amen."

Ramsay took the "Amen" as his cue and began filling the bags. While all was quiet, as the mid-September sun slowly descended into its own place of rest beyond the horizon, he played perfectly the song they all knew and had heard so many times before, "Amazing Grace."

When he'd finished, Hailey, a Tennessean by birth whose mother and father were Virginians, in a strong baritone that could have been heard a half mile away, began to sing: "Oh I wish I were in the land of cotton old times there are not forgotten. Look away, look away, look away, Dixieland."

Ropes were positioned under each end of the board Bill's remains were laid on. Ramsay reached down and grasped the rope on one end of the grave while Hailey did the same at the other. They lifted carefully then slowly lowered Bill into the ground.

Annie Chris, with Kate in her arms, watched with a feeling of emptiness. Bob sat next to her on his haunches, as still as the air that filled the valley floor. Hailey and Ramsay began filling the grave. No words were spoken.

They made camp for the night. Hailey had a fire going and water heating in a coffee pot when Ramsay woke early the next morning.

He walked out of his tent. "Where's Annie Chris?"

"She was up before me. I saw her walking up the crick."

Ramsay looked in that direction and saw her walking back with Bob following.

"Ye could nae sleep ma loove?"

She eased herself onto a rock near the fire and said sadly, "No. Bob didn't leave Bill all night. I found him there this morning – we had a talk.

"I promised him we'd always respect this spot – I even told him we'd have a marker made. I don't know if he understood but at least he followed me back."

"Bill'd like a nice marker," said Hailey. "Are you two going back or staying?"

"We're stayin', Mr. Hailey," Ramsay answered. "We want tae thank ye for all ye've done. We hope tae see ye again soon."

"Oh, you will. Bill felt pretty sure you'd settle here and asked me to check on you from time to time. This'll make a fine little ranch but you got a lot to do first. I'll be on my way to town now."

Hailey paused and thought of his final promise to Bill. "Bill asked one more thing of me."

"Aye?" asked Ramsay.

"He wants you two to keep Bob. He was firm on it – said you'd take good care of him. He was right about that."

Ramsay nodded.

"Well, I'll be on my way then. I have to leave this wagon at the Wells barn, board these two mules of Bill's there, take care of Bill's business and head on back to Kelton."

Ramsay tipped his hat as Hailey slapped the lines over the backs of Jack and Tom and headed down Willow Creek to meet the old westward trail, the trail that started so many years ago way back in Missouri.

As Hailey turned west, in the distance, he noticed three Indians, on horseback about a half mile away. They'd seen him first and were stopped, looking in his direction. They stared at him briefly then continued riding south.

Hailey knew they meant no harm. Indians around here were few. Most were resisting the reservation, scrambling just to stay alive. Sooner or later they'd come close enough to Ramsay and Annie Chris's homestead to alarm them but Hailey had little concern that the Indians would harm them.

But he did get to thinking about all the work the Sproats had ahead of them just to survive the winter, not to mention preparing the place for spring and summer farming and he felt he should've prepared them for an eventual Indian sighting. It bothered him leaving them this way and knew it would have bothered Bill. He drew the lines and stopped, turned the wagon around and headed back to where Ramsay and Annie Chris with Kate in her arms were still standing, talking, pointing here and there, wondering where to begin on the arduous project that lay ahead.

"I forgot to tell you about the Indians," he said as matter of factly as he could. "Saw some up the road a ways. They're friendly enough around here. Sooner or later you're gonna see a few. It was their land you're standing on so respect that and respect them and they'll leave you alone. They're poor, for the most part, and don't want trouble. They might ask for a handout. Give them a chicken or a bag of beans. They'll be grateful."

He stepped off the wagon, reached in his pocket without saying a word, pulled out a handful of coins, counted them and handed Ramsay ten twenty-dollar double eagles stamped CC for the Carson City mint.

Ramsay looked at the coins in his hand, looked up at Hailey – puzzled, searching for words.

"It's a loan," said Hailey stepping back into the wagon. "I expect to be paid back. Go into town and buy one of those pre-cut houses – slat houses they call them. You can probably have it up in a couple weeks."

Hailey turned the wagon around and once again headed for town. Annie Chris managed to shout, "Thank you!"

Ramsay looked at his wife as if he'd just seen a ghost. "Do ye know what this means ma loove?" he asked. "Naw living in the dirt like in ma black hoose at Abington, naw leaky canvas roof, naw centipedes and worms crawling around, a dry warm place for Kate." A slow building energy replaced his just humbled demeanor and with it, a guileful little smile came to his lips. "Let's go tae Boise City in the morn," he said.

"Don't you think we should get the fields cleared and plowed and planted before we build a house?"

Annie Chris, practical by nature, managed to squelch his excitement. Her realistic prioritizing was timely, as it most often was, and a stark reminder of matters more in need of his attention.

"I suppose," he said flatly.

He saddled Lucy the next day and rode two miles up the creek with Bob trotting ahead. He wanted a better look at the land and the circumstances he and Annie Chris were about to place themselves in. The hills leading down to the creek were moderately sloped, not forming an abrupt rocky canyon like the one at the Rock Creek crossing fifteen miles back. They'd met the couple that ran the place, the Caufields, on their way through.

Willow Creek ambled through a gentle valley, narrowing gradually as he ascended. The topography had changed considerably from the lava and basalt that dominated the landscape at Rock Creek. The ground at Willow Creek was loamy decomposed granite – much sandier. The creek bottom itself was thick with willows and cottonwoods, but only feet from the creek, just high enough so the creek never encroached, tall sagebrush dominated. The hillsides were heavy with perennial fescue, buckbrush, some annual grasses and sage.

Bob, with amazing discipline, ignored the coveys of fleet-footed quail they came upon, not frightened enough by the dog's presence to take flight.

Ramsay rode Lucy up one of the ridges where he could get a better view of the area. From there he turned and rode back in the direction of their camp and stayed as high as he could along the way. He arrived at a viewpoint that gave him a panoramic view of the drainage below. He could easily tell that any possibility for raising hay or grain would have to come from a stretch that ran about an eighth of a mile up the creek and three quarters of a mile down the creek from their camp.

There was no natural meadow like the one at Rock Creek and, with the relatively small flow from the creek, irrigating for an entire season would be difficult. It was September and the creek was near its lowest level of the year. But he thought that, with what water there now was, he could probably irrigate thirty or forty acres, or about half of it. At the creek's peak flow, usually in June, he might be able to irrigate more, possibly eighty acres. If he planted alfalfa up the sloping hillside a ways, in a wet year, he might be able to get even more of a hay crop without irrigating it. There was a least twenty years of firewood from cottonwood deadfall up and down the creek.

From the viewpoint, he looked at their camp again and thought that a house and barn on the same side of the creek as the spring, nestled next to the hillside, would be perfect.

That night he described to Annie Chris what he'd seen and how confident he felt that a 160 acre homestead here would easily support a thousand ewes.

"Let's not forget what Hugh told us about getting the place up and running first – before we start thinking about sheep."

"I have nae forgotten," he said, feeling her statement was more an enjoinder and less a suggestion. "Are ye sure this is where ye want home tae be?"

"I do. I feel good about it – do you?"

"I like it. Bill had a guid eye – he was richt aboot this place."

"We have a lot to do before winter," said Annie Chris. "Early tomorrow let's take the wagon into town and file for a homestead. We can find the store and get some supplies. I'll write a letter to the Callands tonight.

We can mail it and get a post office box. I'm anxious to see what Boise City looks like and," she said with a playful smile, "we can ask about a house."

As shadows from the rock pillars to their left began to stretch across the valley floor, Annie Chris looked around at the peaceful setting and the creek and said, "I really like it here. I have a good feeling about it my love – it just feels cheery and settled. I've never really had a *home* but I can sense this being our home. It feels good, Ramsay – warm and bright and friendly. You know everyplace in Scotland has a name – let's call it Sunnyside. Do you like that?"

"Aye, it's a guid fit."

They pulled out at daylight the next morning with Kate bundled, still asleep. He estimated it'd be about twenty miles to Boise City, a distance they could travel in one day.

They arrived at a point overlooking the Boise River valley at about four in the afternoon. It was pleasant, not necessarily beautiful, with a green ribbon of trees stretching east and west as far as they could see shrouding what was undoubtedly the river. From where they were, looking down in a northwesterly direction, the trail descended gradually about two miles to the river below. On each side of the river they could see isolated patches of trees randomly scattered about a half mile or so apart. Ramsay assumed they were homesteads and that most of the areas along the river were probably settled.

He felt good that where he and Annie Chris were camped had more potential than any of the ground they'd crossed since leaving City of Rocks. He was ready to file for a homestead claim before someone else did.

In the distance about five miles downstream, he could see civilization – smoke rising in long straight columns. He could faintly see what he thought were buildings.

By five o'clock they'd checked into the Overland Hotel, asked the desk clerk where they could file for a homestead and boarded the horses at a livery nearby. Ramsay picked up a newspaper in the hotel lobby the next morning and read through it while he waited for Annie Chris. Its lead story was about the expected loss of President Grant's Republicans in the up-coming Congressional elections because of the Panic of 1873. Further

95

down the page of the *Tri-weekly Idaho Statesman* was a story announcing the arrival of Caleb Grant, a Californian, the newspaper's newest reporter. Ramsay wondered if the new reporter might be kin to the President. By eleven o'clock they'd filed papers and walked through town locating places like the First National Bank of Idaho, the post office, a lumber and hardware store and a general store.

They rented a box at the post office, wrote their new PO Box number on each of two envelopes, bought postage, mailed two letters, one to Callands and one to Lou, then walked to Standard Lumber where they asked about prices for materials for a slat house.

"Two hundred and fifteen dollars, delivered," said the clerk.

Ramsay looked at Annie Chris, reached in his pocket and felt the richness and weight of the warm gold coins. They felt good in his pocket so he said, "We'll consider it."

"That'll be fine but we can't guarantee deliveries after the first of November."

"Thank ye. We'll let ye know."

"By the way," said Annie Chris, "a dear friend of ours passed recently. Where would we go to have a grave marker made?"

"We can do that," said the clerk. "Price will depend on the size, of course, and how much engraving you want."

Annie Chris looked at Ramsay, "Something simple I suppose?"

"His name was Bill Judy," she said.

"Too late," said the clerk matter of factly. "John Hailey came in yesterday and ordered one. Paid for it too, gave me the instructions and everything. Sure am sorry bout ol' Bill. We all thought a lot of him. Hailey told us Bill killed the stage robbers and got himself killed for the trouble – darn sure a shame."

"What are the instructions?" asked Annie Chris.

"Got 'em right here," he answered as he reached below the counter. "Bill Judy; 1st Corp, Army of Northern Virginia, CSA; born 1846; died 1874."

"He was only twenty-eight years old," said Annie Chris.

They left for home late morning the next day. Kate was content in the wagon. She seemed accustomed to travel. She'd been on road or rail a good portion of her young life. The wagon was loaded with food staples, two milk goats hog tied in the back, two weaner pigs in a crate and six laying hens in a cage. They did have a load.

As they headed out of town Ramsay asked, "Do ye remember when we stood on the deck of the ship in New York harbor?"

"Aye, of course I do."

"I feel even better now than I did then. It seemed tae take so long, getting here I mean. But now those years seem a blur."

As soon as they arrived at their camp Annie Chris stepped off the wagon with Kate in her arms. "Do you remember the first words you spoke to me in the servant courtyard at Braeburn?"

"Naw, what did I say?"

She took one step closer. "You said, 'Do you own this place?'"

"Aye, I remember."

"Well, my love, we own *this* place."

She grabbed his hand. "Come with me up to where the spring is. I know a fine spot for our house."

Ramsay followed her lead. "Here – right here next to the hillside. There are enough cottonwoods for a small log barn and chicken coop. We can use the spring for water. The hillside is far enough from the creek that flood water would never come near it. What do you think?"

"I like it." Ramsay nodded slowly. "Same spot I had in mind. The spring makes all the difference. We can put in a pressure system fer running water in the hoose. I can pipe the water tae the side of the hill and dig a deep cistern, then run a pipe out of it tae a tank in the hoose, when we get it built of course, put a float on it and we have running water – all gravity!"

"Running water? Maybe next year."

Her dismissive attitude annoyed him. She always felt compelled to remind him of the obvious. It was a continuing struggle of theirs, balancing his eagerness with her practicality.

"We need a spot for a garden and an orchard," said Annie Chris, looking around for someplace suitable. "We need to get them in this fall – get some carrots and turnips and fruit trees planted."

Ramsay groaned under his breath.

CHAPTER THIRTEEN

~Fall of 1874~

A staggering amount of backbreaking work lay ahead: clearing brush and roots, plowing and preparing the soil for planting, getting a garden started, building a shelter for themselves and one for their animals, and much more.

They needed help. Long after dark one day, in an attempt to console Ramsay after he'd had come in for dinner hang-dog tired after a day of swinging an axe grubbing his field of sagebrush, Annie Chris said, "Hugh and Cora should be here any day and, I must say, none too soon – you look so tired."

Ramsay nodded wearily.

Late in the afternoon, two days later, while Ramsay was hacking and chopping, he glanced down the creek and saw a buggy approaching.

"Och," said Ramsay twenty minutes later when he met them on the road. "Ye two are a sight for sore eyes."

"Hop on up here," said Hugh. "You have a camp up the crick?"

"Aye. Annie Chris will be so glad tae see ye!"

"I am so sorry that we don't have a proper place for you two to lay your heads," said Annie Chris after greetings, hugs and handshakes.

"We have our tent, we'll be just fine," said Cora. "Is Kate asleep?"

"Aye, she'll be waking soon, I can – "

"Don't wake her," interrupted Cora, "but I would like a peek."

Annie Chris opened the flap of their tent. Cora peeked in. The wide-awake little girl was lying in her cradle playing with her rattle as content as a plump robin on a warm spring day. She smiled at her mother and Cora and kicked her legs.

Cora glanced at Annie Chris who nodded her approval, then reached down to pick up Kate. "Oh my Lord, you are so precious. My goodness, what's that I smell?" She grinned, flashed a questioning glance at Annie Chris who again nodded her approval. Cora laid Kate on the Sproat's bed-roll to be changed.

"Bill was right," said Hugh. "Looks like this'll make a fine little place."

"How long will ye be staying?" asked Ramsay.

"I reckon the weather will have the last word on that."

"We can use yer help – ye can sure see that. Can ye spare the time?"

"We'll do all we can while we're here. We better get started."

For three days, in a light steady rain, the two men cut, chopped, grubbed and hacked at the sagebrush scattered throughout the sixty acres that Ramsay had decided to plow and plant that fall. They saved the wood for firewood.

Annie Chris had already started spading a large garden, but now, with Cora's help, the work went much faster. Annie Chris felt cheerful in spite of the rain, now that she had a woman to visit with and share the work. After three days of spading and removing rocks they had the garden ready for turnips, carrots, broad beans, shallots and spring cabbage.

"We should make a trip to town for some fruit and start it drying before the weather turns," said Cora once the planting was done and the hillside spring had been ditched to the garden for irrigating.

"Let's make a day of it," said Annie Chris.

The women brought back fresh green beans, beets and carrots they'd bought from Chinese gardeners just west of Boise City as well as three bushels of apples, a bushel of plums, two bushels of apricots, a peck of currants, some salted cod and smoked salmon. Their meat would come from the abundant deer and elk near home. Bacon and ham would have to wait until their newly purchased shoats were big enough to butcher.

Two days later they had cored, pitted, sliced and laid out for drying under sheets of cheesecloth the currants and all six bushels of fruit. All they needed now was sunshine.

"Next," said Cora, "we need to dig a root cellar into the side of the hill somewhere close."

The two started digging into a north-sloping sidehill twenty yards from where Annie Chris told Cora the house would be built. The first four feet of digging was easy – until they came up against a wall of soft granite. Now Annie Chris had to whack at it with a pick while Cora shoveled out the fine rock and dirt. After five days of back-breaking work they managed to penetrate two more feet into the hillside then declared the six by eight dug-out big enough, for now. They braced the opening with upright cottonwood posts, covered the top with cottonwood rafters, a layer of willows and lastly, a six inch layer of dirt. Inside they made room for the dried fruit and saved the front for a temporary chicken coop to house the hens.

On the men's fifth day, to take advantage of the moist ground, Hugh quit chopping and went to work turning dirt with the team and plow while Ramsay continued clearing brush. The plowing went well; the ground was just moist enough for the team to pull the plow through the rich earth without much trouble. Bob, confused at first with Hugh walking and no seat to jump up onto, learned quickly to make himself useful by walking alongside the team encouraging the horses to pull in straight lines. The dirt was dark and rich and smelled of a wonderful earthy wholesomeness – hardly any rocks. Hugh said it was a damn sight better than his own.

At the end of each day Ramsay and Hugh gave the horses a ration of grain, hobbled them and turned them loose to graze on the unplowed filaree and June grass on the valley floor. Bob stayed with the horses just as he'd done with Bill's mules. The horses were always nearby in the morning.

Hugh and the team labored hard. They plowed five to six acres on a good day but by the tenth day, the ground had dried so much that progress had dropped by half and had become a struggle for the horses. Ramsay had cleared brush from sixty to sixty-five acres, he guessed, declared it enough for this fall, hitched Hugh's other team to the disc and harrow and began smoothing clods turned by the plow.

They got one more rain near the end of October, enough for Hugh to finish plowing all the ground Ramsay had cleared. It was time to order the slat house from Boise City. It arrived in three wagon loads on October thirtieth.

Ramsay had the floor down and the roof on the house and the new Majestic range they'd bought installed just in time for the first light snow. All four of them now worked on the simple two-room house. It was finished on the eighth of December.

"We know you have to go," said Annie Chris. "We owe you so much. How can we ever thank you?"

"You don't know how lonely it can be without family. It's you who needs to be thanked. Hugh and I are so lucky to have you in our lives. The Lord knows how blessed we are to have you here."

"Please write as soon as you arrive home," said Annie Chris as they exchanged farewells on the cold clear morning of December ninth.

"Of course – one more kiss," Cora added reaching for Kate.

Ramsay stepped up on the first step of Hugh's buggy, took Hugh's hand in both of his and said, "Thank ye. Please be careful."

"We will. We'll stay at stage stops along the way – should be home in a week."

"Be careful anyway," Ramsay pleaded.

~　　　　　~　　　　　~

The winter of 1874–1875 was so mild the temperature fell below twenty degrees only once and for a stretch of just one week. The brief cold spell was followed by the biggest snow fall of the season that left only six inches near the house. It ended with a two-day warm rain. For the rest of the winter, light rain fell about once every ten days with daytime temperatures in the thirties and forties.

January was so mild Ramsay was able to build a serviceable though temporary barn from willows and cottonwoods and a smattering of materials left over from the house.

About noon on the twenty-second of January, Annie Chris looked out the front room window when she heard Bob barking. A rider leading a pack horse was coming up the creek in their direction. Bob was bounding in the rider's direction; Ramsay was walking quickly behind.

Ten seconds later she recognized the rider. It was John Hailey. She put on her coat, stepped outside and waited.

"Mr. Hailey," said Ramsay. "How guid tae see ye! What brings ye?"

"We have an unfinished chore. I've got Bill's headstone with me back there. Do you have time to help me put it in its proper place?"

"Aye, we will make time. Indeed we will."

Hailey dismounted and tipped his hat to Annie Chris.

"You are looking well, Mr. Hailey. It is so good to see you."

Hailey shook Ramsay's hand and the three of them walked to the house.

"You two have done a lot of work here," said Hailey looking around.

"We had help," said Ramsay, his face bright with pride. "Annie Chris's kin from Fort Hall helped us. We'd be in dire straits without them."

"Suppose you're gonna plant oats and a little alfalfa as soon as the mud leaves."

"Probably fifty acres tae oats an twenty tae alfalfa."

"You should get a good crop if the crick holds up."

"Please, Mr. Hailey, come in," said Annie Chris pointing to the front door of their new house. "I have a venison stew warming on the stove. We can tend to Bill after we eat."

After they'd finished, Ramsay asked, "Where are ye heided from here Mr. Hailey?"

Hailey lit his pipe with a stick match, sucked four long puffs to get it going, and leaned back in his chair. "Well, I'm headed back to town to spend some time with the family. This warm winter so far has kept me busy with my freight business. Thought I oughta slow down a little before it picks back up in the spring."

"How many children do you have?" asked Annie Chris.

"Louisa and I have four children: three girls and a boy."

Annie Chris smiled and nodded approvingly at the obvious pride Hailey exhibited in recalling his family.

"Let me ask ye a question Mr. Hailey," said Ramsay. "Do ye know a banker ye might recommend I talk tae when the time comes tae stock the place with sheep?"

Annie Chris rolled her eyes.

Hailey answered, "I'd wait 'til you know what kind of crop you're going to get before you get too serious about it, but as soon as you can put up a hundred or so tons of hay I wouldn't blame you for looking.

"The best banker in the country is C.W. Moore in Boise City. Good friend of mine. He'll be fair and will tell you straight up."

Ramsay looked puzzled. Hailey saw the look immediately and said, "I'll come out in September and we'll talk about it. My advice never hurt anyone."

They unloaded the eighteen by forty-eight inch grave marker from the back of the pack horse. Together they dug a two and half foot deep hole to bury the butt end of the stone at the head of Bill's grave. When they'd finished, the handsome marker measured eighteen inches square.

The three of them stood back from the grave and the new marker and looked at Bill's final resting place. They were silent, each with their own thoughts.

Annie Chris broke the stillness. "Have you seen Lou?"

"I have – saw her a couple of months ago."

"How is she doing?"

"She's fine and says hello."

~   ~   ~

In March, Ramsay went to work cutting ditches and laterals. He, Bob and the team had the ditches cut at the base of the hills on both sides of the creek by the twentieth of March. The weather had been perfect with intermittent rain then a day or so of wind to dry the surface followed by sunshine. Grass was greening everywhere they looked. The milk goats were getting fat; the horses were putting on flesh and shedding dull winter hair, revealing shiny new coats.

The willows were budding and turning yellowish green. Brilliant blue lupine, violet phlox, pink filaree clover and deep yellow mountain sunflowers covered hillsides between the dull gray sagebrush stalks. All the perennial grasses were green and growing tall. The air was rich with the scent of onion grass and sage. But none of the scents could match the aroma of sagebrush after a rain. It filled the air and was strong and hearty with a heavy smell, not delicate or fragrant but distinct – one knows it's sage and nothing else.

Townsend ground squirrels, called whistle pigs locally, scurried about aimlessly while hawks and golden eagles circled overhead trying to decide which, in this smorgasbord of plenty, might be next. An occasional badger could be seen throwing dirt between his legs excavating for fresh meat below the surface. Fleet-footed killdeer scampered about – ten swift steps then stop, another ten steps and stop, all in the pursuit of some unknown urgency.

Annie Chris and Ramsay were happy and incredibly proud of all they had accomplished from mid-September to the end of March. Not only had they survived, they had flourished. The creek was running ten times the water it had the first day they'd arrived. Willow Creek was their creek, Sunnyside was their ranch. The aristocracy seemed a distant memory. They were beholden to each other only.

There was no denying, however, that Ramsay was restless to start with sheep. Although he was proud of their new homestead, farming was not what he traveled all the way from Scotland to do. He missed working with the animals he knew best. He missed their smell, their seasons, lambing, shearing and tending to their needs. He had always sensed a deep understanding or kinship with the gentle creatures and felt there was a mutual bond between them.

At times he thought the longing might be Biblical, almost as if it were what God intended for him, as He must have intended for other selected members of the hundreds of generations before him all the way back to Abraham. He felt he understood the young shepherd David probably better than most other readers of the Bible.

He told himself he could wait – until fall.

CHAPTER FOURTEEN

~September 10, 1875~

"I would like to introduce you to my son," said John Hailey.

A poised, towheaded pre-teen stepped off the buggy, stuck his right hand out eagerly to meet Ramsay's and said respectfully, "Langston Hailey, Mr. Sproat."

"Pleased tae meet ye, laddie."

"Langston and I are headed to Kelton to meet the train. From there he's headed to a preparatory academy in Chicago," Hailey said proudly. Langston nodded.

"Well, guid for ye, Langston. Ye have a safe trip."

Hailey scanned the panorama of the farm. "You've done very well for yourself, Mr. Sproat. What was your yield?"

"Forty-five bushel an acre," said Ramsay proudly. "Thank ye for stopping by."

"Well sir," said Hailey, "I also have business in mind. I've come to collect on my loan and am pleased to see that it should not pain you to pay me back."

"It will nae, thankfully," said Ramsay. "I threshed twenty-two hundred bushels – sold two thousand tae the Army and saved two hundred for ma animals. I got fifty cents a bushel – a thousand dollars. I put up aboot seventy tons of hay from the alfalfa.

"Aye, it has been a guid year. If ye come with me tae the hoose, I'll prepare ye a draft – two hundred dollars? That richt?"

"Two hundred and six Mr. Sproat, counting three percent interest on the loan."

"That is fair. Naw quarrels on that."

~   ~   ~

"Annie Chris!" shouted Ramsay as he walked through their front door. "Look who's here!" Hailey, who'd been two steps behind, stopped at the threshold to wipe his boots. Langston, respectful of his father's private business with the Sproats, waited in the buggy.

"Why Mr. Hailey," said Annie Chris, coming out of the kitchen wiping her hands on her apron, "it is so good to see you."

"The pleasure is mine, Mrs. Sproat." Hailey nodded as he removed his hat.

"Would you like a cup of coffee?"

"That would be very nice, ma'am, but no. We've a long journey ahead and best be on our way."

"Can you sit for a moment?"

"Of course. Hailey pulled a chair from beneath the table.

Ramsay turned to his wife and said, "Fill out a draft for two hundred and six dollars and bring it tae me please."

A moment later Annie Chris handed Ramsay the draft, then excused herself to attend to Kate. Ramsay signed it, slid it across the table and said, "Thank ye Mr. Hailey. Our feet would be resting on a dirt floor richt now if it were nae for yer generosity."

"I have to admit, Mr. Sproat, I stopped by with more in mind than collecting on my debt."

Ramsay looked at him curiously.

"Bill Judy thought very highly of you and Mrs. Sproat. As you know, I was with him when he breathed his last. Just before he died he asked me to sell his worldly goods and distribute the proceeds. He wanted the two of you to have a share but insisted that I wait until you demonstrated enough industry and self-reliance to warrant his bequest.

"So, Mr. Sproat," Hailey reached into the inside pocket of his vest, "*I* have a draft for *you*."

Hailey looked at it one last time for accuracy then handed it to Ramsay.

Ramsay stared at the amount then back at Hailey. "Seven hundred and fifty dollars?"

"That is correct."

"That's a fortune – I had naw idea." Ramsay looked at the draft again and shook his head slowly. "Bill Judy did more for us than we did for him. I'm nae sure I deserve this."

"He thought you did, Mr. Sproat," said Hailey, "and that's all that counts."

CHAPTER FIFTEEN

~Late fall 1875~

Ramsay finished plowing and disking his fifty acres of oat stubble on November twelfth. He plowed twenty additional acres he'd cleared of sagebrush earlier, in September, when it was too dry to plow. He would plant the newly plowed twenty acres to oats in the spring.

Other than a thunderstorm in early August, there hadn't been a drop of rain from the twentieth of June until early October. The October rain didn't amount to much, less than a quarter inch, but it was enough to moisten the ground for plowing. It was followed by another quarter inch two weeks later. The timing of the rains was perfect to complete his fall work.

The weather remained clear and dry well into December then turned cold with a heavy fog settling in, turning the sagebrush-covered hills and plains dull, dark and lifeless. Night turned to day and then to night again without as much as a glimpse of the sun, day after day. The cold fog continued past Christmas. The frozen world seemed gloomy and stiff.

Ramsay began to worry. He saddled Lucy and rode up Willow Creek to its source, then up onto the ridge separating it from the drainage of the South Fork of the Boise River. From here he was high enough to be above the fog. The sunshine was brilliant and lifted his spirits. He squinted against the sun and looked south in the direction of his fog-shrouded home and beyond. He could clearly see the tops of the blue Owyhee Mountains in the distance. He turned north and could see the Trinity Mountains and the Soldier Mountains in the opposite direction. He turned and again looked south, toward the Owyhees; there was nothing between him and the distant blue mountains but a hundred mile sea of gray gloomy fog, roiling over the expanse like a witch's cauldron. The deep fog brought back memories of his homeland, a memory he'd just as soon forget.

He looked back toward the Trinities. The only snow he could see was at the very tops of the peaks. Here it was, the twenty-seventh of December, and no snow. What would he do if this dry weather continued? How would he irrigate an alfalfa crop? Willow Creek's flow had not increased at all since late summer; in fact it seemed to have decreased.

He had to have an alternative. It would be impossible for them to make it without water and water in the southern portion of the Idaho Territory had to come from the winter's snow accumulation and its spring runoff. He could sit and hope but hope did not build a prosperous ranch.

He turned and began the ride home. He left the sunshine behind and slowly descended back into the murky fog.

As he rode, his thoughts turned to sheep. Sheep could make it in this kind of weather. He could get by if Willow Creek didn't run enough to irrigate – he wouldn't need hay or grain in a winter like this; sheep could winter without it. They could survive on the dry feed and brush to the south in the direction of the Snake River. Sheep could be his hedge against drought. He felt a little better as he considered the possibilities. In the back of his mind, he knew Annie Chris would be hard to convince.

Thanks to Bill's bequest, he had enough money to get a start. For the entire two hour ride back to the house, he planned his debate with his wife.

She listened, dispassionate to his case. She heard his words but seemed oblivious to his logic. "You have no idea what it's like down there near the Snake," said Annie Chris when he'd finished. "Sheep can't live on sage-brush."

"I know that," he said, frustrated by the failure of his argument, "but *ye* know what Hailey told us, it's thick with white sage and salt brush. Deer and elk and antelope fatten on it – in the *winter* naw less."

"Have you ever been there? *No.* Do you know what it looks like? *No.* Are you sure sheep will eat it? *No.* Where will they water? Have you even *thought* about that?"

"Aye, of course I've thought of that. Keep yer heid woman," he answered, trying to keep his temper in check. He'd learned from three years of marriage that his wife's reaction to his anger brought only contempt in return and contempt was a poor platform for closing a sale.

"Do ye nae trust me?" he asked, wounded.

"I trust you but you have never even been there. You can't just take everybody's word for things."

"I plan tae go, I have all along – mebbe in the morn, but I will nae unless ye let me take ye and Kate tae town. I could be gone for three or four days."

"I can't do that," she said emphatically, shaking her head. "Kate doesn't need a long trip to town with her fever. We'll be fine. Go."

With a shrug, Ramsay feigned uneasy agreement. Truthfully, he couldn't wait to go and felt she and Kate would be fine.

"Where is the compass?" asked Ramsay the next morning. He knew how easily one could get lost in a foggy featureless expanse, unable to see no more than five feet in any direction.

Annie Chris held Kate, a year and a half old now, wrapped tightly in a blanket and was rocking her gently trying to get her to sleep. She was listless, short periods of sleep came intermittently, she woke only to moan, avoiding the painful urge to cry out loud. She resisted eating and swallowing, confirming Annie Chris's suspicion that her baby had an inflamed throat. Annie Chris made no attempt to rise from her chair, and whispered to Ramsay, "It's in the bureau next to the door."

She paused for a second looking in Kate's pained little eyes and whispered, "Bring me some more of the carrot poultice."

Ramsay retrieved it from the kitchen, leaned down and carefully rubbed a generous amount on Kate's little neck. Annie Chris covered the dressing again with a cheese cloth. Kate's eyes were closed. She'd finally gone to sleep.

"I don't know if I should leave," he whispered.

"There's nothing you can do here. She'll get over it in a day or two. It's a perfect time – might be more of a test if we get snow."

Ramsay cinched the sawbuck pack saddle tightly on the bay, his best pack horse, loaded two large canvas alforjas bags with a sack of coal, a sack of oats, some groceries, ten canvas bags of water and a few cooking utensils, placed his bedroll and tent on top, tied it all down, saddled Lucy and was on his way south at 8:30 a.m., December 28, 1875. Bob was close behind.

He figured he could make thirty miles a day but wanted to take some extra time to zigzag around a little to get a strong feeling for the area's potential. On the second day he noticed a change in vegetation. The brush was shorter and leafier than sagebrush, its leaves white rather than grayish-green. The horses nibbled on it – a good sign. He felt air movement, a breeze, the first in two weeks. Within an hour the fog was gone; he could see for miles over the flat open whitesage-covered expanse, reminding him of the plains they'd crossed on the train.

The Owyhees again became visible in the distance looking south. He headed in that direction hoping to reach the Snake early the next day.

That night Ramsay camped at the rocky rim overlooking the broad Snake River valley. Worried about Kate, sleep didn't come until the early hours of the morning.

He had guessed the river was eight or nine hundred feet below his camp. Unfortunately, he could see no obvious trail or way to get down to it. He needed to find a passage or opening in the basalt to descend because this whole winter range would be worthless if there was no way for the sheep to get to the river to water.

The next morning, New Year's Day 1876, he woke thinking he must be dreaming. He thought he could hear sheep bleating in the distance. He stepped out of his tent, curious, his senses alert. Bob's ears pointed up stiffly, their tips folded over. He was looking upriver as his tail wagged slowly back and forth. Ramsay heard bleating again but no clearer than before.

He caught, un-hobbled and saddled Lucy, tied the bay to a heavy rock, left his camp intact and headed east along the rim. Bob chose to lead. The further Ramsay went the louder the bleating became but he could not see where it was coming from. Fifteen minutes later he saw smoke. As he followed the rising contour of the ground, a canvas-covered wagon slowly came into view. He wasn't alone. He'd assumed all along the closest humans were his wife and daughter, some thirty miles to the north.

As he looked for the sheep he heard, he rode closer to the rim, close enough to see over the edge.

Blending into the snow and dry grass, it was difficult to see them at first. Gradually, the sheep came into view. He sniffed the air to catch their scent but couldn't. They covered the hillside. As he watched, their mass was slowly moving downward in the direction of the river. He couldn't tell how many, but from where he sat, he guessed at least five hundred. A man came into view carrying a staff, walking slowly behind. Two dogs flanked the sheep and kept a non-threatening distance.

He nudged Lucy into a trot, caught a whiff – memories raced. A warm wave came over him as Lucy trotted closer to sound of the sheep. He saw a passage in the rim and knew it was the gap he was looking for.

He saw a wagon less than a quarter mile away. It was no more than a buckboard with a rounded white canvas top, similar to the hundreds he'd seen during his year in Kansas City. Instead of being open at each end like the prairie wagons were, the ends were closed in. A stove pipe stuck through the canvas top. A smaller wagon was hitched behind, with two draft horses, one tied to each side.

White smoke drifted from the chimney. The stove inside was being tended. A bullet could be the cost of intruding. When he was fifty yards away he shouted, "Hello! Anyone there?"

He could hear rustling inside. The door swung open. A woman poked her head out and looked in his direction. A pistol was in her right hand.

"Stop right there mister, if you know what's good for ya," she shouted and pointed the pistol in the air to make sure he knew she was armed.

Ramsay squinted – it couldn't be – by God it was. "Lou! Lou, it's me, Ramsay!"

"Well if that don't beat all," she hollered. She jumped off the tongue of the wagon and laid the pistol on the wagon's floor all in one motion. Her arms were wide open for the hug she intended to wrap around him. She hadn't changed a bit: hair still tightly braided over the top of her head and the same big ear-to-ear grin.

"Happy New Year, Lou!" shouted Ramsay. "Yer a sight for sore eyes."

"What in tarnation are you doing here? No, before you answer that, let's get out of the cold. Come on in and we'll catch up."

Lou stepped onto the wagon's tongue and through the narrow Dutch door. Ramsay followed. She sat on the bench opposite a small wood stove and motioned for him to do the same. Although compact, almost Lilliputi-an, it was inviting with a snug homey feel. The warm sumptuous smell of roasting meat reminded him of her restaurant.

"Let me pour you a cup of coffee," she said handing him a tin cup. "By God it's good to see you! Tell me about yourself. How's Annie Chris and Katherine?"

"We're doin' guid. We homesteaded on a crick called Willow Crick. Katherine's guid – we call her Kate now. She's nae really a baby naw more. She has a fevered throat but she'll be awricht."

"I remember Willow Creek, Bill talked about it."

Bill. Ramsay hesitated at the reminder. He asked reverently, "Have ye heard aboot Bill?"

"I did – cried for a week. John Hailey told me – told me about your place, too. Now what the hell are you doing clear down here?"

"I'm looking for a place tae winter sheep. I don't have any yet but I'm thinking aboot it. It's been a dry winter and there's naw snow in the mountains. I got tae worrying aboot growing a crop this coming summer and thought it might be time for sheep.

"Now tell me about ye. Och, I was so surprised tae see ye," said Ramsay.

"I expect you was. Well, I was cooking supper at my place in Kelton one day last spring and looked up and this here nice looking fella was coming through the door – had on a clean shirt and clean pants, a green scarf around his neck and a black beret on the side of his head. He was clean shaven except for his black mustache and had a big grin on his face when I asked him what he wanted for supper. I smiled back and he said something in a tongue I couldn't understand a word of. I took him by the hand to the kitchen and pointed to the roast I was carving and he nodded and brought his thumb and forefinger to his lips and kissed them and I was in love like I'd never been in love in my whole life.

"Next day we went to the preacher and got married. Between me and Pache, that's my husband's name, and a Mexican preacher, we exchanged our intentions and were man and wife in five minutes. Pache was living in this here campwagon headed out of Wyoming looking for a place to raise sheep. He'd saved a little money working for a sheepman there and was wanting to strike out on his own – heard about Idaho."

"Married! Well here's tae ye!" Ramsay said, lifting the cup.

"Thank you," she said returning the grin with one of her own and a nod. "We bought some sheep from a cranky ol' Swede in Winnemucca and here we are.

"Pache wants to summer the sheep in the Sawtooths, maybe find a little place down low to raise some hay and grain. This here's pretty good winter country for sheep. Now he thinks we shouldn't get too far away so we can come on back easy enough next winter."

"Yer happy, Lou, a blind man could see it."

"Yes I am. When you meet Pache you'll know why. Let me finish with this here lamb shank stew – we'll take it down there to the river and have dinner with Pache."

Francisco Arestegi was his name, Pache (Potch) for short. He had a bear grip of a handshake and an ever-present wine-filled bota bag draped over his shoulder with a leather cord, eager to share it with anyone who appeared to love life as much as he did.

He was Basque. He emigrated from Vizcaya, a northern province of Spain near France and the Pyrenees Mountains. The rugged Atlantic coastline forms its northern border. It is one of the most beautiful regions in the world.

The Basque people are distinctly different from the Spanish and resemble Greeks or Italians more than their smaller, darker Spanish countrymen. They are easily identified by their unique music and dance and their colorful dress. They live in tightly knit communities, working their small farms or going to sea as fishermen. They have their own, very complicated language, Euskara, a language with similarities to no other language group in the world, a language whose origins are unknown.

In the months since they'd married, Lou had taught Pache some English, though his thick Euskara accent remained. Pache had insisted on learning to read English as well as write it. They were still working on that.

"Lou, you bring dinner guest?" shouted Pache, his welcoming arms and thick hands raised, palms up waiting for an introduction while his two dogs wagged their tails at Bob and sniffed him curiously in places dogs often do.

"Pache," said Lou proudly, "this here is my friend Ramsay Sproat – you remember me talking about Ramsay and his wife and baby."

"Oh jes, jes, I remember." Pache grinned. He extended his right hand to Ramsay in a handshake Ramsay thought might crush his hand like a ripe tomato. "Francisco Arestegi, that ees my name. You call me Pache."

"Ramsay's looking the winter range over. He thinks he might get him some sheep."

113

"Ees big country," said Pache waving his arms around in circles. "Room for thousands and thousands of sheep. You know sheep?"

"All ma life. In ma homeland, Scotland."

"Oh jes, I hear of it. You like America?"

"We are very happy here – Mister Ares…"

"Pache – ees much easier."

"The weather is so dry though," said Ramsay, "if we don't get some snow soon, I won't be able tae farm. That's why I'm considering sheep. I have so many questions."

"We sit, eat, drink wine, talk," said Pache.

After starting a small fire, Lou spread out a clean piece of canvas, the size of a table cloth, on the dry grass next to the river. She took a loaf of bread the shape of a Dutch oven, three metal plates and eating utensils out of a bag Ramsay had carried from the camp wagon, filled each plate with a generous helping of lamb shank stew and said, "Pache likes to give thanks before we eat."

Pache lowered his head, the cue for Ramsay and Lou to do the same, paused, mouthed unintelligible words in his native tongue, then said simply, "Amen." He crossed himself, handed the bota bag to Ramsay and said with gusto, "We drink!"

Ramsay was not a stranger to a bota bag. He'd squeezed his share of Scotch whiskey over the years. He took the bag and squeezed just enough to start a stream in his open mouth. Continuing the stream, he gradually extended the bag away from his mouth until his arms were fully extended. He slowly drew his hands back toward his mouth until the bag's small opening was an inch from his lips. He did not waste a drop; the bag did not touch his lips.

"Salude!" said Pache as he slapped Ramsay on the back. "You goot man!"

They talked through dinner and into the afternoon. Ramsay pressed Pache with one question after another. Ramsay learned that Pache's ewes were Spanish Merinos, good wool producers and well adapted to the region's dry climate. He told Ramsay his ewes were bred in the fall to Spanish Merino rams or bucks as they were called in the West; bred to have their lambs in April, north of here, in the general direction of Ramsay's ranch. Pache said he was interested in cross-breeding different varieties of sheep when the opportunity presented itself.

Ramsay learned there were two varieties of forage brush on the winter range: whitesage or winter fat as it was sometimes called, and salt brush or shadscale. Both were edible by domestic animals. Pache said he trailed his sheep to the river to water about once every three or four days and had found at least four passages in the canyon rim accessible enough for his sheep to descend. There could be more, he added. He also told Ramsay that a little snow was a good thing, that his sheep would consume snow for water, delaying a trip down the rim to the river by days.

Pache told him this was his first winter on the winter range. He spent the past summer in the Owyhee Mountains. He had trailed his sheep to Boise City this past October to sell his lambs to the Army then gradually moved the ewes to the winter range.

"Ye bought yer sheep in Winnemucca?"

"Four hundred and fifty. I like more but Lou, she say no – her money." He shrugged in smiling acceptance, palms up.

Ramsay looked puzzled but chose not to pry.

"John Hailey came to see me one day," said Lou. "He handed me a draft for seven hundred and fifty dollars – said Bill Judy wanted me to have it.

"I told Hailey, all right, but I'm gonna cash it and give you back twenty-five for a tombstone. Me and Pache used part of his money and part of mine and bought these here sheep – couldn't be happier if I was ol' Queen Vickie herself."

Pache put a big hand on Ramsay's right shoulder and said, "I know a man selling sheep in Oregon. You got money?"

"Well, darndest thing, John Hailey came tae me too. Bill must have told Hailey tae give the same tae me and Annie Chris as he gave tae ye, Lou, cause he came tae me with a draft for seven hundred and fifty dollars."

"He had a good heart, Bill did. I'd get so damned aggravated at him though. Lord forgive me but I did."

"John Hailey and Annie Chris and I buried him at our place – put the tombstone at the heid of his grave a year later, just last September."

"I got good idea," interrupted Pache. Again he placed a big paw on one of Ramsay's shoulders. "You buy sheep – we be partners!"

Ramsay's eyes opened wide. He looked at Pache who was still smiling, waiting for an answer, then looked at Lou who was nodding, her smile as broad as her husband's.

"Well?" asked Lou.

Ramsay looked at one then the other and said, "Aye!"

The cheap red wine and the gallon that followed went down as smoothly and as comfortably as if it was twenty-year-old Romanee Conti.

Deep dreamless sleep came easily to all three later that clear still night.

CHAPTER SIXTEEN

"Is she worse?" whispered Ramsay. It was nearly dark but even in the dim lamp-light Annie Chris's face was a disturbingly pallid tone, it sagged – she looked ten years older.

She walked outside. Ramsay followed. She sat hard in a chair on the porch; her face fell into her hands. "Give me a minute."

"What is wrong with her?"

"Her fever won't go away and she has a wretched sore throat. She's finally asleep. She got worse the morning after you left. I decided to take her to town in the wagon to find a doctor but as I walked to the barn I noticed two Indians across from the hay field about half a mile away. They saw me and just sat there on their horses watching. Ramsay, I was so afraid. I decided that it would be riskier to leave with Kate than to stay. I tended to her the best I could and prayed. I am so glad you are here."

She looked up at him, frightened as tears streamed down her face. "I am so glad you are here," she repeated. She lifted herself out of the chair. "We have to go – now!"

"Now?"

"Are you questioning me? I've done everything I can think of."

"I'll hitch the wagon. I can be ready in ten minutes."

Ramsay rushed to the barn while Annie Chris went back in to gather what she needed: blankets, more of the poultice and a container of salt and honey she'd used to mix with some water to hydrate Kate. She put the things on the porch.

Ramsay drove to the front of the house. There was no moon. The darkness was total. Annie Chris handed him Kate's things. She went back, carefully placed Kate on a blanket, carried her outside, handed her to Ramsay and stepped into the wagon. Kate stirred as Ramsay handed her back but didn't wake. He slapped the reins and they were on their way.

He told Annie Chris about meeting up with Lou and her new husband Pache but, considering the circumstances, neither was in the mood to discuss the details as they sat silently bumping along in the wagon in the middle of the night with their child deathly ill in Annie Chris's arms.

They were in Boise City by one a.m. and had no idea how to find the doctor. They asked at one of the only businesses open at that hour, a saloon.

Kate slept the entire trip and was still asleep as they knocked at Dr. Ivey's front door at one forty-five. A sleepy looking middle-aged man in a brown robe came to the door. He took one look at the pale little child in Ramsay's arms and said, "Please, follow me."

They walked through the parlor into an examining room. "Lay her here on the table. I'm Doctor Ivey."

Ivey didn't offer a handshake or wait for introductions. "What has been going on?"

Annie Chris told him about Kate's sore throat, the fever and what she'd done for five days to relieve it including the carrot poultices on her neck, the soda baths, a mixture of salt, water, honey and saffron and the onion slices she'd applied to the bottoms of Kate's feet.

He went to a cabinet, removed a stethoscope and placed it on Kate's chest. She startled at the cold but didn't wake. He moved it to her back. A kindly thin blonde woman in a powder blue robe, Dr. Ivey's wife they assumed, walked quietly into the room, sat, nodded with a concerned smile but said nothing.

Kate began to rouse and fuss. Annie Chris asked if she could change her. The doctor nodded and looked intently at the watery deposit in her diaper. He looked at his wife who took the unspoken cue, left the room and returned with the doctor's pocket watch. He took the watch from her and put his finger to Kate's neck.

Moments later he laid the stethoscope and the watch on the counter next to the examining table and asked his wife to bring him the potash. She went to the cabinet, mixed a small measure of powder in a glass of water and brought it to him. He put the glass to Kate's lips, allowing her to sip slowly until she could swallow no more. A small amount dribbled from the corner of her mouth. She seemed too weak to resist.

"Your names are?

"Mr. and Mrs. Ramsay Sproat," answered Ramsay.

"And the child's name?"

"Katherine, we call her Kate," answered Annie Chris, her voice weak and reedy.

"Mr. and Mrs. Sproat, please sit here on the sofa." They sat carefully, their eyes fixed on the doctor as he handed Kate to Annie Chris and sat in a chair next to the sofa.

Dr. Ivey clasped his hands and slowly placed them in his lap: "I need not tell you that she is very ill. The fever has persisted a dangerously long time but I am not sure there would have been anything more I could have done for her other than what you have done yourselves, even if you had brought her to me earlier. We do not know what causes these terrible sore throats that children sometimes suffer from, but we do know that relieving the fever early in the illness is important to a rapid recovery. You are welcome to stay here with my wife and me. If we manage to bring the fever down and pneumonia does not set in, she should recover. But I must tell you there may be damage."

Annie Chris looked at him absorbing the news, barely able to breathe. Ramsay put his arm around her as Dr. Ivey continued. "I have given her chlorate of potash which sometimes helps with fever and ailments of the throat such as hers. We need to hydrate her as much as we can with a light mixture of salt, lemon juice, some crushed raisins and water. It is critical that she replenish the fluids in her body."

Ramsay asked, "What kind of damage?"

"Heart damage sir; it is sometimes called rheumatic fever. The illness can cause damage to the valves in the heart. If that happens, the heart can be taxed and cannot adequately pump blood. The blood escapes through the damaged valves back into the main chamber of the heart. The heart races to get blood into the body.

"I want to be candid with you but I also want you to know that the heart damage I have cautioned you about may not have occurred. I will not know until a week or so after her fever has subsided. Her pulse is very rapid but there is no marked congestion in her lungs which is a good sign. Hopefully, we are not facing pneumonia on top of everything else. Do you have any questions?"

Annie Chris took in every painful word while Ramsay sat stiff as a post. They looked at one another, then Annie Chris turned back toward Dr. Ivey. "I think we understand but we don't know what to ask."

"I know this is difficult for you but you must know what this little girl may be faced with. It would be best if at least one of you stayed here with us for a few of days."

Annie Chris asked, "What will you be able to tell once her fever is gone?"

"I will listen for what are called heart murmurs or abnormalities in the valves. If I detect damage we will discuss courses of action. But first things first: we have to eliminate the fever."

Annie Chris said, "I will stay."

"The two of you must get some rest. You are welcome to our spare bedroom."

"That is very kind of ye, doctor," said Ramsay.

"The next twenty-four hours will be critical. If we can help her break the fever her prospects should be good. Now you two get some rest."

Neither of them could sleep. At five-thirty Ramsay told his wife he needed some air and would attend to the horse, still tied to Dr. Ivey's hitching post.

"The livery won't be open."

"I'll take her there anyway – she needs tae be watered. I might roust someone up so she can be fed too."

Ramsay was standing outside with his horse and wagon as the proprietor slid open his barn door at six. "Ma name is Sproat. Ma wife and daughter are with Dr. Ivey. Our daughter is sick. Our horse needs rest and feed." In those few words Ramsay felt like he'd made a speech.

"You a Scotchman?"

"A Scot, aye," said Ramsay, too tired to correct him.

"Well sir, I'm Irish – name's Tim Shea," he said extending his rough, calloused hand for a handshake. "Bring her on in. I'll take care of her. You look like you could use a cup of coffee. Got a pot brewing on the stove over there."

Tim Shea led Ramsay's horse to a stall with water and fresh hay while Ramsay sat on an upright nail keg Tim had covered with a board to serve as a stool. He stared at the ground, his big hands circling the cup of warm brew. When Shea returned, he poured himself a cup and sat next to Ramsay. He allowed Ramsay to sip the coffee in silence.

Ramsay sat motionless, drawing deep breaths, exhaling in worried sighs. He glanced at the raw rough-cut pine board wall across from the nail keg he was sitting on and noticed a framed sketch of a horse. It looked so much like Lucy it startled him. Tim noticed: "A beauty ain't it. A young girl here in town gave it to me. She saw me give a local squaw an old saddle blanket and asked if she could give me this here drawing she'd done. Said she appreciated my kindness. Hell, that old Injun was in rags and it was colder than a well digger's ass that day."

"It looks like a horse of mine."

Shea walked over to the wall, lifted the drawing from the nail and handed it to Ramsay. "Keep it my friend."

Ramsay took it in both hands, looked closer, and noticed the artist's signature in the corner. "Myra Grant. Grant. . . I've heard that name before."

"Ain't a sweeter gal in this whole town."

"Well, Mr. Shea, I hate tae nae appear grateful but I need tae return tae Dr. Ivey's. Thank ye for the picture and the coffee. I don't know how long ma horse'll have tae be in yer care, nae long is ma hope. Yer rate?"

"Four bits a day. I'll take good care of her – you attend to your daughter."

At seven, Ramsay stepped onto Dr. Ivey's porch for the second time. He'd been up all night but was too worried to feel the weariness that his body somehow managed to ignore. He knocked softly. Mrs. Ivey answered, her ever-present smile, like an undertaker's, still spread across her broad face.

"Please come in. Your daughter's fever has broken, praise be to God."

Annie Chris came around the corner from the kitchen, moved weakly toward Ramsay and wrapped her arms around his waist. "She's going to be all right."

"Guid God. I was so afraid."

"Dr. Ivey is on another call but he said we can go home after she wakes up. She slept well."

"When does he want tae see her again?"

"Two weeks from today."

Within days Kate was eating and taking fluids more eagerly. Color had returned to her cheeks but she was still listless and seemed continually tired. Dr. Ivey had taught Annie Chris to take Kate's pulse and told her to take it twice a day to see if her heart rate might begin to moderate. It had, some, but was still over 120 beats per minute, 15 beats more than normal.

Kate had begun to walk before the illness but now she seemed to have lost interest. She wanted to be carried everywhere. She had also begun to talk some, just as most children do at that age, but now just pointed to what she wanted and whined. She cried very little and smiled very little.

Annie Chris and Ramsay thought she might just be slow to recover but, as her listlessness continued, they wondered if they should return before the two weeks, but decided to trust Dr. Ivey.

They were knocking at his door at eleven a.m., two weeks after they'd left. "How's my little girl doing?" asked Dr. Ivey. "She looks good."

"She sleeps so much and her heart rate has not gone down much," answered Annie Chris.

"Well, let's take a look."

Ramsay grabbed Annie Chris's quivering hands in his and held tight.

Dr. Ivey examined Kate for at least twenty minutes, moving his stethoscope from her chest to her back, then to her chest, then back again. He took a deep breath, looked up at the two of them and said with a long look, "There is damage, I'm afraid, in at least two of her valves.

"I wish I had better news. She could live a long life or she could be gone within a year. We just don't know enough about the condition. We do know that this kind of damage does not heal itself but some people learn to live comfortably with it. For her to survive will require a life with a lot of rest and little exertion, a life as free as possible from other complicating illnesses."

Annie Chris was prepared for the news but Ramsay was not. He stood, walked outside, sat on the edge of the porch, his shoulders bent, his careworn face cupped in his hands. Annie Chris followed, sat next to him, and placed her arm over her husband's slumped shoulders.

PART TWO

Sweet Afton

"Flow gently, sweet Afton! amang thy green braes,
Flow gently, I'll sing thee a song in thy praise;
My Mary's asleep by thy murmuring stream,
Flow gently, sweet Afton, disturb not her dream.

Thou stockdove whose echo resounds thro' the glen,
Ye wild whistling blackbirds in yon thorny den,
Thou green-crested lapwing thy screaming forbear,
I charge you, disturb not my slumbering Fair.

How lofty, sweet Afton, thy neighboring hills,
Far mark'd with the courses of clear, winding rills;
There daily I wander as noon rises high,
My flocks and my Mary's sweet cot in my eye.

How pleasant thy banks and green valleys below,
Where, wild in the woodlands, the primroses blow;
There oft, as mild Ev'ning weeps over the lea,
The sweet-scented birk shades my Mary and me.

Thy crystal steam, Afton, how lovely it glides,
And winds by the cot where my Mary resides;
How wanton thy waters her snowy feet lave,
As, gathering sweet flowerets, she stems thy clear wave.

Flow gently, sweet Afton, amang thy green braes,
Flow gently, sweet river, the theme of my lays;
My Mary's asleep by thy murmuring stream,
Flow gently, sweet Afton, disturb not her dreams."

Robert Burns, 1791

CHAPTER SEVENTEEN

~Three years later~

It started with a chest cold – then it worsened. On a cold January morning in 1879, for the fourth time in her young fragile life, four and a half year old Katherine Cora Sproat was rushed to Boise City to Dr. Ivey. This time there was nothing he could do. Kate died in his home. He, Mrs. Ivey, Ramsay and Annie Chris were at her side.

They buried her next to Bill just up the creek from the house on the southwest side, the sunniest side. Ramsay had planted two locust tree seedlings a couple of years before that were now about as tall as, well, Kate, he thought.

He swung his pick at the frozen ground as viciously as if he were killing a rattlesnake. It took hours to reach the loose dirt beneath and finish digging the grave. He put more and more force into each successive blow, as if the serpent refused to die. Although he was utterly drained, he was disappointed when the assault was complete. He had not yet purged himself of the rage and frustration that filled his chest like an intruder that wouldn't leave. As he walked back to the house with the pick and shovel over his shoulder he wondered if the intruder would *ever* leave.

A continuing hard winter in Eastern Idaho made it impossible for Hugh and Cora to attend. A Methodist minister from Boise City began a short graveside service attended by Dr. and Mrs. Ivey, Pache and Lou, Tim Shea and a handful of new settlers in the area with whom Ramsay and Annie Chris had become acquainted, and, of course, Bob, and Kate's little dog, Chelsea. Shortly after the service began, a buggy pulled up with three people. The bearded driver, wrapped in a woolen coat, his wide-brimmed felt hat pulled down, his collar up over his ears, stepped out on one side while a passenger similarly clad stepped out the other. The passenger reached into the buggy to help a woman, bundled in a blanket, step out behind him. The three walked toward the assembled group while the minister paused to allow the late-comers to join them. Albert and Alma Hawes and John Hailey embraced Annie Chris, then turned to Ramsay and extended their hands in sympathy and respect. The minister continued.

Annie Chris placed Kate's most valued possessions, including a well-worn rattle, beside her in the little coffin. The coffin was closed and lowered into the ground. Seconds later Pache and Ramsay slowly and carefully threw shovelfuls of loamy Sunnyside dirt onto the wooden box in the dark cold hole.

As he did, Ramsay was struck by the memory of the story he'd been told of how some Indians light an inferno under their deceased to send their spirits in a blaze of glory to meet their ancestors in the afterlife. He suppressed an urge to stop the proceedings, but continued shoveling.

One month later her parents placed a small granite marker at the head of Kate's grave. The marker was shaped like a cross with a resting lamb at its base. Kate's full name, date of birth and date of death were inscribed.

Even though her delicate health had required extraordinary attention, those precious years before Kate died were good ones for Ramsay and Annie Chris. Kate somehow knew and accepted that she was different and more fragile than other children and rarely fussed or complained about the limits her parents were forced to impose on her.

Her curiosity about everything associated with the ranch – the horses, the sheep, the crops, the weather – more than made up for her inability to be active in its daily activity. It was hard to imagine of a four year old; she could tell the age of a ewe just by looking at her, knew by its downcast look when a lamb was not getting enough milk and knew by the actions of the horses when a storm was coming.

Both Ramsay and Annie Chris had carefully monitored her heart rate, the strain of her activities, and always made sure she was warm; they both knew she was at risk if she was to catch any of the common childhood illnesses that most every other child overcame in less than a week.

Most of all, Kate loved being with Pache and Lou and begged her parents to take her to the partnership's sheep camp during the spring lambing season and in the fall when the sheep had been trailed out of the mountains and were nearer home. They often complied, hitched the wagon, and headed out as comfortably as possible across the rolling sagebrush-covered foothills near Sunnyside.

Each time, as the wagon would come within a mile or two of where Ramsay knew Pache and Lou's camp would be, they would play a little game rigged for Kate to win. Kate knew it but loved playing it anyway. The first to see the smoke of Lou's campwagon woodstove would win.

"What kind of treat do ye s'pose Lou has for the winner? I bet it's really guid," Ramsay would say. Then almost in the next breath he would point and say, "I see it!"

"That's not smoke Papa, that's a cloud!"

Five minutes later – "I see it!" Annie Chris would say.

"That's not smoke Mama that's dust!"

Finally they would get close enough and Kate would say, "I see it! I win!"

"Kate wins!" Ramsay and Annie Chris would proclaim. "She gets the treat! Hooray!"

Kate clapped her little hands as delighted as if she had just won a new pony.

On one such trip, Lou heard the wagon approaching and all the whooping and hollering and ran out from the camp wagon with that big lean grin on her face, her eyes dancing. "Who won? Who won?"

Kate said, "I did Lou! What is my treat?"

"Well, come on inside and I'll show you but first, where's my hug you sweet thing?"

Ramsay lifted Kate out of the wagon as Lou ran toward her. Kate's arms stretched out to be held by Lou. Lou hugged her and slowly spun her around and around and said, "I knew you would win! Wait 'til you see what I got for my girl!" and carried her, both laughing, into the cozy warmth of the canvas-covered wagon with all the wonderful smells of burning wood and pastry in the oven.

"But wait," Lou said, "a little bird told me you don't like chocolate cake."

"I love chocolate cake!" Kate said, knowing she was being teased and loving every minute of it.

"Well let's open this oven and see if it's done, shall we? But we have to be careful that the cake doesn't fall."

They both crouched on the floor of Lou and Pache's spotless little home as Lou slowly opened the oven door. They both peeked inside. "Do you think it's done?" Lou asked as the warm chocolate smell escaped the oven.

"I think so," Kate said.

"Do you want a bite now or shall we wait?"

"Now! Now!"

Lou, Annie Chris, Ramsay and Kate sat at Lou's drop-down table and gorged themselves with the best chocolate cake, Kate would exclaim, that was ever made. Kate scolded her father as he ritually reached for the last pieces of the cake. "No Papa those are for Pache and for Bob and Cece."

Ramsay withdrew his hand. "Pache does nae like chocolate cake, does he Lou."

"Yes he does!" Kate interrupted. And they all laughed.

About then the Dutch doors of the camp wagon opened and there was Pache with his big happy grin. "Where ees my girl?"

"I'm here Pache. I saved some cake for you and Bob and Cece."

"Oh thank you." he said, "Do you have hug for Pache?"

Kate worked her way around the table and stove and into Pache's outstretched arms with Bob and Cece sitting at Pache's side, their tails wagging.

The following fall when Ramsay and Annie Chris took Kate to Pache and Lou's camp and they ate the ginger snaps Lou had baked, Pache asked Lou with a wink if he could have four.

"Why four Pache?" asked Kate. "You and the two dogs makes three."

"You a very smart girl but I tell you why if you promise secret."

"I promise Pache, please tell me."

"I tell you then. One for me, one for Bob and two for Cece."

"Why two for Cece?"

"That is secret I tell you," Pache said, looking this way and that as if searching for anyone who might be eavesdropping.

Pache motioned for Kate to come closer. She was breathless. "Cece, she ees going to have poopies," whispered Pache. "Need two cookies."

"Mama, Papa, Lou! Cece is going to have puppies!"

Pache stood, put his big hands on his hips and faked exasperation. "Where is secret?"

Kate didn't even hear him as she gave Cece a big hug and got a lick on her face in return. "Cece, can I have one of your puppies?"

Cece had six pups. Each one looked like Bob. Kate picked the runt and named her Chelsea.

Ramsay and Annie Chris had wanted a sister or brother for Kate, assuming a companion for their fragile little girl would be good for her as well as for their marriage. And, although it was never stated aloud, they both feared being childless if the Lord were to take Kate from them.

But the Lord did take Kate and month after month, Annie Chris's monthly period made its unwelcomed appearance.

Their sadness was so deep tears would not come. Their spirits were numb. Communication between them became forced and awkward. Within a few months, Ramsay managed to pull himself out of his malaise. But his attempts to lift his wife's spirits were ignored or dismissed. She wasn't mean or short with him; they talked productively about the ranch, but personal playful conversations, the kind that bind couples together, left with Kate. Annie Chris's grief was deep below the surface, invisible to all but Ramsay. Grief seemed to have consumed her soul. He wondered if she still loved him.

Late one night while they were lying in bed and sleep would not come to Ramsay and he knew his wife was as awake as he was, he peered into the dark, his eyes wide, staring into the void. Though the two of them lay only inches apart, he was beset with thoughts of how distant they had become. The silence in their small bedroom was heavy. Slowly, faintly, he began to hear the softest little scratching sound. Was it a limb brushing against the house or mice in the wall? The harder he listened the louder it became – louder and louder until he thought his head would burst. Finally he said, "I miss ye, ma loove." The sound disappeared. "I am lonely without ye. Is there anything I can do tae bring ye back tae me?"

Her silence was deafening. The scratching began again, faintly at first then louder and louder. It vanished when she said, "I don't know how to describe how I feel. My heart feels empty. I don't know how to refill it – I'm not even sure I want to."

"Aye ma loove, I understand. But we have tae move on."

Her response left him wondering if she'd even heard what he'd said. "Those Indians weren't going to bother us," she said. "They were just looking for food. Why was I so afraid?"

"It was nae yer fault. What would ye have doon? Indians or naw Indians – ye could nae have driven the wagon and carried Kate – ye would have had tae put her in the back bouncing along aloone. Any woman aloone would have doon the same as ye. Ye have to quit punishing yerself."

More silence. In a soft hiss, she said, "How dare you tell me how I should feel."

~   ~   ~

Cora and Hugh Calland made a trip to Sunnyside every year just before Thanksgiving. Ramsay and Annie Chris had never been to their Fort Hall ranch; the trip had been too risky for little Kate. During the Callands' last trip, ten months after Kate passed away, Hugh, drawn and tired-looking, called Ramsay and Annie Chris to the kitchen table where he, seated next to his distraught wife, announced he was suffering from an extreme debilitation of the stomach.

They'd seen the doctor at Blackfoot who'd told Hugh to get his affairs in order. Hugh had found a buyer, a Mormon named Hansen, who offered him a fair price for the ranch, a price Hugh had decided to accept. He labored painfully through the details as quickly as possible. When he finished he paused, looked at the wall over the heads of Annie Chris and Ramsay and cleared his throat to help push back his emotions. He cleared his throat again, still looking at the wall. He was struggling terribly to say what Ramsay knew his pride would not allow. Ramsay thought his wife knew it too and expected her to interrupt the awkward silence. She didn't so finally, Ramsay, almost at the point of tears himself, said, "The two of ye will live with us. We will have it naw other way."

A look of relief filled Hugh's hollow gray face as he stared at his folded hands on the table. Cora finally said, "Thank you" as she placed both her hands over Hugh's.

Annie Chris stood. "Of course, we are family." She walked to Hugh, gave him a warm hug then moved to Cora and did the same. The empathy was communicated physically and accepted emotionally by the Callands as sincere, but Ramsay knew otherwise.

Cora wept. Hugh patted her hand and turned to Annie Chris. "Thank you," he said.

The day after Thanksgiving Ramsay and Hugh sat down to talk. Ramsay suggested that he and Annie Chris follow them home. That way they'd be able to return to Sunnyside with two wagon loads of the Callands' household goods. Ramsay told Hugh they should leave as soon as possible to be back before Christmas; the worst of the winters usually started in the weeks following. "The sheep are in guid hawns with Pache and Lou. It's a guid time tae go."

"I've looked over your house," said Hugh. "We could build a room off the kitchen and add a warming stove."

Ramsay did not know how to tell him that building on to the house would be an expense that would severely tax his resources. His concern was telegraphed in his pause.

"Cora and I would like to pay for it."

Ramsay shook his head slowly. "I still owe ye for the implements."

"They probably ain't worth much after five years of hard use and I certainly got no use for them now – just as well keep 'em."

"I know a carpenter in town looking for work. He can build the room while we're gone," said Ramsay. "I'll ride tae town in the morn and get him going. It'll put me a day behind ye but I can catch up."

Hugh had never been much of a talker. Ramsay sometimes felt he was prying when he asked Hugh questions but Hugh seemed less reserved now and more eager to talk.

Ramsay asked, "Do ye have a guid buyer?"

"I do. He showed me a satchel full of cash. Mormons are homesteading and buying land all over Eastern Idaho. But there's one thing I'm going to tell you that you have to keep to yourself. Don't tell Cora or Annie Chris or the deal will be off for sure. Cora will raise a brand of hell like you've never seen before if she finds out."

"Nae a word – ye can be sure of it."

"Mr. Hansen, the buyer – well." Hugh cleared his throat, looked around to make sure they were alone then continued in a whisper. "He has three wives."

"What?"

"Lower your voice. He has three wives, Ramsay, he told me himself."

"Is that legal?"

"I don't know, all I know is that I want his cash and me and Cora out of there as soon as possible."

"Why would anyone do that?"

"I have no idea. You'd think one wife is more than enough."

Ramsay chuckled and shook his head.

~   ~   ~

It took almost two weeks to get to Hugh and Cora's ranch, taking it slow for Hugh. The weather was cool and clear with only a few light snow squalls, not enough to stick to the ground.

Hugh told Ramsay that Hansen owned a farm along the Snake River about ten miles southwest of his own place and they could stop there on the way and settle up. Hansen had all the paperwork ready to sign to get the deed transferred. They pulled their wagons up to Hansen's small rock house. A dozen or so children were running around in the cool December midday sunshine.

Cora asked, "Do they use their home for a school, Hugh?"

"You know, that might be so, I don't know," he said as Ramsay helped him out of the wagon and up to the front door, hurrying to avoid questions.

Hugh and Ramsay were back in the wagon in less than twenty minutes. Hugh handed Cora an envelope filled with $100 bank notes. They arrived at Hugh and Cora's house just as it turned dark.

It took two days to sort the things Hugh had agreed to leave and pack the things they planned to take. Hugh spent most of that time sitting in his rocking chair nodding or shaking his head, confirming that yes he wanted to take this or no, leave that.

On the morning of the third day on their way back to Sunnyside, as their wagon bumped along on the road left frozen from the night's frost, Ramsay looked straight ahead and said to Annie Chris with a crooked little smile, "They were nae in school."

"What?"

"The children at Hansen's place, they were nae in school."

"They couldn't have been all his – they were all close to the same age."

"He has three wives, ma loove."

"What! Oh my God, does Cora know?"

"Naw."

"If you ever tell her she'll beat a path back to that ranch and rip that deed right out of that man's hands and throw his money in his face."

"She'll nae hear it from me. But I have tae tell ye ma loove, they seem like guid decent hard-working folks – tae each his own."

131

Annie Chris just stared into the wide open spaces of the sagebrush-covered Snake River plain and said with no emotion, "I never dreamed of such a thing."

It took two days longer to get back to Sunnyside from the Fort Hall ranch than it took to get there. Hugh was failing fast. The trip had taken its toll. They arrived at the Caufield ranch on Rock Creek just before dark, twenty miles short of home.

Henry Caufield and his wife had homesteaded along the creek on the wide meadow below Rock Creek's rugged basalt rim. They had a stage stop contract, ran about a hundred head of cattle and put up a little hay. They were comfortable but not rich by any means.

Jesse Caufield offered dinner for the travelers and a bed for Cora and Hugh. Ramsay and Annie Chris slept comfortably under the wagon just as they'd done every night since leaving for home. They had become increasingly worried about Hugh. He sometimes doubled over with stomach pain. He'd lost his appetite. Cora had to almost force food down to sustain him. Weight seemed to be melting off, most noticeably in his face.

The four left early the next morning and arrived at Sunnyside at three in the afternoon. Hugh was in extreme pain when they reached home. Ramsay and Annie Chris helped him into the house and into their bed. Cora and Annie Chris stayed with him and tried to make him comfortable. Ramsay inspected the newly completed room on their house, felt it would do although it wasn't perfect, and went out to care for the horses and unload Cora's and Hugh's bed. He would get the rest tomorrow.

The next morning when Ramsey came into the kitchen, Cora was sitting at the table with an open Bible in front of her. A cup of coffee was between her hands. She had a peaceful faraway look on her face as if listening to her favorite hymn. She spoke to Ramsay softly as she stared out the kitchen window as the sun began to appear in the eastern sky. "It says here in Paul's Letter to the Romans: 'That if thou shalt confess with thy mouth the Lord Jesus, and shalt believe in thine heart that God has raised him from the dead, thou shalt be saved.' Hugh did that, Ramsay, many years ago and he repeated it again last night."

She closed the Bible and placed both hands on it. "Ramsay, anything can happen that can take your life in an instant. Do you believe what Paul said?"

Ramsay knew the depth of Cora Calland's faith and had been grateful that she had never pressed him about his. He poured himself a cup of coffee and sat beside her. "Truth be known Cora, I do nae know what tae believe. I s'pose, like Paul said, it has tae be in yer heart so tae answer yer question, it is nae in ma heart. Mebbe someday but it's nae richt now and if God knows ma heart he knows I'd be lying if I said it was. Ma died young and Pap died by his own hawn. I do nae know if they believed in their hearts. But by her love for me and ma brother, nae knowing a thing aboot what makes someone a saint, I can tell ye this – there's nae been a more saintly woman on this earth. I do nae believe that a loving God would nae take her tae be with Him just because she may have had doubts. Ma pap had demons torturin' him here on earth so would a loving God need tae torture him more? I s'pose it's all just too deep fer a simple man like me tae understand – mebbe someday."

She turned her red mournful eyes to meet his and said with a peaceful smile, "Hugh died at one-thirty four this morning according to the clock on your bureau. All I can tell you is that in my heart I am at peace because I know he is, right now, with his Lord Jesus. We'll have another burying to do now, one next to Kate."

Ramsay placed his hands over Cora's; four hands covered her well-worn Bible.

CHAPTER EIGHTEEEN

~Arestegi and Sproat, Partners~

Three years earlier, on February 3, 1876, a little over a month after Ramsay's return from the winter range to find Kate gravely ill, he'd hired liveryman Tim Shea's sixteen-year-old son to accompany him to Eastern Oregon to help trail back the five hundred ewes he'd bought for two dollars and seventy-five cents a head. The purchase was to complete his end of the partnership agreement with Pache and Lou. Their investment took everything Ramsay and Annie Chris had received from Bill Judy's estate and more. Their new venture into the sheep business had exhausted their savings – it *had* to work.

The partnership stipulated that they would identify each owner's ewes with a distinctive ear mark, combine the two bunches and herd them together as one. Pache and Lou would herd the band of sheep throughout the year's cycle of winter range, spring grazing near the foothills around Sunnyside, summer in the mountains, back to the foothills in the fall and finally back to the winter range. Ramsay and Annie Chris would provide Pache and Lou's groceries and forage from their ranch, if needed, for the sheep in the winter and would supply and care for the breeding bucks. They would split the proceeds from their lamb crops and their wool fifty-fifty. Ramsay and Pache would shear the sheep together in late February each year. Ramsay would join Pache on the spring range during each year's March and April lambing.

Ramsay would help trail the band out of the mountains back to the foothills near Sunnyside in the fall and was responsible for marketing the lambs and wool. At this point, the only two markets were the Army and the miners, both near Boise City. As a market, for practical purposes, the railheads at Kelton, Utah, Elko and Winnemucca, Nevada, were too far away. There was talk about a new rail line being planned that would cross Southern Idaho from Oregon to the Fort Hall area and connect somewhere south to the Transcontinental Railroad. When that happened, all the markets in Chicago, Omaha and Kansas City would be available to ranchers like Ramsay and Pache. Now was the time to increase their sheep numbers to be ready for the bonanza that was sure to come. Both strapped for cash, they decided to increase their numbers by keeping the best of their ewe lambs each year for breeding and grow their numbers enough to eventually run two bands of a thousand ewes each.

Ramsay and Annie Chris's first winter at Sunnyside had been mild. The second winter, the winter of '75-'76, when they'd became partners with Pache and Lou, was as dry and cold as Ramsay had feared when he forged his plan to buy sheep. He planted alfalfa that spring hoping for rain but little came, the creek ran low all year and the stand was thin. He had to cut his oat crop for hay from the additional twenty acres he'd planted. The plants just didn't produce enough grain to warrant threshing. He harvested about fifty tons of hay, barely enough for an extended hard winter, and prayed it would be enough.

The next winter, the winter of '76-'77, was like their first, mild and wet. Through most of the following summer the creek ran a *normal* head of water, whatever normal was in the short period of time they'd been Idaho ranchers.

Ramsay planted more alfalfa that spring. With ample irrigation water in Willow Creek, it took off and he got a good stand. By fall he'd put up 150 tons of hay and had sold the partnership's first lamb crop to the Army for a reasonable profit.

The winter of '77-'78 was cold and snowy. Two separate storms piled up nearly a foot at Sunnyside. The snow stayed on the ground from Christmas through January. The snow depth never exceeded four inches on the winter range – the sheep came through it unscathed. So once again, other than their confinement during shearing, the sheep did not require hay. After feeding the bucks, the horses and their milk cow, Ramsay was able to carry over nearly seventy-five tons of hay into the coming winter of '78-'79.

In the fall of 1880, after four consecutive years of keeping the best of their ewe lambs for breeding, Pache and Ramsay reached their goal of doubling their sheep numbers. They had enough sheep now to split the 2,000 ewe band into two much more manageable 1,000 ewe bands. Two bands would require another herder and camptender. Lou, Pache's camptender as well as his wife, would not be asked to travel alone from one band to another to cook, move camp and help the other herder move sheep from one grazing area to another.

"One more year," Pache told Ramsay one cold spring afternoon as they sat in Pache's campwagon planning for the future. "If I like new herder, if no problems I stay. If no, I look for ranch for me and Lou to buy. We stay friends – everybody happy."

Ramsay hired a Tennessean named Tobias to herd the second band of sheep. Pache and Ramsay split his wages fifty-fifty. Ramsay bought an old wagon for Tobias to live in and converted it into a campwagon similar to Pache and Lou's. Tobias was a solitary sort, or at least he said he was, proclaiming he didn't need or want a camptender – he could do it all himself, welcome news to Pache and Ramsay eliminating the need to hire another man.

Unfortunately, Tobias was not truthful. He'd ride to Lou and Pache's camp about every other day for a meal or to borrow something, leaving his band unattended and too close to theirs. In May of 1881, as each band of ewes and their month-old lambs were being herded slowly north toward the mountains for the summer, Tobias, afraid of losing contact with Pache and Lou, allowed his band to get too close to Pache's. The two bands mixed. Luckily, Ramsay and Pache were able to separate the sheep without too much trouble thanks to the distinctive ear marks that identified each other's ewes and lambs. But, it happened again – twice.

Pache was done with Tobias. The partners decided it was time to sever ties with the Tennessean and find someone else. Two weeks later, on his scheduled resupplying trip, Ramsay drove his wagon load of groceries and supplies to Pache's camp wagon with Tim Shea's son Mike and Mike's friend Dex on the wagon seat on either side of him. The two boys agreed to finish out the season and trail the band back to the foothills in the fall. Like most people across America at the time, the two were still incensed with the news of the massacre of General Custer and his soldiers at Little Big Horn five years earlier. The boys had come of age and enthusiastically enlisted in the Army to fight in the Indian Wars on the Plains and had to report to duty in November.

Unfortunately, the experiment with Mike and Dex wasn't much better than with Tobias. Each had hidden an ample supply of whiskey in his bedroll. Pache spent most of the summer working between one band then the other. Lou said it was time; they needed to look for a place of their own. Pache agreed.

In November Pache and Lou bought a 120 acre ranch along the banks of the Payette River about twenty miles northwest of Boise City, a ranch that had more than enough Payette River water to irrigate their 120, possibly more. Farms cropped up along the river, a good thing, Pache thought, if he ever needed to buy feed as it would be close by. Pache worried about drought and hard winters and wanted the security of ample irrigation water. Ramsay understood but was not as concerned. The vast winter range on the white sage plain above the Snake River would have all the winter forage he'd ever need. Pache said, "Hope you're right."

Pache and Lou arrived at Sunnyside on the afternoon of December 19, 1881, just shy of two years after Kate's death and two days before they were to leave to trail their own band of sheep to the western edge of the winter range, then on to their new ranch in February. Lou knocked on the door. Cora answered with a big welcoming wide-open smile and said, "Lord, is it good to see you two. Let me get Ramsay and Annie Chris."

Lou was tense. Pache found it difficult to make eye contact.

Cora noticed it immediately and asked, "Is something wrong?"

"Nothing is wrong, we would just like to say goodbye," answered Lou. "It's kinda sad I suppose."

"Come in, come in. I'll pour you a cup of coffee. Here, sit down," Cora said, pulling out a chair for Lou. "I'll go get them."

Annie Chris came in immediately, happy to see them. Ramsay arrived about five minutes later.

"What a surprise," said Ramsay. "We planned tae take the wagon tae yer camp in the morn tae get Bob and say guidbye."

They exchanged small talk about the weather and gossip about the coming railroad then Lou took a deep breath and said, "We have news."

"What is it?" asked Annie Chris.

Pache would not look back at her as Lou glanced at him anxiously out of the corner of her eye. She cleared her throat. "We are going to have a baby."

The color drained from Annie Chris's face as she formed a forced smile. "That's wonderful news, isn't it Ramsey?"

Ramsey stood, opened his arms to offer Lou a hug and said with a grin, "Indeed it is ye two! Congratulations!" He glanced back at Annie Chris, the smile frozen on her ashen face.

Annie Chris walked to Lou and hugged her while Ramsey pumped Pache's hand. Pache's grip was firm but did not come with its usual bone-crushing pain.

"We're very happy," said Lou, "and owe you two so much."

"When baby comes we like you for godmother, godfather. You like?"

"Aye, we are honored," said Ramsey reaching for his friend's hand again. He glanced toward his wife for agreement.

Unable to hold them back, tears welled up in Annie Chris's eyes for the first time in a long time. She turned her head and looked out the window toward the little graveyard. She could not speak, could only meekly wave goodbye and walk slowly out the back door toward her garden. Lou rushed to her but Annie Chris waved her off saying, "Another time please."

Ramsey held Bob's collar as Pache and Lou mounted their horses, turned and rode south.

CHAPTER NINETEEN

~1883~

Lucy was first.

Annie Chris ran into the barn where Ramsay was repairing harness and shouted, "Ramsay, something's wrong with Lucy. She's in pain."

"What?"

"She's down by the crick, on the east side, groaning, almost screaming – rolling back and forth on the ground."

"Get Cora and meet me."

There wasn't much about a sheep that Ramsay didn't know but when it came to horses, other than blacksmithing, he had a limited background. Horses at the McIntyre Estate were attended to exclusively by the stable staff. Crofters walked. They couldn't afford horses. Cora, on the other hand, had helped with their ailments and delivered their foals most of her life. Lucy's only foal, a filly named Ruby, now a four year-old, was delivered safely by Ramsay with direction from Cora.

Ramsay ran down the east side of the creek and came upon Lucy within minutes. Annie Chris and Cora were close behind. Lucy was in obvious pain, extremely agitated – rolling then standing up, then down again, rolling back and forth.

"What is it, Cora?" asked Annie Chris.

"It's twisted gut – a kind of colic. She'll never get over it. Her intestines are twisted and she's trying to fix it. She's in agony. You have to put her down Ramsay."

Lucy had helped bring them to Sunnyside, had carried one or the other on her back all the way from Utah. She carried Ramsay on countless trips to Boise City, the winter range, the mountains and had given them a beautiful filly that was now with foal herself.

Ramsay made a slow painful trip to the barn for his rifle, returned, pulled the trigger, released the spent casing, filled the chamber with another cartridge and pulled the trigger again to make sure. He hitched his team, tied chains to Lucy's hind feet and dragged her corpse to the top of the west ridge of the pasture where she had grazed and raised her foal. Once there, he, Cora and Annie Chris cut brush for four hours until they had enough piled over and around her, doused it with coal oil then set it on fire. No words were spoken; words were not needed as they watched her slowly being consumed by the flames.

Within a month, it was Bob. They knew it was coming with Bob; he was old and slept most of the day in the shade, barely able to get up when he had to. He'd lost his appetite and brought up most of what he did eat. Early one morning Annie Chris came into the house after doing chores and asked Ramsay, "Where's Bob?"

"He's nae by the back door?"

"No."

Ramsay walked outside to see for himself. Bob, sure enough, wasn't where he always was. Ramsay whistled. Annie Chris called, "Here, Bob."

Nothing.

They walked to the barn. Nothing. Ramsay looked at his wife and, without saying a word, they walked up the creek to the cemetery.

There, next to Bill's headstone lay the lifeless body of the best friend Bill ever had. Annie Chris eased herself slowly to her knees, lifted and folded Bob in her arms and held him tight. She recalled him in his stare-down with the mules; his first coming to her at the campfire on the Kelton Road; Bob trotting out to the meadow in the dark to tend to the mules and Lucy; his being led into Alma's house; his sad look with Bill's blanket-wrapped body in the wagon during the trip to Willow Creek; and, of course, the love that Kate had for her old friend who would now be buried near her.

Annie Chris held Bob while Ramsay walked back to the barn for a shovel and the small wooden box he'd built months ago when he knew its need would come soon. On its lid he carved simply: "Our Friend Bob."

~   ~   ~

The next morning Annie Chris felt at peace; more peaceful than she'd felt in a long time. The passage of time, the joy of life, the finality of death and, above all, its naturalness was beginning to take hold in Annie Chris. It had been three and a half years since she'd lost Kate; it was time for Annie Chris to let go. She had punished herself enough and, by default, those she loved. She knew it.

Kate never withdrew from life; she lived her short life to the fullest and would want her mother to do the same. *The Lord blesses us with life one day at a time, and to miss the joy of it for even one day is nothing less than wasting the gift.*

In an odd sort of way, losing Lucy and Bob helped her accept it. Cora had written a verse from Ecclesiastes and handed it to her on one of Annie Chris's darkest days. She lifted her Bible from the shelf and re-read it: *To everything there is a season, and a time to every purpose under heaven. . .* She refolded the paper, carefully placed it back in her Bible, walked to the barn where Ramsay was cleaning stalls, put her arms around his waist and said, "I love you."

CHAPTER TWENTY

Although the Sproats were certainly not the first to arrive, within just a few years, settlers began to slowly fill the meadows and valleys that ran off the lower hills. They were beginning to have neighbors.

A small community named Ryegrass, hardly big enough to be called a town, sprouted from the ground like a spring weed twenty-five miles to the southeast of Sunnyside, only ten miles downstream from the Caufield's Rock Creek crossing. In an average spring, Rock Creek sent runoff water through Ryegrass and beyond. But as the foothills dried in late spring, so did the creek at Ryegrass, leaving nothing but dust and tumbleweeds.

Ryegrass had a small general store, a one-story five room frame hotel built to accommodate as many guests, and the usual services that one might expect in a sparsely populated but growing area on the dusty desert plains of Southern Idaho.

Ryegrass's sole existence was due to the anticipated arrival of the Oregon Short Line railroad. The entrepreneurs in town were barely holding on as they waited.

Boise City had grown considerably since its incorporation in 1863. The town had been platted near the banks of the river, less than a half mile southwest of Fort Boise. Fort Boise had been moved earlier that year to its new location, at the base of the foothills, from its previous location about twenty-five miles downriver. The town owed its beginning to its strategic location along the Oregon Trail where the trail crossed the Boise River. The discovery of gold in August of 1862 in the Boise Basin near Idaho City, forty miles to the northeast, and the discovery of silver and gold the following year near Silver City, seventy miles southwest, accelerated Boise City's growth and importance as a trading hub. Later, the most stable growth of all would come as canals began to be dug to divert the Boise River to the dry sagebrush-covered land to the southwest. Those dry plains would become some of the richest, most productive farm land in America.

In December of 1863, Boise City became the capital of the Idaho Territory, much to the dismay of the citizens of Lewiston, 300 rugged miles to the north. People in Lewiston claimed the November Idaho Territorial legislative session in Boise City, charged with establishing a permanent site for the capital, was convened before it should have been, thereby denying rightful representation for the citizens of North Idaho. To add to the insult, in March of 1864 the self-proclaimed Territorial Governor, Clinton Smith, commandeered a contingent of soldiers from Fort Lapwai near Lewiston to break into the acting capital building there, steal the Territorial Seal and official papers and bring them to Boise City. Court challenges failed and Boise City officially became the capital. The town's growth continued in spite of the fact that mining activity had slowed. By 1880, Boise City's population approached 2,500 and farming began to outpace mining, greening the valley as well as the pockets of the merchants and bankers in town.

Boise City suffered a setback when the Oregon Short Line was completed in 1884 and bypassed the town by about fifteen miles to the south and west. The town's growth continued in spite of the slight. When it came to naming their towns, the city fathers of many fledgling towns in the West added "City" to their town's name to spur development. After years of use, the word "City" slowly was dropped from the local vernacular of many of these towns, Boise included.

Forty miles to the southeast, Ryegrass got what it had waited for so patiently: the railroad passed right through town. It was now poised to become a major shipping point for wool and lambs coming from the Sawtooth, Soldier and Trinity Mountains to the north and east, and the Owyhee Mountains to the south. With the new railroad, the sheep business was about to explode.

With the railroad coming, Ramsay was motivated more than ever to increase his sheep numbers. By retaining his best ewe lambs for breeding, he calculated it would take at least another four years to double to two full bands. He began thinking about buying more sheep and talked with his wife continually about it. Annie Chris resisted but knew her husband would be terribly disappointed if she refused. Still, she couldn't help expressing her fears about the risk.

Cora, after living in another couple's home for so long, learned when it was time to become scarce. Call it discernment or intuition or sensitivity: her timing was always perfect. One day she noticed the beginning of a serious discussion and said, "If you'll excuse me, the garden needs some work."

Annie Chris held her tongue until she heard the back door close. "We can't raise enough hay here for the sheep we *have*. What if something happens and we need to feed more hay than we have?"

"We've had sheep since '76, that's seven years," said Ramsay, the irritation in his voice rising with each word, "and nae once did we need tae bring the sheep off the winter range tae feed hay."

"Ramsay, wouldn't it make more sense to buy a farm first, down by one of the rivers with reliable water. *Then* we can get more sheep."

"Is farming what we came here tae do? If so, we should have stopped in Nebraska."

"Another thing," Annie Chris pointed out, oblivious to his frustration, "you'll have to hire at least one more man. Herb and Pete have their hands full and good reliable herders are hard to find – we already know that."

"Ye need tae trust me. Do ye think me a dunderheid?"

"Of course not, but when did we stop making decisions together? Does my opinion not even matter?"

Ramsay didn't answer. He was not moving her. He began to sulk. For two days he barely spoke.

Ramsay's petulance worked; Annie Chris felt guilty. "Why don't you go to town to the bank. Moore, C.W. Moore, I think is who Mr. Hailey told us to see. I suppose Mr. Moore wouldn't loan us money if he thought we were a bad risk."

Ramsay smiled, opened his arms to his wife and hugged her.

Two months later, Ramsay bought five hundred and eighty ewes from a man named Childers who said he was leaving to marry a woman in Denver who refused to live anywhere but Denver. This time Ramsay paid four dollars a head – $2,320. He was deeply in debt to Moore. But, with these new ewes and the ewe lambs he planned to keep, he should have two full summer bands, almost two thousand sheep, by the summer of '84, in time to take advantage of the railroad.

"We will never regret this," he told his wife. "Mony a mickle maks a muckle," he laughed. Annie Chris smiled weakly at the old Scottish saying meaning, penny wise and pound foolish.

The spring and summer of '83 came in hot and dry. The hot weather followed a warm winter with little snow. Willow Creek was running low. Ramsay was only able to irrigate the upper forty acres – his hay production dropped to fifty tons for the season. It was earlier that year that he'd purchased the additional sheep and, with winter only four months away, his worrying nature began to slowly take hold of him again.

It was hot and still the afternoon of August fifth. Cora had baked a pie and planned to leave in her buggy early that morning to visit a neighbor.

"Wouldn't you rather I go with you?" Annie Chris asked.

"I'll be fine dear. I'm in no hurry. Mrs. Higgins would like for me stay and play canasta. Don't worry about me. It's only a few miles away."

"Five miles, Cora. Not a few."

"I brought a few things. I might spend the night and come home in the morning if it gets too hot."

"Why don't you just plan on doing that, then I won't worry about you if it gets late."

"All right then – that is what I'll do. Look for me around noon tomorrow."

The air was so thick and heavy Annie Chris felt she could chew each breath she drew. She spent two hours in her garden after Cora left and walked back into the house covered in sweat. It was so hot she thought she might spend the afternoon sitting in the shade of one of the cottonwoods along the creek and read a book.

Ramsay had been fixing fence in the buck pasture all morning. The project was far from complete but by noon, he too had enough of the heat.

"I'll dig some holes in the creek," he said, "then we can sit in the cool water. Does that sound guid tae ye ma loove?"

"I'll give you fifteen minutes to dig," she giggled, "and we only need one hole."

Ramsay grinned at his wife, slipped out the back door without a word, grabbed his fencing shovel and walked as casually as he could for the shadiest spot in the creek, just below the spring. Fifteen minutes later Annie Chris arrived at Ramsay's excavation project carrying an old blanket, wearing nothing but her boots. He frantically threw sand and rocks from the middle of the creek, like a dog digging for a bone, slowly enlarging his four foot square hole so it would accommodate the two of them.

"How long are you going to make me wait here?" she asked with amusement as she sat naked in the shade of the cottonwoods, her brown arms clasped around her white knees, sweat glistening, her hair limp in the heat.

"One more minute and I'll have a Roman soaker fit for Caesar."

"Well you better hurry," she said. "You never know when John Hailey will stop by."

"Ready!" he yelled as he bolted out of the hole and on to the bank to strip off his sweaty clothes.

He watched his lovely wife, her body as lean and firm as a dancer's, ease herself into the cool shady pool. "Oh my, this feels good," she said, sucking air between her clenched teeth. "Care to join me?"

Annie Chris giggled and splashed him as he removed his trousers. He was soaking wet before one bare foot even touched the water.

It was four o'clock when they decided they were waterlogged and had better get out of the middle of the creek and dry off in the sun.

Ramsay looked south as they lay drying on the blanket side by side. Towering white thunder clouds were building.

"Mebbe we'll get a rain," said Ramsay hopefully, sniffing the air. He rose to his feet. "Let's go back tae the hoose."

Annie Chris stood. He wrapped the blanket around her. She slipped on her boots and waited while he dressed. They walked, hand in hand, back to the house.

About five, lightning began to flash in the direction of the winter range with thunder following. Ramsay tried to time the flashes to approximate the distance. It was about three seconds between each flash and its thunder – the storm must be right over the winter range, he thought. At six-thirty he saw smoke. By nine the whole southern horizon was filled with it; its brushy burning smell, carried by the evening breeze, filled his nostrils. By nine-thirty as the blood-red sun peered at him through the brown sky and was slowly being swallowed by the hills that seemed only an arm's length away, he could tell the fire was headed north, in his direction. The sheep were in the mountains and safe, but not the fall feed in the foothills around Sunnyside and not their home, barn, fields and hay stacks.

Ramsay paced, feeling helpless as he watched the smoke build – getting closer. He felt the wind grow stronger.

146

"Aboot all I can do," he told Annie Chris as they stood on the porch looking at the towering column of smoke, "is hitch a team and disk up the grass below the hay field."

"I'm frightened Ramsay," she said, her arms crossed with her hands squeezed into her armpits. "This looks awful and it'll be dark soon."

"Waiting 'til daylight might be too late," he said as he stepped off the porch. "I'll hitch the team."

"I'll bring a shovel and come with you," she said, a little calmer now, knowing they intended to do *something*.

The fire was now sucking in air from all around it, creating its own wind, pushing northward at about twenty miles per hour – in their direction.

"Bring two," he said.

They were below the hay field with the team and disk in twenty minutes.

As in most years, Willow Creek was dry below the hay field, its wide sandy channel bare of vegetation. A half mile below the field the creek made a ninety degree turn to the east for about a quarter of a mile before turning south again.

If the fire stayed west of the creek bed and didn't cross it, then Ramsay thought he'd have a chance to stop it if he built a westward-running fire line abutting that quarter mile stretch where it turned east.

At the turn in the creek, he dropped the disk into the soil and turned the team due west to extend the creek's natural fire break. He pushed the team as hard as he could and added a half mile of fire line to the creek bed. He knew the four foot wide path cleared of grass by the disk would not stop a fire barreling down as hard as this one. All he could see now were fifty-foot flames – coming right at him. The smoke was so thick he could barely breathe.

Annie Chris did not have to be told what to do with the shovel as sparks and fiery embers blown by the wind dropped randomly and ignited little fires in the dry grass between Ramsay's fire line and the hay field.

The horses' eyes grew huge and horrified. They jumped back and forth, difficult to control. He knew he didn't have time to extend the line any further so he maneuvered a u-turn and headed back. As he did, he paralleled his first disk path, doubling the width of his fire line. Turning the team calmed them a little. He was close enough now to where he'd started that he could see Annie Chris working furiously, putting out spot fires with her shovel.

Ramsay turned the team and crossed his own line back toward Annie Chris and the hay field. He stopped them inside the field, its stubble still green and unlikely to burn, left them hitched and sprinted back toward Annie Chris. He grabbed a shovel and together they ran from one ember-started fire to another, shoveling dirt to extinguish the flames, unable to even scream at one another because of the deep guttural howl of the fire.

It howled and roared to the line like a hungry beast, gobbling up grass and brush, its appetite insatiable. In spite of its hellish race north, Ramsay could see it was contained west of the creek and probably wouldn't cross.

He took his wife by the elbow and pulled her near. They waited. The main thrust of the fire hit his fire line almost exactly where he'd dropped his disk and started the line west. The fire stopped. Its flames slowly abated as they ran out of fuel. But fingers of fire that had followed the leading wall of flame spread west along the fire line like a wave. The wall of flame seemed alive, crawling along the fire line desperately searching for a place to cross and continue its progress.

Ramsay knew he had the fire subdued, but it was still far from defeated. He ran with his shovel toward the end of his line. Annie Chris ran behind him. They reached it just as fingers of fire three feet high inched toward his u-turn. They threw dirt as fast as they could at the approaching flame. The fire was desperate now, looking for fuel to feed its progress. They knew full well that if it went around their line, the fire would generate a new burst of energy and continue north.

Throwing shovel fulls of dirt in a furious burst of hard work, they managed to stop it. The flames receded and quietly died out. Its fuel was gone.

All that was left of the fire was charred sagebrush stumps and choking smoke. They'd won.

They were both exhausted, leaned on their shovels, their sweat-soaked clothing covered with dirt, and ash. Tired and sore, Ramsay shuffled stiff-legged to his wife. Totally spent, she seemed to collapse. He reached beneath her then lifted and cradled her like a child and kissed her.

"We did it," she whispered, her voice raspy and dry from three hours of smoke.

The smoke was beginning to clear. Ramsay peered south into the dark. He looked past the dying flames and sagebrush stumps toward the horizon miles beyond. A bright glow dominated the distance to his right. He turned to the left; another bright glow. Distances were impossible to estimate in the dark – the flames could be near or far. He had no idea. Regardless, worry and dread began to replace his momentary feeling of triumph.

They went to bed at three a.m. He could not sleep. He was up at daylight and walked to the porch to look south. There was no glow and little smoke but the smell of burnt rangeland permeated everything.

Annie Chris slipped up behind him as he stood staring into the distance. "You didn't sleep did you?"

"A wee bit. Did ye?"

"About an hour I suppose. Are you as worried as I am about the winter range?"

"Aye."

"When are you leaving?"

"In the morn – early."

He stewed all day and accomplished little. His was mind occupied with what might be left of the winter range and what he would do if the feed was all gone.

Annie Chris's mind was going in a different direction. She began to consider options.

The next day he loaded a pack horse, lifted himself on his saddle horse and headed south to see what was left.

Ramsay headed into a dead black world, of ash and cinders.

~   ~   ~

He returned from the winter range four days later.

"It could have been worse. Aboot three quarters gone would be ma guess."

"Will there be enough for winter?"

"I hope so."

"Sheep can't live on hope."

Ramsay resisted the temptation to lash out at his wife and was silent.

The fire had little effect on Pache and Lou. They had settled fifty miles away on the property they'd bought along the Payette River, where its steep narrow canyon widened and its water, after a hundred-mile tumble from the mountains above, finally slowed. With ample irrigation water Pache had put up 250 tons of alfalfa hay and bought eight tons of oats from a neighboring farmer. He'd also kept ewe lambs to increase his numbers but was not ready to pay what he thought was way too much money for more sheep. He too had hired a herder and a camptender, men he could count on.

With the feed on the winter range reduced seventy-five percent by the fire, Ramsay got through the winter of '83-'84 – barely. He kept his two thousand sheep on the winter range as long as he could but left earlier in February than he'd planned, the feed gone. His plans to expand his sheep operation would have to wait for at least two years until the white sage and salt brush had a chance to come back from the fire.

As more and more people began to settle in the area, an idea began to form in Annie Chris's mind. She had become friendly with several of her neighbors, many of whom had young children. She and Cora would hitch Cora's buggy and take pies and bread from her oven and fruits and vegetables from her garden to the shut-ins and new mothers in the area. Much of the small talk over coffee as she visited was about children and their futures. It was time to build a school. They could form a school district and ask for funds from everyone within the new district. It would have to be built in an area central enough to maximize the number of people it would serve. There was no other place between Ryegrass and Boise more central than Sunnyside. If Ramsay and Annie Chris would donate a small plot of their ground for the school, they were sure most folks would support it.

With the enthusiastic endorsement of the settlers ten miles to the east and ten miles to the west, a new school district was formed. It easily raised the funds to build a one-room school with a small attached apartment for a teacher. A young woman named Miss Myra Grant, fresh from Normal School, was hired as the school's first teacher in September of 1884.

When he heard her name, Ramsay searched his mind. Somehow, somewhere, Ramsay had misplaced the drawing Tim Shea had given him nearly ten years before. Unable to find it, he shrugged it off as a coincidence.

Miss Grant was a very attractive woman but her attractiveness was concealed in what seemed to be an attempt to appear plain. Her dark chestnut hair was pulled back and always covered. Her clothes were dark and simple with none of the embellishments women often display to announce their good taste and individuality to the world. She seemed remote and preferred to work alone in the small world of her own surroundings. She was quietly and resolutely self-reliant. If something needed to be fixed, she fixed it. She painted, pulled weeds, built a fence around the school yard to keep unwanted horses and cows out and started a garden irrigated by a ditch she dug that led from Willow Creek. She built a swing and a teeter totter for her students. Volunteers brought firewood but she chopped it. She spent her free time hiking the hillsides and trails around Sunnyside looking for perfect shadows with complementing light for her hobby, painting.

There was something distant about Miss Grant that Annie Chris couldn't grasp – her eyes hinted at a fettered kind of sorrow.

~ ~ ~

The store was Annie Chris's idea. She hated being so dependent on so many things she and Ramsay could not control in the sheep business. Ramsay did not object. They opened for business in the summer of 1885.

It was an inexpensively built little one-room frame building with a potbelly wood burning stove placed in the middle of the room. It was built about a quarter of a mile west of the school on the north side of what was now known as the Foothill Road. Annie Chris worked the store almost exclusively while Cora took over the garden, household chores and cooking at home.

Ramsay built it himself and paid for the materials with money he'd received eight months earlier from the sale of the first lambs shipped from the new stockyards along the new Oregon Short Line Railroad a half mile east of Ryegrass.

It took three trips to Boise for Annie Chris to provision the store. It turned over its inventory and was profitable in one month. The U.S. Post Office would be next.

Now that the railroad was completed, new markets were opened and the store was profitable, Ramsay wanted to build Annie Chris a proper new house, a Queen Anne, he thought, with a wrap-around veranda on one side and a corner turret on the other. A house she would be proud of with indoor plumbing and a gravity pressure system. Maybe it would settle her enough to conceive a child.

With a school and now a store, by default it seemed, the new little community became known as Sunnyside.

Volunteers built a Grange Hall. Annie Chris thought a hotel might be next. The school was the heart of the community. The twenty-three students ranging in age from seven to thirteen loved their dedicated teacher whose only purpose in life, it appeared, was to help them learn and grow. The store continued to thrive.

Annie Chris liked the idea of a new house but was stunned by the expense. The Sproats whittled away at the plans, finally settling on a very nice two-story with two bedrooms upstairs, each with a gabled window, a comfortable living room and dining room downstairs, a bedroom and bath to the side of the dining room and a kitchen in the rear. Ramsay won one concession: they would have their veranda. Cora would have one of the upstairs bedrooms. They would have the bedroom downstairs. They would build the new house near their little slat house which would be reserved for a hired man one day. Water for the pressure system would come from their spring piped into a cistern he would build on the side-hill just below the spring. Gravity would deliver the stored water through a pipe to both houses, providing pressure for flush toilets and running water. They'd heard about Edison's electric incandescent lamps but even Boise didn't have them yet, so they made no attempt to build their house to accommodate such an incomprehensible new invention.

Not long after the house was completed he began to feel foolish. Pressures Ramsay had never considered like competition from other sheepmen and increasing expenses forced him to consider adding more sheep to reduce his per animal overhead. The winter range had not yet recovered from the fire and even in the best of years, the flow from Willow Creek would only irrigate sixty or seventy acres. He was thankful for the store and its success but was frustrated by his inability to take advantage of the strong market for wool and lambs. It appeared his only recourse was to buy a farm on one of the major rivers and possibly move.

His outlook was turning gloomy. Then on a warm sunny morning in late November of 1886 she told him. They were going to have a baby; yes, she said, they were going to have a baby. His rush of joy was dampened momentarily by thoughts of Kate, how much he missed her and how he wished she were here to share the joy. He thought of the Highlands and his mother and his father. He looked back at his dear wife, looking up at him with a quivering chin, her hands on her cheeks, tears running between her fingers. He felt proud and humbled and a smile came to his heart. They hugged one another warmly and softly like they hadn't for years.

CHAPTER TWENTY-ONE

A wet snowfall began early the morning of December 27, 1886 and continued through late afternoon the next day. The snowfall was so dense it was impossible to see more than ten feet ahead. Ramsay shoveled snow for hours each afternoon just to get to the barn to milk the cow and feed the animals. It was impossible for Annie Chris to walk the half mile to the store to open for business even if anyone was able to get there. Ramsay was convinced the storm had dumped more than three feet of snow.

Ramsay's sheep were thirty miles south being tended by two herders whose camp wagons were about four miles apart. A camptender traveled back and forth between them, cooking, gathering firewood and tending the horses.

He quietly stewed and worried about the conditions on the winter range. *Merciful God help me. Three men and all ma sheep out there,* he thought. It was thirty-two degrees at the house. *Mebbe it's been rainin' on the winter range. It's always warmer doon there,* he thought.

Ramsay could not know that the conditions were much worse than he imagined, worse even than at Sunnyside.

He routinely made a trip every ten days in his wagon to provision the herders' camps, take hay and oats for their horses and check on the sheep. But if conditions were anything like they were at Sunnyside he wouldn't make it ten feet from the house.

On the 30th the blizzard hit. It blew so hard that day it was impossible to tell if it was snowing or the wind was creating its own storm of blowing snow. On the 31st they woke to a solid white landscape and a cloudless sky – soundless, still and frozen. The thermometer read eighteen below. By noon it was fifteen below. Ramsay and Annie Chris were both consumed with worry. She had to get to the store to light the stove or everything would freeze, if it hadn't already.

Ramsay had to get to the sheep and his men – somehow. He put on layers of clothes under his heavy wool coat and strapped on a set of Hugh's snowshoes from the barn to try to make it up the ridge west of the house. From there, with his binoculars, he would be able to see fifty or more miles south hoping, at that distance, he might see a backdrop bare of snow.

The air was hard and stiff. Each time he inhaled, the hairs in his nose froze, forcing him to exhale through his mouth. Halfway up the ridge he was sweating in the subzero cold. He opened his coat. Vapor rose from inside. He continued.

When he reached the top he was panting, unused to walking in snow-shoes. Within seconds he was re-buttoning his coat. He squinted into the distance as the sun beat down on an unbroken vista of bright pure white snow stretching from horizon to horizon. His eyes scanned the landscape and searched for a break in the white – there was none. The frigid cold was dry and felt like knives piercing his eyes, forcing him to break his stare to blink repeatedly then wipe them clear of moisture. The stillness was eerie and unnatural.

From where he stood on the ridgetop, the snow was only inches deep. Yesterday's wind had partially cleared it. He could see yellow sprigs of grass poking through the snow as his eyes followed the course of the ridge. It could be like this along all the ridges, for miles he thought.

As he gazed south he noticed in the near distance a short column of smoke rising from the chimney at the store that slowly dissipated into the still atmosphere. He looked to the left and could see none coming from the chimney at the school. It was odd, he thought, that no smoke was coming from the school.

He rubbed his eyes. His mind returned to the winter range; he had to think. *How could I get there? A horse could walk the ridges but it would still have tae cross the deep snowy draws in between. A horse would never make it. I could snowshoe but what point would it be if I could nae at least take some supplies tae ma camps?* He told himself he would think of something.

Snowshoeing downhill, it took him no time at all to get back to the house. He found Annie Chris bundled up on the edge of the porch, strapping on another set of snowshoes. She was headed to the store.

"Will you go with me?" she asked.

"Yere nae going out there – it's fifteen below! We can nae risk the baby."

"I'll be careful. I'm ready, let's go."

155

Cora overheard, marched from the kitchen and looked at Annie Chris sternly, "Ramsay can go and knock down a trail with his snow shoes. Maybe you can go tomorrow but not now." Annie Chris did not think about arguing.

Ramsay nodded gratefully then said, "Someone has a fire goin'. I saw the smoke. I need tae go now."

"What? Who would do that?" Annie Chris answered her own question: "Miss Grant."

CHAPTER TWENTY-TWO

Myra Grant was nineteen in 1884, the year she started her first term as the teacher at Sunnyside's new one-room frame schoolhouse. When the snow storm started on December 27, 1886 she'd been on the job for nearly two and a half years. From her last day as a student at Central School in Boise in 1883 until early fall of 1886 she'd been restless, burdened with thoughts of inadequacy, betrayal and anger. She felt trapped, unable to escape her loneliness. She knew how important she was to the children she taught but couldn't help the feeling that she was meant for a different role in life, a role that might have significance beyond Sunnyside, perhaps beyond Boise as well. She didn't know what that might be, but she did know, from the time she was very little, that she wanted to be a voice for change. There were so many wrongs in this world, wrongs against nature, against the weak and the poor, and so little was being done to right those wrongs.

And, like a recurring nightmare, she was unable to shake the thought of the despicable wrong committed against her.

One thing she knew, she could not affect change of any kind as a schoolmarm in a one room schoolhouse at a wide spot in the road along the foothills some twenty miles from Boise, itself a town of only 2,500.

Myra escaped into her work and her art – just for now, she kept telling herself. But as each month passed, she believed it less and another year would go by. For her own sanity and sense of self-worth she chose to be the best teacher she could be, devoting herself to each individual student, occupying her spare time puttering around the school, painting landscapes and children at play. But loneliness and frustration were beginning to gnaw at her core. No measure of hard work could force that sadness of heart away.

The parents, the children, everyone in Sunnyside for that matter, loved Miss Grant and had not a wisp of a notion that anything was wrong. She was still young, not yet twenty-three. They all assumed one day she would meet someone and they would lose her, but that day had not come.

~   ~   ~

The light and shadows were perfect one Saturday morning in early September, four months before the snow storm, so she loaded her satchel

157

with art supplies, put an easel and unfinished canvas under one arm and a folding chair under the other and climbed the hill behind the school. Some time back she'd sketched Ramsay and Annie Chris's new house with the rocky granite spires rising from the hills behind. She had been waiting for the light to be just right so she could capture the colors and the shadows and finish her painting.

It was precisely two o'clock when she heard the voice say. "Excuse me." It startled her. She turned abruptly.

Standing no more than thirty feet away was a tall, lean, nice-looking young man, not strikingly handsome, just pleasant and kind-looking. He had a shotgun draped across the crook of his arm, was wearing a tan wool jacket with leather patches at the elbows, a dark brown felt hat and well-worn brown leather boots. He appeared ordinary but somewhat out of place, not from Sunnyside for sure.

A neatly cropped blonde beard covered his chin. His blonde hair was cut short. For a perfect stranger, something about him was comfortable and engaging.

A quiet, disciplined brown and white spaniel was healed on its haunches at his side.

"I didn't mean to scare you ma'am," he said. His voice was clear and deep.

Myra looked at him curiously but did not respond.

"My name's Langston Hailey. I'm hunting quail. If I'm trespassing just say so and I'll be on my way."

"This property belongs to my friends; I don't think they'll mind. Did you ask them?"

"I did not. With no fence, I just assumed it belonged to the government. Stupid of me not to ask. Is that their house down below?"

Myra nodded.

"I'll head on down there now." Hailey tipped his hat, took a few steps toward the Sproats' house and noticed Myra's easel.

"That won't be necessary. They won't mind."

"You're sure? It won't take long."

"There's no livestock close by so I'm sure it'll be alright."

"All right," he said laughing, "but if Mr. Sproat comes up here with a rifle we might both end up dead."

She smiled. "Do you know the Sproats?"

"I met them a long time ago, with my father. We were on our way to Kelton. Do you mind if I have a closer look at your work?" He stayed at a safe distance, came no closer, and waited for her answer.

"No, not at all." She shook her head slightly to return her hair to some semblance of order. She was immediately embarrassed by her trousers and old oversized navy-blue fisherman's sweater. She straightened the sweater and tried to regain some composure but did not stand.

"My name is Miss Grant – Miss Myra Grant. I teach school here – well not here, down there, at Sunnyside."

Hailey laughed. "I knew what you meant."

"Please pardon my appearance, Mr. Hailey. I didn't know…"

"The pleasure is mine Miss Grant. No need to apologize, I'm the one intruding on your privacy."

He placed his shotgun carefully on the ground, looked at the dog and pointed at the ground next to the gun. The dog sat without a sound. Hailey took some steps toward her.

He asked again, "You're sure you don't mind?"

He interpreted her smile and slight shake of her head as her permission.

"That is very nice, Miss Grant," he said. He was quiet for a moment. "I can't count art among things I know much about but I know what I like and I like this. How did you get the light and colors to look just like it did when I got here earlier this morning? It's like – being there all over again."

"Practice, experimenting with different paints and so on – I've been doing this for quite a few years."

"And the house – there's a uniqueness. It's the shadows from the house. They have kind of a human quality. You must have added that purposely. Makes me wonder if there's a hidden meaning or something. Am I seeing too much?"

"You're very perceptive Mr. Hailey. All I can say is that it's personal."

"I apologize again. Of course it's personal. I'm so sorry. I'll just be on my way and stop bothering you."

"Mr. Hailey, please, you are not bothering me. In fact, the flattery is nice. Thank you."

"I think it's beautiful and it wasn't my intent to flatter you. I'm not crazy about the job you did on your cheek though"

Her hand reached up and wiped a broad swath across her cheek. Nothing.

"The other one," he said, his blue eyes never leaving the canvas.

"Oh well," she said, chosing to ignore the smudge.

He scanned the painting, searching, looking for something. With his eyes still on the canvas he said, "Where will you be adding the buffalo?"

"What? Buffalo?"

He laughed. "I'm joking. I remember you when we were children. Your wildlife paintings were posted in stores and in our school. There were a lot of buffalo. You probably don't remember me."

Myra turned her head to look at him carefully, squinting her eyes, trying to place his face. Puzzled, she shook her head slowly. "I'm sorry Mr. Hailey. . . I don't recall."

"It's all right, we were children. I left town when I was thirteen – went away to school, so there's no need to apologize for not remembering." His look softened. "I remember you though."

He paused for just a moment then returned his eyes to the canvas. "It *is* beautiful. This isn't the first painting you've done. You must have others. Are they in a gallery?"

A gallery? She gathered her wits. "Yes, I have others but no, I don't have a gallery." She sounded so amateurish to herself. "What I do is mostly private – for my own enjoyment. A hobby I suppose. I am flattered that you think so highly of it. I doubt it's anything special."

"You are wrong Miss Grant, I think your work is extraordinary."

He reached in his pocket, pulled out a clean white handkerchief, pointed it to her cheek and asked, "Do you mind?"

She reached for his handkerchief, cleaned the smudge from her cheek and handed it back. "Did I get it all?"

"You missed a spot *right here*." He reached to her cheek and ever so gently cleared a paint smudge from her jaw line.

She didn't want him to leave. In an attempt to continue the conversation she asked, "How long have you been away from Boise?"

"Other than holidays and schools breaks, about nine years and in case you're wondering," he said and laughed, "I wasn't locked up in jail somewhere."

"I didn't mean to pry."

"It's not prying. If you don't mind some prying of my own, why are you here? I mean here in Sunnyside."

The question didn't surprise or offend her. She had considered it over and over for two long years. To answer forced her to recall her frustration. All she could tell him was the same story she'd been telling herself. "The children mean so much to me. I have so much freedom to pursue whatever interests me, such as art." She felt disingenuous.

"Well, I admire you for that. You must visit town though, whenever you get a chance. Is that correct?"

"You must not think much of our little community."

"That's not what I meant at all. Forgive me. You just seem . . . sophisticated for such a small community."

"I will take that as a compliment and leave it at that, but you shouldn't underestimate our people here. They are wonderful."

"Again, that's not what I meant. I can be so blunt sometimes. I get that from my father, at least that's what my mother always says. Looking around you can see how hard-working and industrious these people are here."

He took an uneasy breath then asked, "Would I be able to see you again sometime? Maybe we can start over."

"I would like that."

"I'd like to see more of your work. Could I?"

Myra thought of the raw simplicity of her room and how desperately ugly she felt at this moment. "Yes, if you give me a little time. That would be nice."

"Would next Saturday morning at eleven be too soon?"

"My, my Mr. Hailey, you don't waste time."

"Another time?"

"No, Saturday will be fine."

"I'll be on horseback – do you have a saddle horse? If it's nice we might go for a ride."

"Of course," she said, fibbing a little, knowing she could borrow one from Ramsay. "A ride would be lovely. I'll prepare a picnic."

"I'm a picky eater – no pigs' feet or Brussel sprouts." She smiled. He glanced at the mid-afternoon sun. "I should go. I promised my mother quail for her after-church guests tomorrow and I have four – I think," he said as he peered into a canvas bag, its strap draped over his left shoulder, and counted. "No five so far. I'll need at least five more."

He closed the bag, and with a hint of shyness said, "I'm so glad our paths crossed."

Myra stood, wished she hadn't, remembering her old rumpled clothing.

"Again, Mr. Hailey, please pardon my casual attire. I promise to be more appropriately dressed next Saturday."

"Please dress comfortably."

He tipped his hat, walked the few paces to his waiting spaniel, retrieved his shotgun and walked toward the eastern slope of the ridge in search of more quail. He stopped, turned back and asked, "Would you allow me to say one more thing?"

"Of course."

He nodded politely and said simply, "I am glad we met."

Oh Lord, he is such a gentleman, she thought, *what will I do? I don't want him in my room. Where will I display my work? My work – damn it, most of it is so awful.*

CHAPTER TWENTY-THREE

~Four years earlier~

It was a Friday. Myra's civics teacher, Mr. Mott, had asked her to stay after school. He'd like her opinion, he said, on an article he was writing about the Yakima Indians near his home in Washington Territory. He hoped to have the piece published in her father's paper. She liked Mr. Mott and had earned good marks in his class. Besides, he had a genuine enthusiasm for history and government, and he seemed to share her empathy and compassion for the plight of society's less fortunate. Mott was admired by everyone in town. He was asked to speak at the Good Templar's Hall and many ladies' garden clubs and social functions.

Myra planned to study history in the fall at the Oregon State Normal School in Monmouth, 490 miles west of Boise. She felt it best to start her career as a teacher and see where it might lead. It would be her best path, at least at first, to initiate change.

School emptied quickly at the end of the day just like any other nice Friday afternoon, leaving just Myra and Mr. Mott. She sat at her desk in the fourth row and waited for him while he erased the blackboard and rearranged some papers on his desk. He didn't say a word. It seemed awkward. Mr. Mott knew she was there but ignored her. She thought of quietly leaving. Her eyes scanned the room – she'd never seen the shade on the classroom door drawn before. Maybe it was routine at the end of a day. The quiet was intimidating, oddly menacing in a strange way, the room always bustling with the sounds of youth-filled activity. She felt alone and small like she did as a child in Sacramento when her mother locked her in a closet for misbehaving.

Mott walked to one of the student desks in the front row, lifted the chair and carried it to his desk. He moved his chair to the side and said, "Miss Grant, please sit in this chair. I'll sit next to you while you read my article."

She stepped to his desk as quickly and confidently as she could and tried to disguise her uneasiness. He pulled the chair back so she could sit and when she did he slid the chair to the desk so her knees were just under the desk top. He stood behind her chair so that she would be unable to

163

move away from the desk without him moving. "It's in this drawer, let me get it for you," he said.

Mott reached for the bottom drawer and slowly pulled the drawer a third of the way out. His left wrist brushed against her ankle. Then in almost the same motion, he grabbed her ankle, gripping it so hard she thought he'd broken her skin. She tried to scream but the shock and suddenness of it caught her so off guard, all she could do was lurch back and gasp for air. She tried to get up but he had her pinned in the chair. She couldn't move her body because his grasp on her ankle was too strong. She couldn't back out and couldn't stand. Her next thought was to lift the desk off her knees but it was too heavy. With all her might she hurled her fist toward where she thought his head was. She hit his shoulder.

He reached behind her and pulled a long knife from the bottom drawer. All she could see was the steel blade. She quit struggling. He released his grip on her ankle and drew the knife slowly toward her throat.

He grasped her hair with his left hand and pulled her head back, further exposing her throat to the knife blade as he positioned his mouth next to her right ear. "There's no one here but you and me. Screaming will do no good and may get you killed." The smell of his tobacco laced breath gagged her.

He released her hair, reached down to the chair leg and slowly pulled her away from the desk. The knife remained at her throat. Once her knees were cleared from the desk, in an instant, he let go of the chair leg, grasped her hair again and with one sweeping painful jerk pulled her over backwards.

"Be still. You may enjoy this."

~   ~   ~

Myra walked home through alleys that late afternoon. She wanted to run but her legs felt limp – it was hard enough just to walk. All she wanted was to disappear in the heavy May air.

Shamed, humiliated, disgraced, destroyed, violated – there weren't words enough to describe the depth of her disgust. Tears streamed down her face. She knew that her mother would be home preparing dinner. Somehow she had to hide the appearance of all of these feelings and get past her mother to her bedroom.

"Myra is that you?"

"Yes. Would you please draw some hot water from the stove for a bath? I think I'm coming down with a cold. I'd like to soak."

"Come here, I'd like to talk to you about school."

"I'm tired Mother. I'll wait for the bath in my room." It was all she could do to calm her voice.

She tore off her clothes, put on her robe and lay on her bed, her face in her pillow.

She heard her mother walking toward her room. "Myra, your bath is ready. Don't be in there too long."

"Mother please don't come in, I'm undressing."

"Are you sure you're all right?"

"I'm fine, Mother. I'll be there in a minute."

She poured some water from the pitcher into the basin on the dresser and washed her hands and face. She quickly examined herself in the mirror. A large dark bruise was developing on her left arm and an ugly scratch above her left wrist. She could hide these. Two fingernails on her right hand were broken to the quick and were painful.

She collected herself as well as she could, pulled the robe up tightly around her neck, walked down the hall and into the bathroom. She shut the door, disrobed and slipped into the hot bath. She soaked a cloth and covered her face. Within a few minutes she heard her mother's footsteps again.

"Mother, please! Leave me alone for a few minutes," she said in a voice that was louder and more desperate than she wanted it to sound.

"All right, but be quick about it. Your father will be home any minute. Supper is almost ready."

The cloth, for a moment, seemed to cover her shame. She was in her parents' house, in their tub with her mother in the kitchen. She felt alone, vulnerable and full of fear.

"Supper's ready. That water must be freezing by now. Your father is home. Get dressed and come in here."

"I'm going to skip dinner, Mother. I feel awful."

She would spend the entire beautiful weekend, one of the first they'd had in the city since last fall, in her room looking at a book – not really reading.

She couldn't clear her mind of the nightmare she'd experienced. Was it her fault? Did she encourage him somehow or sometime earlier in the year? If she told her parents would they go to the police? If they did, would the police believe her? Would they accuse her of encouraging him? Would they take her word over that of one of the most respected teachers in Boise? Would he deny it – probably, or maybe say it was consensual?

She wasn't badly injured; Mr. Mott could deny the whole thing – of course he would. How could she prove it? Oh my God she thought, would her parents believe her? Of course they would – but could she be sure? Her father worried her the most. She felt she was more of a possession to her father than a daughter. Two fears gnawed at her: a baby and, would any man love her if he knew?

From Friday through Sunday and through the following week, Myra stayed in her room. It was hot. She slept fitfully often dreaming of falling through dark fetid air. She'd startle awake, panting, her bedding soaked in sweat, the memory of his touch and smell nauseating her.

She came out for dinner but said little and returned to her room as soon as she was excused.

"What is wrong with you young lady?" her mother demanded after suffering nothing but silence through another meal.

She whispered, "Nothing."

Finally, tired of this *nonsense*, her mother shouted through Myra's door, "After supper we're going to have a talk with your father!"

For hours Myra struggled with what to tell her parents.

She picked at her supper and said nothing. She cared about nothing – about being a teacher, about her art, about her friends – nothing. All she wanted was to disappear into the walls or the long shadows cast by the evening sun.

"Myra has something to tell us," said her mother.

Myra did not look up. Her fork slowly shifted the beets from one side of the plate to the other, the beets she'd helped her mother can last fall. She was silent.

"Well?" asked her father. "What is it?"

Silence.

"Your father asked you a question, young lady."

She laid her fork gently on the plate, took a slow sip from her cup of tea, rested the cup back in its saucer, looked up at her father and said calmly without emotion, as if she were commenting about a fly on the window, "I was violated."

"What?"

"I said I was violated – forced upon." One tear began to roll down her cheek, the only change in her bearing.

Her mother bolted from her chair, grabbed Myra by the chin, jerked her face to within an inch of her own. "What have you done?"

Myra was silent, even as her mother released her chin with a push.

Her father's face was crimson; his neck bulged at his collar. "Who was it?" he demanded.

"My teacher, Mr. Mott."

"How dare you. Do you expect me to believe that?"

Myra was silent.

"You lying little – " Her sense of civility was all that stopped Myra's mother from saying what was on the tip of her tongue. "I won't dignify you with the awful word; at least those women don't lie about who they are with. Look at you, just as calm as if you had returned from a walk in the park."

"Do you understand who you are accusing?" Caleb Grant asked. "Desmond Mott is the most respected teacher in the community. Do you know how many of his articles have been published in *our* paper? Do you know how hard he's worked for statehood?"

He was silent for a moment. "No, you don't know and obviously don't care."

He continued, his anger growing. "Do you understand what would happen to my career if you were to even breathe this wild lie of yours out loud? Have you told anyone? I mean *anyone?*"

Myra looked him straight in the eye. "No."

"If you know what's good for you, you'll tell me the truth." He hesitated, the words hard for him to form on his tongue "Who have you been – my God, I can't even think it."

"Mr. Mott forced me. There is no one else. There's never been anyone, ever. He forced himself on me in his school room – under his desk."

Simultaneously, her parents each lowered their heads and rubbed their foreheads as if in agony. A long period of silence was broken when Caleb Grant looked up. "So, you think you need to protect this little bastard? Is that it? Do you understand that, at this very moment, he is probably boasting about it to all his reprobate friends?"

The kitchen was silent.

Grant closed his eyes. "We have to make a plan or everything is ruined."

"She could do this again you know," said her mother.

"Don't you think I know that? Let me think."

Finally he said, "We'll wait. I'll think of something. God help us if you're pregnant. Meanwhile, you're going nowhere."

Was this a nightmare? she thought. *A nightmare within a nightmare? Which is worse, the rape or their disbelief? To them I'm nothing but an immoral liar.* She felt nauseous, bolted from the table and ran to the bathroom. She thought her whole stomach would come up.

The injustice was numbing. Their lack of compassion and love was beyond her young mind's ability to comprehend. Lying on the cold bathroom floor she thought of Patsy. She began to understand injustice.

For weeks she sat, stared at a book, then an empty canvas. She slept some and took her meals in her room, leaving its confines only to go to the bathroom. One day she put pen to paper, wrote a note and slipped it under her door. She wrote: *There will be no baby.*

Ten days later her father knocked and said through the door, "I want to see you in ten minutes."

She watched her alarm clock tick away ten painful minutes. She slowly stood, opened her door, walked down the hall to where her father was waiting in his chair. She tried to brace herself for whatever fate her father had prepared for her.

"You are not going to school in Oregon. I've written Aunt Tillie and Uncle Lars. I'm taking you with me on the Winnemucca Stage in the morning. We'll meet them at the depot there. You'll take the train with them to San Francisco and spend the rest of the summer. I've enrolled you at the California State Normal School in San Jose. It's a rigorous all-girls school, one where you won't get in trouble even if you want to. I'll find you a teaching job in some little country school far enough away from here but close enough that I can keep an eye on you. Hopefully, you'll meet some dimwitted oaf there and get married. If we were papists, God forbid, I'd have you in a convent by now."

~ ~ ~

Thirteen months later Annie Chris Sproat headed an assembled welcoming committee at the Ryegrass Depot to greet their new Sunnyside schoolteacher who had just arrived after a long train trip from a distant normal school near San Jose, California.

"Miss Grant, what a pleasure it is to meet you," said Annie Chris as she extended both her hands in a warm greeting.

CHAPTER TWENTY-FOUR

For fifteen minutes after Langston left with his bag of quail and walked over the slope of the hill out of sight, Myra Grant sat in her folding chair, brush in hand, staring at a cluster of mixed colors on a white canvas. She had no idea what her next brush stroke would be. She glanced at the sun. Another fifteen minutes went by. Finally, she packed her gear and walked down the hill.

I can come back tomorrow she thought, as she stumbled along, finding it difficult to concentrate on avoiding badger holes, sagebrush stumps and random rocks. *But what if the light is different? I can remember it and finish it at home. I don't have to finish it, just make progress on it before he comes back. Oh my word, I have so much to do. Where will I display my work? Not in the school or in my room. What will I wear? Every dress I own is brown or gray. I only have a week.*

For the rest of the day and into the next, Myra fussed and planned.

Sunday church services had been held for some time at the Sunnyside Grange Hall at three o'clock in the afternoon with a Methodist preacher from Boise presiding. The community was not yet large enough to support a church of its own, the preacher told the little congregation but, until it was, he was happy to make the buggy trip from town after his ten o'clock service. As long, he would always say, as the weather and his health cooperated – "God willing." And, as Ramsay always said mockingly, "And the collection plate remains full."

The minute she walked into the hall for church, an idea came into Myra's head. It dominated her thoughts throughout the service as she mentally scanned the interior walls of Annie Chris's store.

Each Sunday, Cora prepared pastries and made coffee for the after-church guests who had time to stay and visit.

At coffee, Myra decided she would act on her idea and approach Annie Chris about displaying her art in the store but she was reluctant to interrupt Annie Chris's conversation with Mrs. Caufield. Myra went to the stove for the coffee pot, walked to the two of them and asked if they'd like a refill.

While Myra poured, she asked Annie Chris, "Would you mind if I dropped by to see you after school tomorrow? I have a small favor to ask."

"Why of course I wouldn't mind – remember, I close at five. Is there anything wrong?"

"Not at all – I'll be there at four-thirty."

When Myra returned to the school from church, she set up her easel and began to paint from memory, trying to show progress on the canvas Langston Hailey liked so much. She worked late into the evening and gave up at eleven knowing lantern light might trick her into mistakes.

By four-fifteen the next day, after all the children had gone, she walked the short distance to the Sunnyside store. Annie Chris looked up. "Miss Grant, I almost forgot. I'll be with you in a moment."

Myra strolled slowly around the store, looking at bare walls she'd never paid attention to before.

"Now, what is it you wanted to talk to me about?"

"Myra hesitated. "I have something I would like to share with you." She paused. "I came to you because, well – I know I can, trust your discretion."

"What is it?"

"Well, I have a friend coming to see me on Saturday."

"You do?"

Myra shed a little of her timidity, clasped her hands together and looked lovelier than Annie Chris had ever seen her – radiant even. Her eyes danced as she explained. "I was up on the ridge above Sunnyside on Saturday, painting, when a man startled me. He apologized and said he was hunting quail. He liked my work and asked to see more and I..." she stammered, "...he asked if he could see me this coming Saturday. He is very nice, Mrs. Sproat. And, he seems to like my painting."

"Who is he?"

"His name is Langston Hailey. He said he met you and Mr. Sproat years ago. He was with his father. They were on their way to Kelton."

"Of course – I remember him. What a nice boy."

"He is nice. Very nice."

"His father's name is John Hailey. Do you know who Mr. Hailey is?" asked Annie Chris.

"I've read some about him in the newspaper but I'm afraid I don't know much about him."

"Mr. Hailey is a friend of ours. He accompanied us here to Willow Creek when we first homesteaded. He took a chance on my husband and me and loaned us money to get our start. We may not have made it without him. He was here when we buried our daughter." She hesitated before continuing. "My stars, she would be thirteen next summer."

"I am so sorry Mrs. Sproat."

Annie Chris shook off the temptation to talk about Kate. "If young Mr. Hailey is anything like his father, he is a wonderful man. Did you know that John Hailey served in the Idaho Territorial Legislature?"

"Yes, I remember."

"Did young Mr. Hailey tell you that he is a student at George Washington Law School near our nation's capital?"

"No."

"I read in the paper that he will be staying with his parents this fall while he reacquaints himself with the community. He left when he was young to attend school in Chicago. He plans to return after graduation and practice law."

"We didn't talk about that."

"He must not be the boastful type." Her eyes brightened. "We must get you ready for Saturday. We don't have much time. I'll close early – right now as a matter of fact, and you are going to have supper with us. Cora and I are going to make you into the most beautiful thing Langston Hailey ever set eyes on. Of course, the hard part has already been done. I don't think you know how pretty you are, dear."

"I just wanted to ask if I could display my artwork here and borrow a horse."

"Of course you can, but we have lots of work to do first," she said as she looked through bolts of material and rolls of lace in the dry goods section of her store.

"All I have at the store is calico, cotton prints and some linen," Annie Chris told Cora and Myra after supper. Ramsay had retired to the parlor and his newspaper to let the women visit, clean up after supper and make their plans.

Annie Chris asked Cora, "How soon would you need the material to have a dress finished by Friday at the latest?"

Myra interrupted, "I feel like such a burden to you two. Why didn't I keep some of my dresses?" she asked herself out loud, knowing full well why.

"It makes no difference now my dear," said Cora. "We just have to get you something special to wear – and, by the way, you are not a burden. This is the most exciting thing to happen to me lately. I suppose if I had it by Wednesday – maybe."

"Och," said Annie Chris. "Ramsay's planning to leave for town on Wednesday but won't be back until late. That only gives you Thursday and Friday."

"If you were to help I think we can finish it." Cora paused. "I have an idea. Myra, do you have a pretty white blouse?"

"I have a white blouse."

"Good, then all we'll have to make is a vest and the skirt. We could do that in one day. The vest and skirt shouldn't be difficult."

"We can do it!" Annie Chris said. "And you're going to need riding boots and a proper hat. What size shoe do you wear?"

"Six."

"Good, I have a pair of boots that will fit you but the only hats I have are bonnets." She turned to Cora. "Do you have a nice hat?"

"Just bonnets."

"Ramsay will have to bring us a hat," said Annie Chris. "Now we need to decide what kind of fabric to get and what color."

Cora said, "I think you would look beautiful in dark crimson with a black vest and black felt hat with a little rolled brim and a rounded top – it would be very fetching. I've seen those hats in the store window. What do you think dear?"

"I don't know," Myra answered. "I'm so out of touch with fashion, I've ignored the mirror for so long."

Annie Chris kept moving forward, undeterred by Myra's reluctance to be the center of attention. "Do you have any jewelry?"

"No – well, I have my grandmother's brooch."

"Anything else?"

"No."

"All right. Have we missed anything?" she asked, looking at Cora then at Myra.

Myra shook her head slowly. Cora said, "You will be beautiful dear."

"There *is* one more thing," Myra said looking at Annie Chris. "Do you suppose Mr. Sproat would mind if I borrowed Ruby?"

"Ramsay!" called Annie Chris. "Would you mind if Miss Grant rode Ruby on Saturday when young Mr. Hailey calls?"

"Of course nae," he shouted back. "I'll bring her tae the hoose so she can ride her home. She can keep her all week if she wants – turn her out in the school pasture."

"That is very nice of you, Mr. Sproat," said Myra. "I'll take good care of her."

By eight o'clock Friday evening Cora and Annie Chris had finished the skirt and vest. The light wool skirt was dark crimson with no bustle. Cora had sewn tight pleats in the waist so the skirt was full enough to mount a horse. Belt loops were stitched in to accommodate a wide black belt Annie Chris had that matched her riding boots. The broadcloth vest was plain black with no adornments.

It was time to try it all on – first the blouse. Myra's crisp white cotton blouse had ruffles down the front and at the cuffs and a high stiff collar. It looked like it had never been worn. The skirt and belt were next, then the vest. Cora had stitched six buttons down the front. When buttoned, the vest fit snuggly and accentuated Myra's tiny waist.

Cora had a cream-colored silk scarf that she placed around Myra's neck. Myra slipped her feet into Annie Chris's boots and laced them up. They seemed a little big but her feet felt comfortable.

"Where's the hat?" asked Cora.

"It's in the parlor," said Annie Chris. "Ramsay, can you bring us the hat you brought for Miss Grant?"

Cora and Annie Chris brushed Myra's hair back and let it cascade over her collar and down her back.

"Och!" said Ramsay, his mouth open in wonderment. "Who is this?"

"Thank you," said Myra awkwardly.

"All right," said Cora, "now the hat."

"Lean forward a little dear," she continued, "so I can pin it on."

Myra leaned forward as Annie Chris made adjustments to Myra's hair and Cora placed the little bowler in just the right place.

"There," said Cora. "Now look in the mirror."

Myra turned and walked a few steps to Annie Chris's bureau mirror. She looked at herself.

"What do you think?" asked Annie Chris impatiently.

What Myra saw in the mirror was much different than what Cora and Annie Chris were seeing.

"What is wrong?" asked Cora.

"It's not me. I am so sorry. This isn't the same person that Mr. Hailey met on Saturday."

Annie Chris looked at her with complete bewilderment. She turned and cast the same look at Cora then turned back at Myra. She couldn't think of a thing to say.

Finally Cora broke the awkwardness. "You look beautiful dear. You think about it overnight."

Ramsay was in the kitchen pouring himself a cup of coffee. He smiled as he overheard the conversation, not surprised that Myra would reject the embellishments at the hands of two overeager matchmakers.

CHAPTER TWENTY-FIVE

Myra had replaced the garments that her friends had so carefully made, with a simple brown skirt and a plain light blue cotton blouse, both borrowed from Annie Chris who understood completely saying, "Perhaps there will be another occasion." Myra did give up the tight bun she usually rolled her hair into for an approximation of the hairdo that Cora and Annie Chris had helped her with, but no hat. She rode Ruby with the saddle that Ramsay had put on Ruby's back the evening she rode home after supper.

Langston Hailey's blue eyes sparkled in the bright morning October sun each time he turned in the saddle to face her. Although she had avoided attention for so long, it warmed Myra knowing that this nice man seemed to enjoy the look of her.

They rode up Willow Creek to a wide spot along the creek which, in the spring and early summer, would be a green meadow of less than a quarter acre. They replaced Ruby's and Langston's gelding's bridles with rope halters and long lead ropes so the two horses could graze and tied them to cottonwoods. Myra found a shady spot near the creek and spread her tablecloth on the dry meadow grass, placed plates, knives, forks and napkins on the cloth, then brought out the fried chicken and deviled eggs she'd prepared earlier that morning. Langston went to his saddle bag and lifted out a bottle and two wrapped wine glasses and said, "I brought champagne."

Myra nodded as Langston prepared to open the bottle. They laughed as if they had not a care in the world as the cork shot across the meadow.

He handed her a glass, and poured a little. She lifted it to her lips and sipped.

"Well?"

"It's bubbly. It's good. A little sweet – kind of dry."

Langston filled her glass then filled his own. "Let's toast," he said raising his glass to hers then pausing.

"To what?"

"To my mother."

"To your mother?"

"Yes, to my mother. The one who insisted I come out here for quail. Otherwise I never would have met you."

Myra raised her glass a little higher, smiled then said, "Yes, to your mother."

They sat under a deep blue sky in comfortable silence. They were content just to be with one another as the blessedly still fall air, warm and fragrant with willow, sage and blooming buckbrush surrounded them.

They arrived at the Sunnyside Store at two-thirty and stepped up on the porch. "Wait here please. I want everything to be right."

"Of course."

She walked inside. Annie Chris was at the counter and whispered, "Well?" Her face lit with anticipation. She'd been waiting all day for this moment.

Myra's hands came together then rose under her chin, "He's wonderful."

"Are you going to introduce me?"

"Of course."

Smiling, she stepped back toward the doorway and waved in his direction.

"Mrs. Sproat, permit me to introduce Langston Hailey. Mrs. Sproat is the proprietress of this store. She and her husband own the ranch up the crick."

"It is very nice to meet you Mr. Hailey. Please call me Annie Chris. We actually met years ago when you were a young lad. You were here with your father."

"The pleasure is mine, Mrs. Sproat," said Langston removing his hat. "I remember that day."

"Mr. Hailey would like to see some of my art work."

"I wish I could keep her work here forever. It makes the store look homey and more inviting – like Sunnyside itself. You'll see, Mr. Hailey."

"I've seen enough to know that she has a gift."

They strolled slowly around the store. Langston stopped and looked curiously at each painting.

"I like the ones of the children," he said. "They are different from children in town. These are hard-working youngsters. Going to school is a privilege they appreciate. These aren't just children playing. They're individuals that share something in common." He moved closer and thought for a moment. "I can see it in their faces. You've made a difference. *I* can't say that yet – maybe someday."

He continued looking then said quietly, almost to himself, "Someday."

"You give me too much credit."

He moved slowly to the next one. "Here's the one you were working on last Saturday."

"It's not finished. You distracted me."

Langston turned to face her; his look was soft and affectionate.

"I like this one! Is that Mr. Sproat in the wagon?"

"Yes."

Langston studied the pencil drawing Myra had done of Ramsay standing in the doorway of a campwagon, driving lines in hand, with two large draft horses hitched to its tongue. A band of sheep followed behind with a black and white dog off to one side, the sheep cognizant and wary of the dog's presence.

"I'd like to buy this and take it with me to Georgetown. Almost all my classmates are from the East. Nothing I have seen would better explain to them what life is really like in Idaho. All they can think of is Indians and gunslingers."

"I'm sorry but I've promised it to Mrs. Sproat. She wants to give it to Mr. Sproat as a birthday present."

"What if he walks in?"

"I put it up this morning and am taking it home tonight. It was – just for you to see."

He smiled, turned to a window and paused, thinking. He turned back toward Myra and said, "I have two questions."

"Yes?"

He reached for both of her hands. "First, will you call me Langston? And second, if I come for you next Saturday in a buggy will you come to town with me? My parents have a guest room. I'll bring you back on Sunday after church."

"Yes and yes," she said beaming, trying to keep her composure.

"Good! I have another question. Will you bring something special to wear? I have a surprise."

"What is it?"

"If I told you it wouldn't be a surprise now would it?"

"But what kind of clothes?"

"Just something nice, like . . . something you'd wear to church."

"Is it a party or something?"

"No, it'll be just you and me. No more guessing."

~   ~   ~

Fall in Boise was the most glorious time of year. The days were warm and sunny and the nights were cool. The rapid-growing but messy Lombardy poplars and cottonwoods, planted for shade during the city's earliest days, had been gradually replaced with hardwoods: maple, elm, walnut, box elder, buckeye and locust trees that turned the "City of Trees" into a kaleidoscope of brilliant orange, red and yellow. City of Trees is an English translation of the French term, Les Bois, exclaimed, as the story goes, by French fur trappers describing their first gaze upon the tree-lined river.

Langston stopped the buggy in front of his parents' house, tethered the horse to the iron ring in the short stone obelisk at the curb and helped Myra down. He lifted her bag from the back.

"What a nice home," said Myra looking up at the comfortable, but far from opulent, gray Victorian with cream and maroon trim. They walked up four stone steps and across the front porch. The painted tongue and groove decking creaked pleasantly with each step.

Langston opened the door for her and shouted, "I'm home."

Myra heard the happy high-pitched yap of a little dog coming in their direction. Mrs. Hailey walked down the short hall led by a bouncing long-haired lap dog of some kind. The dog jumped up at Langston trying to get his attention. Mrs. Hailey smiled broadly and wiped her hands on a white apron. Her hair was blonde and pulled up, her eyes the same shade of blue as Langston's. Myra was surprised at how much Langston looked like her.

"Why hello," she said, greeting the two of them, while looking directly at Myra. Her voice was strong and melodic.

"Mother, this is Miss Myra Grant."

"Miss Grant, how nice to meet you. Langston speaks well of you. Please come in. We're expecting you. The guest room is all made up and ready."

"It is so kind of you and your husband to share your home with me."

"It is our pleasure Miss Grant."

179

"Please call me Myra."

"That I will do. Myra, my goodness, what a pretty name."

"Is Father home?" asked Langston.

"He went fishing this morning. He'll be home soon."

"Mother, as soon as Myra changes, we're going out in the buggy."

"Well then, I should show you to your room," said Mrs. Hailey.

"It seems Langston has some kind of surprise for me," Myra added following Mrs. Hailey up the staircase.

Without turning Mrs. Hailey said, "One thing you'll find out about me is that I'm terrible at keeping secrets. I can say this one thing though to help you prepare without spoiling Langston's surprise." She'd reached the top of the stairs, turned and faced Myra. With a wink she said, "You're as pretty as a *picture*."

"Really? Oh thank you Mrs. Hailey."

"What in the world is keeping her?" Langston asked his mother as he stood in the hallway waiting.

He looked up as Myra descended the stairs. She was a sight to behold in her crimson skirt, her black vest and crisp white blouse.

"You look stunning," said Mrs. Hailey.

He'd never seen anything as lovely as the young lady slowly descending his parents' staircase. His mother nudged him, "You're staring." He glanced at his mother and noticed the demure smile on her face, recognizing the guilty look immediately.

"You told her," he whispered.

Langston sighed, looked at Myra and said, "So Mother spilled the beans – you know we have an appointment with a photographer."

Myra looked to Langston's mother for reassurance. Mrs. Hailey simply smiled. "You two have a nice afternoon."

"Please don't be angry with your mother," said Myra after the buggy had left the curb. "She just wanted me to know that I was about to be photographed so I could prepare. She was sweet enough to think of me."

"I'm not angry. I suppose I should have told you myself. You look spectacular by the way."

~   ~   ~

"Why do you want to be a lawyer?" Myra asked in the buggy after the photography session.

"There's a very good example in the penitentiary here in Boise. Last May a jury convicted a boy of killing a man in a saloon in Soda Springs about 300 miles east of here. He was trying to defend his father who was getting the tar beaten out of him by a thug. The boy saw a pistol under the bar, grabbed it and shot the thug dead.

"The youngster was arrested and pled guilty upon the advice of an incompetent lawyer. A jury was convened and found him guilty of murder in the second degree. He was sentenced and sent to prison where he, at this moment, is incarcerated with rapists, murderers, thieves and con artists."

His eyebrows narrowed and his voice lowered. "Myra, this boy is ten years old. His name is Jake Oliver Evans – he goes by Jake. I've visited him many times. His spirits are remarkably good considering he is just a child. The only time he broke down was when he told me that his mother is dead and his father refuses to acknowledge him. I'm the only visitor he's had since May. I've asked lawyers in town to take this up on appeal but so far no one sees the effort worth their time."

"You're a good person Langston Hailey."

He laughed. "Not all the time. Wait 'til you meet my sisters, they bring out the worst in me."

Myra and Langston saw each other almost every weekend the fall of 1886. Although happy during the day, each night, alone, she cried herself to sleep. She felt so deceitful – a fraud. When would she tell him? She knew she had to and she knew it would ruin everything.

After Thanksgiving dinner at the Hailey house, Langston asked her to come with him into the parlor. He closed the two lace-covered glass doors and guided her to a chair next to the warmth of the fireplace. He sat in the chair across from her. "Myra, my mother and father are very fond of you. Even my sisters like you and they've never liked any girl I've ever shown an interest in. You know my family – that's what I wanted. I wanted you to know them and like them."

He looked into the fire trying to find the words. "You have never invited me to meet your parents. I know who your father is. Don't be embarrassed. I don't know and I don't care why he no longer works for the paper. I don't care what he does.

"What is it? What's bothering you? What is it Myra?"

181

She could not find the strength to tell him. Langston was the one decent thing that had come into her life since Patsy. She was just a child back then, she thought. She had shut herself off from the pain of the adult world. Now a wonderful man was offering her a way back – on completely different terms, terms built on trust and respect and honesty and yes, maybe love. She ached to her very core to answer him knowing a lie would haunt her and destroy them eventually. She couldn't do that to him or to herself; the painful, bitter but liberating words would not come.

"Please Langston, it's getting late. I think I should go to bed. Do you mind?"

"Of course not." His face was a mask of confusion and disappointment.

Later that night, upset and frustrated, Langston crossed the hallway to Myra's bedroom and knocked softly on her door.

From inside he heard a weak, "Come in."

He quietly opened the door, entered and closed it softly behind him.

"Will you talk to me?" he whispered.

"Come here."

There was no talking that night. Langston left the room just as the grandfather clock in the hallway downstairs chimed six times.

The ride with Langston back to Sunnyside was the longest of her life. She chattered and made small talk willing to talk about anything but herself. He stopped the buggy in front of the school. He helped her down, reached for her bag and carried it to the door. In the doorway he took her hands in his, tried to draw her close but she gently pushed him away. A look of profound confused hurt came over his face. The look startled her it was so penetrating, coming from so deep inside. He took a step back and said without hesitation, "I love you Myra Grant."

All she could say as she turned to step inside was, "I love you too." Then she gently closed the door.

~   ~   ~

Five weeks later, early the morning of December twenty-first, a Saturday, Myra saddled Ruby for the long ride to the Haileys. Her insides felt as dead as coal. Her heart's rhythmic beating pounded in her neck. She didn't know if it was possible for anyone to loathe oneself as much as she did.

She inhaled deeply then knocked at the Hailey front door. Mrs. Hailey opened it. "My word child, did we know you were coming?"

"I'm sorry, no Mrs. Hailey. Is Langston here?"

"Come in out of the cold. I'll get him. Here, sit by the fire. Please, let me take your coat. Can I get you anything?"

"No ma'am. I won't be long. I would just like to speak to Langston if I could."

"Of course dear – I'll get him now."

"Thank you."

Mrs. Hailey walked from the parlor and glanced back at Myra with a puzzled look of worry and concern.

Langston walked in moments later and shut the parlor doors. He was visibly shocked at her pale white face.

He opened his arms to embrace her. She refused, motioning him to sit in the chair across from her. His familiar scent brought back memories. She lowered her head, placed her perspiring hands between her knees in the folds of her skirt then pressed them together to calm them. The pounding in her neck had coursed its way up into her ears.

She filled her lungs deeply with the warm air given off by the fire, exhaled slowly then began. "I've been a little ill."

"Are you all right? Why didn't you write? I've written you four times."

"It's not the kind of illness you're thinking."

"What is it?"

"Langston, I'm having a child, your child." The look on her face did not change. She did not cry. She just turned her eyes from him and looked at the fire.

"We'll be married."

"There's something I have to tell you Langston. It may change the way you feel about me. I am not what you think I am."

"What do you mean?"

Myra told the whole story. As she told him his head slowly dipped into his hands and remained there.

When she finished she stood, trying desperately to maintain control. Langston lifted his face from his hands and looked up at her. Through new eyes, in an instant, he saw ordinary where he had once seen beauty, he saw awkwardness where he had once seen grace, he saw despair where he had once seen joy and he saw dishonor where he had once seen purity.

"I'll go now. It's a long ride back to Sunnyside."

Langston was too stunned to stand. He couldn't make eye contact. His look of profound disappointment overwhelmed her.

Myra let herself out of the Hailey home, mounted Ruby and headed back to Sunnyside.

Deep inside she knew, from the very beginning, she could never have Langston. She knew in her gut that this relationship had no hope of ending in anything but disaster. She hated herself for not being truthful from the very start, allowing it all to come to this. What in the world did she expect?

She had called him to her bed. *How selfish*, she thought, almost shuddering in shame. It seemed a desperate attempt to grasp at something elusive that wasn't hers and somehow keep it, hold it near before it was lost forever. *Dear God*, she thought, *what kind of person am I?*

She sat alone in her room. School was in recess for the Christmas holidays. Several of the locals including Ramsay, Annie Chris and Cora had invited her to their homes to celebrate – she declined all invitations. Annie Chris became worried and knocked at her door. Myra answered looking drawn and pale.

"I've come down with an illness of some kind, Mrs. Sproat. Being with child, I urge you not to come closer."

"Cora has a house full of food," pleaded Annie Chris. "She's been baking and cooking for a week. Please let me bring you something."

"That would be nice but I have no appetite."

"Nonsense, she has a big pot of soup. I'll be back in an hour."

"If you insist – thank you; that would be nice." Myra hoped that would send her away.

Mr. and Mrs. Caufield from Rock Creek joined Cora, Ramsay and Annie Chris on Christmas Eve.

The Caufields were disappointed that Myra was ill and unable to join them. They hoped to get to know her better.

Not long after the Caufields arrived, the five of them loaded into the wagon and rode to the Grange Hall for church. Myra went to a window and watched as cheerful well-dressed people extended Christmas greetings, exchanged handshakes and well wishes then walked inside. Fifteen minutes later she heard voices sing *Hark the Herald Angels Sing*.

Myra had no Christmas spirit.

After church the Caufields and the Sproats walked to the school. Ramsay knocked on the door lightly, knowing Myra was probably in bed, opened it a crack and slipped some cakes, candies and cracked walnuts inside. Inside was a note which said simply: *Please let me take you to Doctor Ivey.*

Myra sat alone through Christmas and looked at the unfinished painting that had caught Langston's attention three and a half months ago. She could not bear the pain of picking up her brush and attempting to finish it. She couldn't read, she couldn't cry, all she could do was pick at the food. Her thoughts were consumed with the child in her womb and, of course, Langston Hailey and his wonderfully gracious family. *What must they think of me now?*

The rape was not her fault, she always knew that and had never taken on guilt for it, but two things hurt her now almost as much as the rape itself. The first was, and had always been, her parents' refusal to believe in her innocence; the second, and the worst of the two, was Langston's look of disappointment, a look that clearly signaled that, in his mind, she was dirty, defiled – used. She wondered how many thousands of women had suffered the same result. Most, she thought, did the smart thing and did not speak of it. Would Langston tell his family? Myra didn't know Mrs. Hailey well but doubted she was the type to dismiss a grandchild because of *circumstances*. Myra knew it was useless to dwell on it. Langston would return to law school, forget her and live a happy life. He deserved that.

What would the school district do when they found out? Fire her for sure. But she was committed to the children. She would finish the term, hide her pregnancy until spring and then move. Where, at this point, was irrelevant.

On December twenty-seventh, it began to snow.

CHAPTER TWENTY-SIX

~The winter range~

As he snowshoed his way down from the ridge that frigid December 31st, fear passed through Ramsay like ice freezing shore to shore across a lake. His herders, the sheep, smoke at the store, his wife – what could he do? From the ridgetop looking south, all he'd seen was white.

No smoke from the chimney at the school but smoke from the store's chimney – what does that mean? Was Miss Grant at the store? If not, who was? If it wasn't her at the store, she had to be in trouble at the school.

With Cora's help, he'd rebuffed Annie Chris's foolish notion to snowshoe with him to the store. He stripped off his wet clothes, dried himself and dressed for his cold walk.

"Check on Miss Grant before you do anything else," Annie Chris pleaded. "The inventory can be replaced."

"And take care of yourself," added Cora.

He strapped his snowshoes on his boots and was trudging through the three-foot snow within minutes.

"Chelsea, come back here," called Annie Chris to Kate's dog as she tried to follow. Chelsea had never taken to the sheep dog way of life. She became attached to Annie Chris and Myra instead. Chelsea seemed as broken hearted as everyone else with little Kate's death; no one had the heart to force her out with the sheep. She became a woman's dog, not really having much to do with Ramsay or any other man in or around the place. That was all right, everyone understood. She would spend her days either at the school or at the store, depending where the excitement was – it was usually at the school. But every evening at closing time Chelsea would follow Annie Chris back home. Home was home.

Chelsea didn't really ignore Ramsay but she never followed him either unless he called her. This time was different. She ignored Annie Chris's commands to come back and struggled undeterred in the deep snow trying to follow Ramsay as he struggled in the direction of the store.

"Go back Chelsea!" scolded Ramsay.

"Come back here Chelsea!" Annie Chris shouted. The dog paid no attention as it flailed desperately to make headway in the three-foot snow. Finally Ramsay picked her up and carried her back to Annie Chris.

"Miss Grant is just fine," Annie Chris told the struggling little dog as she held her tightly. Annie Chris took her in the house and shut the door while Chelsea whined and scratched to get out.

It took him almost an hour snowshoeing through the deep snow to get to the store, a distance he had covered countless times before in twenty minutes. Smoke was still rising lazily from the chimney. The windows were fogged over, a good sign. He sidestepped clumsily toward the door and tried to avoid the deeper snow that had slid off the steep gabled roof. He noticed two wide tracks in the snow, each track the width of a board. The tracks led to the front door. Between the tracks were deep footprints in the snow. A small four wheeled garden wagon with boards wired front wheel to back wheel on each side was on the porch just outside the door. He stood at the door in his snowshoes not wanting to remove them just yet, not knowing what to expect from inside. He knocked politely, even though it was his wife's store.

The warmth rushed at him from within as Myra opened the door. He was relieved to see her standing comfortably at the threshold, warm and safe in old work clothes without a coat.

"Mr. Sproat, take those snowshoes off and come in," she said cheerfully, as if she owned the place. "I have some coffee and soup on the stove. Is everyone all right at your house?"

"We're all fine," he said as he stooped down to unlash the bindings. *What a remarkable recovery* he thought. He hadn't expected this level of cheerfulness from someone who had only recently been desperately ill. When the snowshoes were free of his boots he leaned them against the porch, brushed off the snow and walked inside. He glanced quickly around the room and sighed gratefully that everything seemed just as Annie Chris had left it. The only thing out of the ordinary was a large pile of firewood neatly stacked against the wall near the stove and a pile of blankets folded on the table that Annie Chris used to unroll and measure bolts of cloth.

"I hope Mrs. Sproat doesn't mind," said Myra as Ramsay looked at the table. "I've been sleeping here – the floor is so cold at night."

"Ye hauled all that wood in here with that sled?"

"I did, most of it from her wood pile. Mine at the school is just too far away. I dragged one load – took me two hours. There's not much at the school that needs to be kept warm so I thought it best to conserve wood and keep the store warm – and me too."

"Ye must be feeling better. How long have ye been staying here?"

"I *am* better. I've been here since the twenty-eighth I think – the day after it started snowing. I knew it would be difficult for you to get here with all you had to do at home. I've been getting along fine."

With a look of concern she asked, "What about your sheep, Mr. Sproat – and the herders?"

"There's naw way of knowing other than going tae see for maself."

"How would that be possible in this snow?"

"I have a lot of thinkin' tae do aboot that."

They ate their soup and made small talk about Christmas and Annie Chris's pregnancy.

"I better go back tae the hoose," said Ramsay. "I do nae want the folks tae worry. They'll be relieved knowing yer're doin' fine."

Ramsay stepped through the doorway, sat on a stool on the porch and strapped on his snowshoes. When he finished he stood.

Before he could say goodbye Myra said, "I'm going with you."

"What?"

"When you go to your sheep – I'm going with you."

"Naw yere nae."

"There's no one else Mr. Sproat. Everyone for miles and miles is struggling just like we are, just to stay alive. You can't go alone – you know that. If I don't go, you *can't* go. I'm going with you Mr. Sproat."

"I'll hear none of it. Langston and his family would never forgive me."

"There is no more Langston, Mr. Sproat. I'm going with you."

Ramsay stepped off the porch into the snow and peered at her as if she were a stranger. She had not moved, her arms were folded, her look defiant, daring him to disagree. He took six more steps, twisted his neck and looked back – she was still standing in the cold with the same look.

Finally she shouted, "Do you have a sled or something we can make into a sled? The wagon I put runners on is not the answer."

He walked on without saying a word.

While Ramsay stood on the ridge above his house only hours before, he had puzzled about this very thing. How could he get supplies to his herders along with enough gear to keep himself from freezing? He would have to spend at least four or five nights in the snow. A horse would never make it. He thought of Myra's garden wagon and it came to him. *Ma big weebarrah – of course, in the deep snow I can take the wheel off its axle and pull it like a sled; on the bare ridges I can put the wheel back on and push it. That damn weebarrah'll hold a lot.*

~   ~   ~

"That explains her illness," said Annie Chris after Ramsay told her that Myra and Langston's relationship had ended. "The poor thing – I should have guessed. I could see heartbreak all over her face."

Ramsay gathered himself and prepared for the resistance. "I'm leaving, early in the morn – for the winter range."

Annie Chris stared out the window, focused on nothing, seeing nothing. She felt she would choke on the fear that was welling up inside her. She continued her stare and said blankly, "I knew this was coming. You're leaving me, with child, to walk thirty miles into that white hell to a certain death? You know that don't you?"

Cora was silent.

"What choice do I have? I can nae just sit by the fire and do nothin'. How could I live with maself?" Ramsay anticipated another onslaught. "Miss Grant – she wants tae go with me . . . I will nae allow it."

A glimmer of hope returned to Annie Chris's face. "If I weren't with child I wouldn't hesitate a second."

"Yere nae serious."

"I have never been more serious in my life."

"Naw, I'm going aloone."

"Like bloody hell you are."

"Ramsay, she's right," said Cora. "You'll die alone. Together you'll have a chance. Miss Grant probably thinks this will be a personal test of some kind. It will help heal her heart and lift her spirits. Let her go with you."

Ramsay had a lot to do before morning.

Myra was busy as well. She gathered crackers, oatmeal, macaroni, coffee, a waxed loaf of cheese, a few other things that wouldn't freeze, a slab of bacon and a small can of coal oil. She placed all her bedding plus two new blankets that Annie Chris had on a shelf onto a large piece of canvas. She would roll it tight the next morning and secure it with rope. She was ready. She knew if Ramsay didn't attempt the trip tomorrow, he wouldn't go at all.

She also knew that the two women in the household up the creek would agree – she was Ramsay's only chance. She stoked the fire and was in bed at eight-thirty.

By six-thirty in the morning, Myra had stacked a large pile of firewood near the stove after making two trips to the woodpile, just in case Annie Chris decided to stay at the store. She ate a big breakfast and made three trips to the back window peering into the dark looking for Ramsay, scraping off a fresh layer of ice each time. She glanced at the thermometer placed outside, near the window: twenty below zero.

At seven-fifteen she put on her heavy sheepskin coat, grabbed her lantern and walked out the back door onto the porch and looked north hoping to see Ramsay.

There in the darkness an image slowly came into view. She saw Ramsay leaning forward, walking slowly in her direction. Within seconds she could see him pulling something. Then she giggled as the funniest sight she had ever seen slowly came into view. At the far end of two leather straps was a wheelbarrow without a wheel. The other two ends of the strap were wrapped around Ramsay's chest like a harness. He was pulling like a mule. Perched on the top was what looked like an Eskimo wrapped in blankets with a dog in her arms. Myra squinted hard. It had to be Annie Chris – it *was* Annie Chris and Chelsea. Chelsea whined and yipped when she saw Myra standing on the porch. The humor of it suddenly vanished when she realized that what she was looking at was a reminder of what lay ahead.

"I see yere ready," said Ramsay, trying to mask his annoyance at being outvoted three to one.

"Good morning."

"Good morning Miss Grant," said Annie Chris after Ramsay had helped her off the wheelbarrow with Chelsea struggling in her arms. "Are you sure you want to do this?"

"I am, Mrs. Sproat."

"Cora has plenty of firewood and I see you've brought in plenty for me. Thank you. I'll get by just fine for a week or so. There's more food here than I could ever eat."

Ramsay looked through Myra's provisions. "We can leave the coal oil. I have a can on the weebarrah."

He replaced Annie Chris's things with Myra's and the provisions Myra had set aside, tied it all tightly on the wheelbarrow, turned to Myra and said, "I'm ready if ye are."

"I'm ready."

"Let me help ye with these snowshoes I brought for ye, then we'll be off."

He turned to his wife and opened his arms. She folded herself in his embrace, leaned away and commanded flatly, "You come back here safely. Do you hear me?"

"I will. We both will."

"Please be careful," she said, her voice muffled in the shoulder of his wool coat as she hugged him again, for what she prayed silently in her heart would not be the last time.

She turned to Myra and hugged her even harder, then placed her hands on Myra's shoulders. "Thank you Myra Grant. If there are angels here on earth you would have to be one of them."

CHAPTER TWENTY-SEVEN

Annie Chris held Chelsea by the collar as the little dog struggled to follow Ramsay and Myra into the sea of white ahead.

At that very moment, Shorty, Pete and Herb left the shelter of one campwagon on snowshoes they'd made from canvas torn from the cover of the other. They led their horses, and hoped that once off the winter range and down along the river, they'd be able to ride instead of walk, in their attempt to make it to the little river town of Cleft, fifteen miles away.

For too long it had been impossible to get to the sheep. They'd assumed the worst and knew there was nothing they could do now but save themselves. Out of food, they had decided the night before that it was unlikely Ramsay could rescue them. They would leave in the morning.

Early on Ramsay replaced the wheel and was able to push the wheelbarrow on the windswept ridges. They made good time as they followed the west side of the creek. About halfway to the Oregon Short Line Railroad tracks, where Ramsay planned to spend their first night, the wind came up. Slowly at first, building momentum gradually, it became a blizzard. Their progress nearly halted. He was forced to remove the wheel, harness himself to the wheelbarrow and pull with Myra in the lead doing her best to blaze a trail through the snow by knocking it down with her snowshoes. It was hard work – she gasped for air and could feel her heart pulsing as she struggled forward.

Now, with a twenty mile-an-hour wind blowing snow in their faces and piling drifts into the swales and undulations, with biting cold and creeping exhaustion beginning to cloud his thinking, Ramsay began to have doubts. They had to make it to the Willow Creek bridge under the tracks or they might never make it at all.

Fifteen minutes later, Ramsay could tell Myra was confused. He yelled as loud as he could for her to stop but she couldn't hear him. Pulling as hard as he could, almost running in his snowshoes, he grabbed her by the shoulders and stopped her. He could easily read the confusion in her eyes but not fear. He hollered, "Are ye awricht?"

"I don't know which way to go!"

He reached into the pocket of his snow-covered coat and pulled out the compass. He handed it to her and shouted, "Keep the needle pointing north and at yer chest – it will take us south!"

She nodded, positioned herself and the compass and began to walk, taking two steps for every one of Ramsay's to knock down as much snow as she could so his pull would be easier.

An hour past dark, after trudging through sand like powdery snow with wind gusts of thirty miles an hour or more, without even knowing where they were, they came upon an abrupt rise in the landscape. They'd made it to the railroad tracks. But there was no bridge. Myra turned to Ramsay when he caught up with her and shouted, "Left or right?"

He looked both ways then motioned for her to hand him the compass. He looked at it blankly knowing full well it would do no good. The creek-bed ran a little southeast and they hadn't crossed it, so they'd probably met the tracks west of the bridge. He pointed east. Myra began walking – the small railroad bridge, no higher than seven feet above the creek bottom, was only fifty feet away.

Ramsay had never been more relieved in his life.

The east wind had whipped blowing snow under the bridge beneath the downstream end and filled it three quarters full. The north end, or up-stream end of the under bridge passage, was free of snow, with the bare sandy creek bottom visible and unbelievably welcoming in the dark. Ex-hausted, they sat and leaned against an abutment under the bridge. The big snowdrift at the lower end protected them from the wind. They were grate-ful to be alive.

They sat for five minutes, breathing hard. Finally Myra said, "Mr. Sproat, we made it – we made it."

Ramsay's relief was tempered by the reality that they had at least fif-teen more miles to go before they'd reach Pete's campwagon. "We have tae get a fire and supper goin'."

They both began to pull wind-blown weeds and brush out of the snow drifts and stack them on the bare sand under the bridge. When Ramsay had enough to start a fire he soaked the heap with coal oil and lit a match. He had a fire going in seconds. He untied the packed wheelbarrow and Myra found a bucket, the frying pan and coffee pot. She packed as much snow as she could in the bucket and coffee pot and placed them near the fire. From the haversack she'd carried on her back, she removed a slab of bacon, a loaf of cheese and a tin of crackers. She sliced a dozen slices of bacon off the slab and had dinner sizzling while Ramsay placed the canvas he'd covered the load with on the sandy ground. He rolled out their bed rolls on top of the canvas. The wind continued to howl but not in their shelter, provided courtesy of the Oregon Short Line Railroad.

A period of silence passed while they worked, both bone tired from the brutal day they'd managed to live through. Neither had the energy to talk. Finally Myra spoke. "Do you think the men will be all right?"

"Och, I pray that they are. Was it six days ago this all started?"

"I think that's right, but today seemed like six days all by itself."

"Nae truer words were ever spoken Miss Grant."

"Please call me Myra," she said as she carefully placed a big packed snowball in the bucket and turned over the frying bacon.

"Awricht but fair's fair, ye have tae call me Ramsay."

"I can't do that, I was taught to respect my elders."

"Elders?" he said feigning indignity. "I'm naw more than ten years older than ye."

"Ten years perhaps but I'm so tired after today I feel like I'm ninety."

He wondered if she harbored regrets about coming. "The morrow will be a better day and I think the men and the sheep will be awricht if it's only been six days."

"Tomorrow will be a much better day. I know it will."

They ate and drank their coffee in silence as the unrelenting wind blew fiercely outside their shelter. Ramsay cleaned up while Myra sliced more bacon for breakfast. She looked up. "When will a train come along?"

"I think there are two each day, mebbe three. I can never remember. But they can nae stop – ye know that don't ye?"

"Oh, I know. There's nothing they could do if they did stop. I was just wondering."

"We have tae let the fire go out. We can nae waste the coal. Did ye put enough blankets in yer bedroll? I have plenty if ye need more."

"I'll be all right."

They each crawled into their beds silently, their bodies too tired, their minds too spent to allow sleep to come immediately. Ramsay stared up at the big wooden timbers that supported the train tracks, dimly lit by the dying embers of the fire. "I want ye tae know how kind it was of ye tae come with me. Ye are a brae one lassie. Ye were richt – I never would have made it without ye."

"It would have been a death sentence to go alone."

"I pray I did nae sentence ye tae an early death by agreeing."

"We'll be fine. Look what we accomplished today – eight, maybe ten miles? We're right where you wanted us to be."

Lost in thought, he absent-mindedly rubbed his two-week-old blonde beard. "We might have tae stay here the whole day if the wind is still blowin' like this in the morn. There's a wee rock hoose aboot ten miles from here where we can stay the morrow's nicht but I wonder if either of us can make ten more miles if the wind is still blowing."

"Tomorrow will be better Mr. Sproat – believe it."

"Once we leave here in the morn, the further we go the less sense it will make tae turn back. All the sheep in the world are nae worth yer life and those men can fend for themselves just as well as we can. I want ye tae understand that."

"Let's get some sleep Mr. Sproat. Trust me, tomorrow will be better."

There was something he wanted to say to Myra. He wrestled with himself in the dark for ten minutes searching for words. Finally he stated simply, "I am sorry about Langston."

"So am I."

The mention of his name jolted her into thoughts of her pregnancy, thoughts she'd managed to suppress all day. She'd barely considered it since the after-Christmas snowstorm left her snowbound at the school. Somehow the bitter cold and the new blanket of snow covering everything within sight had strengthened her. She'd felt energized; the sickness had left her.

From the moment she became convinced of her pregnancy to that first night when snow piled three feet outside the school she could think of nothing else. Other women felt optimism and joy, she knew that, but she felt possessed by evil. At times her self-loathing frightened her; the thoughts seemed to come from a stranger occupying space inside her. But the storm was like a portent – it gave her purpose. As she shivered in her room, the woodshed fifty feet away under three feet of snow, she was driven by a stronger urge – survival.

She had opened the front door that morning and stared at a wall of snow piled against it. Most of the tools she used to maintain the school were in the woodshed, including her shovel. All she had inside was a small four inch-wide scoop for emptying ash from the school's stove. It would have to do. She bundled up and prepared for a teaspoon-like assault against the massive frozen barrier between her and the woodshed. Breathless, four hours later she laid the scoop aside and picked up her shovel.

Early the next morning, with a renewed sense of purpose, a large flat nosed shovel and her garden trailer loaded with firewood, boards wired to its wheels, she headed for the Sunnyside store.

~   ~   ~

Had she been foolish to risk the baby to save someone else's livelihood? Did today's exertion put her child at risk? What about tomorrow and the next day and the next? She couldn't ask Ramsay to take her back. She couldn't ask him to go on without her and she certainly couldn't go back alone. It made no difference now – she had to go on and, beyond a whisper of doubt, Ramsay could not be told. Sleep finally came.

Ramsay woke before daylight and lit a match next to his pocketwatch. It was six. In the dark, from under the bridge, he peered through the oddly lit upstream passage they'd easily walked through the evening before. The relentless wind had whipped snow around the bridge during the night. Except for one small window, Ramsay and Myra were now completely entombed by the bridge above them, the abutments on each side and the snow walls that now closed off the ends. Ramsay crawled out of his bed. Myra was awake. He looked through the hole at a clear snowless sky lit softly by a full moon, its brightness reflecting off the landscape almost like daylight.

"Will ye start a fire while I dig our way oot?"

"Of course."

Ramsay dug furiously for ten minutes with the small shovel he'd brought. Myra had the fire going just as he broke through. "Look," he said motioning for her to look through the passage he was clearing for them to exit their snowy tomb.

"Oh my," she said, wide-eyed, "it's beautiful. It's like the world is covered with satin. Look at the moon. Oh I hope I can remember how gorgeous this is so I can paint it someday."

She said, "It's a wonder how the world can be so menacing one day then so beautiful the next."

"Ye understand, don't ye," said Ramsay, his eyes focused on the clear sky, "the change in the weather gives us a chance."

"I know! We can celebrate with a big breakfast. I'll have oatmeal and bacon ready in twenty minutes."

Ramsay dug while Myra cooked. He gradually increased the passage enough to crawl outside, then began clearing a path up the railroad embankment. Daybreak came. Ramsay looked hard to the southwest and hoped to see Twin Buttes, the most familiar landmark on the winter range. Pete's campwagon would be about a mile southeast of the prominent double butte rising 800 feet above the desert floor. The peaks reminded every man who ever gazed upon them of a pair of upturned breasts.

The sun rose over the foothills and slowly replaced the moon's delicate blue light with blazing rays that turned the satiny snow into trillions of glistening crushed diamonds. Ramsay could now clearly see Twin Buttes in the near distance. The buttes seemed to get closer and closer the longer he looked, deceivingly close in the cold morning air. The buttes, he knew, were more than ten miles away. He took a deep breath, exhaling a stream of white vapor, then turned away from the light to make his way back for breakfast.

"Wrap yer scarf around yer face. The sun will burn it tae a crisp if ye don't. Here, put on this cap and pull the bill doon tae shade yer eyes."

"Why, it's a Confederate kepi, Mr. Sproat. It's very handsome. Where did you get it?"

"Belonged tae a frein – he'd be proud it's being put tae guid use."

Ramsay wrapped a bandana around his face, tied it behind his neck and pulled the brim of his broad felt hat down to shade his own eyes. Myra smiled beneath her scarf at the image of what looked like a bandit in pictures that appeared so frightening in the dime novels sold at newsstands in Boise.

~   ~   ~

They trudged south on their snowshoes, Myra in the lead, Ramsay behind pulling the wheelbarrow, in the direction of Twin Buttes. The compass was not needed today.

They were about a half hour south of the tracks when they heard it. They both jerked their heads to the west but could see nothing. "My God, it sounds like it's going to run over us," said Myra, her watery eyes straining through the cold.

The sound of scores of steel wheels rolling over steel rails preceded by the rumble of the engine's pulsing pistons turning even bigger wheels grew in intensity in the frigid morning air. Still, they could see nothing. Finally, in the distance, they saw first a cloud of snow moving east like a summer dust storm. Moments later they could see the rotary plow in front of the locomotive throwing snow. They saw smoke and finally the locomotive. The train was traveling slowly, barely ten miles an hour. They looked at its dark brown passenger cars, the windows fogged over by the warm breath of the people inside. Myra asked, "They don't see us, do they?"

"Naw – they're too warm and cozy tae even look."

One passenger did look. He rubbed the frost from his window to peer out. He noticed something in the distance he thought might be people in the midst of the sea of snow. Langston Hailey shook his head, thinking the brightness of the snow was deceiving his eyes.

CHAPTER TWENTY-EIGHT

At five o'clock they arrived at the one-room twelve-by-eight rock house that reminded Ramsay of the house he was born in and lived in until leaving Scotland forever. They'd had bright sun with no wind the whole day but were just as tired when they arrived as they were from the blizzard the day before. Ramsay had to dig the snow away from the doorless opening in the front for them to crawl inside. They sat for ten minutes until the cold had penetrated their sweaty clothes. A fire was an immediate priority.

"How far tomorrow?" asked Myra once the fire was going and her shivering had stopped.

"Aboot eight miles tae Pete's campwagon. If the weather holds through the morn we should make it before dark."

After a dinner of bacon, biscuits and coffee, Myra pulled a book from her haversack and sat back against the stone wall of the little house to read a few chapters before the fire went out.

"What are ye reading?"

"*The Scarlet Letter*. Have you read it?"

"I'm nae much of a book reader – just newspapers and a few magazines and letters. What is it aboot?"

"I'm reading it for the second time. It's very personal."

"Ye do nae have tae tell me."

"It's all right. It's a story about a woman who was shamed and treated poorly in her community."

"It sounds sad. Why do ye like such a sad story?"

"Because it helps me."

"Helps ye?"

"I suppose it gives me courage."

"Courage is nae something you lack, Miss Grant."

"Courage to face physical obstacles and courage to face your own fears are two completely different things, Ramsay. I'm always looking for inspiration for the second."

"Yere close tae finishing it. Did ye bring another?"

Myra reached into her haversack, pulled out a second book and turned the cover toward Ramsay.

"*Moby Dick*. I've heard of this one. It's aboot a whale."

"Yes. It's about a man consumed with hatred on a quest to kill the whale."

"The whale kills him, richt?"

"Yes, it's justice, the way I look at it."

"I don't understand."

"He was full of hate for the whale. The whale was just being a whale. Our Indian people – it is disgusting what we've done to them. They were just living their lives as they had always done. And slavery Ramsay, how could we have done that to our fellow human beings? Then there's the slaughter of the bison, almost to extinction. It goes on and on."

Ramsay stared into the fire, stirring it with a stick, trying to absorb what she'd said before answering. "I do nae know what tae tell ye Miss Grant. There is naw excuse fer it fer sure. But from the beginning of time mawn has slaughtered other men fer their lands. I don't expect that this peculiar nature of men will end in the morrow or the next day or in fifty years. But I'm one mawn and all I can do is be the best mawn I can – take care of maself, ma family and ma neighbor. If ye can do more then do it.

"We're a stiff necked people lass. We learn slowly ye know. America has its faults but ye have naw idea what the auld country is like. America is a miracle and I am nae goin' tae waste it. I will make certain that ma children have a better life."

Myra turned away. "I am very tired. Good night."

~   ~   ~

Ramsay didn't see the second campwagon, Shorty's, until they were almost fifty yards in front of it. Snow had blown almost to the top of the four-foot spoked wheels. What shocked him the most was the absence of the canvas top. The wagon itself was full of snow. His three men were nowhere to be found – there were no horses and no dogs. It was ghostly. He poked around in the wagon box, tense, bracing himself for what he did not know – relieved to find nothing alarming. It was four o'clock; there was no reason to stay here.

"Why would they take off the top of the wagon?" asked Myra. "And the stays – they're gone too."

"I have naw idea, unless they wanted it for something tae help them leave – a tent mebbe? Whatever it was, I hope it helped."

They walked on in the direction of Shorty's campwagon, hoping the men would all be there. Within minutes they came upon small mounds of snow – scores of them. They stopped at one, fearing what it might be. Ramsay untied the shovel from the load and began digging. His shovel hit something solid. He scraped ice off what lay beneath to discover that it was a wooly carcass. He surveyed the expanse of open snow and counted fifty mounds from where he stood. His gloved right hand went to his face. He took off his hat holding it in his left hand and rubbed his eyes. *What a mess,* he thought. *Pache was richt.*

Myra put a hand on his shoulder. "Let's not assume the worst. We need to get to the other campwagon."

Within an hour and many more mounds, they could see the campwagon in the distance: canvas top intact, but no smoke from the chimney and no horses. Within a hundred yards of the campwagon, they came upon a deep, fresh trail in the snow headed southwest in the direction of the river. They stopped and looked both ways, trying to understand what could have made the trail. It looked as if it had come from the foothills. The trail was littered with frozen sheep droppings pounded into the snow by, what must have been hundreds of hooves, intermittently covered by horse tracks. Ramsay looked closely; there were two distinct sets of horse tracks.

There was no drifting snow on the trail. It had to have been made since the blizzard stopped. Ramsay's spirits rose. But how could sheep do this? The snow was higher than even the largest of his sheep. It was obvious that horses had followed the sheep. It must be equally obvious that the men were riding the horses – why wouldn't they? It all started to make sense. He looked at the trail more carefully and peered at it for signs of human footprints. He walked twenty feet in one direction then twenty in the other. No evidence of man – none at all.

"This is very encouraging Ramsay. The men could be in the wagon but I doubt it. Don't you think they rode on horseback following the sheep toward the river? I bet the wagon is deserted – we have to go see."

The campwagon was empty. The only signs of life were drifted-in horse tracks leading up to it and fresh tracks going away. There were obvious depressions all around the wagon partially filled by drifting snow. Most of Shorty's things were still inside but there was no evidence of an attempt to pack up and leave. At least two feet of snow covered the canvas top. There hadn't been a fire in the stove for several days.

"They must have left on the horses but if they did, where are their tracks around the wagon? There were none on that trail." He squinted and rubbed his brow, more confused than ever.

"I don't know, but it's about dark. We should stay here tonight then follow this trail in the morning. We can't do anything in the dark."

"I need tae shovel the snow off the canvas first or it'll be on top of us 'fore we know it."

A half hour later they had the top free of snow and a fire going in the stove with water heating on the stovetop. Ramsay rolled up Shorty's bed roll, put it to the side then hauled in Myra's and his.

Still trying to figure this out, he said, "Here's another thing. They had a saddle horse and two work horses. If they left on that trail wouldn't they have at least packed their bedrolls and a few things on the horses? It would have been easy enough for them tae walk on the trail packed down by the sheep. But there were naw human footprints."

"We'll know soon."

She made supper. Ramsay unhooked the hinged table from the wall, lowered it and let its table leg meet the bench they were sitting on. He sat down.

"This is a nice wagon – very roomy."

"I built it like a campwagon ma freins had – a couple who were ma partners. They are in the sheep business themselves now, on the Payette River – doing very well. He warned me aboot depending too much on the winter range. I did nae listen."

Over the past two weeks Myra had almost allowed self-pity to conquer her and she was beginning to see signs of it in Ramsay. Although she understood it was the opposite for him, the storm had actually rescued Myra from herself. How odd she thought, the same storm that took her mind off her grief, had added pain and misfortune for Ramsay.

She asked, "Don't you think the sheep have gone to the river? Wouldn't it be better for them there?"

"Looks that way. We'll see."

"I have a hunch the men walked on some kind of snowshoes they'd made from the other wagon, met the trailing sheep and the horses and got on the horses. That would explain why there aren't any footprints."

"But the other wagon was covered with snow and there were naw fresh tracks. If they'd followed the sheep they would have followed them after the blizzard. There would have been tracks around the other wagon."

"Please don't make this worse. Just a short time ago we thought all the sheep were dead. Think of that trail outside. It's not even close to being as bad as we imagined it. Let's just hope the men used good sense and didn't panic and do something stupid."

"I hope yere richt."

For the third night they crawled into their bedrolls in their clothes. He lay still on his back, his mind racing. He couldn't figure out how sheep could have plowed their way through three feet of snow. He forced it out of his mind and thought of Myra and all she'd done for him. He turned to his left side. "You are a brae lassie Miss Grant."

"Good night Ramsay."

CHAPTER TWENTY-NINE

They'd packed their things in the wheelbarrow and were at the hard snow-packed sheep trail by daylight. The sun came up in another cloudless still sky, colder than the morning before. The trail in the snow left by the sheep was at least ten feet wide and went straight southeast as if engineered with a transit. Myra and Ramsay removed their snowshoes.

Myra stepped around lightly. "Lord, what a relief to get these things off. My legs feel like they weigh nothing. I feel like I'm floating."

Ramsay drove his heel into the trail, trying to determine how hard the snow was. "I'm putting the wheel back on," he said, smiling at his wheelbarrow.

"What? I'm so used to you pulling it like a mule . . . surprised you don't smell like one too."

He looked at her mischievously, walked to the side of the trail, grabbed a handful of snow and threw it in her direction. She grabbed a handful on the other side and threw it at him, doing a much better job in retaliation than he did in his initial attack.

They walked side-by-side for hours saying little. The only sound was the crunch of their footsteps on the icy trail and the metallic squeal of the wheelbarrow's wheel rolling ahead of Ramsay over the same ice. By early afternoon Ramsay could see glimpses of the jagged basalt rim that loomed above the north side of the Snake River. An hour later they stood at the rim and looked over the broad valley below and the snow-covered Owyhee Mountains in the distance. He'd ridden to Pache and Lou's camp years ago from this very spot.

As his eyes scanned the landscape below him he noticed, as far as he could see in both directions, tufts of dry grass and sagebrush along the steep descent to the river that had been laid bare of snow by the wind. Also, at the rim, the tracks they'd followed scattered in all directions. Some went straight down but just as many fanned out along the sidehill.

"Mr. Sproat, look – way out there to the right! Do you see it?"

"What?"

"Hand me the binoculars."

He reached for the binoculars while he squinted in the direction she was looking.

She wiped the moisture from the lenses and scanned the right side of the valley near the frozen river.

"What is it?" he asked.

"It's an Indian camp – four or five wickiups."

"Sorry, but I don't care aboot renegade Indians richt now. I have tae find ma sheep and ma men."

He walked thirty feet to the left and noticed some of the tracks had changed. Sheep tracks still dominated but there were others as well. He looked closely at one then walked a few feet further and looked at another. They couldn't be anything else. They were elk tracks. He walked down the hillside slipping here and there over boulders hidden by drifted snow. He went as quickly as he could without falling; his eyes focused on the hillside, first in one direction then the other. Finally he saw movement in the distance – shcep. Hundreds of them grazing on the dry grass and nibbling on sagebrush.

His spirits took an enormous leap. He made his way through the snow and rocks up the hillside he'd just descended. Gasping for breath, he stumbled up to Myra. "They're here – all over the hillside! I saw them!"

"Ramsay! Did you see thc men or the horses?"

"Naw but the sheep were led out by elk, Myra – elk! Can ye believe it? There were a lot of them but I could see nae a one. The sheep saw the elk, Myra, and followed."

Deep in thought she asked, "How far is Cleft?"

"Aboot ten or twelve miles upriver – why?"

"Here, take the binoculars. Look at the Indian camp to the left. It can't be more than two miles."

"Aye, aboot two miles would be ma guess."

"There's steam coming up by the camp. There must be a hot springs. If the herders saw what we're seeing when they got here, don't you think they'd go to the Indian camp and save themselves ten miles or more?"

"Naw if I was wagering. Most folks are afeart of Indians."

"Your sheep are fine for now. We have to go to the camp. Your men might be there."

"I don't know aboot that. Ye don't know what bloody hell those savages have a mind for."

"They're not savages. They are much more civilized than we are. You'll see. Follow me, I'm going down there."

"Wait a bloody minute."

She bounded down the hillside in the direction of the camp without a reply.

She had descended a hundred yards before Ramsay realized she was serious and not coming back. He followed, tripping and stumbling over icy slick rocks, trying to catch up.

As they approached the bottom the snow got deeper, again requiring the snowshoes they'd strapped on their backs. The Indians had seen them coming. Two walked through previously packed snow to meet them and waited about a quarter of a mile from their camp.

Myra approached the Indians confidently just as she was taught by Patsy. Both were wearing heavy woolen coats procured from whites. "Hakaniyun," she said.

Ramsay's head shot in her direction as she greeted them in Shoshoni. The two Indians and Myra talked back and forth for several minutes in a mixture of languages while Ramsay stood by feeling like a bystander in a foreign country.

They motioned for Myra and Ramsay to follow them back to their camp. Four wickiups were positioned around a central fire. The hot springs was only twenty feet away between their camp and the frozen river. Five men and eight women were waiting. There were no children, at least none they could see.

Myra began speaking to the two leaders again. They spoke back nodding. With that the others nodded. Two women brought pottery platters full of some kind of stew for them to eat. Ramsay knew the familiar smell. It was mutton.

Myra bowed and said a few words of obvious gratitude, lifted the stew to her mouth, smiled, took in a mouthful, chewed and swallowed. She motioned for Ramsay to do the same. He mimicked her, smiling, bowing, chewing and swallowing. It was pretty good, he thought.

Never in his life had Ramsay felt so vulnerable and so conspicuous. Myra's obvious comfort in the presence of their hosts took the edge off his fears.

When they'd finished their stew, Myra smiled and spoke to the women who smiled back and bowed. She turned to the two men who'd led them to the camp and spoke. They nodded in unison.

Only then did Myra turn to Ramsay and speak: "The two who led us to the camp are Standing Bear and Two Bulls. They told me that elk did lead your sheep off the winter range, but when the elk smelled their camp they turned upriver and left. They explained that in hard winters it is common for elk to come out of the mountains to the river but the snow was so deep they were unable to pursue the elk in a hunt. Your sheep had no fear of humans and stayed. They butchered one yesterday. Two horses were behind the elk and walked right into the camp. They are with their own horses not far away. I'm sorry Ramsay, they said there was no sign of your sheepherders – the horses came in riderless."

Ramsay now knew that Cleft was the men's only hope. His search for them, at least for now, was over. He felt strangely at peace. He'd done all he could. He couldn't have gotten to them any sooner. He knew what Annie Chris and Cora would say: *their fate is now in God's hands* – and he believed that.

His mind turned back to Myra: "Ye speak their language?"

"I'll explain later. Ramsay, these people were on the brink of starvation until your sheep came down off the winter range. They prayed many prayers of thanks for the blessing. I told them the sheep were yours and that you were honored that they could eat their fill and would allow them to eat as many as they needed to survive the winter. They promised to take good care of them and consume only what was necessary. To show their gratitude, they will herd your sheep back in the direction of Sunnyside as soon as the snow melts. We can stay here with them as long as we want and ride your horses back home as soon as it is safe."

CHAPTER THIRTY

It stayed cold and dry for ten days. Ramsay spent most of those days with his sheep while Myra mingled with the Indians learning more of their language. He let the sheep graze freely and scatter as far up and downriver as he safely could, trying to stretch the feed, knowing the dry grass on the steep hillside wouldn't last long. On one bright windless day he walked along the hillside from one end of the band to the other and tried to count his remaining sheep.

He'd placed one black sheep for every one hundred ewes in each band to allow his herders to keep a reasonably close count of their bands. He counted seventeen blacks or approximately seventeen hundred sheep. He'd lost nearly three hundred. In a normal year at least ninety percent of his ewes would be pregnant, giving birth to their lambs in late March and April. He worried that the cold, the lack of feed and stress might cause that percentage to drop dramatically. Those that survived were, it appeared, his younger ewes, somewhat of a positive he thought. He knew he was now totally at the mercy of his percentage of live births and the market in the fall. A big drop in the price of lamb and wool could finish him. He shot two stalking coyotes, just as desperate to get a meal as every other creature in this icy world. *Sorry coyotes, I've had enough losses.*

Somehow, before this happens again, he thought, *I have tae get irrigation water tae raise enough hay and grain. I can nae go through this again. It may have been a mistake homesteading so far from the rivers.* He'd heard talk of the prospect of building canals to bring snowmelt from the mountains near Camas Prairie to the sagebrush steppe southeast of Sunnyside. *Mebbe I should buy land near Ryegrass and wait for a canal tae be built? But what if it never happens? Or mebbe I should buy farm land near Pache and winter near where he is?*

Canals and ditches were already being built, diverting water from the Boise River. *Should I look for land there?* He'd often looked down at the Boise River from the ridge above Sunnyside and acknowledged the impossible engineering task of diverting its water around the steep rocky cliffs to his place. *Sunnyside will never be more than it is richt now. We may have tae move – sell out.* He hated those two words; they were synonymous

208

with failure. *Sunnyside is home.* He was now arguing with himself. *We built a ranch and a community out of nothing damn it. We can nae leave. Annie Chris will nae leave. Our child is buried there for God's sake. Another child will be born there. But, damn it, this place can nae run the sheep I have now, let alone more.* He stopped the mental torture for a moment. His thoughts returned to the proposed Camas Prairie canal. *The new canal would be the answer but that has tae be years away – mebbe decades. How different this land is from Scotland, where rain is a pain in the arse and snow is only on the mountain tops.*

He kept a comfortable distance from his Shoshoni hosts while Myra talked with them, making friends with each. The day after they arrived she had taken on the task of teaching them English. They knew a little to begin with but within four or five days she was speaking to them more in English than Shoshoni. She encouraged Ramsay to make friends and try to learn their language, telling him it would honor them and be a sincere gesture of respect.

Once they spoke more English they began to drag Ramsay into their conversations, at meals and around the fire, and he began to learn a little Shoshoni. They told stories of their ancestors and of how deeply troubled their ancestors' souls must be knowing their land was being taken from their children. Not once did he detect hate, bitterness or anger but he did sense their increasing resignation to their disappearing way of life. The last thing in the world they wanted was to go to the reservation. They did not fear the white man's ways as much as they feared confinement.

When they were alone, Myra and Ramsay talked about what would become of this little band of gentle people. They felt helpless and sad and they had no answers. Ramsay feared for their safety, knowing most whites he knew carried the same prejudices he had before he arrived here.

In the middle of the night on day ten the weather changed. By noon the temperature had risen above freezing. The sky was cloudless and the snow became slushy and soft. Ramsay thought of home. He wondered if Myra would leave with him – she had become so close to these people. She truly cared for them. He had never seen her happier.

"It might be time tae go," he said to Myra the next day when the temperature had risen above forty degrees. "Mud can slow us. It won't be a problem unless it rains or gets warmer."

Myra turned away from Ramsay. Tears welled up in her eyes. She made no attempt to wipe them away letting them fall freely. She spoke to him with her back turned. "I don't know if I can do this Ramsay."

The numerous veiled remarks over the past two weeks, all shrouded in a kind of mystery had left him too uncomfortable to ask her to explain. But the time had come to ask what it was that was troubling her so deeply. "I'm nae sure I know what yere telling me. I'm afraid there's something I do nae know or something I do nae understand."

"I'll tell you – soon."

Two Bulls and Standing Bear summoned them to the fire that evening – the other members of the small band were not there. Two Bulls spoke in Shoshoni: "Our medicine men are on the reservation. But a medicine man of our tribe came to Standing Bear, speaking to him in a vision last night as the moon rose in the night sky. Standing Bear has never been on a vision quest and has no medicine bag but he thinks our medicine man spoke to him powerfully. He wants you to hear the medicine man's message."

Standing Bear spoke: "The medicine man spoke to me as if through water, talking from within a still clear pool. He told me it was useless to resist the white man's ways. It is not our world anymore – it is the white man's. He said there is no hope for the old life and to go to the reservation peacefully. He also said something that warmed my heart. He said, in time, you would return to us. He disappeared into the pool of water like mist into the morning sky."

"We know nothing of what this might be but trust the truth of Standing Bear's vision," said Two Bulls. "We will follow his instruction and leave for the reservation when the snow leaves."

Standing Bear and Two Bulls waited for Myra and Ramsay at the fire early the next morning holding Gus and Sonny by their halters and a paint pony with a braided horse hair rope around its neck.

Two Bulls looked at Myra. "This pony is for you. Standing Bear and I do not feel the medicine man would have come in the vision if you had not been here with us."

It was time to leave. Myra threw her shoulders back just as Patsy taught her, holding her head high with dignity. There was bowing and formal goodbyes but no hugging or wailing or grand displays of emotion. She said, "un nangkian yuhuttsi" – thank you.

Ramsay told them they were always welcome at his home. He would return by mid-February to herd his sheep back to Sunnyside. Two Bulls nodded and said they would not leave for the reservation until he returned for his sheep.

As the two rode out of the tiny Shoshoni camp, Ramsay on Sonny leading Gus packed with bedrolls and provisions and Myra on the paint pony, Myra turned, put her fist to her heart and said in liquid clear Shoshoni, "Nuu noohimpe um puninnuhi – you will not be forgotten."

~   ~   ~

Two hundred and fifty years of ongoing warfare to remove Native Americans' claim to their ancestral land was coming to an end, ultimately resulting in the Indians' total defeat. In the Territory of Montana, Chief Joseph, with his famous words, "I will fight no more forever," had surrendered in 1877 in the Nez Perce War after courageously leading his starving people on a 1,200 mile retreat. The Bannock Indians had lost the Bannock War in 1878 and the Big Camas Prairie along with it. In 1879, the Sheepeaters, a branch of the Shoshoni tribe that lived in Salmon River country, some of the most rugged land in the world, lost the Sheepeater War, the last major Native American battle fought in the Pacific Northwest.

The reservations carved from their ancestral homelands by the white man were their homes now.

CHAPTER THIRTY-ONE

Ramsay sensed words would not help as the two of them rode through his sheep toward the crest of the hillside and the winter range beyond. The slushy elk trail they followed headed northeast. They were forced to leave it within a mile for a more northerly heading toward Sunnyside. All the white sage and salt brush was visible. The snow had melted and settled to a depth of less than six inches. The sheep would do fine now, he knew. The three horses kept a steady pace in the moderate weather, unhindered by the remaining snow. Four of five more days of weather like this and the horses would be struggling through six inches of mud, a much more difficult test.

Ramsay hoped they could make it to the rock house by nightfall. They made better time than he expected. Myra was still quiet; he respectfully did not disturb her thoughts.

The little rock house came into view around five; they were there twenty minutes later. Ramsay dismounted Sonny and began unpacking Gus's load. Myra slid off the blanket covering the paint's back and began hauling bedrolls and provisions into the house. Still nothing was said. Ramsay grabbed his ax and walked toward the nearest brush and began hacking for firewood. Thirty minutes later he had a fire going just outside the doorless house.

Myra put the water bucket and coffee pot, both filled with snow, next to the fire and busied herself preparing dinner, still deep in thought.

Ramsay cleared a spot of snow near the fire, big enough for them both to sit. He spread out the canvas and sat slowly and stiffly after a long day on horseback. Once he was comfortable he caught her attention and patted the spot next to him. She did not sit. "A guinea," he said finally.

"What?"

"A guinea for yer thoughts."

"You mean a penny," she said, forcing a laugh.

"In Scotland it's a guinea but I'm beginning tae think it might cost me a pound."

"Ramsay, I am at such a loss. I have no idea what to do with my life."

"Why does it have tae be so hard? Ye are a bonnie smart lass with a heart of gold. There is nae a man I know who would nae cherish ye. But mebbe it's nae a man ye want. What do ye want Myra?"

"Let's talk tonight." She handed him a plate of warmed mutton stew and lowered herself onto the canvas. "I'll tell you everything."

They sat close together on the canvas staring at the fire saying nothing. He threw a few more sagebrush trunks on the fire and waited. She gazed into the flames barely moving.

As the fire was dying he reached for another chunk of sagebrush – she placed her hand on his forearm and said, "It's time to go to bed."

They quietly crawled into their bedrolls. The fire had gone out. On his back in the dark Ramsay looked up toward the mortared rock slope of the dark gabled ceiling. He assumed it was up there somewhere, it was so pitch black dark.

Myra took a deep breath, let it out slowly and said, "I met a Shoshoni woman in Boise when I was in school. She lived alone in a bark wickiup by the river. She sold dried fish and fruit on the streets in town. To most people she was subhuman and was treated that way. For them, I suppose, seeing her rags and meager ways made them feel superior.

"I knew very little about her but thought it would be interesting to paint her portrait. I tried for weeks to capture her dignity and her simplicity. The more I got to know her, the more frustrated I got because I knew it was only her image that was slowly coming together on the canvas. As hard as I tried I could not duplicate her spirit. It seemed painfully hidden. I finally gave up and spent the remaining time I had with her learning about life and love and respect and the Shoshoni people and their language."

She paused and looked toward the stone ceiling as if there might be a window up there somewhere, a window through which the perfect words might be revealed. Her voice dropped to a whisper. "Then everything changed."

Ramsay listened in the dark as she told him about Mott and the rape and Myra's parents' rejection, about Normal School and about her *assignment* to Sunnyside. When she finished, Ramsay remained quiet. Finally she asked, "Are you all right Ramsay?"

He inhaled deeply. "There is nae a thing more precious than a child. Ma wife and me lost one and it nearly broke our hearts. Now yere telling me that the parents of a lassie whose heart knows naw equal threw theirs away? I don't know what tae say. God forgive me for ma actions if I ever meet yer father."

More silence in the dark – long silence.

"When I came to Sunnyside I was numb. I resigned myself to a life alone. I was so lonely Ramsay – you have no idea. Then I met Langston."

He waited.

"I'm having a child, Ramsay. Langston knows – he knows everything. I told him about Mr. Mott. I had to tell him. But I couldn't tell him about my parents. I just couldn't – my father is still trying to make a name for himself in Boise. They *are* my parents. I constantly fight with myself to forgive them. Langston made the only decision he could make. He's gone, back to Georgetown by now."

Myra could hear Ramsay's short breaths through clenched teeth.

"And he said nothing?"

"No. When I left he was slumped over with his face in his hands. There was no point in prolonging it. I said goodbye and left."

Myra could not see Ramsay but she could feel his heat. "In Scotland we have a name for a son-of-a-bitch like that. A knob – that's what he is, a knob."

"I don't know what that means Ramsay, but I know it is not kind and I take offense to it. Caring for a defiled woman was not his fault. I should have told him before we went as far as we did. I lured him into my bed, Ramsay, and it was terribly wrong of me. He was a perfect gentleman."

"A woman defiled? A bloody wicked crime was committed against ye and ye say ye are defiled?"

"That's the way it is and you know it," she hissed. "Don't act like this is the first time you've ever heard of such a thing. Did I whine and say society is unjust? Did I Ramsay? No, it's the way it is and I have to live with it. Fairness has nothing to do with it – I'm a woman."

She softened. "But Langston owns my heart Ramsay. It is so hard to be away from him, and I'm carrying his baby. I have to make my own way now. I know that with every little kick within my belly I will think of Langston. He will be impossible to forget. We'll see if I have the strength."

He felt ashamed of his complaining and self-pity about his ranch. He knew nothing of pain and hopelessness and despair. Even in Scotland and, yes, even with the death of Kate. What would she do? A single pregnant school teacher? She would have to leave – he knew it and he knew she knew it.

"I want to finish the school year with the children. I can hide it until school is out, then I will leave."

"We'll figure out something, Myra."

"Is that why you think I told you?"

"Naw," he said, his voice crystal clear. "I would hope ye told me because I deserved tac know – because we are freins. If I can do something for ye I will do it, and so will Annie Chris and Cora."

CHAPTER THIRTY-TWO

Ramsay dismounted Sonny at about noon. They were less than two hours from home. He walked down the embankment of the Willow Creek railroad bridge and noticed a trickle of water flowing underneath. Most of the snow was gone. To stretch his legs, he walked down the embankment beneath the bridge, the same embankment he'd earlier had to shovel his way through to get from the creek bottom to the tracks at the top. He stopped in the moist sand with the bridge timbers directly above his head and stared at the remains of their long-dead campfire. Myra walked to him from behind.

"We will help ye," he said in a monotone, his eyes fixed on the fire's charred residue that seemed months old instead of days.

"This is not your problem. I am responsible for this."

Ramsay turned from the ashes and faced Myra. "We talked aboot this last nicht. Why is it so bloody hard for ye tae let us help ye?"

"Weren't you listening? Do I have to say it again? I'm an outcast. You can't change that."

Ramsay didn't give in. "Have ye forgotten what it means tae be a frein?"

Myra's shoulders dropped. "I didn't forget – I never knew."

"Come here." He took a step toward her, lifted his hands and motioned her forward. He wrapped his thick arms around her. Her arms dangled life-lessly at her sides. "Ye can nae be serious if ye think Annie Chris and I are going tae just wash our hawns of ye. Come tae our hoose morrow nicht. We'll talk."

~   ~   ~

Shadows were growing as the school and store came into view in the distance just as the orange sun met the hilltops. Fifteen minutes later they heard barking.

"It's Chelsea," Myra said with a hint of joy in her voice.

Chelsea ran past Ramsay and Sonny, past Gus and stopped at the feet of the paint. She jumped and barked and wagged her tail furiously until Myra relented, slid off her horse, lowered herself to one knee and accepted Chelsea's wet licks, her arms holding the happy little dog.

"I missed you too little girl," she said as she remounted.

Annie Chris heard Chelsea barking just off the front porch of the store. She thought little of it until the barking trailed off as Chelsea ran south. *Could it be?*

When they left the morning before the blizzard, Annie Chris had no idea how long they might be gone but was prepared for at least a week, maybe two and hoped it would be less than that. When that first week passed she began to worry. Each new day without them built on the worry of the previous day. What should she do? Alerting the sheriff was the first thing to come to mind but what could he do? She felt increasingly helpless – and more alone.

"Chelsea, come back here!" Then she saw them – first a horse with a rider, then one riderless then another with a rider. There was no road in that direction, only a trail. *No one comes here that way – Ramsay and Myra?*

She looked harder, squinting into the distance. It was Ramsay – she was sure of it. *Was that Myra? Thank God – they made it.*

She stepped off the porch, and ran to meet them, waving both arms in the air. Ramsay jumped off Sonny, grabbed her in his arms as they met in the slushy snow. "Oh my God," she said, "it is so good to see you. I've been sick with worry."

"I'm home ma loove."

"I missed you so much. I am so glad you're home – and safe?" she added looking at Myra.

"We are fine Mrs. Sproat. It's good to be home. I can't wait to take a bath."

Ramsay asked, "Are ye awricht ma loove – and the baby?"

"We're fine."

"Have ye heard from the herders?"

"No. What's wrong – where are they?"

"I don't know. In two weeks, we saw naw a sign – nothing. I have naw idea where they are. We're hoping they went tae Cleft. I'll be ridin' tae town tae see the sheriff soon."

"What about the sheep?"

"It's a long tale. It could have been worse. I'll tell ye aboot it later."

"What about the school Mrs. Sproat – has someone filled in for me?" asked Myra.

"Aye, Cora did. She proved to be a very capable substitute. But the children will be eager to have you back. Whose horse is that?"

"I'll explain in a bit after I take Miss Grant back tae the school. I'll help her unload and come back and walk ye tae the hoose."

Myra and Ramsay rode to the school in silence. He tied the horses to the hitching rail just outside the school; untied Gus's pack, distributed its contents on the ground, lifted Myra's bedroll onto his back and walked into the school. Myra followed with the rest of her things.

Luckily, it was a Friday. It gave Myra the entire weekend to herself.

He laid her bedroll on the floor inside the door that led to her room at the rear of the classroom. On his way out he walked to the pot belly stove in the classroom, opened its door and stacked it full of kindling. He reached for the can of coal oil she kept near the stove, splashed a little on the wood and set a match to it. The fire took off immediately. He walked out to the waiting horses, repacked his things and retied the lighter load on Gus's back for the short ride to the store. He remounted Sonny. "I'll put the paint in the barn with Gus and Sonny. They all need a full stomach and a rest."

Myra nodded and looked up at him – her eyes tired and mournful. She seemed ten years older. Ramsay dismounted, walked to her, put his hands on her shoulders and said, "We will make this richt. I do nae know how but we will."

"You know I can't stay."

Ramsay was silent.

"You better be going, Annie Chris is waiting."

"I'll be back for ye at four in the morrow. Ye'll be having supper with us. And I'm nae askin' ye, I'm tellin' ye."

At the store Ramsay dismounted. He walked with his wife, hand in hand, in the direction of home. "How bad is it?"

"Near as I can tell, we lost aboot three hundred. The rest are being cared for by a wee band of Shoshonis that were close to starving."

"Shoshonis? You mean Indians?"

"Aye, Bannocks."

"You can't be serious. You left them with Indians? What in the world were you thinking? They'll all be dead or sold to other renegades. You didn't Ramsay. Tell me you didn't."

"Ye do nae understand. They could nae be in better hawns. This paint horse is theirs. They did nae even ask us tae return it but I will."

"Seventeen hundred sheep for a paint horse? I don't think that's a deal a banker would approve. What in the world are we going to do now?"

"I said the sheep will be fine – they'll be fine. I trust these people. Ye'll just have tae believe me."

"How did you even come to – what would you call it – an understanding? With Indians you can't even talk to?"

"Myra speaks Shoshoni."

"What?"

"I said Myra speaks Shoshoni."

"A school teacher helped you put this remarkable deal together?"

Ramsay resisted the urge to respond with something equally as unkind but thought better of it. "I have tae go tae town, mebbe Sunday, tae let the sheriff know aboot the missing men and hire some herders. I should go in the morn but can nae cause Myra's coming tae supper. We have to help her my loove – ye and me and Cora. Her life is in shambles. I'll tell ye and Cora aboot it. Give me a few minutes tae care fer the horses."

Cora greeted Ramsay at the door with a hug and a rosy-cheeked smile. "Thank the Lord you're alive. Supper is ready – lamb stew. I bet that sounds better than whatever you've been eating the last couple of weeks. I want to hear all about it."

"Aye, mutton stew. Let me wash up a wee bit."

Ramsay sat across from Annie Chris at his usual place at the kitchen table.

He felt he owed Annie Chris to begin with the Shoshonis. "We found the sheep on the fourth day." He lowered his voice. "We ne'er saw the men.

"Most of the sheep, turns out, followed a herd of elk makin' their way doon from the mountains. There was three feet of snow. The sheep all would have died if it were nae for the elk. When we found them they were scattered along the slopes that drops doon tae the river. There was a wee bit of dry grass along the hillside. The wind had blown most of the snow off so they were survivin'. I did nae know it at the time but they were being watched over."

"By who?" Cora asked.

"I'm getting to that. Myra looked out along the river and saw an Indian camp. Within seconds she was runnin' doon the hillside. I was scared tae death and hollered at her tae stop but she would nae listen. I had tae follow her. She was going so fast I could nae catch her.

"Two Indians were walking towards us. She was still ahead of me. When they met she said something in their language. I caught up. I had naw gun or a thing other than ma fists. I was so afraid for her.

"I walked up tae them carefully. Myra was talking tae them – explaining and pointing tae the hillside and the sheep. They nodded and talked back tae her. I could nae believe she was standing there with two Indians talking tae them in their own tongue. This went on for fifteen minutes. Then Myra told me we were going tae their camp. Naw arguing said she. There was nothing I could do but follow.

"Within fifteen minutes we were in the middle of their camp. All they had was a few wickiups around a fire. There were some women but naw children. One of the women offered us a bowl of stew – mutton stew." Ramsay looked at Cora and smiled.

"Finally Myra turned tae me and explained. The sheep had come doon off the winter range with the elk. The Indians did nae see any men but their horses both wandered into their camp."

Ramsay shrugged. "The elk had taken off up the river when they smelled the Indian camp. Myra told the Shoshonis that the sheep belonged tae me. They butchered enough tae keep from starvin'. They told me they were thankful.

"When Myra was a school girl in Boise she learned Shoshoni from an auld Shoshoni woman that lived by herself aloong the river. That's another story all together.

"She formed a bond with those Shoshonis that was . . . well, ye just had tae see it tae understand. We stayed with them until the weather cleared enough for us tae ride the horses home. We only had the two and I had tae pack Gus with the camp so I would have had tae walk. The Shoshonis must have figured that so on the day we decided tae leave, they brought us the paint for Myra tae ride.

"So you see, these Shoshonis were a blessing. They herded the sheep before we got there and kept them from scattering, or we'd have lost them all. We owe them a boondle."

"What a story," said Annie Chris. She thought of the time she was alone when Kate was so sick.

"If it were nae for Myra I do nae know what I would have doon."

"So you must have gotten a count somehow."

"I counted the blacks one day – there were seventeen."

"So we lost three hundred."

"Give or take a few."

"When I go tae town on Sunday I'll try tae hire a couple of herders and take them tae the sheep with me as soon as I can. The Shoshonis said they would begin herding them in our direction when the weather gets better. They could be on their way any day. I'll take the paint with me when I leave."

Ramsay leaned back in his chair trying to relax a little before beginning the second half of the story. Cora and Annie Chris were quiet. Finally Annie Chris asked, "What's this about Myra?"

Ramsay pushed his chair from the table, stood up, coursed his hand through his thick hair and said, "I need a whiskey."

CHAPTER THIRTY-THREE

He found his bottle that hadn't been touched since Pache had been there last, poured a couple of inches into a glass and sat down.

"Ye should know by now that I would nae have made it without her. Have I made maself clear?

"She fought the storm and the cold as well as any man – better than most. But, she was troubled aboot something. It was nae 'til we were almost home that she told me."

He took a nip from the glass. "As I sit here in our warm kitchen with a roof over ma heid, with sheep grazin' on the winter range, with two of the dearest women on the earth before me, you must know that our frein Myra has nae idea where she will go or what she will do with her life."

"It broke my heart to see her so crushed when she and Langston parted," said Annie Chris. "She took it so hard."

Ramsay stared into his glass of whiskey. "It's worse than that.

"Myra will be havin' a child – *his* child."

Annie Chris lowered her head and placed the tips of her fingers to her temples.

Cora stared, unblinking, at her coffee cup. The pink in her cheeks was chalk white.

"Are we supposed to know?"

"She knows I am telling ye this."

"And Mr. Hailey just left her? How dare he?" questioned Cora. "Good Lord, he wasn't raised that way."

"There's more." He looked at the ceiling. "We've all been wonderin' why Myra came here – why she was so private. She hardly went anywhere."

"And why she's stayed here as long as she has," Cora added.

Ramsay knew he had a delicate job ahead. He inhaled the warm homey air he'd missed so much, exhaled slowly. "She hasn't seen her maw and pap fer years."

"Why?" asked Cora.

"They wanted her out of their lives. They cared more fer their standing with the stiff necks in Boise than their own child."

Ramsay lowered his elbows to the table and continued. "Her maidenhood was taken by force – in her last year of school in Boise – by her teacher naw less."

"Oh my Lord," said Cora.

Annie Chris mumbled, "God help her."

"Her parents called her a liar – and worse. I will nae use the word. They accused her of blamin' her teacher tae protect a boy. They sent her off tae a teacher school in California fer a year tae keep her oot of sight then got her a job – here."

"And she told Mr. Hailey the whole thing," said Cora.

"Aye."

"That explains her sadness before Christmas."

"She protected her parents – she has more honor that I would've had," he added.

"A single teacher with a child," said Annie Chris shaking her head. "No parent with a child in school will stand for it."

"Aye."

"What are we going to do?"

"First of all," Cora said, "we need to remind ourselves what Jesus said to the crowd that was about to stone the adulteress."

Ramsay had become accustomed to the fact that Cora could be counted on for an appropriate Biblical quote to fit about any situation.

"Let any one of you who is without sin cast the first stone."

"She can live with us and raise the baby," said Annie Chris. "We can always find a new teacher."

"She will nae do it. I know her. She has the will of a mule."

"Maybe the Sunnyside community will understand," said Cora. "Maybe we can make them understand."

"You know Hattie Rasmussen and Lura McFadden. They would rather have Jezebel herself teaching their children," Annie Chris scoffed.

Ramsay turned to her. "There's that place on the river near Cleft that's fer sale. We could buy it and partner with her on it."

"She can't afford that and neither can we," Annie Chris snapped.

"It's Myra Grant – we could nae find a better partner."

"Partner for what? What's there – eighty acres, *maybe*? Myra needs help not charity, particularly charity we cannot afford."

223

Ramsay had never been good at verbally sparring with his wife. More often than not, she closed their confrontations with a sharp retort that he could never answer with an appropriate swift reply.

She wasn't finished. "We have troubles of our own. We just lost three hundred sheep. That place is at least thirty miles from here. How will you get what little hay it *might* raise over here where we need it? She can't run it herself – with a baby? We'd have to move there and leave Kate, our home, Hugh, Bill, the store.

"Besides, if we invest in anything it should be a hotel right here in Sunnyside. I'm sorry Ramsay, there's just too many things that can go wrong with sheep. Haven't you learned that yet?

"I know I'm sounding heartless but one or two bands of sheep, at the most, is all Sunnyside will ever run and this is our home. We can't leave – this is where our dead are buried. We have to make the best of what we have. We need water for more sheep and there's precious little here."

She took a breath. She knew she was ignoring the point of the whole discussion – to help Myra. But she needed to relieve pent-up frustration: decent crops one year, disaster the next; good markets one year, bad the next; fires, snow, Ramsay gone, finding good herders and the constant battle with predators.

She felt compelled to finish: "The store is doing fine, we have a post office and with a little hotel and a band of sheep we can make a good life for ourselves – without the risk."

It was Ramsay's turn. She knew him well, loved him dearly and would allow him the respect he was due. Ramsay was not a complicated man, never moody or quick to anger and she'd never seen even a hint of violence in his nature. He readily accepted blame when it was his but he never dwelled on his errors or thrashed himself for them. His sense of right and wrong was as rigid as a post. He cherished his independence but, as the first in his family to shed the chains of serfdom, he felt a powerful obligation to his forebearers to build a sense of dignity in the family name they were never given the chance to build for themselves. Ramsay was in the middle. The burden was his and he accepted it willingly and, with pride. He was determined to have something meaningful to pass to his descendants. Annie Chris understood this and lived with the burden he placed on himself. She had always been skeptical of risk, preferring safe avenues and practical approaches. The comforts of the life for which they'd worked so hard were not to be jeopardized.

"How did all this talk end up aboot us? The Cleft place may nae be fer her, or us, but I'm telling ye richt now, cause ye seem tae want tae make this aboot us, and nae Myra, mark ma words woman, ma children will nae be hotel clerks or shop-keepers. Somehow, I will build a ranch I can be proud of, that ye can be proud of and, most of all, our children can be proud of – one that our son can take over and raise a family on. When we're auld and gray we can sit back and feel guid that we built something guid, that will last, proud as we watch our children and their children build guid lives starting with our hard work. Ma pap left nothing to show fer his labors and his time on this earth. We, ye and me, can change that – fer our children and their children. We've worked hard tae get here. Naw one can deny it."

He could feel his temples pulsing, his face was hot. Annie Chris was quiet. He shook his head and repeated softly, "We've worked so hard tae get where we are – and I'm naw finished."

The kitchen was silent.

"Let's keep this about Myra," said Cora.

Ramsay breathed deeply to try to calm down.

"I have an idea," she said. "Mrs. Caufield told me the owner of the boarding house in Ryegrass is looking for a woman to run it. Ryegrass is a lot like Kelton. A new town on the railroad, people coming and going, freighters and miners, no one pays attention or really cares about anyone's past. It could be perfect for Myra and she'd be close enough that we could see her and the baby occasionally."

"We can ask her aboot the boarding house in the morrow," said Ramsay. "I do nae have any other ideas. But fer sure, I'd be afeart something awful if she were tae just leave. We can nae let her do that. I'm going tae bed. Mebbe in the morn I'll feel better."

Besides being bone weary and mentally spent, Ramsay's two weeks away from home left him frustrated with no easy answers for Myra. And, if that wasn't enough, he was angry with his wife.

~ ~ ~

Ramsay pulled Cora's buggy up to the school at four o'clock. Myra was waiting just inside the doorway. A cold heavy wind was blowing from the east, an indication that a storm might be brewing. It was still January and the respite they'd received in the weather, which gave them time to return home from the winter range, would only be temporary. There would likely be lots of winter left.

"I told them everything. They feel the same as I do."

Myra nodded.

They sat down for dinner. Cora said grace, and asked for a blessing for Myra.

"There is no need for you to go through the pain of retelling your story," said Annie Chris.

"Thank you."

"I want to say this one thing though," Annie Chris said for Ramsay's and Cora's benefit as well as for Myra's. "We are your friends and we understand. We do not judge you – we love you and want the best for you and your baby. What has befallen you could have befallen either me or Cora or anyone else in this community for that matter. Unfortunately, there are some who will lack understanding."

Ramsay interrupted. "The three of us talked. Cora has an idea. Ye tell her Cora."

"Mrs. Caufield knows a woman who owns a boarding house in Ryegrass and is looking for a woman to run it. Her name is Julia Mabe. If you're interested, it'd probably be better for me to inquire than you. Some people just look for reasons to be nosy. I'll write her tomorrow if you'd like. I'll just tell her I know of someone who might be interested."

"All right," said Myra, indifferently. "I appreciate your help. If the job's still available when the roads are passable I'll make a trip there and talk to her."

"We'll all go," said Annie Chris. "We can make a day of it."

"If you don't mind loaning me your buggy, Cora, I'd rather go alone."

Two more inches of snow fell that night, but not enough to stop Ramsay from going to Boise the next day to see Marshal Nicholson and look for sheepherders.

Ten days later a reply to Cora's letter arrived from Mrs. Mabe. She said she was in no hurry because the hard winter had slowed business to a crawl in their little town. She would have to hire someone by May as she needed to return to her family ranch on Wilson Creek for the summer months.

It wasn't until March twenty-second that Myra was able to take the buggy to Ryegrass.

~   ~   ~

The winter of 1886 – 1887 had taken a massive toll across much of the West. Four inches of snow fell in San Francisco and stayed on the ground for a month. Not even the oldest of the old timers had ever seen that. Temperatures dropped to seventy below in some areas of Southern Idaho. The severe winter even dealt future President Theodore Roosevelt a blow when he lost sixty percent of his thousand cow herd on the ranch he owned with partners in the Dakota Territory. It wasn't at all surprising to Marshal Nicholson that Ramsay's sheepherders probably died and that their remains would likely never be found. He'd heard reports of people losing their way near their own homes and freezing to death trying to get back. He told Ramsay that coyotes and buzzards would be fat this spring with the pleasant chore of cleaning up thousands of thawing livestock carcasses just in the Boise Valley alone. Although the marshal meant no disrespect by his comment, describing their fate as such was very unsettling to Ramsay. Nicholson said he'd add their names to the list of "missing" that would be published in the paper.

Ramsay shook off sadness and asked, "Do ye know where I could find a couple of guid men looking fer work?"

Nicholson told him to check at the boarding house on Grove Street.

Ramsay knocked at the door. A disagreeable heavy-set woman with a tartan rag tied around her melon-shaped head opened the door. A dirty white apron surrounded her ample belly and bosom.

"Ain't got no rooms," she barked.

Before the door was slammed shut Ramsay quickly interjected, "Please, I'd like tae hire a couple of sheepherders."

She opened the door. "I got a couple guys here that owes me. Seem like okay sorts. I'll get 'em if you give 'em an advance to cover what they owe me."

"Fair enough."

"You'll like 'em." She motioned for Ramsay to step through the doorway. "I'll send 'em in."

Ramsay had just sat down on the horsehair settee in the parlor when the woman walked back in with two men in well-worn but clean clothes. He stood.

"They owe me eight bucks each – just thought you oughta know that."

"Yer names lads?"

"He's Andrew MacDuff. I'm James, his brother." His accent was unmistakable.

"Scots, aye?"

"Aye, indeed we are sir," said James.

"Ye ever worked sheep?"

"Aye, some – at home in Aryshire sir but we are miners fer the most part. Come tae America five years ago. Mined coal in Pennsylvania then mined in Colorado. Lots of strife in the mines there, bad as home. Can nae find minin' work so we're happy fer any work we can get."

"Ye talk much Andrew?"

"Nae much; prefer tae work."

"Twenty bucks a month room and board awricht?"

Andrew nodded, James said, "Fair enough."

"Ye owe the woman here eight bucks each. I'll pay her and take it out of yer pay – that sit richt with ye?"

Andrew nodded, James said, "Fair enough."

"Awricht then, get yer things, throw 'em in the wagon out there and let's be off."

Ramsay paid the old gal who only grunted. They were in Sunnyside just after dark. He told the brothers to sleep in the barn and they'd spend the next day provisioning and be off early the following morning.

In the five days since Ramsay had been there, the snow had almost disappeared on the winter range. The recent snow that had passed through the foothills had missed, thankfully, the winter range altogether. Ramsay was surprised at how little mud there was, owing he thought, to the previous year's extremely dry summer and fall.

He liked the two Scot brothers. They talked about home and their families and the coal mines in Aryshire and how they'd hoped for a better life in America but hadn't found it yet. They hadn't been able to send much money home and worried about their parents. Their pap was laid-up and couldn't work. They might have to go back and take care of them unless their circumstances improved.

Ramsay explained that they were replacing three men who weren't with the sheep when he snowshoed down from Sunnyside right after the blizzard. He had no idea where they were now or if they were even alive. He told the two about the Shoshonis who'd cared for his sheep and were caring for them now. He said he had a campwagon in pretty good shape that they could use and that he would stay with them until they knew what to do and where to go.

They passed the first campwagon, the bare-topped one, at mid-afternoon the second day. As he turned southeast for the other campwagon he glanced southwest. Off in the distance, he felt sure he could see sheep.

When they reached the campwagon it was in good enough shape to spend the night. "Which of ye is the best cook?"

"I am," said James.

"Awricht James, ye'll be the camptender and Andrew ye'll be the herder. Andrew, ye come with me in the morn to look fer the sheep."

They left for the sheep at eight, each on horseback, Ramsay leading the paint. At eleven o'clock they approached the sheep. Ramsay could see what looked like hundreds of them scattered out grazing contentedly on white sage. In the distance he saw a man on horseback then another. They rode directly for the Shoshonis.

"Hakaniyun," said Ramsay.

"You are back so soon," said Two Bulls.

"The weather is better so it is time tae move the sheep closer tae home. This is Andrew. I will help Andrew and his brother learn the ways of sheep and leave them when they are ready. I am grateful fer yer care. They look well. Myra and I are grateful fer the use of yer horse. I hope ye are pleased with his care."

Two Bulls and Standing Bear nodded as they looked at the paint. "Myra is well?" asked Standing Bear.

"She is guid."

"The sheep you counted on the hillside are here, all but two," said Standing Bear. "We will now leave for the reservation. We wish you and our friend Myra well."

"Un nangkian yuhuttsi," said Ramsay as the two Shoshoni rode south in the direction of their camp.

Ramsay was comfortable leaving for home after four days; the Scots had learned quickly. He left a saddle horse and the team, told them he would return in a week with more provisions and another team to move the topless wagon back to Sunnyside.

At six months, Annie Chris's pregnancy was progressing well with no unpleasant surprises. She and Cora switched every other day between home and the store. After the last snow, the weather turned cold again. Daily mail service from Boise had resumed, the well-traveled road now packed and frozen hard. Almost no one took the snow-covered road to Ryegrass – it remained impassable.

Andrew and James had slowly and carefully brought Ramsay's sheep within five miles of Sunnyside when the first lambs of the 1887 lamb crop were born. Green grass was poking through last year's bleached-out stubble flattened by heavy winter snows. Lambing was going well. Ramsay's fear of aborts and weak lambs from stress on the winter range proved unfounded. Predator losses were few – the coyotes didn't seem too pesky this spring, fattened from their unexpected winter bounty of livestock and wildlife deaths.

Rumors circulated that markets should be strong this year and next because so much of the West's livestock had died in the catastrophic winter of 1886-1887. The rumor made Ramsay hopeful and he needed hope; he felt he was making no progress.

PART THREE

"They shall not hunger nor thirst; neither shall the heat nor sun smite them: for he that hath mercy on them shall lead them, even by the springs of water shall he guide them."

Isaiah 49:10

CHAPTER THIRTY-FOUR

Myra arrived in Ryegrass at noon on Thursday, March 24 to inquire about the boarding house job. Cora had agreed to substitute until she returned.

Main Street, Ryegrass, was not much more than she expected. The Oregon Short Line's railroad tracks paralleled the street about a hundred yards south. A newly built white frame train depot, its roof gabled at each end, sat between the tracks and Main Street.

As she drove into town, the buggy was charged by two dogs – one a brown and white short-haired mongrel with a big head, the other, a brindle, smaller and quicker. The brindle led the attack. A third, a long-hair mongrel, kept a safe distance and barked. The two attackers tried to nip at her horse's heels but, at their first attempt, the brindle was sent sprawling across the wide dusty street by a well placed blow from the horse's recently shod left hind foot. The other slinked away in retreat.

She saw two men on horseback headed her way from the far end of Main Street and a man and a woman in a buggy headed east out of town. It was quiet in Ryegrass, Idaho. The boarding house was easy to find as was the general store that displayed a hand-painted sign notifying all that it also served as the U.S. Post Office.

Myra's first impression of Mrs. Mabe, a narrow-faced woman with a pinched up little mouth, was not good. Adorned in elaborate but unkempt clothes, she appeared to be a woman trying her best to be stylish and relevant regardless of the fact that she lived in this forgettable little town. Her clothes smelled of body odor and Hood's French Perfume. After routine introductions and a reminder that she was referred to the job by Mrs. Calland of Sunnyside, Myra said flatly, "I must tell you Mrs. Mabe, I am not married and am expecting a child in September. If you are not able to hire me, I would appreciate knowing it now."

"Oh my," said Mrs. Mabe shocked at Myra's bluntness. "I don't know."

"When will you know?"

"All right, well – my husband is in town today," Mrs. Mabe stammered. "I should, eh . . . discuss it with him. Why don't you come back about four?"

She cleared her throat then added, "I will need a reference and, I'm sorry but – a few details, about your, eh, current status, would be helpful."

"I am so sorry to have wasted your time, Mrs. Mabe. Good day."

Myra was not surprised or offended with Mrs. Mabe's response. She decided to walk around the little town a bit, as her interview had taken so little time.

A poster on a bulletin board caught her eye as she walked past the sheriff's office, four doors down from the boarding house. It read: *Sheriff's sale, Nine a.m., March Twenty-Fifth. One hundred sixty acres on Rock Creek beginning two miles up the creek from the Caufield place. Minimum bid – unpaid taxes accrued.*

She walked to the hotel and paid two dollars for a room for the night.

Myra was the only bidder at the sheriff's doorstep at nine the next morning. At nine-thirty she and the sheriff began negotiations regarding the unpaid taxes and what a valuable piece of property it was by his reckoning. Finally Myra said she'd pay last year's taxes – her last offer. In reality, it was nearly all her three years of savings from the Sunnyside School. Sheriff Winters decided to forgo the taxes in arrears for the four prior years just to get the property back on the tax rolls.

Myra wrote him a draft from the bank account Ramsay had set up for her at C.W. Moore's bank in Boise.

"Congratulations ma'am," said Sheriff Winters handing her the deed. "We wish you and Mr. Grant the best in your new venture."

At ten-thirty she was in Cora's buggy headed back to Sunnyside, deed in hand. *I have a lot to do*, a strange and unfamiliar mixture of excitement and anxiety seemed to fill her.

~   ~   ~

"Ye did what?"

"I said I bought a ranch. Well, not really a ranch, it's a hundred and sixty acres with a meadow. The sheriff said the meadow has about forty acres."

"What happened with Mrs. Mabe?" asked Annie Chris.

"She didn't seem to like the idea of hiring a single woman with a child."

"How much?" Asked Ramsay.

"It didn't cost much. I bought it from the sheriff for last year's unpaid taxes."

"A wee bit odd that the sheriff would sell tae a woman."

"He wanted rid of it. He'd assumed I was married and I didn't try to correct him."

"Where is it?"

"On Rock Creek about two miles above Caufield's."

"I know that place. We cross our sheep just above it on our way tae the mountains. There's an auld hoose and the meadow is nothing but weeds. It's gonna need work."

"I figured as much or there would have been other bidders."

"Ye can nae do all that work, fer God's sake. Yere with child remember? Who's gonna help ye?"

"I was hoping *you* would Ramsay."

"Of course he will," said Annie Chris without hesitation. "We owe you much more than that."

"Ye know I will." His embarrassment at his offhand remark was palpable.

"All I want is a little help."

"Ye can always count on me, ye know that." It appeared to Myra that he might be a little provoked by the suddenness of her unconstrained action. He might feel slighted as well, she thought, that she didn't ask for his advice before she ventured into something as significant as buying a ranch.

"If you'll go with me we could look over what I bought and figure out what I have to do to make a living there."

"I most certainly will. I'm as eager tae see it as ye."

CHAPTER THIRTY-FIVE

Langston Hailey's mind had not been on the newspaper he held in front of him on January 1, 1887 as he sat next to the frosted window in the passenger car of the train that chugged its way through three feet of snow east of Boise. It wasn't on law school either. The shock and sadness that had overwhelmed him after hearing Myra's story had turned into a deep anger. The woman who would be the mother of his child had had the worst of all indignities violently forced upon her. He was not about to dismiss it.

If the snow storm that followed less than a week after Myra's confession had not blocked almost every road out of Boise, he would have been on one of his father's stages headed to North Yakima. Thankfully, he had time to calm himself and think, or he would have been there, hunted Mott down and killed him. By the time good sense had overcome hot blooded revenge it was time to return to school.

He agonized about leaving. His conscience was like a cancer consuming him from the inside out. He'd packed and unpacked his bags twice. His mother knew something had gone awry between him and Myra and was worried about them both, but when she asked, he refused to talk about it. His father had little interest in his social life and told him to get himself to the train depot and get back to school. He complied, but felt like a snake.

The train had been painfully slow. It took thirty hours to get to Pocatello, forty-five hours through Wyoming and forty hours through Nebraska, in travel time alone, not counting all the hours they had to stop for repairs, refueling, restocking and adding water. They waited an entire day and night in Green River, Wyoming, while the train crew worked to thaw out the water tower's feeder pipe that filled the train's boiler. Frustrated, they gave up and filled the boiler with buckets. By the time the train reached Omaha the effects of the terrible winter of 1887 had been left behind.

During this entire journey, Langston had nothing to do but think. It hadn't taken much sleuthing before he left Boise to find out who Myra's teacher had been and where he'd gone. It wasn't until the train had finally made its way out of the bitter cold and windy town of Rawlins that he decided killing was too good for Desmond Mott. But if he could do nothing else, he would not let Mott's despicable deed go unanswered. That would be the first step. He was unsure what the other steps would be but this he did know, Desmond Mott's predatory days were about to come to an end.

He could not relieve his mind of the dreadful circumstances of the last five years of her life; her isolation, her parents' abandonment and the burden of unwarranted shame – and now a baby, his baby. She had to loathe him – someone else she had trusted had abandoned her when she needed support. He tried but he could not concentrate on his studies after arriving back at George Washington Law School. Myra was always on his mind – as was Desmond Mott.

On April third he received a letter from his father. As a routine business practice, John Hailey read the Public Notices of the various newspapers where he conducted business, including Ryegrass. In the letter he included a clipping that read: *One Myra Grant has, for taxes accrued, purchased, at Sheriff's auction, a one hundred and sixty acre parcel on Rock Creek ten miles north of Ryegrass.*

The clipping puzzled him: *Is there someone else? Her last name was on the notice – her name hadn't changed. If there was a husband they surely would have married before they bought property. It's not her nature – she would never marry just for appearances. But how could she have done this – alone? It's rare for a woman to buy property.*

Could he really live his life without her and could he allow her to carry and give birth to his child without him? Two days later he was on the westbound train.

On the train he composed the following letter:

Dearest Myra,

> *I have no words to explain my abhorrent behavior these past four and a half months. You have constantly been on my mind. My contrition is deeper than you will ever know and I pray that you find it in your heart to forgive me. Nothing would please me more than to see you and apologize in person and for the two of us to be together. Those wonderful days last fall were the happiest of my*

life. Regrettably, I will understand if you refuse although I fervently pray that you will not.

I left my studies at George Washington and am returning home. At this writing, my train is leaving the city of Cincinnati. I will post this letter at the next station and stand hopeful that I will be with you soon.

Held Deeply in My Heart with Sincerest Affection and Love,
Langston

Langston stayed on the train at Kuna, the nearest rail stop to Boise, knowing his letter would likely be in a mail sack on the very train he arrived on. He had business with Desmond Mott to attend to that would keep him away for nine or ten days, time for him to return and hopefully, find Myra's reply waiting. He stayed on the train to the end of the line in Baker City, Oregon. At a local livery stable he arranged for a saddle horse and pack horse, bought provisions including rope, a forty-five caliber Army Colt revolver "The Peacemaker" and a sharp four-inch Camillus pocket knife. By early afternoon he was underway on his 235 mile ride to North Yakima, Washington. He rode into the town five days later.

"I'm looking for a man named Desmond Mott," Langston said to the clerk in the North Yakima post office. "Do you know how I might locate him?"

"Whatcha want Mott for?"

"We have some business."

"You'll find him at his place a couple of miles east of town. A little orchard – lives alone in a rundown log house. Fruit trees have all gone to hell. Mott just sits on his porch and drinks. If your business is collecting on a debt you're wasting your time – he ain't got a dime."

"Thanks for your help," said Langston, tossing a Morgan silver dollar on the counter.

The little log house was set back from the road and looked just as the clerk had described. Apple trees were haphazardly in bloom and overgrown with random dead bare branches.

Langston turned off the road and rode up the weed-infested lane toward the house. The wind in his face carried the sour smell of garbage. A man with a shaggy brown beard and stringy hair sat on the porch, the stub of a black cigar planted at the right corner of his mouth. A dirty blanket was draped over his legs. A cider jug sat next to him on the porch's plank floor. Langston expected snarling dogs to come running out baring their teeth but none appeared.

"Who are you?" slurred the man.

"Name's Langston Hailey."

"What do you want?"

"I want to get a good look at the son-of-a-bitch that raped Myra Grant."

"Well, you got your look. Now what the hell you gonna do about it?"

"I don't know yet Mott. I might take you into the law, might not – depends on you."

"You got a gun?"

Langston gestured with a nod to his right hip.

"Then why are you just sitting there like a goddamn dunce? Go ahead and use it."

"Get out of the chair Mott – now."

"If you're going to shoot, get it over with. Shoot."

"Get up, Mott," Langston said again, his right hand firmly gripping the holstered Colt.

Mott threw the blanket from his legs, revealing wheels on each side of the chair and two shriveled legs bent at bony knees.

"If you want me out of this chair you're going have to get down from that goddamn horse and help me."

Mott read the surprise on Langston's face. "Ground's harder than you think when you hit it from the top of an apple tree. Go ahead shoot – I haven't the guts to do it myself."

Langston released his grip on the Colt, turned his horse and headed back to North Yakima. Mott took another pull on his jug.

~   ~   ~

Langston felt nothing. He didn't feel cheated out of his revenge; he didn't feel Myra was vindicated, he didn't feel the trip was wasted or that the trip was worth it. He felt empty.

He'd never detected a desire for revenge on her part. He doubted that her knowing Mott's fate would change her life in the least or change her feelings towards either him or Mott. Rancor was just not in her character.

He pushed hard, made the trip to Baker City, returned the horse and caught the train to Boise, all in five days. He could think of nothing but her. She should have his letter by now. He began to think that, in her mind, he was probably not much better than Mott – and, he concluded, she might be right.

Myra had loved him and trusted him. She gave her heart to him freely and openly and he turned away from her in the most horrible way. Mott, on the other hand, had stolen from her – and cared nothing for what his theft left behind in its wake. Was Mott worse? He was not sure but a deep shame filled him. To have been stolen from is one thing, to give and be rejected is another.

Five days after leaving Mott in his wheelchair Langston was back in Boise.

His father was furious with him for leaving school. He barely listened. His mother hugged him then handed him a letter with no return address. He walked upstairs to his room and opened it slowly. It read:

I cannot allow your guilt to be the only thing that binds our lives.
Myra Grant

She said exactly what he had expected. He was not surprised.

Two days later he rode up to Myra's wobbly barbed wire gate on a horse from the Ryegrass livery he'd arranged for when got off the train. It was Wednesday; she would be in Sunnyside teaching. He dismounted and released one end of the wire gate from the post. Once the tension was gone, twenty feet of fence on both sides of the gate collapsed. He led the horse through the gate then, with considerable effort, reattached it.

An hour later, he was again struggling to close the gate on his way back to a bank in Ryegrass.

He walked into the bank and told the fat man behind the counter he'd like to speak to the cashier. "I'm the cashier," the man said. "Name's Cannon, Francis Cannon. What can I do for you?"

"There's a woman named Myra Grant who recently bought a property on Rock Creek."

"Haven't met her but I'm aware that she did indeed buy the parcel. Are you Mr. Grant?"

"My name is Langston Hailey."

"Pleased to meet you Mr. Hailey," said Cannon struggling to lift his 350 pound bulk from his chair, his face expressing both surprise and respect. He extended his hand. "It's sure an honor to have you here in our town Mr. Hailey."

"If Myra Grant approaches you for a loan, I want you to approve it. I will guarantee the loan."

Cannon cleared his throat uneasily. "What about her husband? I'm sorry but we here at the bank do not extend loans to women, Mr. Hailey."

"You must not have understood me sir. The loan will be guaranteed by me."

"But Mr. Hailey, it's our policy – "

"Sir, your policy does not concern me. Do you want my business or not?"

"Yes, Mr. Hailey, we'll take good care of Mrs. Grant."

"Thank you. Send me a telegram if and when she comes in and then mail me the documents to sign."

"Yes sir Mr. Hailey. I certainly do appreciate your business."

"There's one more thing Mr. Cannon. Myra Grant is not to know that her request for a loan is being guaranteed by another party. You approve it, have her sign the appropriate documents, arrange for the funds and mail the documents to me for my signature. Is that clear?"

"Yes Mr. Hailey, I understand completely. Will you be placing a limit to her request?"

"Whatever she wants."

Langston headed to the depot and boarded the waiting train. He intended to spend the summer at hard labor working for his father hoping that long hours with a pick and shovel would clear his head and help him find a way to approach Myra before September knowing now she had every reason to despise him as much as, if not more, than she did Mott.

CHAPTER THIRTY-SIX

Her sight unseen property was a mess. Enough people had told her that including Ramsay. For years he'd crossed Rock Creek just above it as he trailed his sheep. It was barely habitable even for a backwoods hermit, she was told. She was prepared for the worst but first, she had to see it for herself.

Myra and Ramsay formed a plan. Ramsay would leave for Rock Creek on Saturday morning April 16th in his buckboard and come in to the property at the downstream end. Myra would dismiss her students early, the day before (Friday the 15th), ride Ramsay's horse Alfie, lead his mule Jasper and spend the night camped at a spot Ramsay had given her directions to. Jasper would be loaded with Myra's camp gear. Ramsay said, "I got too many critters and nae enough hay. Keep 'em. I'll let ya know if I need 'em back."

Saturday, she would come in to her property at the upper end. If they planned it correctly, they'd both arrive at the house early in the afternoon.

They had a lot to do with less than a month before the end of the school term when Myra planned to move in and permanently occupy the property. They would assess what had to be done to make the place livable and leave for Sunnyside late Sunday.

Ramsay's buckboard would be loaded with Hugh's old worn but serviceable farm implements. In subsequent trips he would haul some building materials and salvaged lumber from the old slat house. It had been vacant for the last five years waiting for a hired man they were never able to afford. The house had never been stout, had served its purpose and was about to fall down anyway.

She'd see her ranch on Saturday but first, Myra wanted to see the surrounding country to get an understanding of what she was up against. She didn't know what the ranch's potential was, if there was indeed potential, but among the options she'd considered was running cattle. Would the upper end of Rock Creek sustain seventy-five or eighty cows from April to December? The Caufields ran their little herd there, its size limited only by the amount of hay their meadow would produce for the winter.

Would there be country enough for more cattle? It was all government land and just because Henry Caufield ran his cattle there didn't give him exclusive rights to it. It belonged to her as much as to him. He might even welcome a good neighbor. They could look out for each other's cattle and help gather them in late fall. She would just have to see for herself.

The plan was to get everything they could in place for a good start on the improvements and the meadow. All they'd need then was the labor to do it. Ramsay had a young fellow in mind who he thought would do the work: fix the fences, clear the ditches and rebuild the dike that would divert irrigation water from the creek to the meadow. Junior Comstock was his name. Junior could farm it himself under a partnership agreement with Myra. Ramsay and Myra would work on the house.

On Thursday afternoon, April 14, Ramsay rode into the schoolyard leading Alfie and Jasper. Having them a day early would give Myra time to pack, load the animals and be ready to leave early Friday afternoon.

"You know," said Myra, "I've been meaning to talk to you about that poor horse. What self-respecting horse is called Alfie? Good Lord, couldn't you have come up with a name better than that?"

"What's wrong with Alfie? It's a guid Scot name."

"Not if you're a good-looking horse like him. No wonder he's always hanging his head. A horse's name has to say something about him. Look at those spots. They're kind of in a line – like buttons. I'm going to call him Buttons."

"I suppose yere gonna rename the mule too. Named this one Jasper after a stubborn auld SOB I used tae know."

"Jasper will do just fine."

"Ye ought tae know that, as stubborn as auld Jasper is, he's a pretty guid mule fer a mule. Ye can pack him, harness him, ride him – aye, auld Jasper's a guid one."

She dismissed the children at noon on Friday, April 15th. At one o'clock she rode to the Sproats' on Buttons, leading Jasper. Ramsay, Annie Chris and Cora were on the porch waiting. Annie Chris's pregnancy was more evident every day. Cora looked tired and supported herself with a cane. Ramsay stepped off the porch and over to the mule. He checked the pack ropes and knots to make sure everything was tight and secure.

"How'd I do?"

"Pretty guid fer a schoolteacher."

"Not for much longer."

"Well ye better heid out. Ye have the map I drew ye?"

"Have it right here in my pocket."

"Guid, the wagon's loaded and I'll be on the road by seven in the morn. I'll be there around one."

Myra spurred Buttons forward and was off on the trail that led up Willow Creek. She would ride northeast for a couple of hours then turn due east and cross the many draws and drainages between Willow Creek and the Rock Creek canyon. She was no more than fifty yards above the Sproats' house when Chelsea ran after her.

"Chelsea, come back here!" shouted Annie Chris.

"Go back Chelsea," said Myra to the little dog, looking up at her from Button's heels.

Myra freed her right foot from the stirrup and started to swing her leg over to dismount when Annie Chris shouted, "Let her go. She's your dog now."

Myra wasn't surprised by the rugged vastness of the country. After all, she'd been in Sunnyside for almost three years. She and Annie Chris had ridden miles up Willow Creek on two different occasions to help deliver groceries and supplies to the sheepherders.

What she'd never seen was the South Fork of the Boise River as viewed from the ridgetop above the headwaters of Rock Creek. It was about two miles from the ridge down the mountainside to the river below.

Myra had so much to do and, with a baby coming, she doubted that a trip to the river could be made before next year. She stopped Buttons and listened to the distant roar of the river below and gazed at the thick stand of ponderosa pine on the mountainside ahead that stretched east and west as far as she could see. Ramsay had assured her that what she saw below would be good cattle country and Henry Caufield's one hundred or so cows didn't come close to using all the feed.

At one-thirty the next afternoon she stopped at the gate marking the entry to her property. She struggled mightily to open the tangled wire mess of a gate, led the animals through and did her best to fasten it closed with a length of old wire she found along the fence line. As she worked on the gate all she could hear in the quiet of the canyon was Rock Creek's stream rippling over stones in the creek bottom. Chelsea lapped a long drink.

She glanced around and felt a drop in temperature as long mid-afternoon shadows from the steep canyon walls slowly filled her surroundings. *This country is so big and so steep and so desolate.* For the first time she felt a twinge of fear – *I am really alone.* Out of the corner of her eye she spotted a badger run into a clump of brush a short way up the hillside inside her fence. Another badger followed. *That's an odd place for a badger hole.*

Chelsea lifted her head from the creek just as the last badger disappeared into the brush. The little dog knew from experience not to tangle with a badger and stood whining softly with her ears perked up.

Myra shrugged, lifted herself onto Buttons and with two short nudges was headed across the dry meadow in the direction of the tired house that was coming into view.

Ramsay was there unloading the last of the implements from the buckboard when she rode up.

"Guid tae see ye," Ramsay straightened his tired back and stepped down from the wagon. "I suppose yere a rancher now. How do ye like the sound of it?"

"I think I'll like it much better when this place begins to look more like a ranch and less like some kind of squatter camp."

"Ye'll be surprised how nice this place'll look once we get the meadow cleaned up, get some water on it and get some paint on the hoose."

Myra turned her head toward the house and stepped off Buttons. "All right, let's go have a look."

She and Ramsay stopped just short of the rundown steps that led to the house's entry. Its door lay open to the inside and leaned on one rusty hinge. Myra slowly surveyed the front of the small single-story frame house. Its bleached and weathered boards were badly in need of paint. Her eyes ran from the steps up to the simple gable and then back down again. She walked around to the side, stepped back a pace to get a good view of the roof and noticed missing shingles and missing chimney bricks.

There was no evidence the house had ever had a yard or fence to keep whatever might be wandering around from helping themselves to the inside. Ramsay followed her as she walked to the back. A sad looking privy was about twenty-five yards away. It leaned to the left as if it were about to fall into its own hole. A chicken coop stood between it and the barn. A healthy crop of weeds occupied the ground in the coop and thrived on the manure-rich soil beneath. She walked around the other side and back to the front.

"There's glass in all five windows," Ramsay said optimistically.

Myra stepped onto the first step and bounced her weight up and down to test its strength. "Seems sturdy."

She did the same on each of the two other steps then walked through the front door.

The smell of mice was the first thing she noticed.

"I swept up the mouse droppings – the nest too – ye can still smell it though."

She didn't say a thing, just looked around skeptically. The dining area was to her left; the kitchen area was to her right. They were combined in one room.

In the kitchen area was a Majestic wood-burning stove, a short counter with a porcelain sink next to it with shelves below and a corner cabinet with glass doors. The rest of the house was empty. The interior at one time had been painted white but years of neglect had turned it into a sooty gray. There were two bedrooms and an area that served for both dining and sitting.

"Two bedrooms," said Ramsay, "small but most beds'll fit."

She opened the back door and walked carefully down the three steps to the ground below.

"It'll do just fine." She smiled. "I imagined worse. I can make it a home."

"I figure the roof needs patched, some siding needs replaced and the chimney needs fixed. Paint inside and out and it should be a snug little hoose fer ye. I'll bring some scrap lumber from home tae fix the barn and build a new privy," he added. "That privy back there is so rotted I'm afraid ye might fall in.

"The fence is nae as bad as it looks. New braces and corners, a few new posts and with the wire stretched up tight it'll be as guid as new.

"Myra," he said, changing his tone. "Ye made yerself a handsome deal. This is a nice little place. Here's tae ye."

"Do you think so?"

"Indeed I do," Ramsay said respectfully. "Indeed I do."

With those few words of encouragement Myra felt better than she had in months.

"Let's fix the door, clean up the place a tad then camp here fer the nicht. We'll rise early and take the wagon tae Clarence Comstock's place. It's along the way aboot two miles shy of Ryegrass. He and his son Junior are expecting us. We'll talk over the partner idea. If his dad'll be favorable tae the idea then I expect Junior will be too. Junior stopped going tae school so this oughta be a guid thing fer him.

"If he's willing, he can come back with us and bring everything he'll need tae stay a bit and we'll line him out on what needs tae be done in the meadow. We'll leave Jasper and the harness. After two or three passes with the disk he'll have the weeds knocked doon – probably take him three days. Then he can rake up the loose weeds tae burn. He should have a start on the plowing by the time we get back here Friday."

"You're coming back on Friday?"

"With ye of course – yere gonna start painting and I'm gonna start on the roof. Ye got me fer three more weekends lassie then I got ma own work tae do so ye better work ma arse off while ye got me."

"You're a good friend, Ramsay Sproat."

At eight fifteen the next morning they drove the buckboard through Clarence Comstock's gate off the Rock Creek Road. Ramsay had explained that Clarence and his son didn't have much but were honest and hard-working. Mrs. Comstock died several years before and the two of them were making do the best they could with a garden, a milk cow, a few hogs and some chickens. Clarence was a good carpenter and earned cash by doing odd jobs around town.

"I remember this place," said Myra. "I drove the buggy past it when I came to see Mrs. Mabe. I noticed it because of the yellow house and it was so neat and tidy."

"Ye'll like these two."

"Hello there, Mr. Sproat," said the short tow-headed teenager. He had a row of blonde fuzz over his upper lip and blemishes across his chin. "Come on in," he said in a voice that belied his youth. "Pa's out back. We been butchering a hog. I'll go get him." His protruding Adam's apple bobbed with each syllable.

They stepped through the doorway of the neat but Spartan home that obviously lacked a woman's touch.

After a minute or two they could hear a pump handle crank and water fill a bucket.

Ramsay reached out his hand as a short, stocky moon-faced bald man with deep blue eyes and a big smile walked into the front room. Clarence grasped it and shook it enthusiastically. "Guid tae see ye again, Clarence."

"Good to see you too, Ramsay."

"Myra, this is Clarence Comstock and his son, Junior. Clarence, this is Myra Grant, the lassie I told ye aboot in ma letter."

Clarence nodded and said, "Nice to meet you, Miss Grant. I heard you bought the Roscoe Gilbert place up Rock Crick."

"I did."

Comstock nudged his son who made a red-faced bow. "Pleasure to make your acquaintance, Miss Grant."

Myra nodded appreciatively. "The pleasure's mine."

"Ol' Roscoe weren't too keen on hard work," said Clarence. "I heard the place, well, needs some work."

"That's a kind way of saying it, Mr. Comstock," said Myra. "Truth be told, it needs a lot of work."

"No one gets up there much. I never did anyways. Gilbert just up and left one day, I was told. Owed Earl Tallman at the store in town darn near seventy-five dollars. No one's seen nor heard from him since."

"Son," said Clarence, "Miss Grant here is the one I told you about. Listen to her good. Sounds like a good offer to me."

"Now you go finish up scalding that hog, son. I'll be with you shortly. I reckon Miss Grant'll want to take you on up there to Rock Crick today. That right, Miss Grant?"

"If he's willing."

"I'm willing," Junior grinned.

"Go on then. Get your work done. They ain't gonna wait all day."

Clarence turned to Myra after Junior left. "He's a good boy and'll do what he's told. I taught him all about hard work. You feed him good and he'll work all day and all night if you ask. But he's just a youngster, still wet behind the ears so he's like most youngins that have weaknesses for things that look good and sound good.

"Junior says he can't abide school no more. Says he's as much a man as any man and wants to strike out on his own. I ain't gonna argue with him but the truth is, he ain't a man just yet. He'll make a good one though – when his time comes.

"I ain't accusing ya, Miss Grant, of being someone that'd take advantage of a boy like Junior but there ain't much good been said about that Gilbert place. But as his pa, all I ask from you is to be honest with him. If the place ain't gonna make it, let him go."

"That lad of yers," said Ramsay, "could nae be in better hawns. And another thing, ye did nae ask *me* aboot the place so I'm telling ye, fer the richt person, it'll turn a tap and Myra here is the richt person."

"If you say so, Ramsay Sproat."

It was late morning. Myra and Ramsay had a lot to do before they returned home to Sunnyside so Myra could teach the next day. First, they had to take Junior to Rock Creek and get him lined out to prepare the meadow to plant and irrigate. He followed them on his own saddle horse. Ramsay asked if the horse was broke to harness. Junior said the right thing: *Not yet.*

"Until he is," said Ramsay, "the mule will work hard fer ye all by himself."

Ramsay showed Junior the implements and walked around the meadow with him, suggesting how he might best disk up the weeds.

"We'll be back late Friday. Ma guess is ye'll have the weeds knocked doon and burned by then and made a couple of passes with the plow. Ye got hay and oats in the barn fer the mule and yer horse. Above all, be careful. We'll see ye on Friday."

"I'll get along just fine. Got one question though – how hard can I push that mule?"

"He'll give ye nine guid hours a day. More and he'll nae be worth a damn the next."

"You and me, Miss Grant, is gonna get along just fine," said Junior, acting all grown-up. "We'll have a crop in that meadow in no time. You'll see."

"I think we will too, Junior. I left enough food in the house for you to make it through Friday. After I dismiss the children from school in mid-May, I'll be here the rest of the summer."

Ramsay and Myra were back at the Sunnyside School at ten Sunday evening. Since she'd left Sunnyside late Friday she'd ridden Buttons and led the mule across the steep breaks that drained into Rock Creek, camped along the creek the first night, met Ramsay at the abandoned house on her property, surveyed what had to be done on her new ranch, spent her first night there, hired Junior, got him lined out, left the mule for him and made the long buckboard trip with Ramsay back to Sunnyside with Buttons tethered to the back.

It had been almost four months since she'd left the small band of nearly starved Shoshonis. They'd been on her mind a lot of late. She wasn't sure how she could communicate with them but decided to try a letter. The next evening Myra sat down with paper and pen. She wrote Standing Bear and Two Bull's names on the envelope, placed it in another and addressed the outer envelope as follows: Standing Bear and Two Bulls c/o Quartermaster, Fort Hall Indian Reservation, Fort Hall, Idaho. She placed a note in the outer envelope to the quartermaster asking him to please deliver the contents to the addressees and kindly read them the letter inside. The letter read:

Dear Standing Bear and Two Bulls,

I pray you and your people found your way safely to Fort Hall after we parted and hope you are comfortable and happy there.

I am writing you with news of changes in my life. During Ramsay Sproat's and my stay at your camp I neglected to reveal that I was expecting a child. I am sorry for not being forthcoming but the subject was too painful for me to share at that time. My baby will come in September.

The baby's father is a good man who lives in Boise but he only wants me because he feels sorry for me. I have decided to raise my child on my own.

You may remember me telling you that I am a teacher. In the ways of the white man, a woman with a child and no husband is not allowed to teach the children of others so I will no longer be the teacher in Sunnyside. I have purchased a small ranch not far from the town of Ryegrass and with the kindly help of the Sproats I am in the process of making it productive.

Well, that is my news; some of it sad but most of it happy. I pray that our paths will cross again.

Sincerely,
Myra Grant

CHAPTER THIRTY-SEVEN

Myra and Ramsay returned to the Rock Creek ranch on Friday, April 22nd. Annie Chris had come with them. Ramsay's buckboard was loaded with lumber taken from the slat house, a flat of shingles and some paint, two dozen bricks, mortar mix, twenty fence posts and enough food from Annie Chris's store for Junior to get by for at least a month. Annie Chris wanted to see Myra's place and talked Ramsay into letting her come along for the ride.

Cora looked frail. Her legs were swollen and sore but she said she was feeling well enough to mind the store on Saturday while they were gone. Annie Chris would not have it. She would leave the store unlocked, she said, with a notice to her customers to take what they needed and leave a note listing what they'd taken. She'd just add it to their bill. She'd done this before when she had to leave the store unattended and her customers appreciated it.

Earlier in April, Ramsay had taken Cora to Boise to see Dr. Ivey, who concluded that she had dropsy caused by inflammation of the heart. Ivey said the only treatment was to drain her legs by surgically inserting tubes. The procedure could be done in his office but it would be painful and time consuming. He mentioned an oral mercurial diuretic as an alternative but warned her that he'd seen adverse side effects and was reluctant to treat her with this medication. He would drain her legs as best he could to give her some temporary relief. He wanted her to know that the swelling would likely return, calling for repeated treatments. He cautioned her that the treatment would be arduous. Regardless, he said, she should do her best to keep her legs elevated, drink lots of water and to not put off calls to use the bathroom.

After two hours of enduring the painful process, Cora thanked Dr. Ivey and told him that she would forgo any future treatments and rely on prayer instead.

Annie Chris had hoped Cora would be up to helping after Myra's baby was born but as time passed, she doubted Cora would even be able to help with Annie Chris's own baby.

~   ~   ~

Ramsay and Myra were eager to see what Junior had accomplished while they'd been gone. They could actually smell the rich freshly turned earth of the meadow before it came into view. Two hundred yards later they saw Junior walking behind Jasper, guiding the plow by its handles with a row of dark dirt peeling off the side of the one-bottom moldboard plow. Ramsay pulled the wagon up close to the house. Myra eagerly stepped into the back of the wagon to begin to unload her things.

"Ye should show Annie Chris around," said Ramsay. "It will nae take me long tae unload."

"It's not much," Myra told Annie Chris once they were inside, "but with some scrubbing and some paint I think it'll be just fine."

"Aye, it *will* be just fine," said Annie Chris. "Your table and chairs will fit perfectly and with your rocker by that window – well, I think you'll really like it."

"My bed will go in here. When the baby is old enough it can have this bedroom."

Ramsay carried in the things they'd need for the next two days, including bedrolls. After his last load he said to Myra, "Are ye ready to walk up the meadow and meet with Junior?"

"Yes! I can't wait a minute more!"

"I'll clean up that old stove and get supper going," said Annie Chris. "I'm so anxious to meet Junior."

Junior had cleared the meadow of weeds. Piles of black ash were scattered across the meadow about every fifty yards. It looked great. He'd made about five or six passes with the plow starting at the west end of the meadow, gradually working his way east toward the creek.

"Junior," Myra shouted, "this looks wonderful! What a nice job you're doing. Thank you."

"No point in thanking me ma'am – we're partners you know. Quicker we get this meadow growing something good, the quicker you and me is gonna make some money. I ought to be done plowing by Tuesday. Got Juniper, my saddle horse, broke to pull so when I'm done plowing he and the mule oughta be able to pull the disk with the harrow behind it. I expect by the time you're here for good I'll be ready to get the ditches cleaned and rebuilt, then a dike put in the crick. All that'd be left is to drill in the seed and corrugate the meadow. Crick water'll do the rest."

"Well," said Myra, "whether you like it or not, you've got me excited. When you get close to the house, come on in. Mrs. Sproat will have supper ready and wants to meet you."

"I scrounged up enough old lumber to make some benches," said Junior. "I'll bring them in for us to sit on while we eat."

After supper and after Junior had gone to the space he'd claimed as his quarters in the barn, Ramsay said, "Most everyone around Sunnyside knows ye bought this place and will be moving here fer guid as soon as school's out. I've heard talk about a going-away party – naw one knows aboot yer baby as far as I know."

"Please, no party – please."

"It wasn't me. I know how hard that'd be. I'll tell 'em yere too busy."

"Thank you."

Ramsay stood. "I'm gonna turn in and let ye two visit. Guid nicht."

"You know Cora's not well," said Annie Chris after Ramsay had retired. "I was hoping she'd be able to help with your baby but I think that it would be asking too much. I doubt she'll even be able to help with mine. Would you consider staying with us for a month or two when the baby comes? We could help each other."

"No, Annie Chris, but thank you."

"Why?" Annie Chris asked, stunned by her bluntness.

"This is my home now. I'll get along fine."

"Then my baby and I will come here and stay with you."

"That'd be nice of you but I don't think so."

"You'll need help."

"I've already checked – there's a midwife in Ryegrass. I'll be fine."

Annie Chris shrugged – she could argue about this later – so she changed the subject. "Have you heard from Langston?"

"He wrote. He wants to see me."

"Did you write back?"

"Yes. I could tell he was feeling guilty so I told him no. Can you understand, Mrs. Sproat? I don't want his guilt and pity. I want this baby to grow up with parents that respect each other. He doesn't respect me and I don't blame him."

The next morning Ramsay worked on the roof while Myra painted. Neither would allow Annie Chris to do anything that required standing so she sat uncomfortably on one of Junior's benches with her feet up and knitted. Junior continued to plow.

By mid-day Sunday it was time to leave for home. The roof and chimney were repaired and all the damaged and rotted siding had been removed. Next weekend Ramsay would replace the siding and start digging a hole for a new privy. Myra would finish the interior and start painting the outside of the house.

On Thursday evening, May 12, Myra and Ramsay finished loading his wagon with everything she owned. The next day, the last day of the 1887 school term, she would step into the wagon with Ramsay and leave the little school behind.

Choked with emotion, she sniffled through her last goodbyes to her students. Most of their mothers and some of their fathers crowded against the back wall of the tiny school. Handkerchiefs had been removed from almost every pocket. In spite of Annie Chris's admonition, cakes and pies, coffee and lemonade lined the work table under the front window. Annie Chris baked a sheet cake knowing it was futile to restrain the outpouring of emotion. She stood along the wall and sniffled with everyone else.

Myra's sadness at her parting was not just because she would miss these people. She felt deceitful, perhaps even dishonest, that she'd been unable to reveal the truth. But what else could she do? She didn't want to embarrass them and spoil their good intentions, particularly in front of the children. In time they would all know; then what would they think of her after their generous and heartfelt sendoff? Cheated probably – that thought saddened her even more.

Myra and Ramsay left at five and rode quietly in the direction of her new life. The first thing she did after her arrival that evening was sit down with Junior and have a talk about her condition.

Junior was embarrassed but managed to say, "Pa told me I shouldn't be surprised if this might happen. Said he'd heard a rumor started by that ol' busybody in town that owns the boarding house. He said sometimes this happens to good people. As far as he was concerned there ain't none better than you – he liked you straight off and said if you was in a fix like that, to just go on about my business that it weren't no one else's matter but yours. That's what he told me ma'am and that's what I'm doing."

"Thank you Junior. Your father is a very kind man. I'm sure you'll grow up to be just like him."

"Maybe I shouldn't be asking but . . ."

"What am I going to do when the baby comes?"

"Yes ma'am."

"I'm not sure yet Junior, but I better figure something out soon because the little one is coming in September."

"Want you to know ma'am, I'll help any way I can. So will Pa."

"Thank you Junior."

CHAPTER THIRTY-EIGHT

William Calland Sproat was born on June 15, 1887.

Nicknames were common in America. Annie Chris's first choice was Will, thinking it would honor their friend Bill Judy for whom the baby was named. In both of their minds there was only one Bill Judy, so Bill was not an option. The nickname Will did not sit well with Ramsay. He was afraid his son would be called Willie by his classmates and friends, a teasing reference to the commonly used phallic nickname in Scotland. A name like Willie Sproat was a school yard scuffle in the making.

Annie Chris didn't like the sound of Cal but naming him Calland was her idea so she agreed. Cal it would be and when the two of them announced it to Cora she burst into tears.

Cal had inherited Ramsay's thick bristly hair. Ramsay said when he was a young lad his hair was yellow like Cal's and had darkened over the years to its current shade of muddy blonde.

It was Ramsay's deepest wish that Cal would have the ranch one day but there had to be more of it than there was now. Year in and year out, the store had been the stabilizing income source in their finances and allowed them to keep their sheep. The reality that his sheep, by themselves, were unable to sustain his family was very troubling for Ramsay. The lack of water was his ever-present adversary. Jackrabbits ate most of his water-stressed alfalfa one year with an infestation of grasshoppers finishing it off. Luckily, the subsequent winter had been mild.

Selling out and moving was always in the back of his mind, but their roots were so deeply set in Sunnyside that actually doing it and leaving was more than either of them could abide. The twisted gnawing feeling that grew in his gut as each winter approached became more severe when he faced it with the possibility of an inadequate supply of hay.

Among the first visitors to meet baby Cal were Pache and Lou and their son Santiago, Santi for short. As suggested, they came prepared to spend the night.

Pache and Lou had become enormously successful in the sheep business and had survived the brutal winter of 1886-1887 nearly unscathed. From the beginning Pache had bought as much farm land along the Payette

River as he could and rented what land he couldn't buy. He'd raised hay and grain on all of it and had enough stored over a two-year period to feed his 10,000 sheep through the roughest part of any winter.

They'd been Kate's godparents. Ramsay and Annie Chris gladly reciprocated and asked them to be Cal's. They were delighted. Pache got up from his chair after supper and announced with a wink, "I be back."

He left the house briefly, came back with a bota bag in one hand, a bottle of whiskey in the other, cigars in his pocket and said as he handed the leathery sheep's stomach and a cigar to Ramsay, "We drink!" Three hours and many belly laughs later Pache and Ramsay staggered to their respective beds. Pache and Lou left for home at noon the next day.

Cora went to bed as she did every night and prayed that she would live to hold the new baby in her arms. Her prayer was answered. The Lord gave her eleven days to be with little Cal.

Myra's pregnancy was now clearly evident. Annie Chris and Ramsay agonized over how they would publicly spare her embarrassment at Cora's funeral. The service was held in the Grange Hall in Sunnyside with a private burial at the Sproat cemetery. It was Myra's suggestion that the Sproats offer her condolences to the funeral goers telling them the truth, that she was too busy to make the trip from Rock Creek and assure them she'd said her goodbyes to Cora when she arrived at the Sproat home to meet little Cal for the first time.

The day after the funeral Cora was buried where she wanted to be, next to Hugh, Bill and Kate. Myra held Cal and watched sadly as Ramsay and Pache lowered Cora's coffin into the ground after Annie Chris's reading of Cora's favorite Psalms.

Junior had worked tirelessly. Once every ten days he'd ride to town and bring home supplies and mail for Myra. Aside from those infrequent trips, he was in the fields continuously. Creek water now ran down ditches and corrugates. The newly planted alfalfa and orchard grass seeds had sprouted in the soil of Myra's meadow. Junior had never been prouder. A fifteen-year-old – and he had done it virtually by himself.

At dinner one night Myra handed Junior a dollar more than he normally needed for supplies. "When you go to town tomorrow I want you to come back with your father, if he's willing of course. We need to have a celebration. Here's a note you can hand to Mr. Tallman at the store. It says for him to pick out a bottle of wine for the three of us and a good cigar for your father. I'm going to bake a cake and we're going to celebrate the success of our new enterprise."

"Yes ma'am!"

"Do you think your pa would let you have a small glass of wine?"

"He ain't gonna have a choice in the matter! Just kidding ma'am – he won't mind one bit when he sees all we done here. Truth be told, we oughta be careful or he'll drink the whole dern bottle."

At two the next afternoon Chelsea barked and wagged as Clarence and Junior rode up to the house in a buckboard. Junior's horse Juniper was tethered behind.

"Pa brought this here buckboard for us ma'am. We can sure use it from time to time."

"It's an extra," said Clarence, "an old Studebaker – bought it from an emigrant who'd lost his wife fording the Snake – too cheap to pay the ferryman. He gave up and headed back to Kentucky. It's just been sitting around the place not getting any use. Tried to sell it once but no one wants to pay what it's worth so I thought I'd make the loan of it to you and Junior – gotta take the team back though."

"That is very kind of you Clarence. I'd be happy to pay rent."

"If you'll allow Junior to fix it up, maybe even paint it, that'd be rent enough."

"We can certainly do that. Come on in."

"If you don't mind ma'am I'd like to tend to my team first. Then Junior is just itching something crazy to show me that meadow of yours."

"Got a letter here ma'am," said Junior. "Come all the way from Fort Hall."

Myra looked curiously at the envelope, inspected the stamp, the handwriting and the Fort Hall return address. "Thank you Junior."

She took a knife from the kitchen drawer, sat in her rocker and carefully slit open the envelope. Inside was one sheet of paper with the U.S. Army letterhead. She unfolded it.

Dear Miss Myra Grant,

I am First Sergeant Mazurowski at the US Army Post here at Fort Hall and have been asked by Standing Bear to write this letter to you. The following words are his:

I received your letter. It makes my heart glad to hear that you soon will have a child. You must be sad that your child will not have its father to show it the ways of the world but with a mother such as you, your child will grow straight and true. The Great Spirit cares only that his children are loved and sent on straight paths.

You wrote your letter to me and to Two Bulls. Two Bulls and his wife were unhappy at Fort Hall and moved to the Duck Valley Reservation. We hope that they find the happiness they seek.

I told our tribal council about your letter, how I came to know you and what a good woman you are. There are many women at our reservation who would be honored to help you bring your child into the world. We would all be honored to have you stay with us as long as you want.

There is one woman who would be most honored. She knows you from the past and loves you like a daughter. She is very old, wise and skilled. She said you would re-member her. Her name is Pop-Pank. She said you would know her as Patsy.

Standing Bear

She sat straight, tall and still. Her fingers quivered as she held the let-ter. She looked up at the only adornments she'd hung on the walls of her new home, her painting of Annie Chris and Ramsay's house and her unfin-ished painting of Patsy. Her heart had never felt fuller.

CHAPTER THIRTY-NINE

From 1885 to 1887 John Hailey served as a representative of the Territory of Idaho to the U.S. Congress. The new railroad through Southern Idaho had slowed his stage business considerably. Always the survivor, having endured the decline of the mule-drawn freight business and most of his mining interests, Hailey refocused his commercial sights on farming as his family's future.

Attending to the interests of the people of Idaho had taken more of his time than he had expected. He'd been unable to devote his full attention to the farms he was developing from Shoshone Falls all the way to the Oregon border. Langston was given much of that responsibility.

Langston was in charge of the development of three farms adjacent to the Snake River with its abundant and dependable flow of irrigation water. All three required extensive dikes and ditches to divert Snake River water to the fields. Chinese laborers were hired for the hard work and teamsters were hired to run the teams of horses that pulled the fresnos to scrape up the dirt required to dig miles of canals. With his pick and shovel, Langston labored along with them.

Langston worked furiously. His father's orders were to get all three farms ready for planting in the spring of 1888.

Myra Grant was always on his mind. *How odd,* he thought, *that after so many months, her fragrance still lingers, her image still sharp in my mind.*

Work was the only thing that sustained him. As he lay in his tent, pitched on one property or another he wondered what the woman he loved was doing at that very moment and wondered if his child would be a boy or a girl. They belonged with him.

He'd told his parents everything. His mother told him she loved Myra like a daughter and would pray for a loving reconciliation. His father said that, regardless of what happens between the two of them, he and his mother would never dismiss or refuse to acknowledge their grandchild.

There was no harm in prayer but he knew that getting her back was going to require action; what that action might be continued to escape him.

~　　　~　　　~

After delivering Myra's letter then inspecting Junior's hard work, Clarence and Junior returned to the house ready for a celebration. She heard the knock, looked up from her chair and said softly, "Come in you two."

She did not stand. Her eyes were red.

"Anything wrong ma'am?"

"Nothing's wrong Junior. I just received the happiest news – in the letter you brought me."

"Can you tell us?"

"She'll tell you if she wants," Clarence scolded.

"No – it's all right." She grinned. "We have another reason to celebrate this evening so let's get on with it!

"Mr. Comstock, will you open this bottle? We'll have to toast with these old glasses."

She took the opened bottle from Clarence and poured each of the three glasses half full. "A toast," she said grinning. "To Clarence Comstock, Jr., the best partner a rancher could ever have."

"I'll drink to that," said Clarence.

They touched glasses and each of the three lifted the cheap table wine to their lips.

"And another toast – to Clarence Comstock, Sr. who raised one of the best young men in the Territory!"

"That's very kind of you to say Miss Grant. He *is* a good boy."

"And my last toast – to an old friend who I thought was lost. To Pop-Pank."

Myra explained: "Pop-Pank is an Indian woman, an old friend of mine. She's going to help me with my baby." She pointed at the wall. "That's her. Isn't she beautiful?"

"Yes ma'am," said Junior trying his best to appear to agree.

At breakfast the next morning she asked Junior, "I'm going to town to send a telegram. I'll be leaving in about an hour. Is there anything we need?"

"Yes ma'am. After I get the irrigating done I'm gonna finish up on the front gate. If you'd stop at Pa's he's got some old railcar hinges. They're in the barn hanging over the manger – bring a couple with you, please.

"Except for hanging it, I ought to be done with the gate by the time you get back. Maybe you can help me."

~　　　~　　　~

It was a Monday, the ninth day of August 1887. Myra arrived in Ryegrass at eleven and went directly to the depot to buy a train ticket to be sure she'd have a seat ten days later. After changing trains in Pocatello, the Eagle Rock bound train, she was told, would arrive in Blackfoot, the stop nearest the Fort Hall Indian Reservation, at approximately five-thirty p.m. The Western Union telegraph office was located in the depot. She asked the telegrapher to send the following message to Sergeant Mazurowski.

STANDING BEAR. STOP. GIVE PATSY MY LOVE. STOP. I WILL ARRIVE AT FORT HALL BY TRAIN ON AUGUST NINETEEN ABOUT 5:30 P.M. STOP. PLEASE HAVE SOMEONE THERE TO MEET ME. STOP. MYRA GRANT. STOP.

The telegraph completed, Myra sat on a depot bench and wrote a letter to Ramsay and Annie Chris, detailing where and when she was going. She walked to the General Store and posted it.

Junior was working on the main gate entrance to her property when she returned.

"My Lord, Junior," said Myra, as she surveyed the finished gate lying on the ground. "That is a handsome gate."

"I ain't sure about that ma'am but it'll be a darn sight better than that mess we had before. Fixed the gate at the upper end too – had to build stone braces with a wire gate between. Saved the last of Mr. Sproat's lumber for this here gate – it gets used the most."

"We have some paint left over," said Myra, "I think I'll paint it. Won't that look nice?"

"Well, I suppose it *would*," Junior answered as if he hadn't given the matter any thought. "Got to get it hung first."

"I've got the hinges right here."

Junior bolted the hinges to the gate and to the gate post and stood back.

The gate sagged about a half inch – that was all.

"You do the honors ma'am. See if it'll open and close – easy like."

"Works like a dream. A baby could open it."

She stood back and admired his work. "I think it's beautiful. I'll paint it tomorrow."

"You oughta have a sign too, let'n everyone know whose place this is."

Myra smiled. "Grant Ranch? Rock Creek Ranch? What do you think?"

"We gonna have cattle?"

"That's the plan."

"Then we gotta have a brand." Myra was silent; she'd always known a registered brand would be necessary for livestock, but had been too busy to give it even a lingering thought.

"I been thinking this one over," he continued. "A brand oughta say something about who owns the land. It can't be too complicated and it can't be closed in like a 'O' or an 'R' or it'll burn a sore on the critter. I thought about 'G' but it's too closed in, then I thought about just 'M.' But a brand's gotta have a little sashay you know, a little strut, so how about *Rockin M*?"

Junior reached for a stick and drew an M in the dirt with a quarter circle beneath it.

"Rocking M – I like the sound of it."

"Pardon me but you ain't saying it right. It's the *Rockin'* M, not the *Rocking* M. Gotta say it right or you'll sound like city folk."

"The Rockin' M Ranch – perfect. I'll make us a sign tomorrow."

"Don't write it out ma'am – just the M with the quarter circle under it is all you need. You know, like the brand will be."

"I'll cut two forked willows to form the M and a curved one to attach below it for the quarter circle. There's some old chain in the barn we can use to hang the sign from the cross bar.

"Maybe I'll make two and put one at the upper gate."

"Let's go look at that upper gate when we're done here. See if you like it."

Myra led Buttons through the new gate and with a proud grin, swung it closed. She mounted Buttons and headed to the upper end of the Rockin' M as Junior and Chelsea walked beside her. They walked along the west ditch that supplied water for the meadow. The alfalfa and orchard grass was now easily eighteen inches tall.

"Good Lord, Junior," said Myra looking across the expanse of the meadow, its lush green contrasting the stark buff colored hillsides surrounding it. "You have done so much with this meadow. You should be proud."

"It sure wasn't me that done it all. Rock Crick always runs water and deserves more credit than me. One thing about this place, you're the first one on the crick; you'll always have water. Everyone else is downstream. The alfalfa's gonna start blooming any day now so I'll have to start haying. Pa found a used sickle and buck rake but they're gonna cost twenty bucks. I ain't got that much but you can take it out of my half of the hay if you want."

"Don't worry Junior. I can scrimp a little. You go ahead and buy them."

As they approached the back fence, Myra spotted two large columns of stacked rock, one on each side of the gate. From a distance they looked like short pillars of stone, each about eighteen inches in diameter. Junior had formed two cylindrical shells of netwire and filled them with rock to provide solid braces to stretch the fence from.

"Those rock pillars look stout. How long did it take you?" asked Myra as she drew rein.

"One day is all and they're braces ma'am not pillars. No problem finding rock around here."

"I think I *will* put up a sign – maybe on that brace there."

Before Junior could respond, his eye caught Chelsea chasing after a cottontail. Myra turned and looked. Chelsea, in close pursuit, disappeared behind the rabbit in a clump of brush up the hillside. It was the same clump, Myra remembered, that badgers had run into when she'd dismounted to open the gate on her first trip to Rock Creek.

Myra watched and waited. Chelsea didn't come out. Worried, she looked at Junior who shouted, "Chelsea, come back here!" Nothing.

She dismounted, cupped her hands and shouted, "Chelsea, get back here!"

Junior took a step forward to find her just as Chelsea darted out with a big dog grin – no rabbit, but content in the chase.

Chelsea stopped in front of Myra panting, water dripping off the hair on her chest and legs. A puddle formed in the dust where she stood. She shook and sprayed water in all directions. Myra and Junior looked at her bewildered by the sight of a soaking wet dog that had just run out from a bone-dry clump of brush on an arid hillside.

Junior looked at Myra – puzzled. "What the hell?"

CHAPTER FORTY

Myra stared at the brush.

Junior took a few wary steps up the hillside as if a cougar or a grizzly might be there. Myra followed. "We can't just walk up there and stick our heads in. We have no idea what's in there. I'll ride back and get something – a shovel or an axe."

"No, I'll go, I can go faster. Takes you fifteen minutes to get on that spotted horse of yours."

"Good thing men don't have babies," she whispered, "they'd never get out of bed." She added, "Bring back the rifle."

"Don't you go in there 'til I get back!" he yelled.

"Don't you worry!"

Myra walked a few more steps up the hillside. Chelsea followed. When she was within twenty feet of the tangled mixture of sagebrush and buckbrush she stopped and caught her breath. Chelsea stepped forward; Myra reached for her collar and held her tight. Myra listened hard – for what, she was not sure. She heard nothing but the creek and the buzzing of insects.

Twenty minutes later Junior rode up the hillside and dismounted. He had an axe, a shovel and his Winchester.

He leaned over and carefully parted the brush. He peered inside, braced to jump back if necessary. "There's a hole back here! Looks like a cave or something – barely big enough to crawl through."

Myra stepped next to him. She rested a hand on his shoulder to brace herself. She peered in but could see nothing but black.

Junior broke off enough brush to allow himself to get on his knees and look closer in the hole. "It goes way back."

Myra eased herself to her knees next to Junior and looked. "Don't you even think about going in there without checking for snakes."

"Snakes are all out chasing mice and other little critters this time a year – won't be no snakes in there now."

"I don't care – you're not going in there without a torch or something. I'll get you one."

Junior rolled his eyes. "All right. I'll be right back."

266

This time Junior had a willow stick, a gunny sack, some baling wire and a can of coal oil. They both peered in the hole again deciding just what they would do next.

"It smells funny in there, mossy and damp," Myra said.

"That's what caves smell like Miss Grant," replied the fifteen-year-old expert on such things.

She wrapped the gunny sack around the stick while Junior secured it with the wire, twisted it tight then soaked it in coal oil. He lowered himself to his stomach with the unlit torch in front of him and poked it inside the cave. He shook it around trying to raise a ruckus just in case he might have been wrong about the snakes.

Junior inched along on his stomach with only six or eight inches above his back to maneuver. Once inside, the cave opened enough for him to get his arms up to his shirt pocket to reach for a stick match. He struck its sulfur top with the corner of his thumbnail then lit the torch. It surprised him how big the expanse was in front of him, once the torch lit up the inside. He could actually rise to his hands and knees and crawl further. There was evidence of years of animal droppings. The further in the more distinct the musty wet smell was – odd, because the floor of the cave was dry.

Five feet, five feet more, now he could hear the echo of his own movement coming back at him from ahead. Three feet more, he could see the cave opening up, its ceiling rising enough for him to stand in a stooped position. He stopped just in time or he would have stumbled into a cavern at least twenty feet across. Alarmed, he took a step backward, almost falling and dropping his torch. He lowered himself to the security of his hands and knees, crawled to the edge, stretched his torch across the expanse and looked down. Peering into the blackness, he swore there was a pool of some kind below. He felt around for a rock, found one about fist size and threw it. A loud hollow splash rose up from below then echoed through the emptiness – water, about five feet below was his guess. He found a bigger rock and threw it. A bigger splash. He stuck the torch as far out and down as he could to get a better look. He could hear the ripples from the rock he'd thrown lapping against the walls of the cavern. *Big ol' puddle, maybe bigger than Echo,* he thought. Echo Cave was a well known local lava cave eight miles east of Ryegrass that partially filled with ground water early in the year but was dry by fall.

Gotta get back before the torch goes out. As he turned to leave he noticed that, five feet to his left, the cavern wall sloped gently downward in the direction of the water. *So that's how Chelsea got wet in here.* He inched his way back through the opening.

"Well?"

"Miss Grant, you got a nice little cave in there. Good sized puddle too. Puddle ain't a good way a calling it – bigger'n that – more like a little pond I'd say. Seen 'em before ma'am. Been in lots of them in my years – it's a good one. Don't know what you can do with it though. Just a curiosity I suppose."

It was funny how hard he tried to sound worldly and grown up.

"I'll look for myself after the baby's born."

"No hurry ma'am – not much to see."

Junior helped Myra onto Buttons and gathered their things. The two of them headed back to the house just as shadows filled the canyon.

~August 19, 1887~

Junior and Myra left the Rockin' M at five a.m. to catch the eight o'clock train headed for Pocatello. In Pocatello she would change to the train headed north to Eagle Rock and leave the train at the Blackfoot stop.

Junior stopped the wagon outside Ryegrass's small depot.

"Do you have any questions?" Myra asked over the rhythmic huffing of the idling locomotive.

"No ma'am. Got all that hay to put up while you're gone – sure nuff oughta keep me busy."

"I want to talk to you about something, Junior. I hope you aren't offended."

"I can't imagine you ever offending no one ma'am."

"That's nice of you to say but there *is* something I want to tell you. I understand you felt you needed to quit school, but it has bothered me that I might have been complicit in some way. So, ever the schoolmarm, I have a project for you while I'm gone. You are a smart young man and I'm sorry to say that I have not yet seen you with a book. So, I have a book for you to read."

"I know how to read and write and I know my numbers."

"Junior, please take my word for it. There's so much more to an education than just learning to read and write."

She reached in her bag. "I'd like you to read this book while I'm gone. It's a wonderful story about a boy and an escaped slave. When you've finished I want you to write a report for me telling me all about the story and what it means to you. Will you do that for me?"

"I'll try ma'am – ain't too good at that sort of thing though. *The Adventures of Huckleberry Finn* by Mark Twain."

"I know you can handle most anything, including this book."

"I gotta ask you something ma'am," he said, changing the subject. "Remember us talking about buying cattle?"

"Yes."

"If it's all right by you, ma'am, I could ask around some?"

"That would be good. I've been thinking about that. I'm not sure where we'd get the money. I hope after you get the hay harvested I might be able to convince a banker to make me a loan. The Rockin' M is a hundred percent better now and ought to look more valuable to a banker as collateral. I do like the sound of that. Don't you Junior? Rockin' M – I can say it over and over and never tire of it."

"No use having a ranch and a brand if we ain't got cattle."

"You go ahead and inquire. We'll talk about it when I get back."

"I'll take good care of things, Miss Grant."

"I know you will, Junior. Don't forget about *Huckleberry Finn.*"

"You take care of yourself, ma'am," he said with a quiver in his voice. Other than his ma or his pa, the best person he'd ever known had just walked toward the main depot door.

CHAPTER FORTY-ONE

Patricia Louisa Grant was born on the Fort Hall Indian reservation at eleven fifteen a.m. on September 24, 1887. She weighed eight pounds two ounces, was twenty-one inches long and perfect.

Patsy, a skilled midwife most of her life, was very old but quite spry for someone her age, Myra thought. Her pure white hair and bronze leathery skin made her look more like an Egyptian mummy come to life than the deliverer of new life for her people. She directed her two helpers' every move with the skill and authority of an army general directing maneuvers on a battlefield. Myra knew in advance that the child would be Patricia if a girl or Patrick if a boy. No one was more proud of a child than Pop-Pank was of little Patsy.

Myra was thankful she had a month to renew her friendship with old Patsy before the baby was born. Patsy told her she left Boise to die among her people. She found an old discarded dress in a trash can, dyed it black, used a portion of it as a veil and, disguised as a grieving widow, boarded a stage bound for Blackfoot. She knew she would never have been sold a ticket or allowed to board the stage had anyone known she was an Indian. Her spirit, she said, was now at peace, blessed with the presence of her dear Myra. Patsy said that she would be praying now to join her spirit ancestors.

Myra wished it were possible for her old friend to meet Langston although she knew Patsy would look at him with unmasked skepticism. This made Myra sad because she knew Langston was a good man.

She wished it were possible for Langston to share in the joy of the birth of their daughter. He was on her mind during the idle days before Patsy's birth and even more afterwards as she cuddled and nursed the miracle of their new baby.

Two days after the delivery, Myra wrote a letter to Ramsay and Annie Chris to announce Patsy's birth and to inform them she planned to return to Rock Creek in early October. She handed the letter to Standing Bear, and asked him to give it to Sergeant Mazurowski to post.

Standing Bear and his wife were doing well on the reservation. He was offered credit through the government to purchase a small herd of cattle they ran along the lava meadows north of the small community of Eagle Rock along the banks of the upper Snake River. Standing Bear and his wife liked the solitude and the peace away from encroaching civilization. They spent all but the coldest months of the year on the open range with their cattle. They were happy, he said. Her new ranch, Myra told him, was located on one of the few creeks with water enough to raise forage for the cattle she hoped to buy. She felt fortunate because ranching was a struggle for most in her area unless the ranch bordered one of the large rivers.

He and Myra talked about cattle and what he had done successfully in the business and what he'd learned through his mistakes. He told her the same thing he'd been told by a more experienced Indian rancher: Spread her risk by not running all cows or all yearlings but a combination of both.

Standing Bear offered to help her once she found cattle to buy. She said she had a good young man helping her but thanked him for his offer.

She bid them all a stoic farewell on October 10th. She boarded the train back to Ryegrass. Junior had received the letter she'd written him and was waiting for her at the depot.

"That sure is a pretty little baby ma'am – maybe the prettiest I ever seen. What's its name?"

"It's not an *it* Junior," she laughed. "*Her* name is Patricia – Patsy for short. I named her after a good friend of mine, the Shoshoni princess. It's her likeness on the wall in the house."

"I have three surprises for you," said Junior once they were well on their way home. "Here's the first."

He handed her an envelope.

Myra laid the baby on her lap, opened the envelope and removed three sheets of paper neatly written with Junior's very legible handwriting. At the top of the first page was the title. The first line read: *Report*. The next line read: *by Clarence Comstock, Jr.*

She silently read his report. "This is very good, Junior. I am so proud of you! Did you enjoy the book?"

"Yes ma'am I truly did. I learned that doing right might not be what folks want you to do, might not even be legal, but I have to trust myself when I know something ain't right. Huck knew he might burn in hell for letting Jim go but Huck had honor, ma'am, and knew it weren't right to turn Jim back into slavery. That's what I learned ma'am."

"That lesson is the most important lesson anyone can ever learn in life and you are fortunate to have learned it so early. You have made me very proud."

"Ma'am, I got another surprise."

"Tell me."

"Ma'am, I found some cattle for us to buy – good price too."

"You did?"

"I sure did. There's eighty-five head – fifty-five cows and thirty yearling steers. Good price too, nine bucks a head for the cows and five bucks for the yearlings. That's six hundred and forty-five bucks. They're in Oregon, a little town called Jordan Valley. I can get my pal Tommy to go with me. We can trail 'em back here before the end of November if we leave real soon."

"My word Junior, you have been busy!"

"Well, what do you think?"

"We'll need to talk to the bank. I guess we can do that any day now. I talked about the cattle market with my friend at Fort Hall and as I recall from what I've learned, what these folks in Oregon are asking seems fair. Any more surprises?"

"One more – wait'll you see the stack of hay I put up. Figure close to seventy-five tons. Not bad for the first crop. There's some weeds in it but it's still hay – it'll either make a turd or help push one out."

"Junior!" Myra scolded. "Where did you learn to talk like that? Oh, never mind."

"Haven't put the hay up for sale yet – waiting to see what we end up doing about them cattle."

"What else Junior? You look like you have something else you want to tell me."

"Yeah, there is. The same day you left for Fort Hall a man rode up on horseback. A real nice sort. He looked different – not from around here. He said he's been developing farms on the Snake River and wanted to look at your place. I told him that it weren't for sale. He said he weren't looking to buy it. Said he knows you. I told him you left for Fort Hall – wouldn't be back for a month or longer. I didn't tell him why you went and he didn't ask. He asked if he could walk around the place a bit. I told him to go ahead but not to walk in the meadow. He said he wouldn't. I asked him what his name was and he said it didn't make no difference. He spent about an hour lookin' then got on his horse and left."

"Junior, that was Langston Hailey. Langston is Patsy's father."

~   ~   ~

Langston had stopped his horse inside the gate on his way from the Rockin' M back to Ryegrass. He dismounted, opened it, led the horse through and closed it. As he did he glanced up at the sign suspended by chains from the gate's twelve foot high horizontal cross bar. It was in the shape of an M made from the crooks of two large willow branches laid together and a bowed willow branch attached below it. An hour before he had been so impressed by the gate itself he hadn't noticed the sign above it. *Her brand, the Rockin' M.*

He nudged the horse toward town and left Myra's ranch behind.

It seemed so far in the past now – that day in December when Myra *confessed* her story. So much about Langston Hailey had changed. He understood now the enormous risk she'd taken. She'd revealed her trauma and heartache to someone she loved and trusted and by doing so, knew she would become totally vulnerable to him and would be placing her entire future, and her heart, in his hands. He had failed her – all he thought of was himself.

He returned the horse to the livery in Ryegrass. What would he do next? Should he buy a ticket to Fort Hall? Why Fort Hall? She had told him about the Indian woman she'd befriended in Boise and had teased him occasionally by speaking to him in Shoshoni. Was there a connection between the reservation there and Myra? It puzzled him and made him fearful for her. He'd questioned the young man on her ranch about Fort Hall but the boy refused to speak of it. Langston recounted the abbreviated conversation in his head: *Why Fort Hall? Can't tell you mister. Does she have friends there? Can't tell you mister. Will she be safe? Yes.*

Should he board an eastbound train to Fort Hall? He needed to clear his head. He needed help, counseling of the heart, the kind that can only come from a mother. He bought a ticket to Boise.

"I'm in agony. I miss her and I'm so fearful for her; about to have my baby – alone. I need her and our baby in my life. Should I go find her?"

"There is an important question you must ask yourself, Langston," she said. Her sternness startled him. "Would you be feeling the same if she were not carrying your baby?"

"Yes, of course Mother. Of course."

"Think about that. Are you sure? This is a woman who, regardless of circumstances, has known another man. Can you dismiss this from your heart for the rest of your life and never hold it against her? You must be sure of your answer. If you are not, you must acknowledge your child *and my grandchild* with your support and love but let Myra Grant find someone who loves her for who she *is*, not for what she *has*. What if the child does not survive? Would that change your heart?"

"No. I love *her* – period. Nothing will change that."

"All right then – You should make a trip to Sunnyside and have a visit with Mr. and Mrs. Sproat."

~   ~   ~

"I know these people," said Ramsay. "Trust me, she's in guid hawns. She's havin' the baby in the best of care. It's hard nae tae worry but she's with people who loove her – fer who she is – nae a thing more, nae a thing less."

"Should I go there?"

"No," said Annie Chris without hesitation. "Give her time."

"Damn it, I've given her time. Months of time. I can barely wait another minute."

After a deep breath he said, "I'm sorry Mrs. Sproat. I'm just so worried."

"Arrange to meet with her after she returns."

Langston's hands were on his knees, his head bent, as he sat at the Sproat kitchen table listening. He lifted his head, looked at Annie Chris and said, "Thank you. The waiting is brutal. I hate it but I suppose that's what I'll have to do."

CHAPTER FORTY-TWO

On Friday October 14th, Myra waited with Patsy in her arms as Junior hitched the buckboard. They were headed to Ryegrass to speak with the banker. She'd written a letter to Ramsay and Annie Chris she intended to post to announce that Patsy was ready for visitors.

During the ride in, Junior cautioned Myra that banks don't usually make loans to women and to minors, even those with more than enough collateral. Myra told him they'd do the best they could to convince the bank they'd be diligent ranchers and worthy customers. The banker would want to see the ranch, she was sure, and all the improvements and would be eager for their business once he did. Their only alternative, if they were turned down, would be to sell their meadow hay each year and try to save enough to buy cattle outright. It could take years.

"Mrs. Grant! It is so nice to meet you! What a beautiful little boy you have there," Francis Cannon said gushing. He extending his hand from the sleeve of a black suit coat, much too small for his ample girth.

Myra was surprised at the friendliness of this puffy-looking man with small dark eyes. About twenty hairs were plastered over the top of his glistening bald head.

He looked at Junior, "Aren't you Clarence Comstock's boy?"

"Yes sir."

"How is your father?"

"He's doing fine sir."

"How about your mother?"

"She's been gone for five years sir."

"Oh that's right – so sorry about her passing. Well, what can I do for you today?"

"We're here to inquire about a loan to buy some cattle to stock my ranch on Rock Crick. Junior and I are going to be fifty-fifty partners."

"Well now, I think we can help you with that. How much do you need?"

Junior glanced at Myra. She stared straight ahead. He looked back at Cannon and said, "Well sir, there's fifty-five mixed breed younger cows that are bred to calve in March. They're in Jordan Valley and the fella wants nine bucks a head. That'd be four hundred and ninety-five dollars. And there's thirty yearling steers that he'd let go for five dollars a head, if we take the cows. That'd be a hundred and fifty dollars. So, we need six hundred and forty-five dollars by my numbers."

"Makes sense to me. Let's just round it up to seven hundred dollars," said Cannon as he reached into a file in his desk drawer and pulled out a blank note.

He filled in the note. "Mrs. Grant if you'll sign right here we'll get this loan started today."

"Don't you need me to sign too?" asked Junior.

"One signature'll be just fine."

"But there are two signature lines?" asked Myra.

"Your signature will be adequate. Now if you'll be so kind as to open a new account with us Mrs. Grant I'll have your money in the account within a week. I'll send a runner out to your place with a new draft book as soon as the money arrives and you can go to Oregon and buy your cattle. Congratulations!"

Cannon had the note in an envelope and was addressing it to Langston Hailey, General Delivery, Boise, Idaho before the door to the bank had closed behind Myra and Junior. He included a self-addressed stamped envelope for its return. He posted it and walked to the depot to send Langston a telegraph, just as he promised he would.

"I don't know about that banker," said Junior during the return trip to Rock Creek.

Myra frowned. "He seemed a little over-eager. Kind of worries me too. As soon as we get home I'm going to write two identical letters. One for you and one for me, informing anyone who might need to know that you and I are partners on those cattle and that we own them equally – just in case anything happens to me."

"Don't he know you ain't married, calling you Mrs. and all?"

"I don't think he was interested."

The runner from the bank arrived on Monday, October 17th. Junior left with his friend Tommy the next day for Jordan Valley, Oregon. He told Myra not to expect him until late November.

Ramsay and Annie Chris arrived with Cal on the eighteenth. They presented Patsy with a beautiful cradle Ramsay had made and pink blankets

Annie Chris had knit. Cal was four months old now, laughing and smiling. Patsy was thriving but still not sleeping through the night.

Annie Chris looked at Ramsay. He nodded – she spoke. "Langston came to see us in August. You will hear from him."

Myra looked at her toes. "How is he?"

"He asked if we thought he should go to Fort Hall to be with you when the baby was born. We told him we didn't think that was a good idea." Annie Chris paused. "That man loves you and your child – the child you made *together* – and he's distraught. This separation is not good for either of you. You need to be together."

She thought of Patsy's blonde hair and blue eyes – her father's – and said nothing. Patsy woke in the bedroom and started to fuss.

"She wants to be fed."

Frustrated with Myra, Annie Chris said, "It's getting late. We should go."

CHAPTER FORTY-THREE

"It's late in the afternoon, I know, but if you two can spare an hour or so – or better yet," Myra asked as she stood to attend to Patsy, "spend the night? There's something I have to show you."

"I suppose," said Ramsay glancing at his wife. "What do ye want tae show us?"

"It's a cave. It's hidden behind some brush, at the upper end of the place, not far from the gate – up the hillside a ways. Junior and I found it after Chelsea chased a rabbit into it."

Annie Chris shrugged, signaling that it was all right with her.

"What's so special aboot this cave?"

"Chelsea came out of it soaking wet. Junior crawled in and looked. He said there's a pool of water inside. He didn't think much of it – he said that water in caves is pretty common."

"He's probably right," said Annie Chris.

"But it just doesn't seem natural to me," said Myra. "Ground water is what he called it. The cave is about thirty vertical feet from the crick – how could ground water get up that high? Junior said he threw rocks in and they made a big splash. It's been about three months since he went in – if it's really ground water, as low as the crick is now and as high as the cave is and as dry as it's been, surely the pool or puddle or whatever it is, would be dried up by now. If not, and there's still a pool in there, there's something really odd about it." She shook her head. "I don't know, it just really has me curious. I just thought, you being here and all – "

"Awricht," Ramsay interrupted as he rose to his feet. "Get what ye need and let's take a look. If it's still wet, there could be a spring. We'll see."

"You'll spend the night then?" asked Myra.

Annie Chris looked at Ramsay. "I think we better plan on it."

"Aye."

"I wish Junior were here to show you himself," said Myra, "but he won't be back from Jordan Valley for a month or so."

Ramsay carried everything to build torches, an axe, some gunny sacks to crawl on and a length of twine. The women carried the children. Shadows from the west side of the canyon were starting to creep across the canyon floor. They had about two hours of daylight left.

"The cave, it's in *there*," said Myra pointing at the brush-obscured entrance.

Ramsay parted the brush and peered into the darkness. "Aye, it's a cave."

Annie Chris rolled her eyes. "A genius that man."

"Ye want tae look, smart aleck?" teased Ramsay. "It's a wonder naw one ever noticed it before. Who knows, mebbe auld Gilbert knew aboot it. Awricht with ye if I chop this brush out?"

"Sure."

Ramsay chopped while the women laid the children on a blanket. Patsy went to sleep. Cal's eyes drooped – he wouldn't be far behind.

"Awricht," said Ramsay once the entrance was clear. "Someone help me make a torch." They made two. Ramsay squatted down, spread out a gunny sack inside the entrance, put another one under his belt and started inching himself inside.

"Junior says there's a steep drop-off once you're inside a ways so be careful. He almost fell in."

Once well inside, he lit his torch and waved it around for snakes just as Junior had. *Can't be too careful*, he thought. He hated snakes more than even Annie Chris. She thought it was hilarious how Ramsay would jump back at the sight of even a harmless bull snake. No snakes. He crawled in further.

The opening only led to more blackness. In less than a minute he could stand at a crouch. He walked carefully, keeping Junior's experience in mind. He could smell a musty, mossy smell. *Water must still be here*, he thought. He crept carefully to the edge of the drop-off and held the torch over the expanse below. Squinting, it was difficult to tell what was down there, his eyes not fully adjusted to the dark and the torch light. He picked up a rock and dropped it. A large hollow-sounding splash came from below – another rock . . . same splash. He pulled out the twine and tied it to a third rock. He could now see water. He lowered the rock. When the rock had reached water, he jiggled it up and down to hear splashing then let it drop. It went down and down and further down. *What kind of bloody clootie is doon there?* He was afraid he would run out of twine as the rock continued its descent. Finally it stopped – there was slack in the twine. He pulled the rock out of the water and tied a knot as a marker at the spot the twine had become wet. *It must be twenty feet deep,* he thought as he untied the rock and carefully rolled the twine into a ball. When he returned to Myra's house he would measure the distance between the end of the twine where the rock had been tied and the knot he'd marked as the place where the water stopped.

He held the torch again over the cavern, his eyes now much more accustomed to the dark. The water had receded and left a dry water line three or four feet above the surface. *Sticks? Drift wood? Pine cones? And that big board? What the bloody hell?*

He turned and headed back just as the torch started to dim.

Ramsay's eyes were fixed on Myra as he crawled out.

"Well?"

"Damndest thing," he said brushing himself off. "It's a pool awricht – mebbe fifteen, twenty feet deep. But the pine cones is the oddest of all."

"Pine cones?"

"And driftwood and a board – a board that was sawed in a mill. And the smell of the water – that musty river smell. Ye need tae go in yerself. I'll go with ye. Ye'll be fine, just keep yer heid doon fer the first fifteen feet."

"I'll watch the children," said Annie Chris, "then I want to go."

After all three had had their look, they walked back to the house totally confused.

The smell, thought Ramsay, *was like the Boise River in the summer and fall.*

"There's no possible way it could be Boise River water," said Annie Chris. "It must be fifteen miles to the river, maybe twenty."

"Nae straight through the mountain," Ramsay said. "Just five or six the way the crow flies."

"What do you mean, the way the crow flies?" asked Myra.

"I mean straight through the damn mountain. Can either of ye think of another idea? There is nae a pine cone within ten miles of here. How would a pine cone get in there? And driftwood? Ye give me a better thought and I'll give ye a listen."

"I have some ham and leftover lentil soup. Will that be all right?" Myra asked.

There was little conversation as they ate, each absorbed in thought. Finally Ramsay said to Myra, "Here's what I think ye should do.

"If it *is* river water, the water in the cave would rise and fall, same as the river. It might take 'til spring tae see a difference. Ye should measure and compare the water's level once a week and draw oot a bucket each time and save it. Mebbe, over time, ye might learn something. The most convincing thing would be muddy water after a thunderstorm. If it's from the river, the water in the bucket would be muddy just like the river. All ye have tae do is wait fer a thunderstorm. Send us a letter when time allows. I'm as puzzled as ye."

After listening to Ramsay's assessment Myra wondered what Langston would think or what his opinion would be. She missed him.

The next day, after she said her goodbyes to the Sproats, she bundled Patsy, hitched the buckboard and headed to Ryegrass for supplies and her mail. As the wagon bumped along on the rough road she thought, *As soon as I can afford it, I'm going to buy a buggy with springs.*

There was a letter in her post office box from Langston. She slipped it in her pocket and left for home, her heart pounding the entire way.

Once she was settled in her rocker with Jasper the mule in the barn and fed, the supplies put away and Patsy quietly nursing, she opened the envelope and removed the single sheet of paper.

Myra began reading:

Dearest Myra,

> *An hour and a half have passed since I sat at my desk with pen and paper. The words simply don't seem to come. Only poets are skilled at using the written word to communicate matters of the heart. With that in mind, I know it will not be words on this paper that will convince you how much you mean to me. And I know how hurt you were at my reaction to your painfully told story, a rendering that seems like only yesterday to me; my shameful reaction is always present in my mind. I also know what I am about*

to tell you may seem trite and patronizing and much too late but, regardless, it is how I feel and I will not wait to tell you any longer.

I want you and our child in my life, every day, every hour, every minute. Anything less will be a meaningless existence for me. How rare it is to have truly known love and how foolish a person is who has known this rarity and turned his back to it.

I know now nothing will ever replace the void left by your absence, not vengeance, not work, not money, not fame, only you.

Nothing but you and our child can fill my empty heart,
Langston

Myra placed the letter carefully on the table next to her rocker, looked at her baby, now fast asleep in her arms, leaned down and kissed her softly on the forehead.

She rocked her child for an entire hour while the little one slept, traces of the child's sweet breath rising, adding warmth to Myra's softening heart.

She rose from her chair, looked at the photographs of Langston and her on top of her bureau taken nearly a year before and reached for paper, pen and ink.

Dear Langston,

Our daughter is beautiful and as perfect as any child ever was. She is the joy of my life. You have every right to share in that joy and, hopefully, that time will come soon but, along with caring for our daughter, I am fully engaged in making a productive enterprise of my ranch. My heart tells me I am ready but my head tells me to wait. I love you still.

Sincerely,
Myra

CHAPTER FORTY-FOUR

Myra received a letter from Junior on October 27th, postmarked October 24th at the Jordan Valley post office. He said he'd bought the cattle and they were fine healthy stock. The cows, he was told, should begin calving in March. He'd used the seller's facilities and branded them with the new Rockin' M brand that Buster, the blacksmith in Ryegrass, had forged in his shop. He and Tommy would leave the next day to trail the cattle home. He said he would try to spend as much time on the trail as possible and use available forage along the way. There was no need to get her cattle home too early as there was little pasture available in and around Ryegrass and they shouldn't start feeding their hay too soon before winter. He said to look for him at the end of the month. Hopefully the weather would cooperate.

She had established a routine. Every Tuesday she'd go to the cave, measure the depth of the water and bring back a bucket full. She poured each week's contents into its own glass jar and recorded the date. She lined each week's jars side-by-side on a shelf she'd built in the barn. In her first few jars there were small wiggly things in the water but as winter approached, the water became clearer with less of whatever the wiggly things had been. She recorded the water level each week and, over time, noticed a measurable drop. There were no thunderstorms and there probably wouldn't be any until spring so a quick confirmation of Ramsay's hunch would probably not happen soon.

Junior rode up to the house on Wednesday, November 30.

"Get off that horse and give me a hug, cowboy. I've missed you."

"I can sure do that," he said swinging his leg over the cantle. "Got your cattle about two miles down the road – you want to jump on ol' Juniper here and help Tommy bring 'em in? I'll watch the baby. Thought you might want to trail them in the last couple of miles yourself. They're dern good stock, ma'am. You're gonna like 'em."

"I can't wait." She grinned. Junior took Patsy and handed Juniper's reins to Myra.

"Tommy's waiting!"

Myra lifted herself on Juniper and nudged her heels into his flanks. Juniper, thinking he was home at last, was less excited to leave than Myra and required a couple of firm kicks to convince him of the seriousness of her intentions. He reluctantly responded and trotted down the lane with Chelsea following at his heels. Myra could hear the bawling and see the cloud of dust within minutes. Around a turn, a mile past her gate, she saw her entire herd bunched up in a huddle in the middle of the lane. Tommy was behind, barely visible in the dust. He was hollering and slapping the stragglers' rumps with a willow switch he'd cut, trying to get the cluster of bawling bovine flesh to move up the road. She nudged Juniper up the sidehill to go around the cattle and give Tommy a hand.

"Good to see ya, ma'am! I sure could use some help. Having a hard time moving these dern cows – act like I'm trying to drive 'em straight to the hubs of hell. They don't like this narrow canyon I s'pose."

"You've come a long ways. We're almost there."

Chelsea pitched right in, and nipped at the stragglers' heels.

"Good cow dog ya got there, Miss Grant."

"A talent I didn't know she had. I'm as surprised as you are."

She coaxed Juniper close enough to one of the stragglers that she could reach out and slap it on the rump with the ends of her reins. The smell of her cattle, leather, horse sweat, fresh manure laced with dust and the smell of sage, gave her a rush of excitement. Another step forward had just been accomplished. This run-down hovel of hers was becoming a real ranch.

The next day Myra explained to Junior what she and the Sproats had learned about the water in the cave and what she was doing to try to determine its source.

"I'll be derned, ma'am. It's sorta like science ain't it? Never dreamed that water could get here from the river – how the hell could that ever happen?"

"I don't know, Junior, and I'm not sure that's where it's coming from, but everything I've learned tells me it's coming from the Boise River. Nothing else makes sense."

She wrote Ramsay and Annie Chris weekly, detailing the results of her findings.

On January 26 the temperature dropped to single digits. The water level in the cave dropped. A week later, chunks of ice appeared in the cave water but the air temperature inside remained a constant forty-five degrees. She was now as certain as she'd ever been – this was river water.

About nine p.m. on March 4, thunder shook the canyon and bolts of lightning lit the late-evening sky like momentary flashes of daylight. Minutes later it began to rain – hard. Huge rain drops fell, hail followed. As suddenly as it started, it stopped. All told, there hadn't been enough moisture to settle the dust. Myra could hear the thunder trundle off, rolling away gradually and fading into the distance. She grabbed a lantern and ran to the creek hoping it had rained harder up the creek. No rising water. *Maybe it did up in the far reaches of the Boise River. The thunder seemed headed in that direction.*

The next morning she bundled up Patsy and went to the cave with her bucket, hoping for muddy water. None – nothing had changed. It must have just been a lightning storm in the mountains, she thought, with little rain, just like here.

She hesitated, thinking it a waste of time, bundled up Patsy again and went to the cave the next afternoon. She raised her lantern over the cavern and looked down. The water had risen. She looked closer. Driftwood and pine needles floated on its surface. Her expectations soared. She lowered her bucket. After it filled she lifted it from the cavern and placed it next to the lantern. *Good God, it's mud!* Unbelieving, she poured it out and drew another – the same – milky brown water.

She half ran, half trotted, trying to balance the bucket full of water and Patsy. "Junior! Junior!"

Their cattle had been confined on her property all winter and had to be fed each day. One of Junior's daily morning chores was to hitch Jasper to the buckwagon and drive a load of hay to the hungry impatient cows and steers waiting on the rocky flat between the meadow and the upper gate. Calving had started a week before and had been going well. Because the temperature had dropped twenty degrees after the storm passed, Junior had gotten up twice during the night to walk through the herd, lantern in hand, to check on newborns.

Junior was in the midst of the herd that afternoon helping a particularly stubborn wet newborn stand on its own. Steam rose off its back in the cold air. Junior had his finger in its mouth to stimulate the sucking response. Its mother was standing back at a safe distance bawling at them both. Junior pulled his finger from the calf's mouth and stepped back ten feet. The mother cautiously walked to her calf, sniffed and licked it a few times. The calf caught on, lurched on wobbly legs and bumped its nose along its mother's belly until it found a teat and nursed.

"What is it?" Junior hollered as Myra stumbled through the upper gate.

"Look at this water!"

"It's muddy. From the cave?"

"Yes, from the cave! This is Boise River water!"

"All right, it's Boise River water. What are you gonna do about it?"

"I've been thinking about that for months – what I'd do if I was certain it was river water. I need to somehow test it to find out how much would flow out. All I can do is dig open the face of the cave all the way to the cavern, then let it spill out toward the creek. I don't know of any other way."

"That's solid rock. We're talking dynamite and a check dam – this ain't gonna be as easy as grabbing a shovel and throwing dirt."

"I know that Junior. I'm going to need Ramsay's and your father's help for this. Do you realize what this means if that cave produces thousands of gallons of water?"

"Yes ma'am, I do. It means you're gonna be one helluva rich woman."

CHAPTER FORTY-FIVE

Junior had told his father about the cave the past summer. Clarence had dismissed it, just as Junior had, as nothing meaningful or extraordinary. But on March 12th, Junior made his first trip ever to have a talk with his father as one man to another. Clarence Comstock, Sr., his son insisted, needed to see for himself.

Spring rains on top of thawing mud made the Foothill Road a mire, practically impassible from Sunnyside to Rock Creek by horse and buggy. After Myra's letter reporting the results from the thunderstorm, Annie Chris wanted to go badly but the only passable route had to be traveled on horseback, a trip young Cal was not yet old enough to endure on Ramsay's back. Annie Chris stayed home and Ramsay rode to the Rockin' M alone.

Clarence rode to Myra's early the next morning. Junior had told his father about Myra's tests on the cave water and her conclusion that it came from the Boise River. Clarence was skeptical but interested. Ramsay arrived two hours later.

The four of them, with Myra carrying Patsy in her cradle, walked to the cave. Earlier, Myra had removed the remaining brush and grass that shrouded the entry and dug a flat spot nearby for Patsy and the cradle. The black void in the sidehill was now clearly visible from the creek. She had positioned a series of coal oil lanterns leading to the water cavern with more lanterns suspended over the cavern itself from hooks she'd pounded into cracks in the rock ceiling.

It wasn't as clear as daylight inside but it was bright enough for Ramsay and the Comstocks to easily see the pool of water below.

"In January," she explained, "the water level dropped to about four feet below where you see it now, but as the weather warmed and, in my opinion, as the snow pack in the mountains began to melt, it returned to where you see it now. Look – the high-water mark you see there shows that it may rise another two feet."

She dropped her rock-weighted twine, now calibrated in inches, into the water until the rock stopped. She pulled it back up. They all four looked at the water mark on the twine. It read seventeen feet three inches.

Clarence shook his head. Junior said, "I told you so."

Myra said, "I think the only way to test its flow is to open the cavern and test the amount of water coming out. I've thought a lot about this. My idea is to somehow determine the elevation of the bottom of the cavern here. I suppose surveyors can do that sort of thing. After we determine where that elevation point is on the hillside, we'd start near the cavern at a safe enough distance that we wouldn't threaten its collapse, and dig out all the rock and dirt below it in the direction of the creek. That'd leave a channel for the water to go into the crick. We'd have to build some kind of check gate to ease water into the channel and increase its flow until the water level starts to drop in the cavern. Then we'd know how much water we could draw."

She took a deep breath. "What do you think?"

Ramsay stared into the water. Clarence scratched the ring of hair on the back of his bald head then rubbed his hand over his head two or three times. "By God almighty Miss Grant, you sure enough been thinking this thing through. I suppose that should work but there might be another way. There's them big steam pumps they use for hydraulic mining up in the Boise Basin. One of the biggest of them could pump a lot of water out this hole pretty damn fast." He rubbed his bald head. "But they'd be damn expensive and hard to get here and you'd have to hire someone who knows how to run it. Then if you did get yourself a good stream of water you still gotta open up the hole and build what you just described or something close to it. The way I see it, you just as well knock her open and take your chances."

Ramsay was still looking into the water. "It's a big project that'll require blasting and concrete. It'll take big money. Money ye might nae recover if this thing is nae what ye think it is. Ye got that kind of money?"

"No offense Ramsay but do you think I'd be drinking out of cheap unmatched water glasses if I did? I suppose I'll have to go see Cannon at the bank. He'll want to come out here and look it over, I'm sure, and that's fine. He's easy to deal with but I just don't want to assume too much."

"Ain't you heard?" asked Clarence. "Cannon's gone. Got himself fired. Got too loose with the bank's money is what I heard. Got a new guy named Eccles. He's a tough one I been told."

"All right, Eccles then – I didn't care for Cannon anyway."

"Here's the plain truth, Myra," said Ramsay. "This place and all yer cows won't even come close tae giving the bank enough collateral fer a loan on a project like this."

Myra didn't flinch. "All right, I've been thinking about that too."

"Ye've got that look. I can tell ye've got something up yer sleeve."

Myra smiled, hesitant that she might be pushing this too rapidly. "I'd like to propose a three-way partnership – the Sproats, the Comstocks and me." She stopped talking to let them absorb her idea.

She didn't know if the silence that followed was good or bad.

Ramsay looked at Clarence who was almost too surprised to say a word. Ramsay looked back at Myra and said, "A partnership – awricht, let me think aboot that."

"Here's something to think about," said Myra. "Do you all understand the significance of this, if river water will flow out of that cave?"

"I understand," said Ramsay. "Could irrigate thousands of acres – or mebbe naw more than enough tae water yer tomatoes– ye'll nae know 'til ye test it."

"He's right," said Clarence, "but the cost of this thing, good Lord woman."

"All right, Clarence," said Myra. "You're the builder, how much will it cost?"

More head rubbing. "Only a guess mind you, but blasting, concrete, hiring a crew to move rock and dirt." He shook his head. "I worked on a new mine once that took a lot of the same kind of work. I was told that thousands of dollars were spent before one ounce of gold got hauled out of *that* hole. It was way up in the Soldier Mountains, helluva long ways from anything. This is closer to the railroad so it might not take that much."

"Well, I don't know a darn thing about gold," said Myra. "But if that hole puts out the kind of water I think it could, it might be better than gold."

Her face brightened, no trace of uncertainty. "Ramsay, is your ranch free of debt? How about yours Clarence?"

They both nodded.

"All right then, if we add up the value of all three ranches we should easily have enough. We mortgage each one – Clarence, yours is the small-est so you and Junior do the work for your third. Ramsay, yours is the largest so you'd be the primary investor for your third and the hole is on my place for my third. If we hit a flow then we split everything equally."

A long period of silenced ensued. Myra felt her proposal might have come too quickly and frightened them.

"I'll talk to Annie Chris."

"Of course, I understand. What about you Clarence?"

Clarence rubbed his bald head and said, "Well…"

"Come on Pa," pleaded Junior. "You wanna swing a shovel and pound nails all your life? This could be the biggest thing ever to happen in these parts."

Clarence's head rubbing stopped, his chin was up and his face was bright. "All right. Me and Junior's in if Ramsay's in."

~Tuesday, March 27, 1888 – Sunnyside~

"Isn't this your dream, Ramsay Sproat?" Annie Chris asked the next day. "How many times have you told me you want to a leave a legacy for your family? How frustrated have you been for sixteen years – unable to expand the ranch with more sheep because we don't have enough water? How many times have we been knocked down by Lord knows what all – snow, fire, drought, grasshoppers, jackrabbits.

"Water, my love. If we'd had enough water your dream, our dream, would have come true. Water is the only thing that has held us back. This is our chance, my love. Lord knows chances like these are rare. Think about how the land slopes between there and Sunnyside. I bet a canal from Rock Creek could come as close as a mile or two from Sunnyside. That's not far. And what if it doesn't? So what? A nice big farm close to the canal would be easy to manage."

She, sighed, glanced out the window then back at Ramsay, "You and me, my love – we're the same two people that took a mighty chance to leave Turpin and Abington. Do you remember us standing in the dark, then you strutting around like a rooster? My heart swelled with love for you. I didn't think it possible to love someone so much. Well, Ramsay Sproat, I love you more today."

She took a deep breath, placed her face in her hands then looked up at her husband of sixteen years and said simply, "We need to do this."

"Then we will."

A warm wind from the west had blown for five straight days, and the Foothill Road had dried enough for the buggy to make it to the Rockin' M.

Tommy, Junior's drover who'd helped Junior trail the cattle from Jordan Valley, was hired to do the chores on the ranch while Clarence and Junior spent their time at the cave site, measuring, digging and taking readings from Clarence's transit. Ramsay, Annie Chris and Cal arrived at noon.

Annie Chris and Myra had communicated only by mail lately and were eager to see one another and their growing children after a long isolating winter for them both.

Hugs and admiring comments about their children were exchanged at the door of Myra's house. "Come in, please. I'll have dinner ready in a few minutes. Ramsay, will you get Clarence and Junior. I swear those two need to be dragged away from that cave."

After Ramsay left, Annie Chris said with a wink, "We've made a decision but I want Ramsay to announce it."

Myra's eyes formed a bright smile. Her hands went to the top of her head. All she said was: "I was so worried."

The three men washed up outside and came in for dinner at 12:45. All five found a seat at Myra's table.

"I got a bottle of whiskey here." Ramsay grinned as he set a bottle and five small glasses on the table.

He poured a shot in four of the five glasses. He stopped at the fifth. He hovered the bottle over the glass and looked at Clarence who nodded. Ramsay poured a splash in the last glass for Junior.

"A toast. Here's tae our new partnership. May the good Lord look on it kindly."

"Hear, hear," said everyone in unison as they clinked their glasses then tossed back the amber liquid.

"Just so I understand," said Clarence. "Ramsay, you and Annie Chris will share a third, Myra, you'll have a third and me and Junior will share a third. Is that right?"

Everybody nodded their agreement.

"And we'll sell shares of water to farmers and ranchers, is that right?"

More nods.

"All right, when do we go to the bank?"

It came to her suddenly like an abrupt awakening from a dream. It was the future that she cared about now, not the past. The past and all its sadness was irrelevant now.

"There's someone I want to talk to first," she said. She could feel urgency building within her.

She turned to Ramsay. "Are you busy Monday morning?"

"Nae if there's something important."

Myra turned to Annie Chris, ideas coming to her now in rapid spurts of inspiration. "Can you watch Patsy on Monday if I ride back to Sunnyside with you and spend a couple of nights?"

"Aye."

She turned to Clarence. "Will you go straight to the depot when you leave here and send a telegram?"

"Of course."

"What are ye thinking?" asked Ramsay. Her enthusiasm was now contagious.

"Let's go to Boise on Monday. There's someone we should talk to."

Myra briskly wrote out the message for the telegram and handed it to Clarence. It said simply:

Langston Hailey,
Please meet me Monday, April 2th at eleven a.m. in your
office. Please reread my last letter.
Myra Grant

Langston Hailey was away from town on business his father's secretary told Ramsay and Annie Chris at eleven on Monday morning. "Langston left before your telegram arrived. I'm sorry. He will be back in his office on Thursday, April fifth. Would you like me to schedule an appointment then?" she asked.

Ramsay and Myra made an appointment for Thursday at eleven a.m. First they would visit with C.W. Moore, the banker right there in Boise.

"I'm sorry; Mr. Moore is out for the day. Can someone else help you?"

"Can someone talk tae us aboot a loan with yer bank?"

"Yes, please follow me."

A young employee sat across his desk from them. "We'll send an appraiser to your ranch tomorrow Mr. Sproat and I'll send a telegram to our cashier in Ryegrass asking him to appraise your place Mrs. Grant."

"And Mr. Comstock's?"

"Of course. I'll ask Mr. Eccles at our branch in Ryegrass to visit yours and Mr. Comstock's as soon as possible. Mr. Moore will make the final decision. Our appraiser will telegraph his appraisal of your ranch, Mr. Sproat, to Mr. Eccles in Ryegrass. Mr. Eccles will compile all the data and make a recommendation to Mr. Moore. You can expect a decision within the next two weeks."

Myra and Ramsay left Boise for Sunnyside, anxious to return on Thursday.

CHAPTER FORTY-SIX

~Wednesday April 4, 1888~

Three fat cows, each nursing shiny calves, had to be coaxed out of the road before Stanfield Eccles could open Myra's substantial-looking gate. He saw the calves' fresh brands and noticed the same Rockin' M as the sign suspended from the cross pole above his head. He began to feel a little better about what he might expect.

Two hours earlier, after spending twenty minutes in Clarence Comstock's privy and finding little else on the place worthy of a loan, Eccles left for Myra Grant's place without even knocking on Clarence's door. He wondered if it was even worth his time to continue on up the canyon to this place on Rock Creek he'd heard nothing good about.

He said he would do it and he was, after all, a man of his word. He would combine his two appraisals with the Sproat appraisal and offer his opinion to Mr. Moore so Moore could make a decision regarding how much the bank would be willing to loan against this wild scheme that was presented to him through telegraph. As near as he could tell, the bank was dealing with a small-time immigrant sheep rancher and his shopkeeper wife, a woman with a child who not long ago had been a country school teacher, and a handyman and his fifteen year-old son.

The fifteen year-old showed Eccles the Rock Creek property.

~Five and a half hours later~

"What are you doing?" said the indignant woman next in line at the telegraph counter.

"I am so sorry, madam," said Eccles, out of breath. "I know you were in line first but this is an emergency. It won't take Virgil two minutes to send mine."

Eccles appraised the sour look on the irritated woman's face and handed her a silver dollar. The look moderated so he stepped in front of her.

> C.W. MOORE. STOP. ARRIVING BOISE ON TEN A.M. TRAIN TOMORROW. STOP. MEET ME THERE. STOP. EXTREMELY URGENT. STOP. COME ALONE. STOP.

C.W. Moore motioned for Eccles to step into his buggy and shook the reins. Eccles could barely contain himself. "Myra Grant spent six months measuring water levels, collecting debris and taking water samples. There's no doubt in my mind, sir. They're absolutely right. It's Boise River water. Now, how much will come out of that hole once it's opened is anyone's guess. What do we have to lose? If it's just seepage then they'll all be broke and the bank will own at least two nice properties. If it's a gusher, then, well," he said choosing his words carefully, not wanting to overstate, "it will be big."

"Who's going to own the water?" asked Moore as solemn as an owl as he applied his well-honed skill of avoiding the appearance of being even mildly impressed.

"They are. They're not stupid, Mr. Moore. They formed a partnership and will have total control of the flow, if there is any. The hole is on the Grant property – Myra Grant is her name. They'll sell shares of water. She told your office Monday she'll be talking to someone else, she wouldn't say who – probably some other sodbuster – for sure not another bank, they haven't had time. That explains the urgency sir – I assumed you would consider this urgent."

Moore's cigar had gone out so he struck a match across the front of the buggy seat and placed the flame to the end of the cigar. He looked straight ahead and took five long drags to restart it. Columns of blue smoke exited his mouth as the flame increased in intensity with each drag. Satisfied, he removed the cigar from his lips and said, "How much do they want?"

"They've asked for sixteen thousand dollars."

"What are they going to do with it?"

"Open the hole. I asked how, but the kid just said they had a plan."

"They want sixteen thousand dollars and they won't tell you how they're going to use the money? Is that right?"

Eccles was silent. Moore's cigar was now lodged in the corner of his mouth. He sucked twice, blowing smoke with each drag. "What's their land worth?"

"All three places? Twenty, probably more."

"No debt?"

"Grant owes us for her cows. Seven hundred dollars."

"What would be our preferred outcome?"

"As I said sir, there's really not a bad one. If they go broke, we get the properties and possibly the livestock. If the hole's a gusher then we'll have a large new market for farm loans and if it's something significantly less than a gusher we get our money back plus interest. So from my perspective, we'd prefer that their project was a success."

"What about buying up property out there as soon as we know it might be a success?"

"There's not much private property sir. Ninety percent of that ground is government land."

"We want the option to lien Sproat's sheep if it goes over sixteen thousand – then we have a deal. Four percent on the loan – eight percent on anything above sixteen thousand."

Moore pulled on one of the reins, turned the buggy around and headed back toward the train station. "The east-bound comes through at noon. Complete this as soon as possible, write them a draft, then get to the courthouse and check on the deeded ground out there and prepare your branch to be the bank for a lot of new homesteaders."

C. W. Moore, almost inaudibly, mumbled, "Good job, Eccles."

~Friday April 6, 1888, eight a.m.~

"But it's Good Friday, Mr. Eccles."

"You want to keep this job or don't you?"

The runner looked down at his shoes and asked meekly, "When should I tell my wife I'll be back?"

"It's an hour to Comstock's then an hour to Grant's then three hours to Sproat's and three hours back here to my office. That's eight hours. Your ass better be passin' through my door by five o'clock." said Eccles.

"Don't forget," he added, "I want them all here, all of them, at eleven o'clock Monday morning."

Eccles's clock struck eleven rich chimes when the runner knocked on his office door.

"What the hell are you doing here?" roared Eccles.

"The first one, Comstock, said it weren't no use in me going any further. Says they don't need the bank's money no more, sir. Think I'll go on home, Mr. Eccles, if there ain't nothin' else."

CHAPTER FORTY-SEVEN

~The day before – Thursday April 5, 1888, 10:50 a.m.~

Myra sat anxiously next to Ramsay in the waiting area outside Langston Hailey's office. She placed her hands between her knees to keep them from shaking, just as she'd done before Christmas in the Hailey parlor fifteen months before. Ramsay could sense her anxiety; took one of her hands in his, patted it gently and held tight.

For two days, Langston had known he would finally see Myra. He was excited and afraid. Anticipation and tension filled him. His stomach was so skittish he hoped he would not have to excuse himself from this crucial meeting. He was hot and cold. He dried his damp hands again on his handkerchief, and reached for the bell cord behind his desk. The bell above Emily's desk in the waiting room jingled. Emily stood and announced to Myra and Ramsay, "Mr. Hailey will see you now."

Ramsay took Myra's hand, placed it under his arm and followed Emily into Langston's large but modestly appointed office. Langston was standing. *He's lost weight*, Myra thought.

"Please sit. Is there anything Emily can get you? Water? Coffee?"

"Naw thank ye, Mr. Hailey."

Emily smiled and closed the door.

The period of uncomfortable silence that followed as Langston and Myra traded awkward glances was so disconcerting that Ramsay finally spoke up. "Well sir Mr. Hailey, this is why we're here."

Ramsay explained what they'd discovered at the upper end of the Rockin' M and made it clear what they felt must be invested just to determine the potential flow of the water. He explained the partnership and explained the plan to develop, for farming, the thousands of acres the cavern water would irrigate if it produced the flow they expected. Ramsay admitted that the venture could be viewed as risky but the five partners were willing to take that risk based on Myra's six months of detailed investigation.

They were here to ask for a loan, Ramsay said humbly. In the back of his mind he knew Langston had no options – it would be impossible for the young man to reject Myra's request. For a fleeting moment he wondered if it might have been Myra's plan to manipulate Langston. He was ashamed of himself for thinking this; he knew Myra would never exploit Langston and their daughter.

Langston could barely concentrate on what Ramsay was explaining, he was so thunderstruck to have Myra in his presence after fifteen months of painful separation, the most heart-wrenching ordeal of his life. In her ankle-length prairie skirt, brown riding boots and plain white blouse, she was even more beautiful than he remembered.

His ears were ringing and his mouth was suddenly dry.

"Do you mind if my father joins us?" Langston asked, finding it difficult to maneuver his tongue inside his dry mouth.

"Nae at all," said Ramsay.

Langston pulled the small cord. His secretary knocked. "Emily, please ask my father to join us."

John Hailey, nearly white haired now, with the aid of a hickory cane, walked through Langston's door.

After pleasantries and handshakes, Ramsay explained the partnership's proposal again.

Hailey listened patiently with no visible reaction. When Ramsay was finished Hailey said, "Ramsay, Miss Grant, would you mind stepping out for a few minutes so I might speak with my son?"

The two stood and walked into the outer office. Hailey closed the door.

"I'll give you half the money for a wedding present and loan you the rest. You know what you have to do and you damn well better do it now."

Hailey walked into the outer office, stopped and faced Ramsay and Myra. "If you don't mind Ramsay, my son would like to see Miss Grant alone." He shook Ramsay's hand and bowed to Myra and said, "I hope we'll see more of you Miss Grant."

Emily ushered Myra back into Langston's office.

There was nothing in this world for him but this woman. He was terrified but resolute. This was his final chance to win her back. He stepped toward her. "You have no idea how much I have missed you and how sorry I am for my horrible selfish behavior. Please understand that I love you with all my heart. I…"

"I don't want apologies, Langston. What is done is done. I love you too."

His relief was immediate. He stepped closer. "All right then. I want you. I want our baby. I want nothing more in this world. I will never allow my stupidity to separate us again."

He embraced her. "Marry me, Myra. Please, marry me."

"I will, Langston," she whispered. "Oh God yes, I will."

CHAPTER FORTY- EIGHT

"And Moses lifted up his hand, and with his rod he smote the rock twice: and the water came out abundantly, and the congregation drank, and their beasts also." Numbers 32:11

~Six months later – October 1888~

It had taken much longer than expected. The partnership used three surveyors before they found one who was reasonably competent. By then it was almost May and it took him six weeks to complete a canal plan. A network of canals would work perfectly if, of course, there was water enough to ever run through them. Because of the rugged lava that rimmed the canyon, water would have to flow five miles down Rock Creek before the canyon walls sloped gently enough to divert water into a main canal that would course its way southwest and onto the flat. From there, the soil was loamy and relatively free of rock with a gentle slope that ran for twenty-five miles. If the cavern produced enough water to irrigate all this land, Clarence said with a chuckle after he'd looked at the map of the canal plan, "It'll drain the whole goddamn Boise River!"

Although they were both good with forms and concrete, neither Clarence nor Junior had much experience with dynamite. Learning by trial and error was expensive and had become complicated by many mistakes. Luckily, no one was hurt. It took some time but little Patsy had become accustomed to the loud explosions and was able to continue her naps in the midst of what sounded like a battlefield a half mile away.

Ramsay took several days to advise the down-stream neighbors of their excavation project, including the possibility that a large rush of water might soon be coming their way. He would alert them when that day might come so they could clear anything at risk from its path. Most laughed at him sheepishly, saying "Good luck" and "You bet."

Earlier, Myra had asked the Sproats to keep Patsy for ten days following Langston and Myra's private May 20th wedding ceremony at the Sproats' Sunnyside home. But Langston resisted. He'd been away from his daughter too long – he wanted Patsy with them on their honeymoon. The wedding party included Mr. and Mrs. Hailey and Langston's three sisters, Myra and Langstons' four partners, Tommy the drover, Junior's hired man, and Pache and Lou, their son Santi and Santi's little brother Anastasio.

The newlyweds spent two nights in the Overland Hotel. Ramsay and Annie Chris met them at the depot with Patsy, and after send-offs and hugs; the new family boarded the train for the twenty-one-hour first-class coach ride to San Francisco. They stayed at the opulent St. Francis Hotel and were eager to tour the great western city and see its sights and simply enjoy the fact that they were a family.

Langston hired a lawyer for the group who helped them form a corporation. The lawyer suggested hiring a real estate firm in Denver with experience in marketing irrigation water to eager new farmers courtesy of the Homestead Act. He also advised hiring another law firm in San Francisco that specialized in water law and securing water rights. Their new company, the Rock Creek Irrigation Company, Inc., would sell shares of its water to the homesteaders, *if* this didn't turn into the biggest boondoggle in the long history of boondoggles.

The start-up expense by October had reached $16,000. John Hailey's magnanimity had reached its limits. He agreed to extend the partnership an additional $10,000 loan, but no more.

They needed water now and lots of it. If there was enough, they would start immediately building the canals. If the flow was not enough to warrant the expense of building the canals but enough to offer additional water to the downstream farmers, they would forego the canal project and sell shares to the farmers along Rock Creek's channel. This would not be large a project but one that would generate enough money to pay their expenses and provide a measure of ongoing annual income for the new corporation.

If the flow was minimal, they were in trouble. If that was the case, the next plan, according to Ramsay and Langston, would be to bore through the mountain to the Boise River itself and build a six-mile-long tunnel. That would take serious capital from investors in markets far from Idaho.

The structure that Clarence and Junior and their workers were building from the creek to the cave was beginning to look impressive. At a distance, it looked like one side of a Mayan pyramid, stair-stepped a hundred feet down to the creek with a large circular dome at the top. Once the dome was removed, the water within would be exposed to the sky.

Langston was home at the Rockin' M with Myra on weekends and spent most of that time reviewing the project. Ramsay was on site as often as possible without neglecting his sheep business. Clarence, Junior and their workers were there at least twelve hours a day.

"Buster, our blacksmith in Ryegrass, is building the headgate and apparatus now," Clarence explained to Langston one Saturday when all the members of the partnership were together. "He should have it done in a week. We could have it in place at the top a couple of days after that. The last thing, once the gate is in, is to remove the dome and knock out the rock behind the headgate. That'll take a day or two. Once we start opening the headgate and start releasing the water, we should know in a few hours."

All along, Myra and Langston had been the positive ones in the partnership. They didn't ignore the risk by any means, but took it upon themselves to assume success, encouraging the others. They always predicted the most positive outcomes.

"The newspapers from both Ryegrass and Boise have contacted me," said Langston, "and asked to be here when the headgate is opened and the water is released. I wrote them back and said no. I hope that is all right with everyone. I think we're all a little too private for that kind of attention. I'll invite them back soon for a story if we do get water and plenty of it. We'll want the coverage to help promote the shares."

~Monday, October 22, 1888~

The dome of the cave and the rim of rock behind the headgate were removed. The water in the cave was open to the sky. The headgate was the only thing holding the water back now. A metal rod calibrated in feet and inches extended vertically into the cavern all the way to the bottom. A walking path three feet wide circled one half of the rim.

Myra walked up the concrete stairs along the left side of the channel wall. She hadn't felt this anxious since waiting for Langston outside his office nearly six months before. She felt strangely detached from her legs. To avoid falling she had to watch the placement of each foot as she climbed the stairs. Annie Chris was next followed by Ramsay. Clarence followed in fresh trousers and a clean shirt. Junior, in his black cowboy hat, took up the rear.

Waiting below with Patsy in his arms was Langston, his mother and father at his side. With them were four construction workers: Tommy the hired man; old Henry Caufield, their downstream neighbor; Buster, Tim Shea; and, of course, Chelsea.

Pache and Lou were there as well. Lou's right hand firmly gripped Chelsea's collar to keep her from following Myra up the steps while she held Cal in her left arm. Pache was holding Anastasio and explaining to Santi in Basque what might happen at the top of the concrete structure. The curious little boy stood wide-eyed and motionless and waited for something dramatic.

At the top, Junior handed Myra a bottle of "The Glenlivet," an imported single-malt fifteen-year-old scotch whiskey. Annie Chris had splurged just for this occasion. Except for the humming of insects and the rippling of water down Rock Creek, the canyon was still; so quiet, in fact, Myra thought she could hear old man Caufield's raspy breathing far below. She said to herself, *What the hell*, gripped the neck of the bottle, gave it a kiss and with a strong back-hand shattered the green bottle against the top of the steel headgate. Clapping and cheering broke the quiet below.

Myra reached for the headgate wheel, gripped it firmly and closed her eyes. She took a big breath and turned the wheel counter-clockwise, surprised at how easily the wheel turned in her hands. The wheel's axle turned a series of gears and the big steel gate lifted slightly. Water began flowing toward the creek down the stair-stepped channel. Four pairs of eyes stared at the measuring rod. Myra's eyes, the fifth pair, looked to the heavens as if to summon divine intersession and providence. She turned the wheel another half turn – more water. She was still unable to look at the rod.

Another half turn, more water, enough now that she could hear it rushing. No voices from her partners telling her, as they had planned, to stop turning the wheel when the surface of the water began to recede down the metal rod. Another half turn; the rushing water now was loud; still nothing from her partners. She looked at Ramsay who nodded for her to continue. Another half turn – she could feel spray. The air seemed to cool.

Ramsay shouted over the rush of water, "Hold fer twenty minutes tae see what it does." He pulled out his pocket watch and checked the time.

Myra walked the few steps to where her partners' eyes were transfixed on the rod and looked at it for the first time. Five minutes, ten minutes; nobody moved. Finally Buster shouted from below, "How's it looking?" He was either not heard or ignored. The staring continued. Fifteen minutes, twenty minutes. Ramsay looked at his pocket watch again and nodded to Myra to go back to the wheel.

Another full turn; the rushing water was now a torrent. She looked at Ramsay. He knew she was looking at him but his eyes would not leave the rod. Five minutes, ten minutes – still nothing from Ramsay. Another five minutes then, without prompting, she walked to the rod and almost screamed to be heard. "Let's leave it here for a couple of hours!"

Grinning, one by one, the partners walked carefully down the spray-soaked stairs to the waiting group below. Without thinking about it, some had stood on the upstream side of the now rushing water and had to walk up the hill and over the top of the cavern to avoid fording the torrent.

The on-lookers at the bottom rushed to greet them with pumping handshakes and back slaps. Lou ran to Annie Chris, threw her arms around her and said, "I'm so happy for ya honey, I could just bust!"

Annie Chris reached into a bag she'd brought, pulled out another bottle of scotch, handed the bottle to Lou and said, "This should hold you together."

"If I do bust at least I'll bust with a smile on my face," Lou said laughing, as she lifted the bottle to her lips.

Pache, his bushy eyebrows now pure white, matching the hair protruding beneath his black beret, thrust a bota bag into Ramsay's outstretched hand and hollered over the sound of cascading water, "WE DRINK!"

Ramsay squeezed a long stream of the red liquid into his mouth, handed it to Langston who, lacking the practice of a seasoned immigrant, missed his mouth on the first try and shot a stream of wine down his neck, prompting rounds of happy laughter.

Ramsay reached for his pipes and began blowing into the blowpipe, filling the bag with air. He hadn't been sure about bringing his bagpipes but wanted to express his joy in the best way he knew how if the project was a success.

"Mr. Sproat," asked an amazed little seven-year-old boy, "where does all that water come from?"

"We're nae fer sure, Santi," answered Ramsay, "but we think from the Boise River."

"How?" asked Santi.

Pache scolded him in a barrage of unintelligible Basque then said to Ramsay, "My boy, too many questions. You play pipes."

~   ~   ~

Myra's eyes scanned the meadow, the house and the barn. She saw five yearling steers grazing on the hillside. Her eyes returned to the people around her – the people who were most important in her life.

She thought of her mother and father. How different her life may have been if they had stayed in Sacramento. She never knew why they left in such a hurry but it could not have been good. She decided she could be grateful to them for the move.

She smiled at Ramsay happily playing his pipes which looked so oddly out of place among these hard scrabble frontier folks. She felt honored that she would be able to play a role in his lifelong dream.

Annie Chris. Loyal Annie Chris who was standing next to him, her eyes smiling – this lovely thin, dark-haired woman from Scotland who'd been through so much in her own life – her dear friend, who'd stayed by her side through her toughest times. This woman who at the beginning of this remarkable day had caught Myra's attention, softly patted her waistline, winked and whispered in Myra's ear, "I'll tell Ramsay tomorrow."

She thought of old Patsy and Standing Bear. And of course, she thought of Cora.

She smiled and turned her eyes toward Patricia Louisa Hailey being gently held by her father. She watched as Langston carefully placed her on the ground so she could walk on wobbly legs to try to catch her friend Cal.

Myra smiled, content, confident and proud. She thought of the dramatic sequence of events that had occurred in her life and how all those events had led to this moment.

She had prevailed.

A new era was beginning.

AUTHOR'S NOTES

Rock Creek is a work of fiction. The earthquake and the subsequent rupture that sent Boise River water six miles to a hidden cave is not a true historical or geological event.

The idea for the earthquake and the water came from a true story told to me by my father, a third-generation Idaho sheep rancher. Early in the twentieth century a group of investors devised a plan to dig a six mile tunnel south from the South Fork of the Boise River to the headwaters of the small creek, Syrup Creek. Shares or rights to this water were sold to eager farmers who homesteaded or bought land and waited for the water to arrive. The water, theoretically, would irrigate the arid desert land and turn it into valuable productive farmland. The tunnel was never built and the water never arrived.

Syrup Creek joined with another small creek called Long Tom Creek to form Canyon Creek about fifteen miles north of the current town of Mountain Home, Idaho. The tunnel would have channeled river water from the Boise River into Syrup Creek then Canyon Creek then out onto the Mountain Home desert through a series of canals. Many of the canals were built. Grass and sagebrush now hide what remains of the canals, still winding through the arid desert northwest of Mountain Home. The investors' intentions may have been legitimate but, unfortunately for many innocent farmers, the end result was financial ruin.

The drainage the river water would have followed before being channeled into canals is Canyon Creek. Rock Creek is the fictional name I gave Canyon Creek for my story.

Ryegrass is a fictional town that closely resembles my hometown, Mountain Home. Mountain Home began as a small community near the Rattlesnake Stage Stop on the Oregon Trail and was moved to its current site when the Oregon Short Line Railroad was built.

Sunnyside is a fictional town that resembles the small community of Mayfield. For many years Mayfield had a Grange Hall, a school, a store and a hotel. Mayfield fell victim to the ravages of time and progress. The dilapidated Grange Hall still stands.

The Abington Estate and Braeburn Castle are products of my imagination. Details of servant and crofter life in Scotland were gleaned from research with addition information from the PBS series *Downton Abby* and books such as Ken Follett's book *Fall of Giants* and Jane Austen's *Sense and Sensibility.*

My grandfather, the son of a Cornish immigrant sheep rancher, and a sheep rancher himself, had many Scot sheep ranching friends across Southern Idaho. I had always wondered what prompted so many Scots to come here and take up sheep ranching. I learned about the crofters and their sad lives in the process of gathering research for this book. The more I learned the more convinced I became that many must have come here for the very reason that Ramsay and Annie Chris came.

The present town of Glenns Ferry was named after the late nineteenth-century ferry operator Gustavus B. Glenn. The town is located upstream from Three Island State Park, where thousands of emigrants made the perilous island crossing through the swift waters of the Snake River on their way west before the Glenn/Moody ferry became operational.

Annie Chris and Ramsay discussed the possibility of buying land near a proposed irrigation project that was intended to capture nearby mountain snow melt. In the story Ramsay dismisses the idea as being too far in the future to help them. He was right. The Mountain Home Irrigation project, a series of canals and reservoirs that brought irrigation water from Bennett Mountain to the area surrounding Mountain Home, was not completed until 1912.

Fort Hall was a very real fort in Eastern Idaho along the Oregon Trail. It was established in 1834 as an outpost for fur trade, many years before emigrants began to arrive by the thousands in their wagons. The fort served as a military outpost until the Indian threat diminished in the late 1860s after the Fort Hall Indian Reservation was created.

The excerpt about Myra writing to Army Sergeant Mazurowski in 1887, in reality, could not have happened within the timeframe of my story. Fort Hall was abandoned by the Army in 1883. Please remember that *Rock Creek* is a novel and, as with most historical fiction, small liberties are often taken with facts to enhance the story. For more information about Fort Hall read the *Idaho State Historical Society Reference Series; Fort Hall; Number 121.*

Stricker Station or Stricker Store, the stage stop along the Kelton Road, was also known as Rock Creek Station. I chose to use the name Stricker Station in my novel to avoid confusion with my fictional stream, Rock Creek, for which the novel is named.

~   ~   ~

Three of the characters in my story are real. C.W. Moore was a prominent Boise banker whose First National Bank of Idaho, grew to become the largest bank in Idaho before it was eventually absorbed by what is now US Bank. He was born in Toronto, Canada on November 30, 1835 and died in Boise on September 20, 1916. He is buried in the family plot in Boise's Morris Hill Cemetery.

He and his wife Catherine had seven children. The family is still very prominent in Boise and the surrounding area. The Laura Moore Cunningham Foundation, one of several Moore family philanthropies, serves as a significant benefactor throughout Idaho.

John Hailey built the Kelton Road, an early freight and stage road connecting Kelton, Utah, to Boise City and the Boise Basin mining district. In the late 1870s Hailey extended the road to the Wood River mining district near the present town of Hailey, Idaho, named for him and located on ground he homesteaded.

Hailey engaged in a variety of commercial interests in the Pacific Northwest during his long career including operating freight and stage coach lines throughout the region, farming, and mining. He served the Territory of Idaho twice as a representative to Congress: two terms in the mid 1870s and one term in the mid 1880s. He was appointed warden of the Idaho State Penitentiary in Boise in 1899 and was the founder of the Idaho State Historical Society.

Hailey and his wife, Louisa Meyers Griffin Hailey, had six children.

All of the Hailey family incidents in my story are fictional, including the fact that Langston Hailey did not exist.

John Hailey was a prominent Idaho citizen and is fondly remembered as one of the territorial pioneers who pushed for statehood. His tenacity and work ethic crossed the boundaries of road building, transportation, mining, farming and politics and has left a lasting mark that stretches throughout Idaho's history. He was born on August 29, 1835 in Smith

County, Tennessee, and died in Boise on April 10, 1921. He is buried in Boise's Pioneer Cemetery beside his wife Louisa.

The tragic story of the ten-year-old child, James (Jake) Oliver Evans, is all too real. I had to alter his dates of confinement, however, to fit the story. Jake was imprisoned in the Idaho Territorial Prison in August 1885, not August 1886. The Territorial Governor commuted his sentence and released him in May 1886. Read *Prisoner 88* by Leah Pileggi for more about the life of Jake Evans.

The Kelton Road became obsolete in 1883 with the completion of the Oregon Short Line Railroad. The Oregon Short Line extended east through Southern Idaho to Pocatello in the southeastern corner of the state and connected with the Transcontinental Railroad at Granger, Wyoming. Railroad shipping points were soon built in small towns along the route. Kuna, Mountain Home (or fictional Ryegrass) and Glenns Ferry, each of which was mentioned in the story, were three among many.

In 1904, the Lucin Cutoff was built south of the original route of the Transcontinental Railroad in Northern Utah bypassing Kelton. Almost immediately the town was abandoned. All that remains today of the once-major shipping point are a few concrete foundations.

Southern Idaho became one of the most significant sheep ranching regions in the world shortly after the Oregon Short Line was built. Through the end of World War II, sheep ranching was the region's dominant industry.

Of the sheep ranching immigrants, the Scots were among the first to arrive. Many grew their fledgling ranches into large successful operations. Andrew Little, a Scot, came to Idaho in 1884 virtually penniless and grew his ranch into one the largest sheep ranches in the world. His descendants still ranch in the Payette and Weiser River drainages in Southwestern and Central Idaho. Andrew Little's grandson, Brad Little, is currently Lieutenant Governor of the State of Idaho.

The sheep industry suffered a rapid decline shortly after WWII. At its peak, at the beginning of the Twentieth Century, the federal census reported 1,965,500 sheep in Idaho. By 2011, the same Idaho census reported only 185,000 sheep.

The development of synthetic fibers such as rayon and nylon has been widely cited as responsible for the fall of the industry but other factors contributed to its decline including the increased importance of recreation and the environmental movement.

Other than John Hailey, C.W. Moore and James Oliver Evans, the names and character depictions in this story are purely fictional. They bear no resemblance to and are not based on any person living or dead.

ACKNOWLEDGMENTS

Thank you to all the readers who gave their detailed and personal responses to the numerous drafts of *Rock Creek*. Many technical and historical inaccuracies were avoided through their insightful reading. Their encouragement and feedback was invaluable.

I would like to especially thank my wife Marsha who supported me with her spot-on critiques. Rock Creek wouldn't have been possible without her belief in me and her encouragement to persevere.

I hesitate to name all those who assisted me for fear of leaving someone out but I feel compelled to try: Martha Ascuena, Bob Bennett, Rob Bennett, Louann Boyd, Wendy Carpenter, Carol Chipman, Margie Chipman, Hartzel Cobbs, Joy Cobbs, Joyce Day, Ellen DeAustin, Bob Dutton, Fred Gates, Margot Gates, Gretchen Hyde, Cynthia Jenkins, Brooke Bennett Lewis, Roger Lewis, Adelaide McLeod, Bob Porter, Karen Porter, Kimberly Bennett Porter, Helen Robinson, Joe Robinson, Marlys Saltzer, Joanne Simpson, Barbara Turner, Rae Ann Wick and Kaye Yrazabal.

The translations from English to Shoshoni are from the *Shoshoni Dictionary* available through the University of Utah at shoshoniproject.utah.edu.

The character Patsy was inspired by the story of Chief Seattle's daughter in the book *The Short Nights of the Shadow Catcher: The Epic Life and Immortal Photographs of Edward Curtis* by Timothy Egan.

Thank you Dennis Held, editor and writing advisor, Josh Hindson, graphic designer, for designing the cover, Carolyn Fletcher for her photo, Kimberly Bennett Porter for her image on the cover and Jane Freund, book coach.

I am especially grateful for the hours of collaboration and insight my daughters Kimberly Bennett Porter and Brooke Bennett Lewis shared with me.

"There are three rules for writing a novel.
Unfortunately, no one can agree what they are."
W. Somerset Maugham

312

ABOUT THE AUTHOR

RW Bennett is a descendant of four generations of Southern Idaho ranchers. He grew up in the sheep and cattle ranching business and was raised in Mountain Home, Idaho, near the family ranch. He and his wife Marsha live in Boise and will celebrate 47 years of marriage in 2017. They have two married daughters and four grandchildren.

Richard has written numerous magazine and newspaper articles and is currently working on his second novel.

Follow Richard on Facebook at RW Bennett – Author.

Is your book club interested in a FaceTime or Skype conversation with author RW Bennett? If so, contact him at **dickbennett45@gmail.com** to make the arrangements.

Made in the USA
Columbia, SC
17 November 2017